The Dreamer's World

a sleepless slumber

GERARD SIOREK

Book cover design by Gerard Siorek

www.TheDreamersWorld.com

*To Lucy, for the time she invested in reading and editing,
and Julie, for being a dear friend,
and Sarafina, for being the best meow ever.*

CONTENTS

PROLOGUE

"But Daddy, what is the Dreamer's World?" Amanda asked as her father snuggled her underneath the warm bedsheets.

The young princess looked up at him with curious eyes, filled with awe. She understood that this place was important, as her father was entrusted with the duty to protect it—a responsibility that would fall upon her some day when she was older. But she still didn't understand what the Dreamer's World was, or why it was so important. She felt it was about time she learned.

"The Dreamer's World is a very special place," her father explained. "It's a gateway that connects our universe to the other side, allowing the dreamers to come visit us every night while they sleep. It was a gift created by Kausmos, so that they could experience all the wonderful things on this side."

"You mean we have strangers coming here all the time?"

"Yes, they come and visit us, every single night."

"But if they visit every night, then how come I've never met them before?"

Her father smiled. "Because our universe is very big. There are so many places they could be."

"But why does it have to be so big for?" she whined, crossing her arms together.

"It has to be able to fit everyone's dream, no matter how silly or imaginative it may be. It's imperative that every dream has a home."

Amanda rolled on her side, glancing at all the plush animals she had scattered across her bed. She had everything from a cute, cuddly polar bear, to a reptilian beast with sharp serrated teeth that was looking hungrily over the teddy bear and the dolphin. On certain nights, she'd reenact large land and sea battles atop her bed, adapting the plots from stories her father had told her. At times she would play the monster, slithering underneath the comforter, sending the helpless animals over the ends of the earth. And while she played her games, Teckin would watch over her—a mammoth machine towering ten feet tall, with a shimmering metallic body that bore two massive arms and legs, and a comparatively small head. With his two beady eyes he monitored her whenever her father wasn't around. Every night he stood in the exact same corner of her room, keeping his two gargantuan feet carefully positioned within the imprints he had created in the carpet.

Amanda didn't mind his company at all. She had reservations at first, but quickly grew fond of him. There was no reason to be scared. He was the kindest, gentlest robot a six year old girl could have. They would take walks together, discuss nonsensical topics, and he would even help with her chores if no one else was around —truly an indispensable companion.

She rolled back on her other side and saw her father getting up from the edge of the bed. Before he could say goodnight, she called out to him.

"I want to see the Dreamer's World," she said.

Her father stopped and returned to the bedside. He patted her gently.

"You will, Amanda, when it becomes your turn to protect it. It might seem like a long time, but the day will come when you witness the Dreamer's World in all its splendid glory." Amanda frowned. "Now close your eyes and fall asleep, and that day will be one less night away."

He leaned over and kissed her forehead, switched off the lights, and proceeded to leave the room.

Amanda was eager. She would have been ready to leave right then—ready to embark on a journey through the night, and through space, as anything would have been considerably more exciting than going to sleep. Those hours that elapsed while one's body lay inactive were about as enthralling as viewing a black painted canvas in total darkness. But it was different for *them*, she thought. They experienced phenomenal wonders when their bodies became dormant—wonders that occurred here, somewhere in this universe.

She could hardly lie still thinking about it, never mind sleeping. There were these people from another world, occupying every far corner of her universe. And though she couldn't see them, she knew they were out there, hiding like crickets in the thicket. And they kept passing back and forth through this place called the Dreamer's World. She wondered what the point of passage looked like. Maybe it was like a train station, and you had to pass through a tunnel to get to the other side. Or maybe you had to travel over a long bridge, or ride a boat across a sea. She really didn't know.

But she wanted to know.

She threw off her covers and hopped down onto the carpet. She crept silently towards the balcony, while glancing at the doorway to check for anyone that may have been lingering about. Her heart skipped a beat when she heard a deep, hollow voice fill the room.

"Amanda," it said. "Why do you leave your bed?"

She sprung around and saw something shift in the darkness, but it was only Teckin. She shushed him loudly.

"I want to take a look outside," she said, sliding open the door to the balcony.

She stepped outside and surveyed the surrounding town as it appeared two hundred feet in the air. All but just a few shops had their lights still on. The scent of freshly baked goods and grilled meat had long ceased. Only a few stray individuals were left walking down the cobblestone streets, undoubtedly on their way back to their dwellings that stood along the foot of the surrounding mountain range. Beyond one of the tallest mountain peaks was a moon rising into the sky, its bluish aura creeping into the blackness. To the east was an adjacent world, a gleaming orange marble, that too, spilled its color upon the sky. There were similar planets to the north and a couple others to the west. And if one continued to observe the night, they'd see there was a least a dozen planets.

Amanda studied each of them carefully, trying to identify any peculiar characteristics, but they all looked relatively the same. They were all round, with slight color variations along the surface. Two of them had orbiting rings, but that was nothing out of the ordinary either.

She heard clomping footsteps coming from behind. A moment later Teckin was standing beside her. He glanced at the sky and looked back down at her.

"What is it that you search for, Amanda?"

"The Dreamer's World, Teckin. I want to find it."

The machine looked back at the sky.

"You won't find it there," he said. "It's well hidden, as King Clovis would tell you."

"It's not fair that he won't tell me where it is."

"It's not for you to know, at least not yet. There will come a time when this knowledge will be yours to have and yours to protect. But that time isn't now."

"But why not?"

"Because it's ten thirty-four, and you have somewhere you need to be."

Amanda knew where. Reluctantly, she complied, and forced herself to postpone her fantasies for another day.

She went next to Teckin and climbed up onto his foot and clung tightly to his leg. His body was hard and cold, but she didn't mind. All that mattered was the free ride back to her bed. Teckin, already familiar with all of her antics, carried on and trotted back to the bed with the princess attached. After ensuring she was tucked back in, he returned to his spot on the carpet and positioned his feet inside the footprints of the fabric. He would remain there until morning, guarding the young princess as she slept silently and soundly through the night.

———Chapter 1———

Tomorrow Comes Too Soon

A blaring ear-shattering sound filled the room without warning. It took all but half a second before Ryan rolled around and slammed the toggle on his alarm clock, switching off the infernal machine whose sole purpose was to annoy those that sought a few extra minutes of sleep. Furthermore, it had disrupted a dream. He did his best to recall it:

I was on a deserted planet that was covered in sand and rocks as far as the eye could see. The air was unbearably hot and the sky was pale gray. I was thirsty, so I moved out in search of water. I heard the sound of a current, so I followed that.

I trekked through a valley and found a river waiting for me on the other side. That's when I noticed two things: first, an abandoned city in the distance, perhaps no more than two or three miles away. The buildings were hundreds of feet high, rising from the mountain side. They were heavily damaged and crumbling apart; second, I saw a girl by the river, maybe about my age. She looked in my direction, and was startled. That's when the machine that was with her began to approach me . . .

What would have happened next, he didn't know. But it didn't matter, as it was as nonsensical as any other dream he's had lately.

The clock read a quarter to seven and he had to be at school within an hour. It was only his sophomore year, but that already proved to be more than enough. There was something about the mundane and repetitive nature of attending school that made him weary. The thought of being locked up inside a building for seven hours a day, five days a week was like being in prison, as any typical school-hating teenager would say. But Ryan didn't *hate* school—he merely disliked it. After all, he had lunch to look forward to, with those delectable servings of frozen pizzas that came with the two ounce milk cartons. There was also gym, the only class where he was graded according to his athletic ability.

Basketball was his sport. He had consistently made the team since middle school, chalking up plenty of victories over the years. He was widely accepted as being the top player at Rimtale High. Though it was a small school, in an equally small suburban town, but still enough of an accomplishment to garner the attention of Blake Fioravanti, a guy that had become a rival overnight. There was nothing subtle about his desire to steal Ryan's frivolous title away from him.

A casual confrontation in the hall one afternoon resulted in Friday being marked on both their calendars. It was going to be a simple one on one held at the local park. Had his opponent been anyone else, there wouldn't have been much to worry about. But this was Blake, a particular breed of bully in Ryan's eyes. He wasn't the common stereotypical bully—the physical, intimidating, steal-your-lunch-money kind of bully. No. Blake displayed none of those attributes, and yet he gave off that air, that stench of repulsion. Maybe it was his wild, gel-filled hair, with its varnished golden glow. Or maybe it was his immense stature and muscular physique. Or maybe it was those abysmal blue eyes—to have them gaze into your own would instill an immediate sense of inferiority. Ryan had already met with the misfortune of having looked into those gorgon eyes. Their pernicious stare was already taking a toll on him. Yet somehow, someway, he had to endure and overcome.

But those weren't the thoughts Ryan wanted dancing in his head before arriving at school. There were more preferable, welcoming daydreams he could have, such as one that involved that pretty girl that sat near him in English—the one with the dark-rimmed glasses and the silky black hair, who carried around a tote bag with cartoon characters stamped on the side.

Her name was Karina, and that was the sum of his knowledge concerning her. That, and supposedly she had transferred from another school at the beginning of the semester. He wouldn't know. He never asked. For whatever reason Ryan always had complications around girls he found attractive. Karina was no exception. It's been two months since the start of the school year and he has yet been able to utter a single word to her. He could attribute the taciturnity to many things, but perhaps the key reason had something to do with his self-confidence—a thing that Blake has been slowly nibbling away at. It was just another problem added to his agenda, on top of the ones already in his math book.

Ryan sat up and lazily rolled off the edge of the bed, bringing his feet under him just before hitting the floor. He changed into his clothes, throwing on some layers under his new teal shirt, and ran downstairs to throw a pastry into the toaster.

He sat at the kitchen table while he waited. The morning sun crept through the window, filling the room with an orange glow. Ryan was particularity fond of the way it gave the illusion of warmth, despite the cool temperatures of the autumn season. When the toaster popped, he took the pastry, ate it, and headed into the garage.

He grabbed his bicycle from against the wall, mounted it, and rode into the quiet streets of his small neighborhood. It was always quiet this time of year, compared to the summer months when one could see children flocking to the streets in hoards, on their roller skates and scooters, playing street hockey or basketball. Sometimes you would see those young entrepreneurs that sold lemonade on the corner, waving around those big cardboard signs. But now, during the colder season, the town was still and desolate, giving off an almost creepy vibe.

—)—

Rimtale High was just a short distance away, down the main road just outside the development. The buses were pulling in as he arrived. The air was filled with their loud roar, as students chatted and squeezed through the entrance of the building.

Ryan wheeled his bike down the sidewalk and parked it at the bike rack. He was securing the chain lock when he heard a familiar voice call out his name in the distance, powerful enough to overtake the engines and the chatter.

He turned around and saw Megan Lovetta coming down the cement path, her coffee hair fluttering in the breeze. She had on a lavender top, adorned with rhinestones that created a floral design. Over that, she had a black nylon jacket, and on her ears, the tiniest of studs.

She stopped and stood next to him.

"Ryan," she said. "What is this?"

"What is what?" he answered.

"That wasn't a yellow school bus you came riding in. That was a bicycle."

"I knew that."

"I know you know. But when the weather gets chilly, you always opt to take the bus."

"It's not that cold today."

"Please, I can see you got two shirts on under your hoodie. Clearly it's cold enough to go through the extra trouble of finding a second clean shirt."

"All right, fine," Ryan said, knowing it was best to concede. "I'm riding my bike because I could use the exercise."

"Uh huh," Megan said, nodding her head. "Exercise . . . to prepare for your match tomorrow? Is that what it is?"

"That's possible."

A grin emerged on her face.

"Blake really has gotten under your skin, hasn't he."

"No, why would you say that?"

"Because you and I both know that riding a bike for five extra minutes in the morning ain't going to do a damn thing to help you play basketball. You're reaching, Ryan—reaching as far as you can for that extra edge."

"Well, that's the kind of thing that separates the best from the rest."

"True. But I think in this instance, it's an act of desperation. You've got your doubts about tomorrow. It's written all over your face, right next to that splotch of jelly."

Ryan quickly ran the back of his hand across his mouth.

"But it doesn't matter, cause I'll cheer you on regardless. That Blake is seeking trouble. I just know it. And I know you'll be the one to put him in his place. Isn't that right, Ryan?"

"Sure," he said, sounding less than enthusiastic.

That's how Megan was most of the time, an inquisitive truth seeker that wasn't afraid to step in front of anyone or anything— not even a plowing freight train if it just so happened to contain the only piece of evidence that would lead her to an answer. She was bossy and quite adamant about getting what she wanted. It was a trait of hers that she had carried since elementary school, which is where Ryan first had the pleasure of meeting her. There she was one day, frolicking about the black tarmac of the school playground with a basketball in hand. It became routine to see her there playing with the other guys. And from what he observed, she was kicking ass left and right. Eventually he decided to confront this peculiar girl and settle matters, because as everyone there knew, no one could beat Ryan at b-ball. He had a reputation to uphold, and this girl wasn't going to tarnish it.

The next day the two of them played their game. The stakes were high. Emotions were strong.

And Ryan lost.

The rest after that was playground history.

Ryan navigated through the school entrance, went to his locker, popped the lock, and pulled out the books he needed. He picked up on the frequency of a distinctive voice that was originating just down the hall. He looked askance, peeking from behind his locker door. There was Blake, at the center of a very disheartening picture.

He was standing over Karina while she collected her belongings out of her locker. One hand was propped up high on the wall, while the other rested on his hip. He was saying something to her, but it wasn't loud enough for Ryan to hear. And that's just what he needed—to find out that the girl he liked may have already been taken. But Karina never made eye contact. Maybe she wasn't interested. Just *maybe*.

The school's physics teacher, Mr. Deskov, had a good reason for the overzealous smile he wore that day. He was excited, as any science teacher would be when a major breakthrough was made in the field. And that's what was happening. The tenth grade was gearing up for a field trip this coming Wednesday to the Museum of Natural and Modern Sciences. For a limited time only, the museum would be holding a special exhibit featuring what many would consider the epitome of human ingenuity—a microwave-sized apparatus, soldered together with steel and copper wiring, decorated with microchips. It traveled from state to state, country to country, safeguarded behind a cube of tempered glass. While seemingly appearing to be nothing more than an innocuous gizmo, it still managed to elicit fear and paranoia among certain groups of people. It was even regarded as the technological discovery that would bring about the apocalypse, all the while lacking any kind of lethal ordnance. It wasn't the proverbial gun that fired the bullet, or even the hand that pulled the trigger; it was something that preceded all of that; it was the thing that granted permission to carry out a certain order, a thing that imbibed knowledge and used that same knowledge as the basis for making decisions. Right now it sat in plain view of the public. Watching. Learning—closing in on the line that separated the living from the non-living. The Mind was waiting for its special moment.

The students were settling to their seats, many rushing in just as the bell went off. Ryan took his at the back corner of the room. When the noise came under control, Mr. Deskov preached ardently to the class.

"As some of you already know, we're in for a very special treat come next week. The museum we're visiting will be holding an exhibition that will be showcasing The Mind, which, I can vouch for, is a very special treat indeed. You may have already heard about it on the news that this revolutionary machine could change mankind as we know it. Now what it does is assimilate all sorts of information. It can see and hear with its artificial eyes and ears, in much the same way as you and I. And just like you and I, it takes all the information that it gathers and formulates it into something coherent. Something that it can interpret and study. However," he chuckled, "unlike you and I, it doesn't forget. It remembers everything it learns, and it uses that information to formulate thoughts and opinions about the way we live and the way we interact with one another. It understands sociology and human nature to a degree we can't even comprehend. The Mind notices trends and can distinguish patterns that we often times overlook. It's able to do this because of its massive database of case studies that it has acquired first hand. We're talking close to a billion people," he said, spreading his hands apart in the air. "In addition to that, it has access to anything ever documented or recorded. Just imagine walking into a library and being able to recollect any piece of information in those books at the snap of a finger, and then multiply that ability times a million.

"If you guys can wrap your head around that, then you can begin to understand the reservations some folks are having. We have many agencies, corporations, and even the federal government investing in this piece of hardware. These people are pushing the idea that this machine will bring about a new era for mankind. Why? Because with this omniscience, this degree of wisdom and intelligence, there will be no erroneous decisions. We, as human beings, won't ever have to preoccupy ourselves with decisions regarding our future—how we spend our money, our natural resources, handling overpopulation, avoiding war. The Mind will be able to give us the answer to all these questions, and more.

"And this," Mr. Deskov went on to explain, "is why we have trancestors roaming about our school this very minute."

Just as he mentioned them by name, a trancestor came zipping in through the doorway like a wild rodent. It was a flat, translucent disc, no more than two inches in diameter, marked with a *no. 7*. On its head was a small trap door, that when opened, revealed a glowing diode.

The little machine swiveled in every which way, propelling itself across the floor of the classroom.

"And there's one right now," he said with a bright smile. "It's watching all of you, looking for something that sparks its interest, so that it can relay all the data back to its mastermind."

The trancestor continued to swerve around the chairs and desks, causing the students to giggle and shuffle as it zipped past their feet. It made its way to the other end of the classroom, slowly coming to a stop. It might have found something of interest, and Ryan feared that it may have been himself. The mechanical critter decided to park itself right beside his desk. The light on its head shuttered on and off. He just looked right back at it, feeling a bit perturbed.

"It looks like it finds you interesting, Ryan," Mr. Deskov jested. The class giggled with glee.

But Ryan found it less than amusing. Sure, this whole project was very fascinating, but does this machine really know what it means to perceive and understand? What exactly was it doing right now? Conducting some form of facial profiling? Assigning values to his expression? His posture? Or even his choice of clothing? Whatever it was doing, it all boiled down to numbers. Ryan knew that much. There was no way it could replicate a human's innate ability to extract power from knowledge, or to observe and reason. Those are skills reserved for people. So he had to ask himself, what did this robot think it was doing?

Ryan stared at it unwaveringly, showing that he was the superior entity.

"Anyway, as I was saying," Mr. Deskov continued, "next week is going to be special, not only because we'll get to see The Mind first hand, but because The Mind will be put to sleep. And I don't mean in the way you put a sick dog to sleep. The Mind will actually be undergoing a cycle reminiscent to the way we humans sleep. It will enter a dormant state for twelve hours, and during that time it will compile all of its data, sort through it, analyze it, and study what it all really means. And after that cycle is complete, it will proclaim its findings to the world."

"Kinda like dreaming?" one of the students called out.

"Oh yes. Dreaming. That's one of the primary objectives of this whole experiment. The way The Mind will compile its data is very similar to the way the human mind processes information during sleep. Studies suggest that our memories have a direct correlation to the kind of dreams we have. And with this study scientists hope to further understand the relationship between the two. There's a whole lot riding on this machine, and if I were a betting man, I'd wager there's going to be a big payoff. So mark your calendars folks, because Friday at midnight, The Mind is going to sleep."

Ryan was listening intently to the lecture, periodically looking over at the trancestor that was still parked by his desk. Soon the little machine fled from his sight and escaped through the door.

He would admit that he spent a lot of time pondering over his dreams. Granted, a lot of them were nonsensical and total rubbish, but a few of them seemed to offer some type of clairvoyance, or a window that oversaw a fountain of untapped power. He could distinctly remember one dream in particular, where he sat at a piano and played a melody, consciously aware of what keys he was pressing. The notes he played were real, the harmony was real, and though he could only vaguely remember the tune upon waking up, it was still knowledge that was carried over from the confines of a dream. He could only wonder what other talents could be brought back to his waking life.

Later that day around noon, Ryan was returning to his seat in the cafeteria with a lunch tray in hand. Megan was already waiting for him at the table with a sandwich she had brought from home. Seated right next to her was the ravenous glutton they knew as Mike Cunningham, who had already consumed his helping, and now had his eyes on Ryan's. He was the kind of guy that always carried a spare pencil, along with paperclips, a stapler, soda tabs, rubber bands, ketchup packets, and other miscellaneous items that only MacGyver could use collectively.

Ryan had known Mike for a long time, since first grade to be exact. He met him on the playground one afternoon, dribbling around a basketball—a fresh, brand spankin' new rubbery scented one. Ryan was drawn to it immediately, like a moth to a porch light. It was something new and that's all that mattered. In short time, Ryan had made a new friend, while also finding some competition. They went out to the courts several times a week, getting in all the games that they could.

But they sucked. Their scrawny arms were hardly enough to toss the ball ten feet in the air, forcing them to use the strength of their entire body to lob each shot. But with consistent practice, they did get better, and as they did, they set new arbitrary goals for themselves, whether it be scoring from the free-throw line, or being able to dribble and sprint at the same time. Soon they were ready to tackle larger challenges. Eventually it was Mike's idea to take on the fourth and fifth graders—the kind of opposition that Ryan didn't dare challenge. He was always worried about humiliation—something that never crossed Mike's mind. But with insistent nagging from his friend, Ryan took the plunge and found himself surrounded by the giants. Humiliating defeats were had, but it was nothing a couple of younglings couldn't recover from.

Megan turned her head and noticed the way Mike was starring at Ryan's pasta.

"You know, Mike," she said, "you'd still have yours if you didn't swallow the damn thing so fast."

"They only gave me like ten noodles. What am I suppose to do? Stare at them?"

"No, but you could try chewing somewhere between the first and last noodle."

She turned the other way, watching Ryan from across the table, noticing how he took the time to savor every bite. "So tell me, Ryan, did Mr. Deskov go off on another tangent in your class today? Because he forgot to teach any physics in ours."

Ryan nodded until he could swallow.

"He was telling us about The Mind and all the things it's suppose to do for the human race. A dawn of a new era and all of that."

"Yeah, that sounds about the same as what I endured. It kinda gives me the creeps, if you know what I mean."

"Maybe it'll kill us all," Mike blurted out. "Like the way they do in the movies."

"Sorry to disappoint you Mike, but The Mind is an intellectual robot. So even if it goes rogue, it's not going to come at us with guns blazin'."

"It's still possible. The Mind just needs a body. Hey, I know, why don't we just swap out Megan's brain for his?"

"Now why would we replace a perfectly good brain when there's one in desperate need of an upgrade?" She clenched her fist and began knocking on Mike's skull. He let out a weak yelp. Right away she knew something was wrong when Ryan didn't seem the least bit amused. Then again, he hadn't been saying anything at all.

"What's the matter, Ryan? You're like on your third noodle."

"Don't count my noodles."

"I know what's wrong. It's Blake. The pressure's building too fast. You're about to pop."

Ryan made a few indecisive motions with his head. He didn't really want to admit to anything.

"Or maybe it's something else," she said, squinting her eyes. "Another psychological aberration that you haven't disclosed yet."

Ryan shook his head while swallowing another fork full of pasta. "There isn't one," he mumbled.

"C'mon, we don't have to interrogate Ryan," Mike said. "He'll tell us what we need to know."

Megan ignored him and continued. "She's pretty, ain't she?"

Ryan was ready to shake his head until he realized that she was asking a question based on preconceived information.

"She's got silky black hair and emerald green eyes. She's a little on the shy side, transferred here at the beginning of the semester. Ring a bell?"

"No bells," Ryan said.

"Oh, you can't deny it, Ryan. I've seen the way you stare at her as you pass her in the hall. And then there's you talking about wanting to join the Yearbook Club all of a sudden. You know who else is in there? Take a guess."

"I don't have to guess," Ryan said, as his voice trailed off. His attention shifted to the tall window panes at the front of the cafeteria. Blake was marching down the hall, chatting with a couple other guys. He came into the cafeteria, waltzing in like a billionaire arriving at his own party. The group split and Blake took off in his own direction. He combed through his hair with his hand before helping himself to a seat among a table full of girls.

"What are you looking at, Rye?" Mike asked.

"Nothing. Just Blake."

Mike swiveled around in his seat immediately. Megan, too, was curious enough to do the same. She spotted the golden totem with the silly haircut right away. Her eyes narrowed into a gaze of contempt.

"What a flirtatious jerk," she muttered under her breath. "Everyday he tries to get with another girl. It's like some kind of contest with him. He's adding trophies to his trophy case for every one he acquires. And these stupid sluts are so dense that they don't see themselves as the game in this savage hunt."

"I take it you don't like the guy," Mike said.

"I wouldn't like him if he were the last guy on earth." She looked at Ryan. "Which is why I want *you*, Ryan, to humiliate him tomorrow. Don't let him score a single basket, ya hear me?"

Ryan kept his calm and continued to enjoy his meal. He wasn't feeling that fierce competitive fire in his belly, at least not at the moment. The only thing he felt there was his stomach acid going to work.

"That sounds harsh, Megan"

"It does," Mike said. "Do you treat all transfer students this way?"

"He's not like any transfer student I know. He made a name for himself practically overnight. He's just so damn amiable, so damn charismatic, and yet it sickens me."

"Maybe you should be the one to play him," Ryan said. "You can put him in his place."

"Yeah," Mike said, "right at the bottom of the high school social hierarchy,"

"You know I can't," Megan said. "I'm not at that caliber of play."

"I don't know why you didn't keep it up. You were pretty good" Ryan said.

"The novelty of being the only girl able to kick a guy's ass in basketball had run its course. The attention was nice while it lasted, but eventually people stopped caring. So now I'm going to let you hog the spotlight for a little bit. Now take the torch and keep it burning. Keep it burning real hot."

"I'll do my best, coach."

"Don't try to get smart with me, Ryan, cause there I have you beat."

"That's right," Mike said. "She got another hundred on her last vocabulary test."

"What did you get?"

Mike paused.

"A seventy-eight," he admitted quietly.

"Doesn't matter what he got," Megan said. "He's probably forgotten all the words by now anyway."

"Not uh. I still remember hullabaloo: a commotion, or a fuss. All I had to do was think of Megan and that incident at the salon where they screwed up her hair. So easy."

"Well, if everyone's perception of you depended heavily on your appearance, I think you'd care too about a couple of miss-cut bangs."

Ryan's attention had waned as he searched avidly for Blake again, as if he were on reconnaissance duty. That was roughly the extent of his preparations for the past couple of days. That, and a push-up or pull-up here and there. He was on the fence about what an adequate amount of training would be, or if he needed any at all. There were two voices inside his head fighting to be heard. One argued that he was more than ready, that Blake would prove to be nothing more than a pushover. There was no physical evidence to suggest otherwise. But then the other voice cried that it could be a massacre, and Ryan would be conquered by his adversary. Blake was a beast, and he was just beginning to show his true colors.

But Blake was gone. He wasn't at the girls' table, or any other table. He didn't seem to be anywhere in the cafeteria. He was gone, just like that.

"What is it now?" Megan said petulantly, trying to find what Ryan was looking at.

"He's gone," Ryan said.

"Gone," Mike repeated. "Like a ghost."

Megan gave him an ugly grimace.

"Five bucks says he's behind a stairwell."

"Nah. He's too classy for that. The teachers' lounge is more up his ally."

"And just how exactly is he suppose to get in there?"

"He's got connections."

"He's got *connections?* Mike, do you realize how ridiculous you sound?"

"Well, villains do have their ways, you know. Sometimes they are able to defy all logic."

"Wait, so he's a villain now? I think you should go back to your movies, Mike."

"But it's all true—"

"False alarm," Ryan called out, as he stood up to throw away his empty tray. "He's over in the snack line."

"That's swell, Ryan," Megan said, beginning to feel exhausted. "Real swell."

For the remainder of the school day, Ryan kept a vigilant lookout for Blake, not sure what exactly he intended to accomplish by doing so. He passed him in the hall at least twice in between classes, and each time he projected himself as that arrogant guy without a care in the world. There wasn't a single thing that could deter his jaunty attitude, and Ryan knew that spelled trouble for tomorrow. As the hours counted down, Ryan felt the tension and nerves within himself grow ever so potent. It was similar to the anxiety that preyed on him whenever he had a big presentation to deliver. But this was even worse than that because there were no means by which he could prepare himself. There was no book, no encyclopedia, no person that could help him. The only way he could quell his worries was to find a way to overcome his self-doubts, and only he could do that.

It was so silly, he thought, that a lump of cells and neurons—that thing referred to as the mind—could be capable of so much, yet at the same time hold so many reservations. It had the potential to do many things, but in order to do them, the mind would have to grant itself permission.

—)—

Later that afternoon, after the school bell had permitted everyone to leave, Ryan exited the building and hurried through the crowd to get to his bike. But before he could even wrap his hands around the handle bars, Megan shouted his name. He saw her coming down the walkway, with Mike following closely behind, a basketball in his hands. He knew she was up to something.

She came beside him. "Now hold up just a darn second," she said, burlesquing the tone of a sheriff. "Where you think you're off to?"

"Nowhere in particular. But the final destination is probably home."

"You wouldn't be thinking about going to P.B. Bastions, would ya?" Mike asked, with a rumbling stomach.

"P.B. Bastions? Nope. But I wouldn't mind stopping there on the way."

"Awesome," Mike cheered. But Megan didn't share the elation. She grabbed Mike by the arm and whirled him around so that they were looking face-to-face.

"Mike," she said, "I know short-term memory is something you struggle with, so I'm going to try and be patient. Now tell me, do you know why you're carrying that basketball right now?"

Mike pretended to think about it before nodding his head.

"Good. Now give me the ball," she said, and he did as he was told.

She turned and faced Ryan. He was clutching the handlebars,

wondering if now would be a good time to make a break for it.

"Now listen, Ryan, and listen good. I know you think you're better than me, and I know you think you're better than Mike."

"I don't think that at all!"

"I'm talking about basketball, Ryan. The jury's still out when it comes to everything else. But I'm talkin' basketball."

"She took a blow to her pride," Mike said," when she was forced to recall the truth at lunch today."

"It's not about that. It's about helping Ryan, as sappy as that sounds. I want to see him perform on the court one last time before he's forced to retire tomorrow."

Ryan put on a doleful face. "Are you trying to say I'm going to lose?"

"I'm saying you're going to lose, *if* you don't cross it out as a possibility. You have to decide that you want to win."

"But how do you know I can win?"

"Because you can."

"But just because I can doesn't mean I will."

"You will if you want to."

"I want to, but that doesn't mean that I will."

"Ryan!" she shouted in frustration, "enough with the semantics. You're pissing me off."

"Be careful," Mike said, "or you might become the bad guy."

"I wouldn't want that to happen."

"Then listen and follow me," Megan proclaimed.

Ryan, feeling skeptical and fearful, decided to succumb to her demands.

—)—

The three of them traveled across the school grounds, looping around to the backside of the building. In the distance was a vast plain, as well as a running track and football field. The cool autumn wind swept through the land, rustling the blades of withering grass, and the tall evergreens that lined the property. The noise of the after-school traffic had become all but a distant sound. Coming up on their path was a short footbridge, which granted passage over a narrow stream into Pinesburrow Park—the place where Ryan spent a great deal of his childhood. He enjoyed everything about it, from the swings to colorful elaborate jungle gyms, to the picnic huts, and nature trails. If Ryan and Mike weren't playing basketball, they were finding new ways to get themselves lost in the wilderness. They'd stray from the main trail in search of things that weren't marked on the map (so to speak). Eventually they did make a grand discovery: a large desolate lake, bordered by a sandy shoreline. There was even an abandoned cabin tucked away at the far side, that remained mostly inaccessible due to the natural overgrowth of the woods. Soon they learned swimming was the easiest way to access it, at least during the summer months. The cabin became a sort of club house for the two of them, and eventually the three of them. Though to Megan's misfortune, she was forced to jump through a long list of hurdles before being entrusted with the location of its whereabouts. It was a time none of them would ever forget.

The park was a safe haven, as far as Ryan was concerned. Now in recent years it had transformed into a battleground, a site of many intensive basketball games. And come this time tomorrow, it might evolve into something much worse. For all he knew, the field would hold some sort of bloodbath, except he had no idea whose blood it would be.

They were deep inside the park now, among the younger children that were scampering through the premises. As they marched through, Ryan felt Megan wrap an arm around his shoulders, urging him to up his pace. "C'mon, Ryan," she said in a motherly tone. "Don't be scared."

But Ryan was scared. Sort of. Those towering basketball posts now seemed to look a lot more like flag posts that marked the entrance to some forbidden territory. Their nets even fluttered hauntingly in the wind.

Ryan took a couple of daring steps onto the court and tried to better his state of mind by relishing his most satisfying victories. There was quite a few of them actually. One on ones, team games; he even sent people home crying (presumably). What was he afraid of again?

He saw Mike and Megan going through their stretch routine. They were gearing up for something.

"Remind me why we're here," Ryan asked.

"To initiate you into our new after-school study group. What does it look like, Ryan?"

His eyes shifted to Mike, who had already taken off with the basketball and begun taking shots.

"I think Mike's here to play basketball," Ryan said, "but that doesn't explain what you're doing here."

"Isn't it obvious, Ryan?"

"But you just got done telling me you don't play basketball anymore."

"What, that means I can't still score on you?"

Mike stopped in his tracks just after catching his own rebound. "Don't listen to her, Ryan" he said. "She's been training behind your back all these years just so you won't see it coming when she manages to beat you again."

"Sure, Mike, as if I had nothing better to do."

"Then what's going on?" Ryan asked.

"I'm here to play you, Ryan, regardless of how much you outclass me. Just think of it as a warmup before your big match tomorrow."

Ryan chuckled. "Please. I bet Timmy could put up a bigger fight."

"Oh, look who's the tough guy now. Are we going to hear

that kind of talk tomorrow? Think again, Ryan. I know you can beat me, and I know you can beat Mike. But the question is, can you beat the two of us together?"

"What do you mean, a two on one?"

"Precisely."

Ryan shrugged. "Seems kind of silly to me."

"It's not silly. If you want to beat Blake, you're going to have to step your game up to the next level. You got to be twice as fast, twice as accurate, and twice as spunky."

"Spunky?"

"Yes. Spunky."

Ryan tried to keep a straight face, but it collapsed into a burst of laughter.

"She's serious," Mike said. "C'mon, you get first ball."

He bounce-passed the ball to Ryan, who was barely able to catch it. Once he got a hold of himself he dribbled the ball out to the three-point arc. He stood there, surveying his surroundings and his position relative to the basket. Megan was approaching him with the defense while Mike lingered around the key.

"When you're ready," Megan sneered. She leaned forward with knees bent and arms out at her sides.

He studied Megan's stance and recognized right away that it was poor. Her legs were spread too far apart and she was looking into his eyes instead of the ball. He took no time to capitalize on the situation.

He bounced the ball right between her legs and reclaimed it on the other side. Before Megan could even realize what happened, he was half way to the goal. She turned around and saw that Mike picked up on the defense, being careful not to allow Ryan to pull off the same stunt twice. He stayed with him as he dribbled left and right, buying enough time for Megan to rejoin the defense. Ryan noticed that she was coming up on his left, unintentionally setting up a perfect pick and roll. Ryan drove down the left lane, and as soon as Mike took chase he collided straight into Megan. After that it was an easy two-point layup.

"Two nothing," Ryan teased.

"Don't get too cocky," Megan said. "It's not over yet."

Ryan smiled and dribbled the ball back out.

"Switch it up,"Mike called out. "I'll cover him."

Ryan dribbled from side to side, gauging Mike's defense. He was staying close to him, ready to catch him if he took a break in either direction. That's when Ryan faked a break to the right and crossed over to the left. Mike was left behind which prompted Megan to step up. She anticipated that Ryan would drive all the way to the basket, and positioned herself accordingly. Ryan spotted her movement and stopped abruptly and pumped a fake shot. Megan leapt into the air, flying helplessly while slapping away at nothing. Ryan went ahead and took a clear shot, landing another two easy points.

Megan was left flustered, obviously not ready to be so easily overcome.

"Real good, Ryan. You're doing really good."

She signaled Mike as Ryan took the ball back out. Right away she got back on defense, playing him really close. They smiled at each other while Megan waited for just the right moment. She waited for Ryan to go for another break, and just as she saw his arms shift, she reached in, just narrowly tapping the ball. But it was enough to knock it out of Ryan's control, giving Mike the opening to retrieve it. Ryan gave pursuit, but Megan was already standing in place to intercept, and Mike was granted a clear path to the basket.

It was Megan's turn to tease.

"How'd you like that, Ryan?"

"Looks like I got to be more careful."

"Be as careful as you need to be, cause I ain't cutting you any slack."

It was now her turn with the ball. She knew she didn't have a chance at shaking off Ryan, so at the earliest opportunity she made a long pass over to Mike, allowing him to score with a lay-up.

"That's just dandy," Ryan said with a forced smile. "Now how about you try taking a shot now."

"Challenging me, are ya?"

Megan dribbled along the outer edge of the three-point arc, and little by little tried to inch her way closer to the basket. Ryan kept close, but still far enough to bait her into taking a shot, which is exactly what she did. She dashed around him and tried to get off a shot, but it launched horribly. Ryan knew the trajectory would be way off, and it was. He didn't even attempt a block. The ball struck the backboard with a thud and bounced down the court, where Mike watched it go by.

"Megan!" he yelled, throwing his arms in the air. "The hoop. Aim for the hoop."

"That's what I was doing!" she yelled back. "But Ryan here screwed me up."

"But I gave you a free shot," he said.

"Yeah, after you knew I was going to miss."

"How could I know that?"

"Cause I suck."

"You don't suck. You're just . . . less good than me."

Megan chased after the ball. She pointed back at Ryan as she ran.

"You better save those words, Ryan. Save them for when you're real hungry, because when that time comes, I'm gonna feed them to you."

Mike hustled over to Ryan and exchanged glares. "Save some for me too, will ya," he said, and then hurried back into position.

They continued to play their game, taking turns scoring and bouncing retorts off one another, all while basking in the light of that warm afternoon. Ryan had almost forgotten that this was to be treated as a warmup, as preparation for one of the biggest games he'll probably ever have to play. He was feeling confident, but at the same time he knew that feeling would change quickly the moment Blake laid eyes upon him, with those crystal blue marbles that had the power to evoke fear and dread into the hearts of any who stared into them—or maybe just people whose name just happened to be Ryan Satterfield. In any case, he knew that tomorrow his life would find its way to the crossroads between success and defeat. Which way he'd go, he didn't know.

Blake sat at the far end of the clearing, scoping out the courts, preemptively indulging in his triumph. Seated beside him was some voluptuous girl whose name would be unimportant by the end of next week. But for the time being she clung to him, as if her affection meant anything to him at all. Her luscious lips opened to produce a soft alluring sound.

"I don't get your obsession with this kid," she said. "You got me right here. What else do you need?"

He grew a belated grin, which left her wondering if it was as a result of what she said or what he was looking at.

"What?"

"Nothing," he said, and chuckled. "I just think it's kind of cute that he believes he has a shot at winning tomorrow."

"What does it matter who wins anyway. It's not like it means anything. This is a freakin' playground."

"You're right, it doesn't mean anything. But he doesn't know that. Our poor champ here is going to be playing his heart out. He's going to be playing for respect, his pride, his reputation. And you know what? He's just going to go ahead and throw all of that away. It's going to be so sad. "

The girl laughed.

"Then why even do this? Why even go through the trouble?"

"Cause I don't like the kid," he answered promptly and coldly. His face became serious. He felt a ball of hatred abruptly manifest inside of him. "And because I just feel like it."

"Oh yeah? Well I feel like doing some things too, except it doesn't involve being in a public park with a bunch of five-year-olds running around."

He gave a smile of acknowledgment, finally taking his eyes away from the court. Before leaving he stopped to observe Ryan one last time, and relish the misfortune that he would issue against him this time tomorrow.

CHAPTER 2

SABOTAGE

The following morning came and it filled Ryan with great trepidation. He awoke feeling rather nauseous, effectively eliminating any thoughts of eating. The only thing he could dwell on now was Blake, and the unfaltering influence he had over his mind. Couple that with the preoccupation of getting together with Karina and you have what it feels like to be a wet cloth wrung dry. That was how his brain was feeling right now. It was getting twisted and contorted in every direction by the slew of unanswered questions that continued to gnaw on him. He didn't know what tomorrow would be like, much less the day after, and even less the day after that. He could be dead by then for all he knew. But despite all that, he'd have to deal with today first.

Ryan left the house, in no hurry, and arrived at school just minutes prior to the bell. As he traveled through the halls he kept his head low, to ensure he didn't see Blake until the allotted hour.

While accessing his locker, he felt an incessant poking on his shoulder. He turned and saw Mike standing there with a mischievous smile, and a folded sheet of paper in his hand. He was up to something for sure. Ryan knew the look all too well.

"I got it," he said. "I got it right here."

"What do you got?"

"Our secret weapon."

"Secret weapon?" Ryan scratched his head. "I don't remember that being on the agenda."

"It's to give you that extra edge you'll need for your game today. It's the best I was able to come up with."

"But—"

Mike handed Ryan the folded sheet of paper, anxious to await his feedback. Ryan opened it and saw that the contents were composed like a letter—a letter with a bunch of hearts and smiley faces scribbled in every corner. He made a valiant effort to read it.

Hey Sweetzies,

I been seein' ya round school, and what I've been seein' I like. You don't know me, but I've been a fan of yours since ya first got here. Heehee. And I know about your game after school today. And you can bet your sweet buns that I'll be watchin'. Depending on what I see, I might even hand out mah number, and maybe you and I can hang out alone sometime. I'll see you soon. XOXO.

Ryan gently folded the letter and held it out for Mike to take back.

He didn't really know what to think. It was a weapon all right, though he wasn't sure how effective it would be, or whether or not such a thing was even humane.

"So what do you think?" Mike asked. And just as he was about to reach for the letter, it was snatched out of Ryan's hand, like a hungry seagull spotting a french fry. Ryan was relieved to see that it was only Megan. She opened it right away and began to read it. A big smirk soon emerged.

"Uh oh. Looks like someone is getting popular with the ladies."

"Hardly," Ryan said, snatching the letter back. "It's Mike's." Megan looked askance. "I mean, it's from—Mike wrote it. For Bla—to Blake. It's a weapon, you see, to put some pressure on him."

Megan crossed her arms. "Tell me you're kidding."

"I'm not kidding. It was Mike's idea."

"You don't need a weapon, Ryan. *You* are the weapon."

"He's a little low on ammo," Mike said. "I'm just trying to level the playing field."

"By trying to sabotage the match? Seriously, Mike, Ryan doesn't need any more ammo. He's got an M16 going up against a Colt pistol."

"But I can still die without ammo," Ryan noted.

"You're being silly, Ryan. Just like hatch-scheming Mike over here."

"Well, let me ask you this," Mike said. "Is there any harm in trying?"

"No, but that doesn't change the fact that you're wasting your time. Ryan doesn't need to depend on your dumb tactics. He'll win because he's better than Blake, not because he stuffed his locker with love notes. Am I getting through to you, Mikey?"

The warning bell rang, indicating that there was only a minute left to get to class. Mike snatched the letter from Ryan and tried handing it off to Megan.

"Here!" he pleaded. "Slip this into Blake's locker. It's on the way to your class."

"Mike!"

"Quick! Four-nine-one! It's our only shot!"

She tensed up, clenching her lips tightly together. She grabbed the letter from Mike and stormed down the hall, into the jostling crowd.

"We're set," Mike said. "All pieces are in play."

—)—

Later that morning, Ryan and Megan were back in the cafeteria, the boisterous chamber of chatter. They couldn't even hear themselves think, much less hear the sound of their own chewing. They were still awaiting Mike's arrival, which meant that he was running late—a strong indication that something was amiss.

Megan was working on her salad when she noticed Ryan barely working on his hoagie. He was chewing slow—alarmingly slow.

"I just don't get it," she said. "All this worrying and anxiety is simply unwarranted. Go out there this afternoon, play him, beat him, and he'll have no choice but to leave you alone. Then you'll be able to put this whole silly thing behind you."

Ryan didn't say anything at first. He continued chewing while organizing the thoughts in his head. Whichever way he analyzed it, it all boiled down to the future and the degree of uncertainty that accompanied it. The way he understood it was that each and every event would beget the next. If one bad thing happened, it could be followed by something just as bad or even worse. He wanted to avoid falling into that plunging spiral of disaster. It was a shallow and superficial way of thinking, but losing this match today could impair his confidence to do other things, namely to speak to Karina. Call it cowardice, paranoia, or whatever else, but these were the sensations that were attacking him.

"I heard from someone, that Blake was MVP at his old school," Ryan said.

"You heard? From who?"

"I don't know the guy, but that's what he said."

"Is that what you're worried about, Ryan? Being demoted?"

"It's more complicated than that."

"I'm sure it is, Ryan. I'm sure it is. But think about this: what's really going to change if you lose?"

He thought about it. He didn't want to reveal the truth, so he gave a makeshift answer.

"At the very least, I'll have myself a rival. Every good guy needs a rival."

"And so does every bad guy. And fortunately for you, the good guys tend to win out in the end."

"Lucky me I guess."

They shifted their attention when they noticed a fresh lunch tray descending upon the table. Mike wiggled into his seat and went to work on his meal. No joke, no comment, no eye contact, no nothing. Ryan may have been fine with that today, but Megan certainly wasn't. She didn't seem happy about it. Not one bit.

"What's the matter, Mike?" she asked. "Got another sixty-eight on one of your quizzes?"

"It was a seventy-eight."

"Yeah, whatever. Now tell me what's going on."

Mike kept his lips tight, opening them just temporarily to take a sip of his milk.

"Tell me, Mike," she said, growing more impatient.

Mike swallowed, and finally looked at her eyes.

"I . . . spoke to Blake during second block."

"And?"

"Well, I attempted to get some intel out of him regarding the letter, you see, since I know he switches textbooks between his first and second class."

"Uh huh."

"I was real casual about the whole thing. I was all like, so I hear that there's this girl that's really in to you, and all that. Then he's like, tell me something I don't know. Then I tell him, she's kinda shy, probably not the type that would come up and admit it. So he's like, but maybe she can write, and I say yeah. Then he gets all smug in his chair, tells me that he got more fan mail today, and that it's been difficult to follow through with all of it. So . . ."

Megan sighed.

"So basically you wasted your time. He's not even going to bat an eye. See, what did I tell ya?"

"Yeah, but—"

"But he tried," Ryan said. "That's suppose to be the thing that counts, right?"

"But what?" Megan said, addressing Mike again.

"There's uh, more."

"More?"

Mike swallowed again, except this time, he had nothing to swallow.

"Apparently when you slipped Blake the letter, one of his friends noticed. So . . ."

Megan's eyes grew wide. Her jaw dropped, and her fists tightened. She leaned over the table, dropping her arms with a heavy thud. Ryan feared the aggressive posture. In an instant, she had become scarier than Blake. He hoped she wouldn't eat him, or hurt him, or physically harm him in anyway.

"So *what*?!" she whispered furiously.

Mike lowered his head.

"S-so Blake is now kinda under the impression that the letter ca-came from you."

After hearing what he had to say, Megan returned to a collected mood. The anger seemed to have been expelled completely.

"Kinda, or *is* under the impression?"

Mike bobbled his head from side to side.

"Is," he shrugged.

Megan nodded with acceptance. She even had a smile on. But Ryan knew that was no smile. It was the face one would make when they were forced to do something regrettable.

Ryan placed his hand on her shoulder and issued his plea.

"Please don't kill him," he said. "He's a really good friend."

She paused and thought about it.

"Please," Ryan begged again.

"All right. Fine. I'll cut you a deal. I'll spare the life of this young delinquent if you go up to Blake and tell him the truth."

"The truth?"

"You tell Blake that this whole letter-writing nonsense was your idea."

"But it was Mike's."

"Then tell him it was Mike's idea."

"No," Mike squealed. "Can't tell him it was me. You'll compromise my cover. He'll be on to me if I ever have to pull off another covert operation."

Megan sighed.

"Then tell him it was Ryan's idea. Pick one and get a move on it."

"Wait," Ryan said. "I don't think this is such a good idea. If Blake thinks I was trying to cheat, and I still manage to lose, that won't look good. In fact, knowing that I tried to cheat will never look good. We got to keep this whole thing under wraps. Just for now at least, until I can figure things out."

Megan became vexed. Again she opened her mouth, fumbling to get something out.

"Look, Ryan, I'm not filling a role here. I'm not going to play the girlfriend of the biggest prick in the school."

"But you have to. Just for a while. I promise."

"Yes," Mike said. "For a while. It'll be cool having someone on the inside."

"Quiet, Mike. It's your fault I'm even in this mess."

"Play the role," Ryan begged. "Play the role."

Megan grew tired, and had already reached a point well beyond frustration.

"All right, Ryan. I'll be your actress—under one condition."

"What's that?"

"I get fair compensation."

"What can I give you?"

"What can you give me?"

Ryan grew silent. He thought about it, and derived at an answer.

"I'll owe you a really big one."

Megan rolled her eyes.

"A big one. Yeah. I gotta find myself a new agent."

CHAPTER 3

THE BIG GAME

The impending hour drew near, as indicated by the clock hands that crept steadily past each number. Ryan kept a close eye on them, watching as they ticked and tocked. He wanted them to stop, but no force in the universe could have made that possible. They would keep ticking, counting down the hours and the minutes, slowly merging the future with the present.

Ryan thought about what Megan had said. She was a firm believer in him, which was mildly comforting. She was sure he could win. The potential was there—potential that hinged on execution. He certainly had the skill and celerity necessary to win, but he knew it would take more than just that. Decision making was also important, and so was the ability to read his opponent. Though in this particular instance, it was more about mind games than anything else. And Ryan was afraid that Blake already had him beat in that regard, basically stripping him of the most critical advantage.

—)—

The dismissal bell rung, which now left Ryan with mere minutes to prepare himself. But there was nothing left he could do at this point. He took a pit stop at the restroom, mostly for the sake of stalling. He wished for anything to happen, anything at all that would postpone the match—a rainstorm, a tornado, or the sighting of a wild bear. But all the cowardly wishing did was amplify the fear. It was clear he had no choice but to face whatever the future held for him.

He stepped outside the school, and saw Megan and Mike waiting for him at the bottom of the steps. They were chatting among themselves, stopping the moment they spotted Ryan.

"What was the hold up?" Megan said with her hands in the air.

He came down the steps slowly.

"I had to pee."

"That's great," Mike cheered. "Way to rid yourself of that extra weight."

"I get the feeling the difference won't be significant," Megan said.

Two students on bicycles came riding by. One of the guys called out, "don't keep us waiting, Ryan." They continued to ride down sidewalk, towards the direction of the park.

Ryan detected something wrong with that statement.

"What does he mean by *us*?"

He looked at Megan and Mike, as they exchanged glances at one another.

"He probably means nothing by that," Megan said.

"Nothing?"

Mike explained, "Well, you see, Blake, as well as a few other guys have been hyping this game up. A lot of people know about it, which means there's probably going to be a bit of a crowd watching."

Oh, that's just great, Ryan thought.

—)—

The journey across the field was a dreadful one. The cool wind swept across the plain, becoming colder with every step. There were students up ahead, making their way over the footbridge into the park. Ryan followed them, wondering how many more were already on the other side. Whatever the number was, Ryan was certain it'd be too many.

He crossed the bridge, passed through the thin copse of trees and saw the basketball courts on the horizon, sprinkled with the colors of a crowd. They mingled among themselves, guys and girls, people he knew, people he didn't. There was already a ball in play, with several of the students taking shots. As Ryan got closer, he could make out more of the faces. There must have been at least fifty people there, but there were only two names he was interested in. His eyes juggled from one person to the next, until they landed on one particular group of girls—among them, Karina.

She shouldn't have been there, he thought. What were the odds of her coming by on her own? Blake must have talked her into it, if only so she could witness Ryan losing. But how did he know? He couldn't have. His interest in Karina was a secret. Either way, her presence would still pose a problem.

Things grew increasingly dim as Ryan spotted his renowned adversary. That cold, cunning behemoth lolled against the goal post, with his arms firmly crossed. He hadn't so much as bothered to look at the other guy who was speaking to him. His eyes were pinned on the arena. He kept shifting his weight from one foot to the other, blowing out puffs of air. He didn't show the slightest hint of apprehension or concern. It was as if the outcome was already determined and he was just waiting to acquire his trophy.

Ryan felt a hand rest on his shoulder. It was Megan.

"Just remember, Ryan," she said, "that you got all the tools you'll need, and all the materials you'll need. It's just a matter of putting everything together."

"That's right," Mike chimed in. "You got the wood, the nails, the hammer—now just put all that stuff together."

The words of encouragement were not helping Ryan.

"That's great," he said. "But what exactly am I putting together here?"

They both searched for an answer. Megan was first with the delivery.

"A coffin," she said.

"I see."

"And that's a coffin for Blake, not you. So be sure to get the dimensions right."

"Of course."

Mike slapped his back.

"You'll be fine, Rye. Don't think about it too much. Just do what you do best. Force 'em into early retirement."

Ryan wasn't convinced, but he approached the court anyway. He took short strides until he reached the crowd. One by one the heads turned, and each sparked a reaction—either one of joy, excitement, or contempt. There were cheers of encouragement, mixed with a couple of slanderous remarks, undoubtedly supporters of the opposition. Ryan did well to filter those out. Actually, he filtered almost everything out, except for his visual on Karina. He glanced at her, noticing that, she too, happened to be looking at him.

He marched onward, stopping when he reached the three-point arc. He waited for Blake to acknowledge him, to say something. But instead, that pompous grin emerged once again, letting Ryan know he should feel intimidated.

Blake took a step forward, maintaining his air of superiority. The crowd responded, and the clamor slowly subsided. Soon it was dead silent. He stood over Ryan, exchanging stares.

He waited a moment, and then projected his message. "It's all just a dream," he said, breaking the silence. "That's what this is. And after our game, you're going to wake up in another world. It might not be a better world, but it'll be the one you deserve to be in. So play carefully, Ryan."

Some *oohs* erupted from the crowd. Their volume escalated, but Ryan didn't let it bother him.

"That's just fine, Blake. Now make it happen."

The crowd roared as they applauded with enthusiasm.

Blake grinned, and snapped his fingers. A ball came bouncing in his direction. He caught it and fired a strong pass to Ryan. Any stronger and it would have slipped through Ryan's hands and struck him in the gut.

"So what are we playing to?" Ryan asked.

"Doesn't matter," Blake answered, "cause you're going to quit before we get there."

The crowd erupted again.

Ryan didn't say another word. He dribbled the ball out to the arc, turned around and faced his opponent.

Blake was hunched forward, hands on his knees, baiting Ryan into making an impetuous move. Ryan realized what he was trying to do, but that wasn't going to stop him from making a break for the basket.

He dashed forward, dribbling the ball to his right. If he could at least be the first to score, that would bolster his confidence. But it didn't seem like it would happen.

Blake stayed on him. He wasn't going to get off a clean shot, so he decided to do the next best thing.

He stopped dead in his tracks, hoping Blake would be slow to react. He leapt back, and took the fade away shot. The ball barely left his fingers before he heard a heavy plop that sent it bouncing away.

Ryan was now convinced the threat was real. There was a vicious bite behind the bark. Victory was no longer within arms reach.

He panicked.

Blake waltzed around him before his feet could even touch the ground. The ball was now in his possession.

He dribbled out to the arc and turned around, still showing that conceited grin. Ryan avoided the gaze at all cost, paying attention solely on the ball. He watched as it traveled up and down the court, slipping through and around Blake's legs. Little by little it inched its way closer to the goal. Ryan wanted to reach in for a steal, but it would have given Blake an opportunity to run away with an open shot. He was left without a plan.

He saw Blake leap off the ground, his arm forming an arc that pointed towards the basket. The ball spun off the ends of his fingers, soaring through the air in a perfect trajectory that would put it through the goal, with a graceful swoosh to boot.

Cheering broke out from the crowd, an ecstatic outcry. The sounds struck Ryan harder than a hailstorm. The support clearly wasn't in his favor. And when he realized that, it made his poor start that much more daunting. He felt like an exile, trying to fight for acceptance, but his chances were bleak at best.

Blake took the ball back out, his grin growing more wicked and spiteful. It was becoming more and more difficult for Ryan to bear.

Blake hung around the three-point arc as Ryan watched him. A tight defense wasn't necessary, or so Ryan thought. But he would soon discover the folly of his assumption as he saw Blake take the shot. There was nothing he could do about it now, except watch as the ball soared across the sky and land through the hoop—except that wasn't what happened at all.

The ball clanged against the rim, and bounced around a few times. It was clear it wouldn't go through, but Ryan had already made the mistake of not going for the rebound. Then, like some ravenous jungle cat, Blake sprinted past him, snatched the ball, and rushed in to secure another two points.

It was downright embarrassing, completely humiliating. He was plunging into a deficit he doubted he could recover from. He imagined what Mike and Megan must be thinking. It was probably as hard for them to watch as it was for Ryan to play. And Karina—if anything she must be laughing, and if she was, he'd rather not look to find out.

Blake projected his voice loudly, enough for all to hear. "What's the matter, champ? Falling down a slippery slope? Some words of advice: if you got an ice pick, now would be a good time to use it, cause it's going to be a long way down."

But Ryan had no ice pick. He had nothing right now. He was stripped of every mental fortification, every comforting reassurance, his confidence to play basketball. All of it was gone.

Once again Blake was in possession of the ball. Like last time, he hung around the arc. Ryan waited for another shot from downtown. He was ready to collect the rebound this time.

The ball launched through the air, and before it even reached its apex, he ran to retrieve it. He was relieved to see that it was another botched shot. Though strangely enough, Ryan found himself alone in the pursuit of the ball. Blake hadn't moved at all. Ryan then realized that Blake had simply, in an act of mockery, donated the ball to him.

That's just wonderful, Ryan thought. That was exactly the kind of tactic that he had come to expect from Blake. Honorably speaking, it didn't matter now if he made the next shot or not, as he did not earn possession of the ball. No less, he scored his points, and listened to the cheers of pity from the crowd.

He took the ball back out, and saw Blake keeping a weak defense. He may have gotten away with a fast layup this time, but he had already decided on another play.

He took two steps before Blake lunged forward to intercept, but he missed.

Ryan froze, quickly catching the ball in his hands, realizing his mistake after it was too late. He couldn't dribble again, as it would have been a travel. On top of that, he was far from the basket. There was no way he was going to make the shot.

The crowd roared with excitement. A barrage of snappy remarks were fired from every direction.

Ryan tried to breath, tried to relax, but the colossal fiend hovered over him. Whatever shot he attempted would be awful, but he had no choice.

He leapt out and away, getting off an underhanded shot before landing back on the ground. He stared at the ball, and within a second, he knew it wasn't going through that hoop. No. Instead it ricocheted off the backboard, producing a hollow thud that almost sounded comical. It was humorous enough to stir laughter among the spectators. And to follow it up, Blake caught the rebound again and scored.

What was the score now? Eight to nothing, not counting the freebie? How could he be doing so poorly. It had to be some sort of nightmare. It just had to be. He desperately wished he would awaken, but that wasn't going to happen. Every facet of this experience was too lucid and vivid to be a fabrication of his mind. The suffering, the humiliation, all of it. It would be a juncture in his life, a staple of his memory that would be preserved indefinitely.

"Let's end this, champ," Blake said, "before someone gets hurt."

Ryan waited for him to take the ball back out and execute his next play.

For the next five minutes Ryan watched as Blake scored one basket after the other. The relentless assault would not stop nor abate. No matter what kind of strategy he utilized, it always seemed as if he were playing directly into his hands. It was only by a stroke of good luck that he pulled off a single jump shot—one which Blake may have let happen. But those points were a piddling contribution to his current score. The game was a massacre, just as he had feared. He was being outclassed in a way he could never imagine, in a way he could never live down.

With his curiosity getting the best of him, he glanced at the spot where Karina and her friends were standing just a short while ago. Now they were notably absent, no where in sight. There seemed to be no reason to continue this disaster of a game. There was nothing left he could hope to accomplish. It was time to fold. Time to cut his losses and go home.

He approached Blake, with shoulders slouched and his head hung low. He never thought he'd have to utter these words, but there was no other choice.

"I'm done, Blake," he said. "You win."

Blake stood there with his arms held out, aghast and dumbstruck, but clearly pretending. There were cheers all around, and rapturous cries from his loyal female supporters.

Blake covered his mouth with his hand as Ryan dragged himself off the court.

After Ryan weaved his way through the half-booing, half-cheering crowd, he was intercepted by Megan and Mike. He could barely summon the strength to look them in the eye. There they were, forced to watch that abysmal performance despite all their efforts to assist. He could tell that they were unprepared to deal with a disaster of this magnitude.

"Don't take it so hard, Ryan" Mike said, picking up his pace to keep up with Ryan's hasty walk. "You had an off-day. It happens to everyone."

"Yeah," Megan said. "On a good day, that score would have been the other way around. There's no way Blake is that much better than you. You know that."

"I *knew* that," Ryan corrected. "Now I know better."

"You're kidding yourself, Ryan. We all know it shouldn't have played out that way. You were just intimidated, that's all."

"She's right," Mike said. "Just take some time off, play him again. I'm sure you'll do better."

"Right. I can try going for a perfect zero."

"This isn't golf, Ryan," Megan said. "This is basketball, a sport that you excel at."

"I'll try to believe that."

"You have to believe it, cause it's the truth."

Ryan walked hurriedly across the field, leaving the two of them behind. He thought he heard them say something to each other, but he didn't care right now. His mind was too busy making sense of what had just transpired. He was bitter, he was angry, but not just because of the loss he suffered, but rather with the way it was dealt. It wasn't just a defeat, but a moral defeat. It was a declaration of Blake's superiority. Every day from this day forward, Ryan would have to yield to him, and in turn, lose whatever foothold he had in making progress with Karina. His chances of getting together with her were now a distant dream, lost in a field of ones that have already been shattered.

That evening he spent his time alone, keeping to the confines of his room. He sat at his desk, making a paltry effort to finish what was left of his math homework, all the while the clock counted down the hours left in the day. The sun had long descended behind the horizon, making way for the effulgent ornaments that decorated the night sky. The moon hung within the borders of his window, emitting its ethereal glow. And beyond it, light-years away, were the sparkling trinkets known as the stars.

The nightly beauty had drawn Ryan into a daydream. He looked into the sky, as if he were staring into a wishing well. Out there was a sea of undiscovered wisdom, an outlet of strength and power that the world had yet to understand. The future is what piqued his interest. Perhaps it existed out there, somewhere, interconnected through a thousand different trails, each coming to a crossroads that led to yet a thousand more. But to make it problematic, the only indication as to where to go was the rickety sign posts that were weather-beaten beyond any recognition.

Is that how one finds their future?

Ryan wasn't sure. It was exhausting to think about it. So rather than dwell over what his feeble mind wasn't ready to understand, he decided to retire to his bed, where by luck of the draw, he may be able to find himself in a more desirable locale. That's what could happen after his lids closed and his body fell dormant. And such is what occurred on this very night—a night that he would remember as a night that set a most treacherous journey in motion.

That night Ryan fell asleep and he began to dream.

Chapter 4

The Man with the Motorcycle

Ryan felt a hard frigid surface against his palms and face. He blinked his eyes a few times, trying to bring his vision into focus. Everything was dark, and he could only vaguely make out the furnishings in the room. There were long, black desks, paired with chrome stools. There were no signs of activity, except for the dim, dancing lights that must have been coming from some apparatus atop the desks.

He didn't think much of his surroundings. No thoughts had come to him just yet, except for one—this was not his room.

He pressed his stiff, aching body off the ground and climbed onto his feet. Now he could see the broad monitors that stretched across the tabletop. They projected lines of information that scrolled ceaselessly, as well as graphs that plotted all sorts of data. Ryan figured they were all compiling something simultaneously. What exactly, he had no idea.

As he made sense of his environment, he noticed how large the room really was, and how it was comparable in size to the gymnasium at his school. The outlying walls were geared from floor to ceiling with computer consoles, and more digital displays, all which were littered with equations and graphs. Next to them was shelving that held glass tubes, beakers and containers, filled with all sorts of alien substances—some as luminous as radioactive gel, and others as black and murky as sludge. Next to that was a glass cabinet stocked with scalpels and needles, and other sharp medical (or torturous) instruments.

Following the trail laid out by his curiosity, he navigated around the desks. He stopped when he noticed something shimmer.

At the center of the room was a sunken pit, an inverted silver dome that was seemingly the focal point of everything in the room. Every desk, every monitor, even the cables that ran underneath the translucent tiles gravitated to this spot.

A man was suspended over the center of the pit, but not by any rope or wire. He was levitating, trapped in midair. He hung lifelessly, his head drooped, his black hair spilling over his face. He had a lean, spindly body, and wore a dark maroon shirt with a battered leather jacket, with black pants and black boots. The whole ensemble hung like an outfit on a peg.

Ryan wasn't sure if he was dead. Though if he was, it'd be unlikely they'd leave him there as decoration. One way or another, it didn't concern him nearly as much as finding a way out of the room. From what he could see, there was a glass door at the other end. However, to reach it, he would have to cross paths with the dark figure—which should have been easy enough, given their immobility.

But Ryan took no chances. He walked briskly past the desks, past the pit. He glanced back once, and promised himself he wouldn't again.

"Hey!" yelled a hostile voice. The sound echoed throughout the room.

Ryan nearly jumped out of his sneakers, his heartbeat escalating to a pounding palpitation. His instinct was to run. And he ran, all the way to the far door.

He stopped to examine it, and saw there was no handle, no obvious way to open it. There was a security pad on the wall, but he wasn't getting through that. He was stuck.

There were no other options, he thought, but to turn around and address the voice that had called out to him.

He looked at the man in the pit. His head was lifted high, his face now visible. His skin was ashen, with protruding veins that carried black blood. He had pronounced cheekbones and a sharp chin. Overall a withered face, though still a face that couldn't belong to anyone older than thirty. But what drew the most attention were the savage, bloodthirsty eyes. The pupils were shrunken pinheads. The irises were a nebula of black and red. They stared at Ryan for what felt like an eternity, filled with surprise and curiosity.

The man said, with a gentler tone, "You don't have to be afraid. I want to get you out of here."

Ryan stepped closer to him, taking solace in the fact that he was still trapped inside a contraption that was seemingly a product of wizardry.

The man took a deep breath. "Get me out of here, and I swear I'll help you."

Ryan dithered over what he should do. Freeing him seemed like a bad idea, one he could easily regret, so he stopped advancing. The man must have picked up on his reservations, because his voice grew agitated again.

"Listen to me, Ryan. There's only one way out of this room, and only one person that can get you out. So if you don't want to leave your fate up to chance, then free me."

Ryan kept his distance. He became curious about one thing.

"How do you know my name is Ryan?"

The nuances of the man's expression indicated that it was a slip of the tongue.

"That's not important right now. What is important is that I get off this station."

"We're on a station? Like a space station?"

"Yes, like a space station. But don't get the wrong idea. These people aren't exactly here to photograph stars."

"So what are they here for?"

"Doesn't matter. All you need to know is that it's important we get out of here. And from the looks of it, you're in a really good position right now to make that happen."

Ryan was skeptical, but he felt he had no other choice. There was no way to get out of this room on his own.

"What do you want me to do?" he asked.

"I want you to take one of those desks and slide it into this pit."

"Slide it into the pit?"

"Don't question. Just do it."

Ryan walked over to the nearest desk, wondering if he could even move such a thing.

"Remove the equipment. It'll make things easier."

Dislodging one piece at a time, he brought the different components to the floor, while minding the cables that were coiling around his ankles. Lastly, he attempted to move the monitor. Due to its bulkiness, he found it difficult to establish a firm grip. It was a heavy thing, heavier than what he anticipated, because as soon as he pulled it over the edge of the desk, it came crashing down, exploding into a thousand glass shards.

He panicked over the potential consequences if someone were to find out.

"Forget about it," the man hollered.

Ryan threw his weight against the desk, trying to get it to budge. With a steady exertion of force he was able to get it moving, little by little. Soon the desk tottered over the brim of the pit, and with another hefty push it dropped inside.

The desk jolted towards the center of the pit with a tremendous velocity. It looked like it would collide with the man, but it didn't. At the last second, he brought his legs up, and right before impact, he kicked his feet out and pushed off the surface of the desk, tumbling out onto the floor. The desk continued to oscillate back and forth, gradually coming to a rest at the center of the pit.

The man crawled back to his feet, fumbling to keep a steady walk. He sprawled his arms and cracked his joints. He approached Ryan, and gave a nod of appreciation, then continued towards the glass door.

Ryan followed.

"So how do we get through—"

Before he could even finish the sentence, the man had lifted his elbow and fired it with a bludgeon of force. From where Ryan was standing, it appeared as if the door was taken out by a stick of dynamite. Bits and pieces were scattered across the floor like pellets of hail.

"Hurry," the man said, quick to leave the room. Ryan, still feeling ambivalent about his decision to release him, obeyed the man.

Together they raced through an open corridor. It was ridiculously long, as if without end. Its meticulous architecture bore no resemblance to Ryan's conception of a space station. The floor was black marble, with an immaculate surface. On either side were strips of burgundy carpet, detailed with dark sinuous lines that curved and twirled, forming abstract shapes and fractals. The beige walls towered overhead into arches. There were shallow alcoves on either side, and intricately carved columns that climbed to the ceiling. Together they created a beautiful environment—a kind of elegance that was almost haunting.

Ryan continued to chase the man down the hall. All was silent, except for the clatter of their footsteps.

They took a turn at the end of the corridor, and then another. By then they had passed a variety of doors, each different in their own way—sliding glass doors, wooden doors, wrought iron doors. Some of the bulkier looking ones had slits covered by a sliding panel.

Ryan heard a rattle, followed by a muffled voice.

He stopped and searched for the source of the sound. The man stopped too, but only to tell Ryan to hurry. But Ryan couldn't help his curiosity. He backtracked a couple of steps and was able to identify the tall metal door from which the sound came.

He approached it cautiously.

"What are you doing?" the man whispered loudly.

"I hear something."

"We don't have time for this."

Ryan could hear the faint call from behind the door.

"Someone's locked up," Ryan said. "Maybe we can free them . . . if you think they don't belong here."

"Now isn't the best time to be helping strangers."

"But I helped you."

The man made a disgruntled groan before approaching the door himself. He slid open the panel and saw a pair of tired, beaten eyes looking back at him.

"Who are you?" the man asked.

The captive sighed when he saw the man he was looking at.

"Trust me," he said. "For my sake, it's better that you don't know."

"You want to get out of here, don't you?"

"Yes."

"Any reason why I should help you?"

"Because we share a common enemy. And because I can tell you how to get to where you're trying to go."

"Yeah? And where's that?"

"You're searching for your motorcycle. It's in one of the aircraft hangars. The entrance is marked. You'll see a pair of tall doors. Just follow—"

"I know where it is."

The captive raised an eyebrow. "You do? Well then, there's only one other thing you'll need."

"And that is?"

The man slipped an electronic key card through the slot. It was a translucent, rectangular device with some sort of embedded chip. Ryan watched as the other man took it.

"Take this. It'll grant you passage into the hangar. Remember the digits 4-7-2-6. And while you're at it, you can also use it to unlock this door. Just slide it through the reader."

Ryan watched as the black-haired man examined the card for a prolonged amount of time. He was ready to tell him to go through with it, but ultimately didn't have to.

The man swiped the card and dialed the digits on the keypad. There was a low beep, followed by the sound of a latch unlocking. The captive was ready to push the door open, but the other man held it firmly shut.

"Count to sixty before stepping out."

"Fair enough," the captive replied.

The black-haired man stepped away from the door, then checked to see if it remained closed. When he saw that it did, he beckoned for Ryan to follow.

Together they threaded through the passageways, deeper into this palatial labyrinth that seemed to have no end. Ryan was struggling to keep up, as the man moved ever so swiftly. No matter how hard he tried, he felt as if he were being bogged down, as if he was running through water. After thinking so much about it, he forgot why he was running in the first place. Why was he following this man? What was this place, and why was he here? None of it made sense. His mind wanted to drift, and travel somewhere closer to home.

He got his wish when he started to see new things appear all around him. There were signs and storefronts, benches and fountains, people ambling all about. The air was filled with the scent of fried foods. It must have been the mall, he thought. That's exactly what it was. And there was a reason he was there. He needed to buy something, but he couldn't remember what. Maybe if he sat and thought about it.

Up ahead the man stopped and turned around, the piercing eyes looking back at Ryan. Suddenly Ryan found himself back in the space station.

They were standing before a pair of tall doors, just like the captive had described.

Ryan watched as the black-haired man used the key card to open the lock. There was a quiet whirr as the two doors slid apart.

Inside was the hangar, an enormous facility that spanned the distance of at least three football fields. From wall to wall, there were monstrous machines of all sorts, things that Ryan had never seen before. They resembled aircrafts, in an abstract sort of way. They were pods that grew amorphous limbs, connecting to shapes that spiraled and twisted, and sprouted fins with claws. They were as sharp and fierce as the fangs of a wildcat. Their bodies were coated with a charcoal-colored luster that shined brilliantly under the warm lighting. Some were bolstered by supports, with panels removed. Inside were legions of silver tendons, like an artificial system of muscle.

As Ryan understood, the man was searching for his motorcycle—an item that would have been distinctly out of place in a facility like this. He started to ask himself what could have made it so important.

They each branched off in different directions, searching around and between the different aircrafts. Ryan followed the east wall and came to a section that was partitioned for smaller vehicles. That's where he saw a motorcycle propped up on a mechanical lift.

It was a black sports bike, one that had seen its fair share of use. The enamel was brittle, and portions of the chrome trim and fenders were beginning to rust. The vinyl seat was tattered and the tires worn. Yet it must have been a beautiful machine in its heyday. Even now, it appeared vigorous, ready to spring to life, like a panther lying in wait.

Ryan called out to the man, and watched as he hurried over.

"Is this what you were looking for?" Ryan asked.

The man nodded.

He walked over to it and grabbed the underside of the body. As if it were made of cardboard, he lifted it off the frame and set it gently on the floor.

Ryan was stunned. Yet again he witnessed another remarkable feat of strength, only reinforcing his belief that there was more to this man than he let on. He was nothing short of an enigma, much like this place he was trapped in.

The man stood over the bike, lost in a daydream, his hand caressing the torn seat. When he realized, he quickly mounted the machine. He took his finger and pressed it against a small touch panel located by the dash—an obvious modification. There was a silent beep, followed by a monstrous roar. The machine had sprung to life, letting out a cry that communicated it was ready to obey the will of its driver.

He turned around, and looked over at Ryan.

"If you trust me, climb on, and I'll do my best to get us both out of here alive."

For some strange reason, Ryan did trust him, despite only knowing the man for a short while. Underneath the fiendish visage, there was some underlying quality that hinted towards benevolence. The man wanted to do good, and Ryan would grant him the opportunity.

He climbed onto the back seat, and just before he could grab on to the guy's jacket, the bike squealed across the floor. It swerved around the aircrafts, continuing to pick up speed, eventually passing through the center of the room. From there they rode towards the west wall, stopping momentarily to unlock a security door that led into a new corridor.

A whole new wing of the station unfolded before them—a grandiose hall that managed to surpass all the splendor of what Ryan had already seen.

The passageway was expansive, a cathedral with a never-ending aisle. The ornate columns rose to form arches that tapered towards the ceiling's end, an area cast in shadowy darkness. At either side of the passage, tucked away in their own alcoves were a bundle of enormous pipes that traveled the length of the wall. They were black, each with the girth of a subway tunnel. They growled and hissed silently, propelling a powerful current that also emitted a wave of heat.

The bike continued to increase in speed, rapidly approaching a hundred miles per hour. Though no matter how fast they rode, the walls around them hardly seemed to pass by.

Ryan was amazed by everything he saw. As they raced down the passage, he saw sunken partitions on either side, followed by a set of doors. They passed them one by one—fifty, maybe even a hundred of them. He could only imagine that each one led to another hall, another wing of the station. But the man did not change his course. He continued to follow the burgundy carpet all the way down.

After a lengthy ride, they turned into the next passageway. Here the eastern wall transitioned into a vast seamless window that rose a hundred feet. It provided an immaculate view of what was outside: a shroud of night cast over the endless scope of space. There wasn't a thing to see except for minute traces of distant stars, burning with a glittering light.

After a lengthy ride they reached the end of the passageway, which opened into a large hall. It was another room of immeasurable size, composed of multiple tiers all interconnected by short stairways. At each level were spacious areas with ample seating, with black vinyl couches and glass tables, and even raised plant beds that harbored exotic vegetation. The highest tier had a running fountain that spilled water down each declivity, which was then collected into a pool at the lowest level.

Ryan held on tightly when he saw that the man was going to take the stairs head on. The bike bounced furiously up each flight, eventually slowing down as it reached the middle tier.

The man looked both ways, at the pair of tall, opulent doors on either side of the room. He gazed at them attentively, much to Ryan's curiosity.

"Are we lost?" Ryan asked.

"Lost? No. I'm thinking more along the lines of found."

"Found?" he repeated nervously.

The bike sprung back to life, lurching forward with a burst of speed that ripped the fabric of the carpet. The man climbed the remaining flights of stairs, settling at the top. He parked before another door, one equipped with a security lock. Ryan figured they were going to enter, but the man issued a different set of instructions.

"Get off," he said. "Get off and stay out of sight."

"But what—"

"Just do as I say."

Ryan obeyed, and scurried over to one of the marble plant beds. He peeked from behind the ferns, waiting for something to happen.

A low rumble traveled through the walls in the room. It grew louder, keeping a steady rhythm.

Something was approaching.

The east and west entrances simultaneously produced a mechanical whirr, forming a seam along the center of each door. The rumbling intensified, revealing itself to be the sound of footsteps marching in unison.

Like a severed pipeline, a gush of soldiers swarmed the room, flanking from the east and the west, assembling themselves in a formation at the base of the first tier. Each of them were outfitted in black uniforms, with tailored breastplates and arm guards. Over their eyes they wore a black-tinted visor, which was part of the headset that wrapped around the back of their heads. In their arms they carried an assortment of intricately crafted rifles, equipped with bayonets that gave an otherworldly glow.

Ryan was sure something disastrous was about to go down— something that could mark the moment of his demise. He had visions of cruel torture, a merciless trial, and even death itself. Maybe it was for breaking that monitor. Or worse—aiding in the escape of two prisoners.

The black-haired man stood just a few feet away, surveying the threat from up high. Ryan expected a peaceful surrender from him, as what other choice did he have?

But no. He had other plans.

He pinned the throttle, and the motorcycle roared a terrible roar. The rear tire spun rapidly, sending the bike forward. It traveled down the first flight of stairs, passing by like a blur.

The soldiers below had established an aggressive formation, with weapons in hand, ready to deliver punishment. The riflemen in the rear had their guns drawn and pointed at their target.

They fired a round of shots that zipped across the room. Several shots clanked as they nicked the body of the bike.

They were going to kill him, Ryan thought. Just like that, they were going to kill him.

He flinched at the sound of each shot. With one eye peeled, he peeked from behind the cover of the ferns.

The man descended another flight of stairs, then another. On the brink of reaching the next, his body sprung into the air, lifting the bike along with it. He was soaring, straight into the crowd at the base of the stairs.

The bike began to change.

The front and rear side of the body shifted and turned, screeching and whirring, rearranging itself in a way that brought the wheels together. The two handlebars folded into one, forming the hilt of this would-be weapon. Another section extended from the other end, which unleashed a long, narrow shaft. From there emerged the ruthless blade—stark, with a shimmering sharpness that demonstrated this was an instrument of devastation.

The man, still in the middle of descent, now held the vehicle as a sword. He lifted the weapon, and held it just behind his right shoulder, with the tip of the blade pointed skyward.

He waited for the perfect moment.

The time came.

He swung the blade with vehement force, covering a seven foot arc. A dozen men were hurled to the ground, scattered about like pins. Those less fortunate, standing in range of the open blade, had their bodies ripped apart, with their innards splashing all over their comrades like a torrential downpour.

He followed through with his swing, allowing the blade's end to reach its vertical peak before swinging it back the other way.

Another set of bodies were knocked across the floor. Corpses were beginning to accumulate. But the remaining soldiers did not waver in their resolve. They regrouped and persisted with their assault.

They attacked viciously from all sides, attempting to use their melee weapons on the man, but each blow was parried and deflected by the sheer range of his weapon. Rifles were fired, but the shots did nothing more than graze the skin.

The man followed through with another swing, and yet again with another, always drawing back the weight of his weapon towards the center of his body. Minding his balance, he lunged forward, thrusting the blade into the body of one soldier, then immediately retracted it to level the foes that stood behind.

Ryan, though deeply horrified, couldn't help but watch. The man was a beast, nothing short of an absolute monster. With every second the bodies piled higher, the blood slathering across the floor like detonated paint buckets. The soldiers that occupied the field of battle dwindled in number, until there were only a handful left.

Then came a thunderous stomping from the next room. It grew louder with every step, bellowing and growling.

The man could hear it approaching. He turned around and spotted the monstrosity as it took its first step into the room.

It was quadrupedal animal, five meters high, that took the physical characteristics of a frog, tiger, and gorilla. It had a long, broad face, a blunt snout, and two powerful forelimbs and hind legs. The epidermis glimmered from secretion, and was covered with blue and black striations that formed a disorderly pattern.

The creature pounced forward with impressive agility, and bellowed angrily.

The man readied his weapon.

The animal cocked its powerful arm and swept it through the air. The man dropped to the floor, just in time to feel strands of his hair being grazed by the animal's skin. He then leapt back on his feet. With his weapon in hand, he rushed in to pierce the torso.

He thrust the blade forward, digging it deep into the body, provoking a shrilling scream from the creature. But before he could retract the blade, the animal's massive arm returned for another blow. With a clenched fist, it struck the man like a battering ram, sending both him and the bike hurling across the room.

Barely fazed, the man climbed back onto his feet and hurried to retrieve the motorcycle. He lifted it and rushed back towards the creature while dragging the blade in tow.

A clenched fist was fired again.

The man ducted under the arm, then lifted the blade off the

ground. He followed through with a deathly swipe.

The blade tore cleanly through the flesh, forming a long gash along the creature's belly. The animal growled with fury as it returned a volley of its own.

The counterattack was quick and strong, occurring before the man could react. He was thrown once again into another corner of the room, clipping the wall of a plant bed and falling face first into a glass coffee table.

He shook off the discomfort of his landing and clasped his weapon again. But rather than assault the creature a second time at close quarters, he kept his distance, biding his time until the animal could find him.

He hoisted the weapon high in the air, elbow bent, pointing the blade skyward. With his thumb he struck a switch, which revved up the engine. The wheels turned, slowly at first, then faster and faster. They produced a whirlwind of energy, screeching and grinding, sparks flying. The bike then produced one last roar.

The animal spotted him and charged, moving deftly on all fours.

Timing was everything. He waited for the animal to come near, and when the moment was right, he swung the weapon forward. The motorcycle squealed as it generated a mass of heated particles. The energy surged through the body, where it was channeled and sent through the tip of the blade. The particle mass shot across the room in the blink of an eye, striking the creature dead-on.

A white flash filled the chamber as a fiery ball engulfed the surrounding area. The ardent flames exploded in all directions, singeing the walls, consuming the carpeting, the trees and the ferns. A collection of smoke gathered at the ceiling. Clumps of juicy matter lay scattered across the floor, broiled pieces of meat still cooking in the blaze.

Ryan, though far from the blast, could still feel the heat quite strongly. From what he could tell, the threat was vanquished. The soldiers lay dead, and the creature was slain.

The man, looking somewhat fatigued, stepped outside the zone of fire and ash and began climbing the stairs. It appeared safe for Ryan to come out from hiding—that is until he noticed a new figure enter the room, stepping through the scorched debris.

"A magnificent performance, Zephner," the figure proclaimed. "Keeping the cleaning crew busy I see."

Ryan retreated to his cover behind the ferns.

The man called Zephner, turned around to face the gentleman that stood before him.

He was an individual of moderate height, in his forties, with a lean body and a small, rounded face. His eyes were crystal blue, his hair black and neatly combed over. He wore a black, knee-length military coat that was left unbuttoned. The collar stood high, covering the nape. The lapel was wide and prominent, tapering down the length of the coat. On each shoulder were golden epaulettes with long dangling laces. Underneath his coat he wore a tight-fitted black shirt and a pair of black slacks. But the most peculiar thing about the outfit was the metal insignia that he wore over his left breast—a semicircle with a talon-like extension that curved over the flat side, with a spearhead shape protruding from the underside.

The man stood proudly, with a grin on his face.

"You know, we had high hopes for you. We really did—hopes that you'd be the one with the knowledge. But after our comprehensive observations, we've assessed that you are of no value to us."

"That's not my problem."

"Oh, but it is. Think about it. You're expendable now."

Zephner felt his muscles grow tense. A part of him wanted to snap.

"Listen to me," he said. "You're going to provide me with an aircraft, and allow me to leave this station uncontested. If you don't comply with these simple demands, you're going to become the cherry on that charred mountain of corpses. Am I making myself clear?"

The man broke into a hearty chuckle.

"My, Zephner, you've been amusing. It's been a special treat having you aboard. If only you knew where you stood now, you'd see you were in no position to be making demands."

"I'm in a very good position," Zephner snapped back, strengthening the grip on his weapon. He took a step forward, dragging the blade along the floor. "Your neck lines up perfectly."

"I'm afraid truncating me won't do you any good."

"I think it will."

"No. No, you see, our itinerary has already been set. We'll be arriving at our destination shortly, with or without me."

"Shortly? I haven't given you permission to go anywhere."

The man chuckled again. "Humorous as always."

Embittered by the comment, Zephner raised his voice. "Where the hell are we heading?"

"Our bearings are set for 275-G."

Zephner rummaged through his mind, trying to recall the location. He had heard of it before, and after giving it some thought, it finally struck him—a shocking revelation.

"What the hell is this?" he said, raising his voice. "That's a star!"

The man looked away. Immeasurable sorrow spontaneously filled his face. His demeanor took a complete one-hundred and eighty degree turn.

"Yes," he said. "It is a star. Quite the sparkling gem if I do say. It looked especially beautiful as part of the Cronellia constellation, as it was once seen from the surface of Ridaiya."

"Do you not have an ounce of sanity left? It's a star. You'll be doing us all in."

"It must be done. There's nothing left for either of us now. Unless of course . . . "

"Unless what?"

"Unless you surrender the boy."

Zephner became enraged. He felt there was little he could do to control the anger that simmered within. That bastard—how did he even know about Ryan?

"The boy is what matters now," the man went on. "Perhaps he could tell us what you could not."

"But at the same time, you're willing to just let him die? You would get nothing!"

"Yes, but it wouldn't really matter. Our Lord's desire will still see fulfillment, only it would be later rather than now."

"Then why do this? Allow us to leave, then do as you wish."

The man shook his head. Tears were ready to fill his eyes. His voice trembled.

"You don't understand. In the eyes of Lord Triocks, I will have failed. He would not be pleased. Oh, I swear to you he would not be pleased. I will no longer be worthy of the gift. It'd be best if I handled my own punishment, while I still have the power to do so, and at the same time, issue a just comeuppance to those responsible for my fate."

"No," Zephner said, trying his best to contain the anger. "You're going to let us go, and you're going to do it now!"

The sorrow left the man as quick as it had come. A new, overly ecstatic grin took the place of his frown.

"Now!" Zephner yelled, his patience faltering. "Release us now!" he yelled louder, grabbing hold of the man's collar. Though the man's grin only grew more rapturous, reaching a level of lunacy.

"Oh, Zephner, you can't stop it—neither you, nor any of the others you align yourself with. His moment of glory will come to pass. His eternal wish will see consummation. All those that have plighted to his cause, and that are found worthy, shall reap the rewards of this most marvelous unveiling."

Not able to endure another demented utterance, Zephner pulled the man close, only to shove him with a jerk of his arm.

The man flew, his feet coming up off the floor. He came to an abrupt stop when the back of his skull struck the edge of the fountain wall. The fracturing of the bone was heard, and the blood stain visible.

The man was dead. Regardless of intention, it didn't appease Zephner's irate emotions. Even in death, the man kept that stupid grin, looking as if he were most pleased with himself. But even worse, the station was on an ill-fated course, straight into the heart of a red giant.

With the captain out of commission, Zephner had to take matters into his own hands, as he had no intentions of walking through death's door.

Ryan, who watched the terror unfold from afar, knew little of what awaited them. All he knew was that Zephner was racing up the steps in an awful hurry. For the first time, he looked fearful. Of what, Ryan didn't know, but it scared him just the same.

Zephner reached the top floor, rushing to the door that stood behind Ryan. He fumbled to get the key card out of his jacket.

"What's going on?" Ryan asked, almost afraid to find out.

Zephner didn't respond, and only focused on inputting the numbers into the keypad. This made Ryan worry even more.

The access panel beeped, and the door before them opened up, revealing the station's bridge.

Inside was a room with a hundred computers and terminals, all aligned side by side in a semi-arc. The seats and the controls had all been abandoned by the crewmen. They stood dutifully at their stations, frozen in a hypnotic stare. Their arms retained a certain gesture, where they rested their right hand over their left breast, while keeping their left hand propped under their right elbow. They watched as the tiny ornaments of space slowly drifted past them.

Ryan was astonished by what he saw. It was like stepping into a wax museum. Not a single one of these souls even acknowledged their intrusion. They remained where they stood, without flinching, without blinking. All of them kept a fixed gaze on the window, or more specifically, the fiery sparkle that glittered all the more brightly with each passing second.

Zephner rushed up to one of the crewmen, grasped his shoulders and then forced him into a chair. He looked into his eyes and saw an unwavering conviction, a complete refusal to cooperate. He grasped him even tighter, until his thumbs sunk into the cavity between his bones. Still he could not incite any facial response.

"Listen," Zephner said. "You're going to change the coordinates to some place that's not an incinerator. Do you understand what I'm telling you?"

There was no response, nothing but a stern, perpetual stare.

"Answer me!" he shouted and shook him.

"I'm sorry," the crewman said calmly. "I cannot defy the order given to us by Captain Martisse. Doing so would incite the wrath of our Lord."

"Wrath, huh? You want to talk about wrath!"

Zephner grabbed the man by his uniform, lifting him above his head. He cocked his arm back and tossed him into a row of computer consoles. The others glanced at the scene briefly before reverting their attention.

Zephner moved on to the next crewman, handling them rougher than the last. Again he issued his order, but received nothing but a curt reply of refusal. He pushed him aside and went on to the next, and then another, until it became clear that none of them would comply. Their fidelity could not be bent or broken. They could not be dissuaded from their oath of obedience. It was nothing short of maddening.

Zephner looked at the window and the impending ball of doom that drew near. The gassy giant burned more brightly, shining like a brilliant gemstone against a black canvas. He dared not look at it for too long, for if he did, he'd see that it was coming closer—moving as stealthily as the minute hand on a clock.

Time was running out, but no progress was being made. He could have killed all but one person in that room, and still the last man standing would not have given in.

Ryan was still huddled in the corner. Between Zephner's interrogations and the ever-growing star, he figured out what was going on. He could hardly believe any of it, despite the fact it was all taking place right in front of him. Something about it seemed off. It just couldn't be real. It just couldn't be happening. There was no way he was going to die now. Not like this.

Meanwhile, Zephner had exhausted every method of getting through to the crewmen. Few remained standing. Others crawled along the floor, trying to overcome the pains and the aches.

Ryan decided to approach him.

"What are we suppose to do now?" he said, while taking another look out the window.

Zephner was breathing heavily, looking around the room.

"I don't know," he said petulantly.

He scurried over to one of the terminals and leaned over the console. He studied the screen, the graphical user interface, and saw nothing familiar. It was all charts and dials, numbers and measurements, all actively running processes. They appeared to show the status of different systems aboard the station, as well as data concerning their current performance. He tried punching several keys, and played around with different inputs, but nothing was getting him closer to finding a way to change the coordinates. After a while, he couldn't restrain himself any longer, and in a bout of fury, he pounded his fists against the machine.

When Ryan saw the shattered glass sprinkle across the table, he knew they were done for. He thought about the manner in which they would die. The star would get real close, everything would start to get real hot—so hot that they would begin to burn, and eventually combust. It would be a terrible way to die, to say the least.

His body shook and quivered, as he watched the star get closer and closer. He could feel its heat already. The temperature in the room was escalating, a single degree at a time. And with each degree came another bead of sweat down his forehead. Soon his face would be soaking wet, a last-ditch effort by his body to keep him cool.

He went over to Zephner, hoping for some enlightenment.

"What is this?" he asked, not even sure what he was referring to. "This can't be real. This can't be happening. Can it?"

"It's real. And it's happening."

"But it can't be. It doesn't make sense. How did I even get here? How could this have happened?"

Zephner looked at him for a long time, and Ryan just looked right back.

"I know what you want to hear, and I don't blame you."

"Well, then tell me. What is this?"

"It's a dream, Ryan. You're dreaming."

Ryan sighed with some relief. It was enough for him to believe that everything would be all right. Shortly he will wake up in his bed, in the safety of his home. There wasn't anything to worry about.

"In that case," Ryan said, "I guess we can just wait it out. When we die here, we'll just wake up, and it'll be over."

"No," Zephner yelled angrily. "*You'll* wake up. I, on the other hand, have nothing to wake up to."

"But what—"

"Listen to me," he said, placing his hands firmly on Ryan's shoulders. "Don't make the mistake of passing this off as being *just* a dream." He put his hand up against Ryan's chest. "You feel that? That's your heart pounding. That's you being afraid right now. And I can tell you that when you wake up, that feeling is still going to be there. You'll remember all of this, and the toll it took on you—the fear that stems from the danger, the uncertainty of not knowing what's going to happen. It'll stay with you when you wake up, and it'll continue to stay with you for as long as you choose to remember it. So embrace this moment, Ryan, because it's going to define who you become."

He listened intently, but the blood in his body was still rushing too fast for him to think about it lucidly. Perhaps it would make more sense after he awoke. So for now, all he could do was wait it out.

He took a seat at one of the empty terminals, plopped his elbows onto the desk and rested his forehead against the back of his hands. He could feel his own fever, or maybe the room was just that hot already. Either way, things weren't going to get any more comfortable.

He peeked under his hands and looked straight at the star. It was beautiful, an enchanting decoration that complemented all the darkness. It was larger than he could ever imagine. It was bigger than the Earth, bigger than any planet. And yet there were billions and trillions of them just dangling there all over space. Kind of like underwater mines when you look at it in the context of the situation.

After staring for far too long, he looked away. The star was getting too bright. But that didn't change the temperature. It was unbearable right about now. His face was all wet, the collar of his shirt soaked. It was just a dream, he kept telling himself, but that didn't make the conditions any more tolerable.

He looked at Zephner and saw that he, too, was seated at a

terminal, except he had his back turned to the star. He was hunched over, with his arms on his knees, and eyes to the floor, sulking over this hurdle he could not get over.

Ryan opted to look back at the star, however bright it was, and embrace it for all it was worth. It became brighter and brighter, its intensity unfathomable. The heat burned his skin, creating a scorching pain.

Everything became white, then black.

———Chapter 5———

Safety in Hiding

Ryan's head sprung from the pillow like a catapult. His skin was warm, and his hair drenched. He could feel his heart palpitating rapidly. He looked around and saw that he was back in his room, where it was dark, cool, and most importantly, safe.

He wiped his forehead with his sleeve and threw the heavy blankets off of him. He sat there, trying to recall the dream he just had, discovering he could remember almost everything, from the interior of the station, to the long desolate halls, but most of all, the man with the motorcycle. His name was Zephner, and he was really strong. But even more fascinating than his strength was the aura he projected—his manner of speaking, his character. There was a certain depth behind all of it, an elusive quality that was typically absent whenever he had a dream involving people. It was like the man was a real person, rather than a fabrication that had been conjured up by his mind.

Ryan remembered what he said, sort of. Something about not passing the experience off as being just a dream. It was more than that. It was something he would bring back with him when he woke up. Well, if he brought back anything, it was the scare and the sweat.

The excitement must have been too much, because now he desperately needed to pee. So he hopped out of bed and crept silently to the bathroom. He switched the light on, relieved himself, and walked on out.

But not before he noticed himself in the mirror.

For whatever reason, he decided to study himself. Not out of vanity, but because his own face struck him as looking peculiar. He didn't understand why. Everything looked the way it should. His eyes were green, his hair a brownish gold. He turned away and then looked back at the mirror. He was still the same.

He lost interest in his reflection and returned to his room, slipping back into bed.

He allowed his eyelids to fall, and everything became black again. There wasn't anything to worry about now, he thought. He just needed to get some sleep. Expel his thoughts, and get some sleep.

An indeterminate amount of time had passed before Ryan was aware of himself again. He chose to roll on his side, in search of finding a more comfortable position. But it didn't matter how he twisted or turned. The mattress had become inexplicably rough, coarse, and loose, as if it were composed of grains. Furthermore, he could feel a gentle breeze blow against his face. And there was a sound, a gushing of water, an aquatic ambiance.

He opened his eyes and found himself somewhere other than his room again. He saw a long strip of beach that ran as far as the eye could see, where it disappeared into the misty horizon, under the hazy blue sky. He thought he was alone, until he saw a series of man-made ramps that led up a precipice. Civilization couldn't have been far. But still, why was he here? Wasn't he just on that station? Shouldn't he be dead?

Ryan looked out at the ocean. It was almost like an out-of-body experience, because what he saw was impossible. He was left mesmerized.

It was the mother of all shipwrecks—that is if you could even call it a ship. It was a vessel of colossal proportions, a monstrosity of engineering—or a marvel of ingenuity. It was hard to distinguish between the two.

It was the space station all right, occupying the landscape, while being partly submerged in the sea. Though that didn't stop the tallest segment from penetrating the clouds. The whole thing extended to a height and width beyond what Ryan could see. The whole thing comprised a multitude of quadrilaterals, all drenched in a nightmarish black. They were like picture frames of varying sizes, all intermingled, one within the other, coming together at perpendicular angles. The largest, outermost frame held all of the other limbs in place, including that single, incongruous section at the very center. It was like a narrow spin top, with a long, coiling core rising from the center. And each strand of the coil branched off towards different quadrants of the station.

The site left Ryan baffled, for more than one reason, with the primary one being how the station managed to end up in an ocean, when it was supposed to be traveling to a star.

"So you decided to wake up," he heard a voice say.

Ryan turned his head and saw Zephner seated on the sand, right beside his black motorcycle.

"It's you," Ryan said, with bewilderment and excitement. "We're both alive." Though the enthusiasm wasn't reciprocated. Zephner just sat there, keeping his thoughts private. He looked out at the ocean, the wreckage, with a kind of calmness and tranquility that was anything but characteristic of him.

Ryan looked back at the sea.

"I don't get it," he said. Weren't we headed towards a star? Shouldn't we be dead now? Were you able to change the coordinates?"

"I didn't change the coordinates," he said plainly.

"Then how are we here?"

Zephner had the look of an adult that was being pestered by the incessant inquiring of a child.

"I don't know. All I do know is that we've struck the fortune of living another day, just so we can joyride through hell one more time."

"One more time? Does that means we're not out of the woods just yet?"

"Not even close. We're still stuck in the tree, surrounded by a legion of pyromaniacs that would love nothing more than to see our little forest burned to ashes."

"So we're in a bad spot."

"Yes. That's what the metaphor means."

"Sorry."

Zephner remained awkwardly silent before he continued with what he was going to say.

"And there's no reason for you to get involved in any of this. I don't know how you got on that station, but I'm going to make certain that you don't get checked-in to another."

"Another?" Ryan interrupted. "There's more of those things?"

"Stop, Ryan. I'm telling you, don't seek more information than you need to know."

"And that's another thing," Ryan said with indignation. "Just how do you know my name?"

The man muttered an expletive under his breath.

"Trust me, you're better off not knowing. There are just some things that you're not suppose to know. You're ignorant about this place right now, and let's try to keep it that way. Because that's how dreams should be. They shouldn't make any sense to you. They should be riddled with nonsensical oddities and unexplainable phenomenon. And if you ever start to make logical deductions, that's when things start to become very dangerous. So take this as a warning, and a piece of advice. Don't get in any deeper than you have to."

Ryan became quiet, though he was still on the verge of objecting. He was just itching with curiosity, like a kid in a toy store, if every shelf were covered with a blanket. Or maybe a better analogy would be an electric blanket, with the wires exposed. Yeah, you'd get to the toys, but then you'd be burned. But was that worth it? Ryan didn't know. He was never really a big risk taker. He preferred going into situations where he was confident about the outcome. This wasn't one of those situations. Here it seemed like the better idea was listening to the man that managed to keep him alive this long.

"So what should I do now?" he asked, feeling rather lost.

Zephner climbed up on his feet. He went over to his motorcycle and pulled the kickstand up.

"You can come with me."

Ryan obeyed. He stood up and made his way over to the bike.

Zephner fired up the ignition and rolled gently on the throttle. The bike cruised smoothly through the beach, traveling up a ramp along the cliff side and onto an old road.

Ryan turned his head and took one last look at the sunken station. When he did, he thought he noticed an object dart into the sky—a tiny thing that shimmered once before disappearing entirely. Passing it off as nothing more than a trick of the light, he faced forward again.

During their ride, Ryan saw a vast rural landscape, with shallow valleys that seemed to run for miles. When they reached the wilderness he got a great sense of its scale. The trees were exquisitely grand, rising to staggering heights. Their trunks were massive, and their boughs equally so. The leaves capered in the wind like unbridled sails, like a green mass of clouds.

The road meandered around the landscape, with a steep declivity on either side that dipped into a grassy marsh. The water there was channeled into a basin, that rested at the base of one of the hills.

Ryan watched the world envelop around him, as he sat there with sensuous delight. It was a remarkable experience unlike anything he had ever known. At times it'd slip his mind that he was even riding on the back of a motorcycle. He could have been a bird, or a land mammal that was running really fast. There was nothing that told him otherwise, as it was just him and the open road.

For a great while they followed the paved road, increasing in elevation little by little, until they took a curve around one of the valley walls. There on the other side was an entirely new vista—a modern city built around a placid blue bay. Ryan didn't think there was anything unusual about it. When they entered, he saw that it was your typical city, with its fair share of skyscrapers, and people bustling about. There was traffic, with cars lined up bumper to bumper, horns blaring, drivers complaining, commuters jaywalking. Your typical nuisances. It was all humdrum, until he noticed, or thought he noticed . . . could it really be?

Overhead a busy street he saw a car pass by. At least it looked like a car. It was up there, about a hundred feet or so, darting through the air like a really small plane. But it wasn't a plane because it had no wings, at least none that were distinctly noticeable. They were more like fins that gracefully extended from the body, sort of like a manta ray.

It was a big deal for Ryan, as the prospect of flying cars had always fascinated him. And here was one now, cruising by like it were a normality—at least to some extent, as wheeled vehicles still made up the majority of the traffic.

As they rode deeper into the city, Ryan got a clearer view of the bay. There were freighters coming to and fro their berths, unloading their cargo onto the platforms. Further down the coast were long piers with anchored sailboats, and in them, avid fishermen with their poles and lures ready to snag their day's prize. With the high noon sun, and its rays gleaming off the water, it seemed like this was one of those perfect days.

The motorcycle turned at the next street, riding all the way down a busy avenue. Ryan looked around and saw shops and eateries of all kinds, from bakeries to candy shops, to restaurants to retail outlets. It was the central hub for those wanting to keep busy.

The olfactory method of attraction was nothing short of effective at attacking Ryan where he was weakest—right at the core of his belly. The sumptuous aromas of grilled meat enticed him immediately.

Zephner pulled over the motorcycle alongside the curb. Ryan climbed off and stepped onto the sidewalk and took a look around. He was expecting the bike's engine to shut off right about now, but it didn't. It kept running, and Zephner remained seated.

"You'll be safe here," he said. "Just keep yourself occupied until you hear the alarm."

Ryan stood hesitantly.

"And what about you?" he asked.

"I have important matters to attend to."

Without another word, the man pulled away and merged seamlessly back into the traffic. Before long he was lost in a swarm of motorists, completely out of sight. His departure left Ryan in a quandary. The man's face slowly faded from memory. Ryan's orientation and sense of purpose became lost all at once. He had forgotten where he was and why he was even there in the first place. The lucidity of the world had taken a hit, and he now only had a vague sense of his surroundings.

He quickly turned around, in the direction he thought he

heard the murmur of voices, but when he looked he saw only an empty street. He turned again towards the other set of voices, and again saw no one. Not a trace remained of the people, or the vehicles they rode. After Ryan realized this, everything fell silent.

His interest migrated to the front of the establishment by which he stood. To his delight, and curiosity, it was a familiar fast food joint that he instantly recognized as P.B. Bastions.

CHAPTER 6

THE MAKING OF MEMORIES

The big glassy letters perched high on the wall had instilled a great comfort. P.B. Bastions was the place where the three of them had always gone to dine, typically after a hard day at school. It was the only eatery around that served both pizza and burgers, appeasing to either of the two common cravings of ravenous adolescents. It was also the place where Ryan had celebrated childhood birthday parties, some of which were remembered as the best days of his youth.

Through the window Ryan could almost—no—he *did* see a gang of rowdy tots, prancing about in a cheerful gale, with fries in their fingers and party hats on their heads. There were colorful banners festooned across the ceiling, linked together with cutouts of different sport balls. Gifts wrapped in festive paper and topped with glittering bows laid stacked on one of the tables.

After a period of eating and frolicking, it came time to open the gifts. The boy in the teal jersey was now the center of attention. One by one he took each of the presents and stripped it of its wrappings, which were then tossed heedlessly onto the floor. The presents quickly revealed themselves to be things that brought joy to a young boy: action figures, board games, an RC car, a water gun. The look of excitement grew more intensely with each one. Lastly came the present that was handed to him by the boy's parents. It was a medium-sized box, shaped like a cube, wrapped in a sports-themed paper. The boy clawed at it with haste, unearthing the prize within. What he found was a brand new basketball—a simple orange, spherical object crafted in a manner that could provide endless hours of entertainment. At twenty-nine and a half inches in circumference, it met official regulations. And in the hands of a young sports enthusiast, it symbolized a kind of transition, a rite of passage that opened a new threshold for his physical and mental ability.

Ryan observed the scene and was enraptured by its semblance to a time and place close to home. It spoke comfort and puerile glee, the kind that he sought to relive once again.

He approached the building slowly, stepping up to the big glass door. He pulled the handle and allowed himself inside. When he entered, the ambiance was different than what he originally perceived. The place was strangely dark, with only a handful of ceiling lights turned on. The chairs were turned upside down on the tabletops, and the floors were still moist from when they were mopped. There were no children there, nor the sounds of their excitement. No decorations, no presents. The playground located in the adjacent room was empty and isolated. There were no signs that anyone was still here, except for a stir in the kitchen.

The sound had lured Ryan over to the registers. He waited for someone to come along and take his order.

He glanced up at the wall where the menu was posted. He spent some time thinking about what he should order, until he realized the items listed were not foods, but rather notations of different homework assignments. Oddly enough they retained a price point. Read chapter seven from World History was $4.95, and problems 12 to 32 in Geometry was $7.49; study for vocab test was $1.99, located under side orders.

None of the options available appealed to him. He was getting ready to walk out and try some place else, until someone walked up to one of the registers.

Ryan looked at her, the young comely girl in the orange polo shirt and black jeans. Her collar buttons were unfastened, and her brown eyes were heavy with exhaustion, her hair an untidy mess. It was as if she had just been abruptly awakened from a peaceful slumber.

She leaned against the counter, letting out a big yawn. "We were just getting ready to close shop, Ryan," she said. "You and your nightly cravings."

Ryan looked at her with a certain kind of perplexity.

"Megan," he said, "you're not suppose to be on that side of the counter. You're going to get in trouble."

"What are you talking about? I work here now."

"How did that happen?

"I told you already. I pulled a perfect score on the pickle exam."

Ryan wasn't sure what that was, but the answer satisfied him just the same.

"I wanted a pizza," he said.

"That's fine, but I'll have to charge you."

Ryan dug into his pockets in search of whatever cash he could find, but all he could muster up was a handful of coins.

He poured them onto the counter, hoping they would total the cost. Megan looked at it and gave a petty laugh.

"You know what, forget it. It's not like anyone here is going to count the pepperoni slices. Sit down, I'll bring it out."

He was pleased with the kind, though still unscrupulous gesture. He followed her suggestion and found himself a booth alongside the large window panes, right next to the front door. It was the spot they'd always claim when it was available. From there they had a decent view of Pinesburrow Park and the after-school traffic, which was only a tad more interesting than the alternative view of the parking lot.

As he waited he felt the perpetual motion of his life's clock. Time kept advancing forward without any impediment. It was a force so powerful, so frightening that he dare not ponder on it for too long. Though it hardly mattered because the process had become plainly visible to the eye. There was darkness outside, and it was steadily ousted by the rise of the morning sun. A warm autumn glow spilled over the landscape, giving a lustrous coat to the streets and the store facades. The fields lit with fire as the dark silhouettes of the trees stood starkly against the orange sky.

Ryan watched, trapped in a hypnosis. Everything became increasing beautiful. Different colors emerged, giving meaning to the abstract shapes that made up the horizon. It was the orange, the rampant orange that opened up his appetite to a new level. He could even begin to smell its scent pervade through the air. Though after a more careful observation, he traced the aroma to its actual origin.

He saw Megan walking towards him with a large tray of pizza. She set it on the table and took a seat, and without saying anything, helped herself to a slice. Ryan grabbed one as well, lifting it carefully as to not let the cheese slip off. He took a bite and enjoyed it thoroughly.

"So how's that pilfered pizza tasting?" Megan asked.

Ryan mumbled out an answer through his obnoxious chewing.

"It's good."

"No it's not. That's just your mind talking. Now if your taste buds could talk, they'd say it was shit."

"What are you talking about?" he said, taking another bite.

"It's your mind, Ryan. You remembered it tasting good when you were little, and so you think it still taste good now. But if you were being objective about it, you'd realize how crummy it was."

"Not uh. You're just saying that cause you probably have to eat this stuff every day."

Megan shook her head. "Nah. I'm more of a burger gal personally."

"Then have a burger."

"Ryan, it's not time for that."

He glared at her with puzzlement, and she just glared right back, motioning her head to the right.

Ryan looked to his left and saw nothing but the short, metallic napkin dispenser resting there, doing nothing, as it should. But then it made a shrilling scream, an insufferable beeping that Ryan could not withstand. By instinct, he made a quick reach for it and yanked out one of the napkins, causing the dispenser to become silent. Ryan then went ahead and wiped his face with his napkin, as if that had been his intention all along.

He relaxed back in his seat and sat there idly. He didn't want anymore pizza. Megan must have not wanted any more either because she was just sitting there, staring back at him, expressionless. Though if any of her facial features were communicating, it was her eyes. They were squinting and opening in ways Ryan didn't understand. Maybe she was trying to be funny, or maybe there was dust in her eyes. Either way, this ocular exchange soon became awkward, and Ryan looked away.

His eyes drifted to the napkin dispenser again, but this time it appeared different. The front side read like a digital clock. The time was clearly spelled out. It was 7:39. That meant something. He was sure of it. And after taking a few seconds to think about it, he acted.

"Damn, I'm late for school!" he exclaimed, and slid himself hurriedly off the seat cushion.

"Wait a minute," Megan said, but Ryan was already out the front door.

Today would be a terrible day to be late if there ever was one. Why, he didn't know. All he did know was that it was imperative that he show up on time.

He raced down the sun-soaked sidewalk as fast as his feet could carry him, all the way down the block. He passed a couple of shops on his right, each with their windows tinted black. *Closed* signs were hung from the door, while others were marked for sale. To his left was an empty road, without a car anywhere in sight. The town was deserted, but it didn't even raise a red flag. He just needed to run, as fast as he could.

At the end of the block he came across his first traffic light. The damn thing was red, and he was forced to stop. He looked both ways and saw that no one was coming. But the light was red. He wasn't allowed to move. He waited impatiently, keeping his feet dancing in place. When the light turned green, he dashed forward.

He ran all the way down to the end of the block, and again came across another red light.

He stopped, and waited, his feet itching to continue.

The light turned green, and he darted again, knowing for sure he was going to be late.

After what felt like an eternity, he came upon the school grounds. Though they were not what he expected. The place was forlorn and desolated. Not a student, nor a teacher could be found anywhere. The bus lane was empty, as well as the parking lot. The front door was shut, and every window boarded. The brick walls were weathered and fractured, and the trees in the courtyard were parched and denuded. There was a stench of abandonment and neglect, gloom and despondency. There was nothing here, nothing left.

Ryan was too late.

He stared blankly at the site, without any thoughts or words, as if standing before a fresh grave. If only he had gotten here sooner, things may have been different.

From behind he heard Megan's voice.

"Ryan," she said, empathizing. "Don't you remember? The

school's closed now. Forever."

Ryan didn't understand. He couldn't remember.

"Why did it close?"

"Because they didn't get the funding they needed."

"B-but—that's what The Mind was for. The institute gave us grant money to have the trancestors around."

"Yes, but we weren't interesting enough. There was nothing they could learn. Nothing we could teach them. We just weren't important enough. The institute pulled out."

Ryan lowered his head in disbelief. He couldn't process what was going on. He couldn't wrap his head around how something like this could have happened. Then his mind jumped to a different thought.

"I forgot something in my locker," he said, and started down the walkway to the school's main entrance. Megan followed.

"It's not safe to go in there," she said. "He could be waiting. He might see us."

"I'm not afraid," Ryan said, keeping up his hasty pace.

He marched right up the front steps and plowed through the set of doors.

The inside was as bleak and deserted as the outside would have suggested. Everything was filthy, and the floors were dusty enough to obscure the patterns of the tiles. The lights were all switched off, many of the bulbs broken, with their shards sprinkled across the floor. The only way to see was by the light of the sun, which pelted down with full strength through the open chasms in the ceiling.

Ryan stepped forward gingerly, maneuvering around the small heaps of rubble and debris. Megan was still following him closely.

"Careful, Ryan," she said, but he paid no attention.

He kept moving forward, until he reached the main office with the cracked windows. From there he took a right, down the

darkened corridor, which resembled something more of a cata-
comb than a school hallway. The lockers were lined up like a row
of metal caskets. Some of them were bulging outward, as if something from the inside had tried to force its way out.

Ryan tiptoed through, as quietly as a draft, stepping through
the beams of sunlight from above.

He turned the next corner, and again traveled down another
dreary passage. He looked back to check and see if Megan was
still following him. She didn't say anything, but he could tell she
was bothered by his lack of concern for their safety. Either way,
he continued onward.

By the time he reached the next turn, he thought he could
hear something—rubber sneakers scuffling against a hard floor. It
was quiet at first, but got louder the further he walked down the
north wing. After a short distance he began to hear distinct
voices, that of children, chattering and cheering happily. They
were mixed in with other noises—heavy thuds and clacks that
varied in magnitude. Ryan neared the source, and as he did, the
dissonant arrangement of sounds got clearer and more lively.
There were people here, he thought.

With Megan still following closely behind, he came closer to
the source of the commotion, and discovered they were coming
from the school's gymnasium. He could even see rays of light
poking from underneath the set of closed doors. There must have
been a class in session.

"What are they doing?" Megan whispered. "No one is suppose to be in here."

"Well, someone's here," Ryan said.

His curiosity got the best of him, and so he couldn't help but
reach for the door handle. He pulled it open and a flood of light
spilled out into the hallway. The tumultuous sounds of children's
gaiety escaped all at once, entering into Ryan's ears.

After his eyes adjusted to the light, he saw that the gym was full of children, little younglings no older than six or seven. They were separated into groups, with each participating in a different activity. There were jump ropers in one corner, and handkerchief jugglers in another. And running laps around them were those riding in roller racers. They were as glad and carefree as any child could be, relishing the moment without fears or worries of any kind. They had one objective, and that was to have fun with their peers.

That was all well and good for Ryan, who wanted to insert himself into the swarm of merry children. Eventually he found a way, when he noticed a most enticing object.

There, at the far side of the gymnasium were a pair of kids, a boy and a girl, dribbling around a basketball. They each took shots at the goal, missing them, then going after one another for the rebound. Ryan observed that they weren't very good. They continuously committed travel violations, their dribbling was clunky, and their shooting technique was all wrong.

He approached them, and Megan followed after. She looked at the two kids and made a startling discovery.

"Hey, Ryan," she said. "Look at that. It's us."

He paid no attention. It was just a trifling detail. Nevertheless, he went to confront the boy.

"You're doing it all wrong," he said. "If you want to beat her, you have to shoot like this."

He grabbed the ball from him and demonstrated the proper form. With arms and knees bent, he held the ball close, letting his fingers rest gently on it. He brought it over his shoulder, and with the strength of his arms and legs, he shot it, letting it roll off the ends of his fingers. It soared through the air and fell gracefully through the hoop with a swoosh.

The young boy was impressed, but discouraged.

"That's too hard," he complained.

"You have to practice. It'll get easier over time."

Ryan noticed Megan had already retrieved the ball and was crouching next to the young girl.

"Listen here," she said, speaking into the girl's ear. "This is what you gotta do."

Her voice then fell to a whisper. The girl nodded obediently during the instruction, eventually growing a mischievous smile.

Megan stood up and walked away, prompting Ryan to come along with a pat on the back. He followed reluctantly, as he would have preferred to see the two kids battle it out. He turned his head one last time to see the young Ryan in possession of the ball. The boy would make him proud, he was sure. But before he could take five more steps, he heard a painful cry. He looked back and saw the youngster on the floor, curled in the fetal position.

"What did you tell her?" Ryan inquired immediately.

"Nothin'."

"Whatever it was, it was a foul."

"Ain't a foul if no one is there to call it."

Ryan sighed, and kept walking.

They were about to reach the set of doors when Ryan spotted a lone basketball that sat idly on the floor right alongside the wall.

There was nothing unusual about this particular basketball. It was round and orange, just like any other. It was relatively clean, showing only minute traces of dust and dirt. The black bands were clear and solid, and the dimples were well intact. No, there wasn't anything unusual about it at all. That is, until he saw the ball begin to roll in his direction.

It moved towards him, uninfluenced by anything in the gym. It was an autonomous decision. The ball chose to get close to Ryan. It rolled until it nudged the tip of his sneaker. Immediately, Ryan felt a strong connection, and knew they had to be together. It was as if he encountered a stray puppy, and just like he would with a stray puppy, he took it for himself.

Megan watched as he picked up the ball and made off with it, as if it were his.

"So you're just going to take that?" she said.

"I think I'm suppose to have it."

"I'm not sure what gives you that impression"

"It came to me. Didn't you see?"

Megan shook her head. "You have a silly imagination, Ryan."

Together they stepped into the dark hallway, where they were once again swallowed by their dreary surroundings. They retraced their steps quickly. Ryan, dribbling his new ball, was too distracted to realize where he was or what he was even doing here. Megan couldn't help but seize the opportunity to mess with him.

In the midst of a bounce, she reached in with her hand and snatched the ball, right from underneath his nose. She let out a laugh and capered away, deeper into the dark, and then around the next corner where she could be seen no more.

"Hey," Ryan yelled, but to no avail. She was out of sight. But he could still hear the bouncing of the ball.

He followed the sound down the hall, then around the corner. It never got any closer or farther. The sound maintained a steady volume. At the brink of every turn he caught only a glimpse of her dark coffee hair, as it fluttered and shimmered under the rays of sun.

He ran as fast as he could. Faster and faster.

Around the next corner he went.

Her hair disappeared again.

He chased her, calling her name.

Then he stopped.

There she was, in the shadows, only her face catching the tenuous threads of light from above. Her merry attitude was gone. All that was left was a pair of frightened eyes and a trembling jaw. She was caught, ensnared by the clutches of something large, massive, a corporeal creature in the darkness. Both her arms were held firmly against her body, by a pair of powerful hands.

Megan was desperate, whimpering and struggling to break away, but her efforts proved fruitless.

"Help me, Ryan," she cried out.

Ryan saw her distressed, but he hadn't the slightest idea what he could do.

"Help me, Ryan," a second, deeper voice said with mimicry. "Help me."

Ryan remained silent, enduring the ridicule.

The voice reverted to a regular tone. "Face it, champ, I won. And you know what they say: to the victor go the spoils."

"Ryan, do something," Megan cried out again. But still he could do nothing but watch.

He saw the monstrous arms grasp her even tighter, picking her off the ground. Their heads were now touching cheek to cheek, the figure's face still under the cover of shadow. Slowly, it brought forth its head, revealing its malicious grin under the beam of light. Its lips were moving in for the kiss, as Megan continued to struggle free.

Ryan felt he could endure no more. Some form of retaliation was in order. It would be rash, as there was no time to think it through. He went ahead and acted on his first impulse.

He lunged forward at the figure, with his fists cocked back. The ribs were wide open, a perfect target. He fired a fast hook, but it didn't connect. Instead he felt a gush of pain across his face —a powerful blow that sent him crashing against the row of lockers, producing a clang that rattled his ears. He was left dazed and disoriented, but could still hear Megan calling his name. When his vision returned, he saw the figure walking off with Megan in its arms, pulling her into the shadows.

Ryan, still sitting in defeat, sought a way to fight this foul fiend that knew no limits. Strength alone wouldn't be enough. Wits, maybe. But where would he find that?

He felt a nudge against his fingers, and turned to see that it was the basketball he was holding just a minute ago. It rubbed and nudged him, like a pet begging for attention. It wanted to be held. It wanted Ryan to utilize it in some way. Though only one idea had entered his mind.

He picked up the basketball, and then in one seamless maneuver he threw it with all the force he could muster. It fired like a bullet, ripping through the air. It struck squarely the back of the figure's skull, inciting a painful and vindictive growl. The arms loosened, providing just enough slack for Megan to break free. She fumbled as she hit the floor, steadying herself just as Ryan came rushing up to her.

"C'mon, let's go!" he exclaimed, wasting no time in getting his feet moving again. Megan raced alongside him.

Ryan could feel the presence of the monster nearing rapidly. It's howls and snarls were only a breath behind them, its stomps loud and thunderous—a one-animal stampede. The ground rumbled, and the lockers on either side rattled on their hinges. They could not run fast enough.

They threaded over the stones and rubble, at times staggering on the dusty surfaces. They kept running and running, their hearts racing frantically. There was no end to this hall as far as they could tell. The perilous trail of darkness ran forever. Even the locker numbers climbed steadily; they were well into the thousands. No end was in sight.

The fear and panic had slowly taken its toll on Ryan. He was frightened and exhausted. Carelessly, he slipped on a stray locker door, and took a hard fall against the floor. He groaned from the throbbing pain in his knees. Megan noticed and stopped to assist.

"Get up, Ryan!" she urged him, as she lifted him off the floor.

Ryan struggled back on his feet, then made the regrettable mistake of looking back at the thing that chased them.

Whatever semblance it had to a human was now completely

gone. Closing in on them was a dark mass that filled the dimensions of the hall, from floor to ceiling and wall to wall. Its arms and legs were black as char, with the girth of tree trunks, its torso a decomposing carcass of some deep seabed creature. And attached somewhere on the frontal side of that foul, repugnant beast was a head that looked like a severed skull with traces of decomposing flesh. The teeth were huge jagged fangs, spilling blood like a feasting predator, and its hair wild as a lion's mane. But it was the eyes that evoked the most fear. They were empty glass marbles that radiated a preternatural glow. They were hungry for meat, thirsty for blood. Their ravaging gaze did not break.

Ryan darted instantly, sprinting faster than before, deeper into the darkness.

He felt something latch onto his arm and hold him back. He looked and saw Megan trying to pulled him towards a door.

"In here," she said, as she pulled on the handle and dashed inside the classroom. She slammed the door behind her.

Ryan was still on edge, wondering what they were going to do from here.

"We're trapped in here," he said to her.

He could still feel the floor rumbling, and now the light fixtures clattering. The beast was approaching rapidly.

Megan looked around, peering at the walls. The windows were quickly ruled out as an escape route, for on the other side were howling shadows, dancing in a ferocious blaze that could have been the sky burning. These figures clawed at the windows, shrilling uncontrollably.

She scanned the room for any other exit.

The beast was right outside their room It pounded against the wall, creating a lighting bolt of cracks through the cement blocks. It roared angrily.

Megan needed to hurry. She continued to search. Eventually she found a square vent on the ceiling.

"There," she said, pointing to it. She ran over to the nearest desk and slid it underneath the vent. Then she moved another one next to it.

"One more, on top" she said, bringing over yet another desk. Ryan came over and helped her stack it on top of the other.

The beast's thrashing intensified. The thunderous pounding sent the cement blocks crashing to the floor. Plumes of dust spilled out into the air. Everything was shaking.

"Hurry!" Ryan called out.

Megan stepped on a chair, and then onto the first desk. She then climbed onto the next one, careful not to let the wobbling throw her off balance. Once at the top, she grasped the vent and ripped it out, tossing it onto the floor.

"Hand me the chair."

Ryan lifted the chair and handed it to her. With that she was able to pull herself into the air shaft. She beckoned for Ryan to follow.

Ryan climbed the rocky tower, scaling the first desk, then the second, before reaching the chair on top. He took Megan's hand as she helped pull him into the shaft.

Just as his foot left the chair, a floodgate of water was released, plowing through their tower with the strength of a raging river. The onslaught of water continued to gush past them, eventually subsiding into slow, swelling waves.

Soon after they heard the clacking of rain droplets against the exterior of the shaft. They fell in heavier quantities, sounding like a shower of silver pellets. Then they saw the surface of the water illuminated by a flash of light, followed by a boisterous crack of thunder. The metal walls of their refuge vibrated and resonated.

The two of them looked at each other, still trying to catch their breaths from their close encounter with death. Now with the threat out of the picture, they were able to relax, and listen to the sedative sounds of churning water. Smiles emerged on their faces, and soon they were laughing at their situation.

"We almost died, Ryan. It's not funny," she said, barely getting the words out.

"But we're alive, and that's what counts."

"Like you know anything about counting, Mr. Seventy-Two in algebra."

She rolled onto her hands and knees and began to crawl through the shaft. Ryan followed her lead through the tight space.

The deeper they got, the darker everything became. The faint light that entered through the vent could no longer reach them. Everything was black. The raindrops were still pelting against the metal.

"I'm taking a right," Megan's voice echoed.

"I can't see anything," Ryan responded.

"Just feel your way around."

Ryan extended his hand, trying to find the wall before he could bang his head into it. But instead of touching the cold metal, his fingers came into contact with something soft and round.

"Easy, rye bread."

Abashed by his mistake, he immediately pulled his hand away. Luckily for him, the humiliation would be quickly forgotten.

He underwent a free fall as the panel below him detached from the shaft. Down the two of them went, into the dark undulating sea. His body smacked hard against the murky surface, where the cold water engulfed him entirely. He was spun around, and for a while he didn't know the difference between what was up or down. He flailed his arms and legs, while letting his buoyancy guide him in the right direction.

Shortly he surfaced, gasping for air while battling to stay afloat. He could see nothing, and only hear the sounds of a storm-struck ocean and the clatter of falling rain. That was until a gash of lighting lit the sky, revealing an endless sea filled with black swelling waves. Above were malevolent clouds with drooping tendrils that curled like gnarled fingers.

In between the flashes of light, Ryan searched the waters for Megan. He found her only a few yards away, bobbing in and out of the water like a buoy. She was waving her arm around.

"Over there!" she shouted, pointing to the distance.

He swiveled around in the water and spotted the shore, which was well within swimming distance. In addition to that, there was a stone structure with a tall entrance, brightly lit, possibly inhabited. He was pleased to know that they would be all right.

He kicked furiously through the water, riding the lumpy waves as they rose and sagged, all while battling the heavy rainfall that kept spilling in his eyes. He concentrated on the light and followed it.

After an arduous voyage through the wrathful sea, he was propelled by one last wave that left him brushing up against the beach. He tried to stand but tripped when his feet and hands sunk into the wet sand. With the strength he had left, he crawled far enough away where the treacherous waves could not reach him. Here he basked in the light given off by the nearby structure. With the same light, he spotted Megan emerging from the sea. She too, fumbled onto the sand before being able to stand upright.

Contrary to what Ryan expected, she came forward wearing another one of her smiles. She was completely unfazed by the successive trials they were just dealt. None of it made a dent in her mood. She strolled across the beach, using the downpour to rinse away the wet grit on her hands and arms, as nonchalantly as if she were taking a shower in the comfort of her own home.

It was enchanting for Ryan to see her this way, so calm, despite the nightmarish conditions. She was drenched from head to toe, with sand clinging to her clothing, and hair tangled like a clump of seaweed. It was odd that she would stand for this. It wasn't really like her at all.

"Let's get inside," she said, as she started to hike the sandy slope. Ryan nodded, and followed her.

Together they approached what would be their makeshift shelter. Though in actuality, it was a stone monument, built within a hillside. It had a forty-foot arching entrance, brimming with light, with pillars on either side. There were steps leading down to the shore that had crumbled into fractured slabs that laid interspersed across the sand—broken, weathered bits that could only have taken form from thousands of years of torrential abuse.

Ryan and Megan trudged up the crumbling steps and passed through the entrance. Once inside they became witnesses to the building's splendid architecture. The floor, stretching for seventy yards, was brilliantly laid out with decorative mosaic tiles. They created colorful, spiraling patterns that complemented the interior walls and ceiling, which were made up of marble columns, tapering arches and frescoes. Under every arch were granite statues, tattered and worn by time. Each face was depicted with fear, with eyes that gazed up at some heavenly force. They were men, dressed in armor, brandishing their swords at their unseen enemy, as the aghast maidens cowered on their knees beside them.

The frescoes, on the other hand, were stranger, even bizarre to Ryan. They were meshes of color, abstract forms that wanted to have a likeness to a corporeal being, but were ultimately something else entirely. He also saw paintings of desolate landscapes, woods and mountains, glaciers and oceans. And even though they didn't depict people or animals, there was still the sense that something in those paintings was alive. They emitted a certain energy that made him feel uneasy. Megan, however, seemed delighted by the artwork.

"This place is beautiful," she said to him.

Ryan answered, "At one point, maybe. But it's in ruins now."

"And that's probably somehow your fault."

"How can that be *my* fault?"

Megan shook her head and laughed.

Up ahead, at the end of the main hall, was a room with a towering glass dome that gave vision to the lingering storm clouds up in the sky. Underneath it was a round fountain made of granite, with multiple basins, each diminishing in size as they rose. They had elegant engravings of ancient village folk and armored soldiers, with flora motifs all around. The water in the basins remained stagnant like a pond, reflecting the bright interior of the building as well as a mirror would.

Megan stepped over the wall of the first basin and walked through the water, creating ripples that disrupted the perfect reflection. She gripped the brim of the second basin and lifted herself, throwing her leg over the edge, then the other.

Ryan watched her from the floor, concerned.

"What are you doing?" he called out to her.

"What does it look like? I'm violating safety guidelines. Wanna join me?"

Whether it was a dare or sincere invitation, Ryan felt pressured to follow her lead. He jumped into the fountain and quickly climbed into the second basin, as Megan impatiently hurried to the third. Not surprised, there was a reason for that.

"Last one to the top gets adopted by lemurs."

As if it were the worst fate imaginable, he scrambled as fast as he could. He grabbed the brim of the next basin and pulled himself over the edge, splashing into the pool. He dashed again, pulling himself up over the next with brisk execution. Megan was just a hairline ahead, mirroring his celerity like a shadow.

They reached the top, almost at the same time, though it was Megan who put her foot over the brim first, creating the first ripple.

"Don't worry," she said. "I'll take care of the paperwork."

"It was a draw," Ryan tried to argue, but she didn't buy it.

They both waded to the other side of the basin, catching their breaths. Megan interlaced her fingers behind her head; Ryan bent forward with his hands on his knees. Both of them admired the view they had from thirty feet up in the air.

Megan took a seat against the outer brim. She allowed herself to slouch into the water, leaving little but her head exposed. Ryan, hesitatingly, found a seat right next to her. Together they lay with their heads tilted back, taking in the view of the glass dome and the night sky above their heads, as if it were a planetarium.

The storm appeared to be subsiding. The clouds were dispersing, and the rain was barely a trickle. They were no longer silver pellets, but rather paper pellets. The moon was also searching for its part in this nocturnal spectacle, peaking shyly from behind the disappearing clouds. Megan took notice, and she looked at it adoringly.

She lay there for a while without saying anything. Ryan however, wasn't as interested in the moon as he was watching the rain droplets careen down the side of the dome.

"I love looking at the moon," she said from out of the blue. "So round, so white, just like a sugar-coated golf ball."

Ryan gave it a cursory glance.

"I guess it sort of does look like a sugar-coated golf ball."

"And it's so far away. I can stretch my hand out and I can't even touch it."

"You shouldn't feel bad. Your arms are kinda short."

"But you know what's *really* far away? The stars. Whenever I look at them, I feel so distant."

"But we are distant from the stars."

"I don't mean just the stars. I mean generally speaking."

Ryan exhaled deeply. He turned his head slightly, sneaking a peek of Megan while she lay in a state of quietude. Her head rested over the brim of the basin, her eyes glued to the sky. She was perfectly still, almost a corpse. The only thing indicative of her breathing was the way her chest rose and fell through the water's surface. Never had Ryan seen her so relaxed.

He looked back at the sky and saw that most of the dark clouds had cleared. The stars were emerging and the rain had been reduced to a drizzle.

"Ryan," he heard her say, "what do you think of me? Honestly?"

"What do I think of you?" he repeated nervously.

"Yeah. As a person."

He struggled to come up with an answer. And he knew if he waited too long, his silence would be misconstrued.

"Well," he said, "it's hard to say."

"Equivocating, are we?"

"No, no. I think you're great."

"I don't want flattery, Ryan. I just want the honest truth. I want someone to put it to me bluntly."

"Okay" Ryan said, trying to come up with a response as fast as he could. He found one, but wasn't sure it was the best.

"You're like a coconut," he said. "You got a hard outer shell, and it's difficult to get inside."

"Oh."

"I mean, it's hard to get inside your head, kinda. You know, like, um—"

Megan chuckled. "It's okay, keep going."

Ryan sorted his thoughts.

"I don't know a lot about the way you think, and I never really get a chance to. You're like an offensive player, always forcing the others to play defensively. And you know what they say, the best defense is a good offense."

Megan rolled her eyes. "You and your sport analogies. I'm sorry. So what you're trying to say is . . ."

"You're keeping yourself safe and secluded. You got secrets that are locked up so good that no one has ever come close to breaking the safe. And if they do, there's an alarm system in place that will go off and scare them away."

She chuckled again, and rolled over onto her stomach, disturbing her reflection in the water. She interlaced her fingers and rested her chin on top.

"Really?" she said.

"I think so," Ryan said, looking over at her.

"What kind of secrets am I keeping?"

"For appetizers," he said jestingly, "why do you detest the whole male population?"

Upon hearing the inquiry, she grimaced. To Ryan, it felt good being the one to finally ask questions.

"I don't detest the *whole* male population," she protested. "Just a large majority."

"Any particular reason why?"

She smiled at him. "Let's say I had one too many bad dealings with them in the past."

"Just like that, you're going to shun us all out?"

"Trust me. If you were in my shoes, you'd understand."

"Well, hand me a pair. Tell me what happened."

Megan sighed, and took some time before spilling out the information.

"It was terrible, Ryan. A terrible day in eighth grade." She rolled on her back again and stared at the starry sky. "Everything that could have gone wrong, went wrong. To start things off, he arrives at my house an hour late. His mom was suppose to ride us out to lunch, but her car's transmission decided to die on our driveway. So if we wanted to do anything, it'd be at least a forty minute walk into town. And did I mention the temperature was in the nineties that day? By the time we got to the restaurant, I looked as if I had just came from a gym with a faulty air conditioner. And he, well, he *smelled* like he had just came back from that same gym.

"Next, I was forced to listen to every petty thing he ever accomplished, from his little league trophies, to the time he smooth-talked his way out of serving a detention. But despite his ability to achieve greatness, he lacked the foresight to bring enough cash to cover the bill. I had to chip in about eight bucks."

"That does sound terrible," Ryan said, beginning to regret ever having brought up the matter.

"But that's not the end of it. After that he decides he wants to go play some mini golf. Did I mention the sweltering heat? Anyway, during one of his strokes, he pulls back his club, striking me right in the shin. I mean, who the hell lifts the club more than six inches off the ground to play mini golf?"

"Must have been a steep slope."

"It was the practice hole."

"Oh."

"And then," Megan went on, her voice exhausted, "we agreed to reconvene later that night to catch the Fourth of July fireworks at the field behind the school. Why I agreed to that, I have no idea. The heat must have already done its damage. And to top things off, he must have been under the impression that the day had been a total success up until that point, because amid the booms and crackles, he invited himself to hands-on playtime. And let me tell you, he was playing with toys outside his age group."

"What kind of toys?" Ryan asked, speaking on autopilot.

"I'll give you a clue, Ryan. They weren't G.I. Joes."

After that, Ryan kept quiet, wishing not to pursue with anymore questions.

There was a short silence between them as they both continued to stare into the sky. The menacing clouds were all but gone, and the stars and the moon had fully revealed their celestial beauty.

"So what about you?" Ryan heard her say, sounding more composed.

"What about me?"

"What are you holding back?"

"Nothing at all."

"Seriously, Ryan, you know you got your secrets bottled up inside. And you know one of these days I'm going to pop the cork."

Ryan laughed. "Good luck with that. I'm screwed on with a cap."

"Ha, ha. Very funny. You know I just want to help you."

"Help me with what?"

"Karina. It's a favor I'll do for free."

"I don't know what you're talking about."

"Whatever you say." She lifted herself out of the water and sat upright against the brim of the basin Her wet hair dangled over her shoulders. "So what about Blake?" she added.

The name pierced Ryan's ears like the screech of a chalk board. He quivered as a result, feeling the chills run through his body. He had been here long enough, he thought. It was time to go somewhere else.

"You know, I actually got to pee."

He stood up and shook his arms dry. Then he shuffled through the pool and climbed down into the lower basin. "I'm going to look for the restrooms," he said, before dropping down to the next level. Megan stood up as well, dripping water like a wrung sponge. Upon feeling the air, she sought warmth by huddling herself with her arms.

"I'll be around," she called out, "critiquing the artwork."

After Ryan had parted, she did as she said she would. She explored the area along the periphery of the fountain, admiring each piece in the gallery, in a museum that was bustling with a multitude of sounds that she didn't even know was there.

———Chapter 7———

Discussion

Zephner was shown into the opulent office that was renowned for its fantastic view of the city's northern bay. The noon sun seeped in through the lofty windows, spilling onto the olive-colored upholstery of the armchairs and sofa. All the tables and bookcases had a elegant veneer that gave a brilliant luster. But the room's centerpiece was located along the eastern wall, a grand burgundy desk that could only be suitable for one person: Commander Roland, the top ranking official in this region of the planet Cyannus. He sat at the desk, in a chair that was as big as his ego. His graying hairs and inherited legacy had managed to instill a false sense of political acumen, which Zephner had been able to see right through. Zephner wasn't fond of his character and wouldn't have bothered to come here had he not felt the obligation.

"What do you have for me, Zephner?" Roland asked promptly. "I'm going to need something real good if I ever hope to keep this situation under control."

Zephner had yet to reach the center of the room, and when he did, he stood there dumbly, unsure of whether or not he had any information that would appease the man's expectations.

Roland belatedly offered him a seat, but Zephner declined, opting to stand over by the bookshelf. He looked out into the bay as he spoke.

"I'm afraid I don't know a whole lot. And what I do know probably won't help you."

Disappointment swept across Roland's face immediately. It then transformed into a look of fear.

"Well, darn it, you didn't come all the way over here to tell me nothing. Tell me *something*. Anything that I can use."

Zephner glanced at him, and starred back out the window.

"The people aboard that station were all members of a very radical mission, one that is led by a man they refer to as Lord Triocks. They carry but one thing on their agenda, and that's to find the Dreamer's World."

Roland opened his eyes real wide.

"The Dreamer's World? You mean that mythical place that's been passed through folk legends for millennia?" He read Zephner's silence. "That's absurd. The place doesn't exist. They'll never find it."

"You're mistaken. The Dreamer's World does exist, and with time, they could theoretically find it."

"Oh, cut me a break. We've been through this before, and I have no intentions of going through it again. We haven't the time."

"I was on that station, Roland."

Roland paused and raised a brow.

"You were?"

"I was imprisoned there, for about a month. I was interrogated, each and every day.

"Concerning?"

"The world you don't believe in."

Roland leaned forward, laying his arms flat on the desk. He looked at Zephner inquisitively.

"And how does this substantiate your claims?"

"Aren't you going to ask me first how I got out of there?"

Roland shrugged. "I figured you bludgeoned your way out.

After all, that is your M.O."

"Evidently that doesn't work when you're being held in an anti-gravitational holding cell. The reason I was able to get out was because a certain boy appeared, and was willing to help me."

"Zephner . . ."

"There was no one in that room a minute prior. And there was certainly no way that boy could have been on that station. It was an impossibility unless you consider otherworldly intervention."

Roland turned his head and held up his hand, signaling for him to stop. "Let's put this aside for now," he said calmly. "Moving on—can you explain to me how the station came to founder out at sea?"

"That I can't tell you. All I know is that the captain had a course set that would fly us directly into a star, as a way to escape the consequences of his failure, and take us out in the process. I don't know how it came to land here."

Roland nodded, and then proceeded to stand from his chair. He picked up the glass from his desk and went over by the far window. Now neither of the two men in the room were looking at each other. Roland sighed and took a sip of his drink. He relished the taste thoroughly before he swallowed.

"Have you been in contact with Knivus as of late?"

"It's been a while."

"Did he ever mention anything regarding this mission?"

Zephner shook his head. "He was aware of their presence, but he didn't say much to me about it. Last I heard he had an agent on the inside relaying information. If everything went smoothly, he should know something by now."

"I'm glad to hear that. I'll have to send our liaison to Armon right away."

Zephner looked at Roland quizzically. "What's the matter with our interstellar communications?"

Roland took another sip of his drink and begun to dawdle back to his desk. He sighed again, placed his glass down, and collapsed into the chair. He spoke softly and slowly, as if reluctant to recollect the issue.

He intertwined his fingers, squeezing his thumbs together. "The relay station in our sector is down . . . and it hasn't been down in over *fifty* years."

Zephner looked away, anticipating what he was getting at. The anger was building up inside of him again, ready to whistle like a boiling teapot. Except now there was no outlet by which he could vent.

"Fifty years," Roland said again. "And when you consider the terror that's unfolding, I would say there's a good chance that these people have already showcased their hostility. My guess is that this is a coordinated attack with the intent to disrupt interplanetary communications. Because without the relay station, there's no way to focus and accelerate a signal across these kinds of distances. For now we have no choice to employ archaic methods of communicating."

"We'll do what we have to do," Zephner said.

Roland motioned with his hand and head. "Yes, well. We are going to do what we can. But in regards to delivering a tactical response, we may face a few hurdles. Ever since the misfortune that Lylid suffered, everything has been difficult for our administration. Our military, our intelligence, our foreign influence—everything has taken a hit. Which I guess can be expected when one loses their key export. We're facing financial ruin right now. And though it hurts me to say it, if things get any worse, it's the Garthega Federation that we'll have to look up to."

"Wealth can only take a nation so far," Zephner answered defensively. "It's the decisions their leaders make that determine longevity. And with Knivus calling the shots, I'm not liking their odds for surviving the next generation of war. With him it's all about the machines, and he forgets that they will always lack a crucial quality that sets them apart from their living counterparts. Artificial intelligence is never going to be a substitute for the human mind. But that's something he refuses to believe."

"If it gets us through today, then I couldn't care less. But that's a discussion I can save for some other time. Right now, I have to tackle what's on my plate." He sunk onto his desk, in a posture that showed mental unrest. "And it's more than I can eat."

Zephner looked askance, catching wind of the fact that he was holding on to something else.

"What haven't you mentioned?" he said.

Roland took a deep breath.

"We have an unidentified armada approaching our outpost on Lylid. We've extrapolated their arrival to be within four hours."

Zephner grew more restless, his body filling with rage. He tried to enjoy the scenic view, but it didn't bring him any solace. He clenched his teeth tightly.

"Our presence there is barely enough to handle a pack of wolves. What the hell are they suppose to do?"

"I know, I know. That's why I've deployed the *Obsidian* to contest their arrival."

"What do they have on board?"

"Four-hundred and eighty seven crew and fifty-six armed air-crafts."

"Is that enough?"

"I hope so. Though let me tell you, I have no intentions of firing the first shot. I'm not about to initiate a war with an enemy I know nothing about."

"Smart call."

Roland gave a perfunctory smile and reached for his drink again. He gulped down what remained and stared disappointingly at the bottom of the empty glass. Zephner watched him, studied him, and saw the burden that the aging man carried. He was in up to his neck with the kind of predicaments he wasn't use to handling. In his thirty years in office, there had been no wars, no major conflicts. It was very much that way throughout the galaxy. There had been the flexing of muscles, sure, and the appetite to impose the perception of superiority. But war was unfamiliar, and the prospect of war was terrifying. And no call to arms could be better heard than the one made by having a twenty-mile wide enemy space station in the waters of one's nation.

Roland gazed at Zephner reminiscently.

"I don't suppose this is a problem you'll be able to make go away?"

Zephner didn't recognize the rhetorical tone of the question and answered accordingly.

"We're not dealing with petty criminals or local insurgents. We're up against an ideology, which is a hell of a lot more dangerous. Knocking it in the back of the skull isn't going to make it go away."

Roland looked away and didn't say anything. He put his elbow on the desk and rested his fist against his jaw. Zephner could almost see the gears turning in his head. Though he wasn't sure they were actually accomplishing anything.

"Well, thank you, Zephner, for stopping by. If you learn anything else, you know how to contact me."

Zephner started to head towards the door.

"Don't count on it."

"How about a drink before you leave?"

"I have a long drive to make. Probably not a good idea."

Roland nodded. "Smart call."

Zephner walked swiftly across the room. He was just under the doorway when he heard the telephone ring. Right away he had a strong premonition. There was something about the innocuous ringing of a phone that riled him. Maybe it was the way it served as prelude to whatever message the caller intended to pass on, whether it be good news or bad. As of late, he's had more experiences with the latter.

The phone rung once more before Roland picked it up. Zephner remained in the doorway, unconcerned about whether the eavesdropping was welcomed or not.

Roland answered, "This is Roland."

Zephner turned his head, and analyzed every facial cue he could find. His face was well at first; calm, confident. But then his mouth sunk into a frown. The brows wrinkled, and the eyes fixated on the uncluttered surface of his desk.

"Yes—yes, patch me through."

He paused. Then there was silence. As he waited he noticed Zephner listening in from the doorway. But he didn't care.

A new voice came on the other line. Roland spoke again, though this time he struggled to keep a tone of conviction.

"Yes—this is Commander Roland. Whom am I speaking with?"

Zephner could discern it was one of them. Though he couldn't hear the voice, he could still perceive the vile, twisted principles the individual on the other end of the line stood for. They might as well been standing in the same room.

"Captain Malcus—I think it goes without saying that there are important matters to discuss."

Zephner kept watching, listening. He could sense Roland was growing uncomfortable.

"Tell me, what is it that you seek?"

Roland listened for the answer, then shook his head. "I'm afraid that's something I'm not equipped to assist with—yes, but why does this necessitate a military presence?"

Zephner continued studying the cues, looking out for any

change. Then he witnessed a sudden shift in posture. Roland bent over the desk, laying down his forearm for support. His fingers grasped a loose pen, clutching it tightly. His eyes were filled with the kind of dread that can only be seen in a man whose life hung in the balance. The following words were painfully extracted from his tongue.

"Yes—yes, I am willing to cooperate."

Zephner glowered at him. Either he really was backed into a corner, or showing how easily he could be succumbed.

Roland's voice rose in pitch. "Boy?"

Zephner's interest in the conversation rose to a new level. Given the situation, boy could have only referred to one person. And he wasn't happy about it.

"Please hold just a moment," Roland said, quickly covering the mic. He looked up at Zephner.

"The boy. You mentioned there was a boy. Where is he now?"

He knew where this was heading, and he cringed slightly. It was clear now that Martisse must have sent out a memo prior to his passing.

"I dropped him off a couple of blocks south of here. I didn't think he'd still be involved in this."

"Damn it, Zephner!"

"What do they want with him?"

"The hell does it matter? They're posing a threat that could endanger *a lot* of lives. I couldn't care less what they do with one kid."

Stuck between a rock and a hard place, he opted with what he thought was the most sane decision.

"I can probably find him."

"Then find him!"

He wasn't aware of it, but he lingered there, unmoving. His feet didn't move. He had doubts about what he should do.

"Go now. Go!" Roland urged him.

Who was he kidding. He wasn't going to jeopardize more lives than what he would be saving. He abandoned his reservations and left the office and fled the estate. He mounted his two-wheeled mode of transportation and headed south into the heart of the city. After that he could only hope what he knew about Ryan was enough to locate him.

Chapter 8

Aboard The Obsidian

Ryan advanced slowly down one of the museum's dark, lonely corridors, looking for anything that would point him in the direction of the restrooms. So far he saw nothing but a collection of priceless artifacts, all of which were neatly aligned on either side of the hall. One after another, he saw glass box displays that held all sorts of historical trinkets and items, from stone arrow heads, to clay pottery, to marble busts of (what looked like) very important people. These in particular disturbed him the most. The light in their cases produced stark shadows in the recesses of their faces, and the eyes were blank and soulless. He couldn't tell if they were looking at him or not. Though did it matter? They weren't alive (or so he thought). He did his best not to look at them and to continue down the hall. Though the further he traveled the darker it became. He turned a corner, then another. He hurried faster, remembering again how badly he needed to relieve himself. Soon he found what he was looking for.

High on the wall was a glowing sign that spelled out the word *Restrooms*. At the time it couldn't have said anything better. He approached the door designated for men.

Inside he was confronted with what was, for the most part, a standard restroom. There were urinals to his left, followed by a couple of stalls, and then a row of sinks on his right. But just like the hall outside, it was all very dark. The only thing that granted any vision seemed to be the long horizontal mirror that stretched over the row of sinks. It gave off a frail glow, barely enough for him to make out the surrounding environment. He looked at it curiously, confirming his reflection, and then moved on.

He entered the very last stall, the one against the far wall, just because it was the roomiest. He closed the door behind him, locked it, then realized he could see next to nothing. But it didn't matter. He was safe in here. While being keen to any sounds, he lowered his pants and took aim where he estimated the bowl to be. When heard the splash he became sure of his accuracy.

The stream ended, and he could go back now. Though he only had a vague recollection of where he had come from and why he was there. Actively his mind searched for an answer, putting together different fragments from here and there, and then from somewhere else, from a place he didn't even know existed. All these pieces came together, sculpting a place for his being to occupy.

He turned around in the dark and fumbled to unlatch the lock. He stepped out, immediately noticing that something was different. The restroom had undergone a new look and shape. Everything looked clean and well polished. The floor tiles were huge colored circles, while the walls were porcelain squares. The east wall curved ever so slightly, and now above the sinks were a series of portholes, alternating between mirrors and windows.

Ryan stepped next to one and looked at it closely. As if gazing through a telescope, he saw a cluster of stars strewn throughout the big black sky. Some were tiny, others larger, but regardless of size, they were evident of one thing: he was no longer in the museum.

Without anywhere else to go, he decided to leave the restroom, weaving through the short tunnel-like passage that was the exit.

He emerged on the other side, into an empty hallway. It was

cozy and cordial, shaped like a tubular tunnel with a nine foot ceiling. The walls were a soothing taupe, clean and welcoming. The ceiling was decorated with dome-shaped light fixtures that hung at equidistant intervals. Under his feet was an oceanic blue carpet with fibers that sprouted like bushy grass. Ryan could only think about how fun it would have been to run through it barefoot. But such a thing was probably not a great idea, given that he was an involuntary intruder. He also saw cabin doors on either side, set within the recesses of the wall. If people were inside, he didn't want to be seen, so he scurried off furtively like a frightened mouse down towards the end of the tunnel.

He came up to a four-way juncture, stopping as soon as he reached the corner. He leaned past the wall, searching diligently for anyone that may have been on board. There were two individuals far down the east hall, conversing among one another. He could only make out a few words: something about ship deployment and arrival time.

Not wishing to make himself known quite yet, he hurried past them, seeing that their backs were turned. He followed the corridor, all the way down until he reached a rotunda. The round, open room was thoroughly lit by a sole decorative globe that was embedded into the peak of the domed ceiling. All the light came pouring into the tower.

Ryan leaned over the handrail of the balcony and saw the gyrating stairway that ran past many decks, each encircled by sheets of glass. It ran much deeper than what he could see.

It was time to stop loitering and get a move on it. To where, he had no idea. All he knew was that the only place to go was down, and so he went.

He entered the stairway and descended down each step, hastily, but silently. He passed each deck one at a time, while reading the signs posted at each level. They pointed to additional cabins, eateries, docking bays, training facilities, and more. But there was one in particular that caught Ryan's attention—something called the Gravalon Arena. He was optimistic about the entertainment such a place could provide, and so he got off on E deck.

Through tunnels and turns he followed the signs as they led him deeper into the core of the station. The silence was nerve-racking. The carpet muffled the sounds of any footsteps, so he had to continue with blind faith that he wouldn't be caught coming around the next corner.

On his left he saw the words *Gravalon Arena* affixed to the wall, in slick, silver letters. He was as excited as a kid that had just seen the entrance gate of their favorite amusement park.

Beside it was a door, but not just any door. It was big, square and followed the curve of the wall. Ryan examined it and saw a panel with buttons. He found and pressed the button to open the door. It slid gently across into the wall, revealing the chamber inside.

It was overwhelmingly stunning, greater than what Ryan could have imagined. He took one step forward and found himself inside a hollow globe, doused in a gleaming whiteness that was so pure and vibrant. It was impossible to distinguish whether the walls were twenty feet away or a hundred. It was like floating in nothingness. But after a closer inspection he noticed seams running through the floor in a polygonal pattern. That's when he knew that the room was, in fact, a room.

He paced around, absolutely captivated by the sheer absence of anything. While moving about he noticed the lack of his shadow. He tried making one by placing his hand close to the floor, but still he could not produce a shadow. It was then only logical to conclude that the floor panels were self-emitting. Cool, he thought.

There was a nudge at his ankle. He looked down and saw that uncanny, air-filled bundle of rubber that he recognized as a basketball. He was certain that it was the same one he encountered and claimed for himself not too long ago. He couldn't remember why he wanted to take it. It could have been because it exhibited certain properties that were of interest to Ryan, namely its ability to roll by its own volition. Basketballs weren't suppose to do that; he was sure of it. Either way, he was going to have some fun with it.

With the swing of a bowler, Ryan chucked the ball up the room's spherical incline. It traveled like a pinball fired by a launch coil, climbing higher and higher up the wall. But instead of slowing down, it continued to climb, barely losing any momentum. Ryan stared at it, baffled, as it continued towards the apex of the globe, and then back down the other side to where he first threw it.

Something wasn't right. He tried it again.

He gave the ball another good roll. Once again it completed a full lap around the room. It was strange, but fascinating. And like a child with an unquenchable thirst for amusement, he threw the ball again—but this time with a slip of his fingers. It bobbled instead of rolled, making it look like it wasn't going to be able to make the round trip. And it didn't. It came to a stop right at the peak of the ceiling, the most inaccessible location possible.

Right away his first thought was that someone was going to see this, and know that he was playing around in here when he probably wasn't suppose to. Heck, he shouldn't have even been on this station, but here he was anyway.

He tried figuring out a way to retrieve the ball, but it seemed impossible. It must have been at least sixty feet or so. Maybe if he could chuck something at it and get it moving again. Or maybe find another ball and have them collide. But that would most likely result in the second ball getting stuck. And where was he going to find another ball anyway? It was no good. He had to scrap the idea. But then he hatched a new method, one that was simply ingenious.

He marched forward, directly towards the incline. He started to climb, expecting to meet some form of resistance, in the way of, say, gravity. But that never happened. He kept climbing, higher and higher, never getting the sense he would fall. He could still feel his weight directly under his feet, and it stayed that way until he was standing right beside the ball. Anyone that would have walked in through the door would have seen him hanging upside down like a bat.

He made a complacent smile as he triumphantly lifted the ball off the ground. He dribbled it all the way back down—or was it up? Either way, he headed to the doorway, then dribbled around some more, wishing there had been a hoop somewhere. But he had to make do with what he had: a ball and a big empty room.

There was little else he could do besides dribble it back and forth, and that's what he did. Then, after his next bounce, he caught a glimpse of someone standing in the entranceway. Quickly, he caught the ball and held it firmly in his hands.

It was a young guy in his late twenties, dressed in a navy blue long sleeve shirt, with a pair of beige slacks. He had a cargo belt looped through his waist, which carried a small pistol, and a small gadget that looked like a radio. He must have been standing there for a while, which told Ryan that he wasn't alarmed by his intrusion. He looked more confused than anything, like a visitor at the zoo watching the monkeys do strange things. Regardless, Ryan remained motionless, awaiting some kind of indictment.

The man held his index finger up, as if trying to recall the name of the species he just spotted. His mouth was slightly ajar, ready to say something, but nothing came out.

He caved and finally asked, "who are you?"

Ryan answered cooperatively, "I'm Ryan." Then hastily added, "I know I'm not suppose to be here. But I don't know how I got here either."

The man nodded understandingly. "Looks like that makes two of us. Cause there's no way for a stowaway to gain access to this place. With all the security checks and clearance points, it's just not possible."

"Impossible things have been happening to me a lot lately." He tossed the ball lightly into the air. "Like this basketball. It moves all by itself. It even managed to follow me all the way over here."

"So that's what you call it," Steve said, with his eyes fixated on it.

"You mean, you've never seen a basketball before?"

"Can't say that I have. And I can't say I've ever heard of one either."

"That's odd."

The man chuckled. "You know what else is odd—the way you look like you've just crawled out of an ocean."

The comment reminded Ryan that he was still wet from head to toe. He could almost taste the salty water that he swallowed.

"I *did* crawl out of an ocean," he proclaimed. "I fell in right after I was chased by this monster."

The man continued to muse over Ryan, but not in that incredulous manner that he would have expected. He appeared to genuinely accept his story.

The man spoke again after a studious observation.

"You know, they've always called me the gullible one. And I wouldn't be surprised if I hear it again today."

"How come?"

"Because I think I know who you are."

"I'm Ryan. I told you that."

"You're more than just a Ryan."

"What else am I?"

The man pointed with his finger again. He had it figured

out. The answer had unraveled itself and he was ready to pro-claim it proudly.

"You're a dreamer, Ryan. That's what you are—a traveler from the other side. You went to sleep, you paid the tollbooth, you crossed the bridge, and now you're here."

"A dreamer," Ryan mumbled to himself, seeing how the explanation fit. At the very least it would answer the question of why he had fallen in an ocean, or gotten mixed up with that strange man with the motorcycle. Suddenly he remembered Zephner's voice, and the words he spoke: *It's a dream, Ryan. You're dreaming.* So it hadn't been the first time he heard this explanation. Though seemingly, having left the company of the one person who understood what was happening, he had managed to forget where he was and what he was doing. Hearing it again re-ignited his memory and tied everything back together.

"I'm dreaming," Ryan declared confidently, trying to commit it to memory. "That's what's going on."

The man smiled.

"Either that, or we both have a couple of screws loose."

Ryan gazed around the room, appreciating it all over again with his newfound wisdom. Everything seemed marginally clear-er, sharper, as if he had just slipped on a pair of glasses. Then he remembered something else.

"Megan," he blurted out unintentionally.

The man asked him, "Who's Megan?"

"This girl I was with. I told her I was going to the restroom. But that was at the museum. Now I'm here, very far away from the museum. I wonder what she's going to think."

The man pressed his lips together and gave an empathetic look.

"Yeah, she's not going to be too happy about that."

"But it's not even my fault. I keep *moving*. I'm starting to feel discombobulated."

"I don't think you'll need to worry about that anymore. Because if I'm right about the whole dreaming thing, then that means you're undergoing, uh—that thing."

"What thing?"

The man brought his hand to his forehead. He searched laboriously for the term. It was on the tip of his tongue.

"I got it," he said finally. "Layers of Perception."

Intrigued, Ryan asked, "Does that explain why I keep moving around?"

"It should, assuming I'm remembering this correctly. You have these different levels of awareness. At the lowest level you have the dreamer who doesn't know they're dreaming. They tend to accept what they see and hear, and never bother to ask any questions. You could say they're out of sync with the reality of this universe. They're not grounded, so they often times just drift from place to place."

"I think that is what's happening to me," Ryan said, looking down at himself.

"I bet it is. Then after that we have another level, which I think is what you guys refer to as lucid dreaming. You become aware of the fact that you're dreaming. And you also have some degree of control over what you do and where you go."

"I've experienced that before. But this feels different. It feels even realer."

"Then that could only mean one thing—you're hovering around the third level."

Ryan became even more fascinated.

"What's the third level?"

The man took a moment to put his words together.

"It's essentially a state of perfect perception. It means being able to see this place for what it really is. And not just seeing it, but understanding it as well. You have to be able to comprehend that this place isn't *just* a dream, but something more than that.

To put it into perspective, it's like the difference between looking at a boat and seeing a stack of planks fastened together, and looking at a boat and seeing a vessel that's capable of staying afloat in the water. Though you'll never know that unless someone tells you, and instills you with the wisdom. That's why not everyone who visits here experiences this level of lucidity. You need someone on this side to 'awaken' you, so to speak."

Ryan pondered over what he said, trying to make some sense out of it. At the very least, it gave some credence to what Zephner had said to him earlier.

"This is the first time I've had anyone on this side tell me this," he said.

"That's because it takes someone who knows what's going on to pass out the information. And there isn't a lot of them around anymore. This is an arcane phenomenon that is being covered up by isolationists. It's in the best interest of leaders for the people to believe they are alone, and that dreaming is a thing of myth. And I can hardly blame them. If you flip through a history book, you'll see the countless wars fought on the account of the Dreamer's World. These people were willing to shed the blood of an entire kingdom if they thought their kings had information that could ascertain its whereabouts. And in the end, it's only led to a million dead bodies and a million dead ends. Not a single person today has come any closer to finding it as the people from a thousand years ago."

Ryan shook his head, trying to reestablish his grip with reality, if he could even call it that. There was a lot to digest, and he had nothing to drink.

He looked over at the man again.

"So how did you come to learn all this?"

"Well," the man said, licking his lips. "Let's say I've been sticking my nose in forbidden literature."

"It's forbidden? Really?"

"Not forbidden, but just highly inaccessible."

Ryan felt nervous about his presence here and how it had the potential to stir up trouble. He wondered what they would do to him if they learned he was in their yard. Would they treat him like a fairytale character? Would they apprehend him, put him in an exhibit? Would people come and pay admission to see this boy from another dimension? Or even worse, would they run experiments? Cut him open, dissect his brain? See what's inside? He sure as hell hoped not.

"So what happens now?" Ryan asked, feeling queasy in his stomach. "What are they going to do with me?"

"I'm not really sure," the man said, bringing his finger to his chin. "This is one heck of a doozy. Not sure what would be proper protocol."

"Do you think I'll be able to go back home? Or at the very least, back to the museum?"

He looked at him regrettably. "I can't be sure when we'll be heading back, as we're currently on route to Lylid, to—um, intercept an unidentified fleet."

He didn't like the word unidentified. It sounded hazardous.

"Could they be an enemy fleet? Hostiles?"

"I really don't think so. And even if they are, we're equipped to deal with them quite handily. We're packing the firepower, and guess who's going to be behind one of those guns."

"You?"

"Damn straight. Steve McKindler, 38-S-rated fighter pilot, top of his class. The great white of the air is what they call me."

"And gullible."

He chuckled. "Yeah, that too."

"I feel reassured."

"You should be."

Ryan still had his doubts, though the man did seem pretty confident in himself. Maybe he should trust him.

He watched as Steve walked over to the basketball. He picked it up off the floor and examined it like it was some alien artifact. He felt it, smelled it, and then proceeded to try and dribble it the way he saw Ryan doing earlier. He handled it pretty well, better than what Ryan would have expected.

"They really don't have these around here, do they."

"Nope," Steve answered. "We play with a different kind of ball."

"Like what?"

"Here, I'll show you."

Steve put the basketball down and walked to the center of the chamber. He crouched down and reached for a flat, circular dial that Ryan hadn't noticed. He laid his thumb on it which caused a blue ring to illuminate on the floor. A slim, cylindrical column rose from it, revealing a series of small compartments, each of which held a cerulean-colored ball. They were just slightly larger than a softball, marked with a decorative yellow ring, and two thumb-sized holes in either side.

Steve grabbed one of them and held it up for Ryan to see.

"This is what we play with."

"What do you call it?"

"A gravasphere. Here, go long," he said, ready to pitch the ball.

Ryan scampered a few yards out and held his hands out ready to catch. Steve gave the ball a firm throw and it flew through the air—but not in the manner that Ryan anticipated. What he thought he would see is the ball rise a little, then fall, just like any object under the influence of gravity. But this ball behaved differently. Instead of arcing, it traveled in a perfectly straight line—a line that aimed right for Ryan's face. He caught it, but barely. As soon as it was secure in his hands, he tried letting go of it. And surely as he expected, the ball just remained stationary in midair. If only Newton could see what they've done with his first law.

"Kinda neat, huh?"

"I'd say. How do you play?"

"It's easy." Steve grabbed another ball and spun it into the air, catching it again. "You start off with four balls in play, two for each team. When the match commences, there will be holographic rings spread around the room. You'll have eight players on each side making passes between one another while trying to score, which is done by completing a pass that goes through one of the rings. What makes it interesting is that the rings are always moving around, and changing colors, which can indicate a variety of different things. You have the orange rings which net you points, and you got the yellow that deducts points. A blue ring freezes the others in place, while a red one temporarily makes them disappear."

"Uh huh," Ryan said, already envisioning himself as the next Gravalon super star.

"You got to use all of these in conjunction with one another. For example, if you have two of your guys next to a ring, another guy could trigger a blue one, freezing the other so that the two guys can just make a series of quick passes. The score will go up by one with each pass. But the thing to consider is that you'll earn more points relative to the distance the ball travels. Three feet is like one point, ten feet is about two, then thirty is like six, and so on and so on, until you get to a hundred plus which could net you all the way up to fifty."

"But is this room even that big?"

"Oh, not this room," Steve said, spinning the ball into the air again. "This is just a smaller scale of the real thing. Its only purpose is to bait our guys into getting some exercise. You couldn't fit the real thing in here. The official arena is four-hundred feet in diameter."

Ryan tried to picture how big that was. He thought of a football field and how that was only three hundred-sixty feet. This was even bigger than that. But this wasn't even a field, but a giant globe. It was almost too much for him to visualize. He tried, only to picture hamsters running around in really big exercise balls.

"This is something I have to try out," Ryan said adamantly.

"Definitely. Once we have matters squared away we'll get a game going for sure."

"Great. So what happens now?"

Steve pointed at Ryan again, licking his lip.

"That's right," he said. "You're not suppose to be here. But you know what—before I make mention of you to the captain, there's someone I want you to meet. I have a score to settle and I think you can help me out on this one."

"Glad I can be useful."

"Hey, everyone is good for something," he said with a smile.

They put away the gravaspheres back into the storage container and left the Gravalon arena.

CHAPTER 9

A CLOSED DOOR

A succession of horns blared from every direction, deprecating the reckless maneuvers of a certain two-wheeled motorist. Zephner zipped in and out of lanes, narrowly grazing the cars on either side of him. He was constantly scanning the road up ahead, anticipating where an opening would appear. He leaned into the right line, then back into the left, again nearly scraping another vehicle. To the motorists, he was driving recklessly, but he knew perfectly well there was no risk of a collision. Among his keen senses was the ability to detect the slightest shift in movement. If a man was going to throw a fist, he'd know as soon as the muscle twitched; if a gun was going to be fired, he'd know as soon as the finger applied pressure to the trigger. So he was completely comfortably racing through the heavily congested traffic.

At the next corner he made a left turn that took him towards the bay. There he took another road that ran parallel with the coast, one that overlooked the beach, the ports, and all the freighters and sailboats.

He picked up his fair share of looks as he rode another half-mile down the road to the Museum of Antiquities, an exquisite stone building that was constructed within a rocky hillside. Massive columns flanked the entrance, which stood at the top of a long flight of stairs. People were coming and going, many of them noticing the motorcyclist hopping over the curb and onto the sidewalk.

Zephner pinned the throttle and climbed up onto the stairs. The bike roared viciously, and the people in its path sprung away, clearing a beeline to the entrance. He saw a couple leaving through a door, so he sped up to reach it, managing to slip through before it could close. Once inside, he knew he would face resistance. Not only did he have to deal with the heavy crowds, but whatever security was present as well. They would surely have something to say about a man riding a motorcycle inside a museum. But it didn't matter; time was of the essence. Ryan had to be found.

He plowed through the main lobby, which produced shrills and shrieks from every direction. The bike jerked violently from side to side as he avoided the frantic museum visitors. Their volatile reactions were making it that much harder to predict a clear route, but he did find one eventually. It led him straight down a long hall, with marble statues on either side, and colorful wall frescoes. He was actively searching the crowd, for any young boy with golden brown hair and a dark teal shirt. But there were none here that fitted that description. So he pressed onward with screeching acceleration, all while dodging the crowds and the priceless artifacts.

The hall opened up into an enormous room with a domed ceiling, and at it's center was a tiered fountain that spilled curtains of water over the brims of the basins. He circled around it, snagging a clear view of everyone in the room, studying their faces and outfits before they could flee. But amid all the scampering people, there was one individual that didn't seem to react. It was a girl in an orange polo shirt. She remained stationary, staring studiously at a painting on the wall. It was only when he pulled up close to her that she looked askance, as if *maybe* she had heard something.

—)—

Megan thought she heard something, while she still waited for Ryan to return from the restroom. As far as she knew, the museum was desolated. That's what she observed and that's what she perceived. She was studying a pretty painting of a house on a mountain side when she heard a faint voice call her name, with a sense of urgency. It continued calling, each time sounding louder and clearer. Soon she heard other sounds: frantic footsteps, a running fountain, even an engine growling.

She turned around and was floored when she saw a museum bustling with people. In front of her was a man in a black leather jacket, standing alongside a motorcycle with the engine thrumming impatiently.

She wasn't scared, even though it would have been reasonable. The other people in the room were certainly alarmed. But her head was too hazy to figure out why that may have been.

She gazed at him with immense curiosity. The red, fearsome eyes, however sinister, projected a kind of comfort and familiarity. He wasn't a villain, or a man who wanted to hurt her. He was someone she could trust.

Zephner looked back at her, becoming perturbed by her unresponsiveness.

"Megan" he called out again. "You have to tell me where Ryan is."

Megan looked at him blankly.

"I don't understand, what's going on?"

"Listen," he said, taking hold of her shoulders. "You're dreaming right now. You have to understand that. Use your senses; feel the solid ground beneath your feet, listen to the voices in the room. Anything."

"I'm dreaming?"

"Yes, you are."

The word resounded in her head. *Dreaming*. If that's really what was going on, it would explain a lot. Just now she realized she was soaking wet. She backtracked through her memory and was able to recall the abandoned school, and the plunge into the ocean that followed. The juxtaposition of the events made no sense, but with hindsight, she understood that it shouldn't have. Suddenly she felt more immersed in the world she was in. The ground *was* solid, and her ability to think lucidly helped her feel stable. She remembered that Ryan had gone to the restroom, and that he was yet to return.

"Now tell me where's Ryan," Zephner urged again.

"I don't know. He went to the restroom, but it's been a real long time. What's this all about? Is he all right?"

She saw him hesitating.

"There's no way to guarantee that unless we find him."

She could gather from his tone that things were worse than he was willing to admit. It made her feel uncomfortable very quickly.

"I saw him take off in that direction." She pointed towards the western hall. "Maybe we can find him."

"I sure hope we do."

Megan stared at him some more, still intent on unraveling the man's knot of secrecy.

"I know you, don't I?"

"That doesn't really matter right now," he said, jumping back on the motorcycle. Without an invitation, Megan went ahead and climbed onto the backseat. She held onto the man's jacket, ready to takeoff.

"What are you doing?"

"What does it look like? I'm coming along. If you're telling me that Ryan is in trouble, then I need to be there."

Zephner didn't argue. He kept his mouth shut and pulled away. The tires screeched and spun as the bike took off. Megan clutched his jacket just before she could topple backwards. The exhilaration of cruising through a museum while on a motorcycle left her with her heart in her throat. The people flew by with blinding speed, shrieking and dodging out of the bike's path. The air brushed against her face, and her hair fluttered wildly. She could feel her nerves tingling and her stomach springing into her chest whenever she thought there was going to be a collision. But that never happened. Turned out this man was a pretty damn good driver.

They turned at the next corner, blazing past a collection of marble busts. Up ahead a man in uniform leapt out from a con-joining hall. "*Hold it*", he shouted, just before stepping out of the way. But Zephner didn't ease up, and just kept on going. Only then did Megan realize the severity of her actions and the penalties that it could entail.

Megan leaned forward and spoke into his ear.

"We're so going to get in trouble for this, aren't we?" When he didn't answer, she went on. "If push comes to shove, I'll tell them you had me at gun point, okay? You do have a gun, right?"

Zephner came up to a fork and squeezed tightly on the brakes, reeling Megan into his backside. She let out a painful grunt before sitting back up straight.

"Let's not test out the airbags, shall we?"

Zephner turned his head both ways, scanning the corridors for any signs of a restroom. Over to his left he spotted a sign high up on the wall that marked such a location. He took off again in a dazzling burst of acceleration, leaving Megan clinging on for dear life.

It would've all been worth it if it meant helping Ryan, she told herself. Because, for cryin' out loud, she didn't know what the hell was going on. If this was a dream, like the man had said, it was certainly the most bizarre one she's had yet, in the sense that it didn't feel like a dream at all. At least not anymore.

Zephner pulled tightly on the breaks again, parking the bike right beside the entrance to the restroom. He dismounted it as he gave Megan instructions to stay put.

—)—

He hurried inside the men's room, only to find it empty. Though there was that single stall with the door closed all the way at the end. He rushed to it, knocked on it, and called out Ryan's name. No response. He jiggled the handle and saw that it was indeed locked. Someone had to be in there, or *had* been in there. There was only one way to know for sure.

He battered open the door with a single blow from his elbow, and saw right away that it was empty. From what he could gather, the worst possible scenario had come to pass. Ryan wasn't going to be in the museum, or even this city. There was now exactly an endless amount of places he could be. The odds of ever finding him in time were stacked as high as a tower to the next galaxy. There wasn't going to be enough time; they weren't going to wait. The most he could do now was report his findings.

He left the restroom, only to find a squad of security officers surrounding him with guns drawn. Off to one side, Megan was planted face down on the floor, with her hands ready to be bounded and cuffed. They were ordering him as well to turn around and lie flat on the ground. But he didn't comply. He re-mained standing and stared them down, contemplating what his options were. He could dispose of them in a variety of different methods, but his conscience got in the way of that. Furthermore, he didn't want to endanger Megan. A stray bullet wouldn't have been and issue for him, but it would have been for her. He tried to remain as prudent as his patience would allow.

"I'm carrying out a search under Roland's orders," he said to them. But he was duly ignored, as if he were a crazy person.

Again he was ordered to get on the floor, but still he refused. His blood was seething, and he had to get it under control. He decided the best thing to do was comply now, and then deal with the matter after Megan was out of the picture.

He turned around and dropped his knees to the ground. One of the officers came up to him, grabbed his wrists and fastened the first cuff. His free hand was clenched tightly. He could have . . . if he wanted to . . .

He heard one of the officers take a call on their headset. Judging from the tone there seemed to be some sort of confusion. He heard a few okays and all rights, followed by confirmation that he understood. After that he heard the officer issue an order to the others.

"We're to let them go," he said. "Just got the message from HQ. They got a direct order from the commander. He said not to detain the man with the motorcycle."

The other officer turned to Zephner. "What's this all about?"

"I'm not at liberty to discuss it," Zephner answered as they uncuffed him. "But if you want to be of some assistance, you can do yourself a favor and contact Roland. Tell him we're not going to be able to find the boy, and to take appropriate measures."

The chief officer overheard and commenced the call.

Megan was already up on her two feet, wearing a most unpleasant scowl. She waited for Zephner to make his way over to her before speaking, but he only glanced at her, and then climbed back onto the bike. She glared at him.

"I don't get this," she said. "What boy? Are you talking about Ryan? What do you mean we won't be able to find him? He was here just minutes ago."

"It's kind of complicated. And I don't have the time to fill you in right now."

"So where are you going now?"

Zephner noticed that some of the officers were still hanging around, most likely eavesdropping. He didn't wish to say anything more in front of them.

"Get on," he said.

"Get on? But where are we going?"

"Come with me and I'll tell you."

After some hesitation, she decided to tag along. She climbed onto the back of the motorcycle and felt it drive away, with less turbulence this time. She didn't feel like she was going to fall off, and the museum visitors weren't fleeing in panic. They just watched from afar, with baffled faces.

Megan was still questioning how Ryan could just disappear like that without saying anything. He would never do that to her, not ever. If there was one admirable quality about him, it was that he was reliable and trustworthy. Heck, even back in middle school, he gave up an afternoon of leisurely activities to help her reconstruct her science diorama that she so clumsily tripped and fell on the day before it was due. He was even honest about why he was so late to that one birthday party—he got engulfed by a sci-fi marathon on TV. But now this—what was the explanation for this?

They retraced their route back to the entrance of the museum, then rode out into the street, under the warm sunshine. Megan decided to inquire once more about the situation.

"So are you going to tell me what's going on or not?"

"Just wait," Zephner answered.

"Wait for what?"

"Wait until we're safe."

Megan furrowed her brow, though it wasn't like he could see her face anyway.

"Are you telling me we're in some kind of danger?"

"Yes."

"What kind?"

"The kind that will get us killed if we don't get the hell out of here right now."

She didn't ask any more questions after that. That was enough to scare her out of her wits, enough to keep her eyes permanently peeled. If this really was a dream, she wanted to wake up right about now.

———Chapter 10———

Change of Plans

The *Obsidian* was a magnificent station, as Ryan had learned from Steve. It was shaped much like a sphere, with all the passages and facilities situated around the center. There were close to a hundred loading docks for the plethora of different aircrafts that were on board. Aside from that, the station had a dining hall, a gym, a fitness center, training simulators, and much more. Ryan could almost forget that its main purpose was basically that of an aircraft carrier. Except this one could fly through space, which unarguably made it that much cooler.

Steve hadn't specified where they were going yet, but that was just as well because Ryan welcomed the mystery of not knowing what would be around the next corner. They passed through so many passages that Ryan couldn't help but think that even a mouse could get lost in here.

Ryan hadn't said anything, but Steve took the initiative anyway to get him into a pair of drier clothes. He made a pit stop at his cabin and searched for an outfit Ryan could get into.

Ryan looked around as he waited. The room wasn't big at all. Maybe ten feet wide, domed-shaped, with a lone bunk, and a small cubicle which must have been for the toilet.

"This station is very globular," he joked. "Everything is curved and round.

Steve let out a chuckle. "That's true. I suppose it's because

134

anything spherical is very structurally sound."

"I guess that's important to consider when designing something that's going to be used for war.

Steve dug out a handful of clothes from the drawer. "Take your mind off of war and try these on."

He handed Ryan the clothes: a long sleeve, hunter green shirt, and a pair of beige cargo pants. Ryan changed into them and found that they were snug, even though the pants were a size too big. He looped a belt through his waist to make it fit just right.

—)—

They traveled down to D deck and followed the passages until they arrived at their destination. Here the taupe walls transitioned into tall glass windows that offered a view into a room with all sorts of exercise equipment—at least that's what it looked like to Ryan. He didn't see the metal plates or the dumbbells, just the bare benches. Underneath each of these stations were circular translucent platforms that emitted a weak light. Next to them were racks filled with items that looked like miniature boxing gloves.

The room was empty, save for just a few people. Ryan and Steve approached the entrance doors and watched as they swished open. Immediately Ryan felt a cool breeze brush against his face, while taking in an ear load of the upbeat techno music that was playing. No one seemed to care they were entering. They were all heavily focused on their workouts.

Ryan followed Steve to one of the weight benches, where a young woman was currently doing bench presses.

She was around Steve's age, pretty, well toned, with auburn hair that was trimmed into a bob cut. She had on a dark blue sports top with black sweatpants. She was in full concentration, taking deep breaths with every rep. She wasn't letting Steve's presence distract her.

Ryan watched her, paying close attention to the gloves she wore on her hands. They were blue and round, similar to a hollowed-out gravasphere. She used them as if they were dumbbells, but even if these things were packed with lead, they couldn't have weighed more than five pounds each. She had to be stronger than that, Ryan thought. Her arms were straining, there was sweat running down her forehead. There must have been more to it. Regardless, Steve ran away with the first joke.

"Look at that, Ryan," he said. "I bet you could curl that weight with your fingers."

Ryan smiled, but didn't say anything.

After the woman was done with the set, she let her arms fall to her sides, and the two gloves slipped right of her hands. They hit the floor with a hefty thud. She sat up and wiped her forehead clean with a towel.

"Don't listen to this guy," she said. "He's a professional jester."

Steve was about to respond, but before he could get a word out, he was interrupted.

"And just for your information, the console is set to a multiplier of twenty-five."

Steve looked over at Ryan. "She's a tough one. Make sure you don't ruffle her feathers, cause then she'll come and pluck yours."

"Be quiet for just a second, will ya."

She stood up from the bench and threw the towel around her neck, holding onto each end. She tilted her head to one side, laying her eyes on Ryan.

"Why do I get the feeling that someone as young as you isn't suppose to be here?"

Ryan answered, "Maybe because—"

"You got a name?"

Ryan swallowed the lump in his throat.

"Ryan. Ryan Satterfield."

"And this one here is called Leilah Rockwell," Steve chipped in. "But I can think of a lot of names that are more suitable."

Leilah gave him a light shove and reverted her attention back on Ryan.

"Now tell me, why doesn't that name sound familiar?"

"I think I can answer that," Steve said.

"Yeah?" Leilah snapped. "Tell me why."

Steve took a step forward and held up a vindictive finger. Leilah put her hands on her hips and waited for him to deliver the explanation.

"Remember back at the academy, you used to give me lip about my beliefs concerning a certain otherworldly phenomenon? I was always reading up on the volumes discussing Kausmos and the Dreamer's World, and because I did, you made fun of me. You called me names, you scribbled things on my assignments, you gave me a *dream* journal. It was one gibe after the next. But you know what? Today I'm zippering up your bag of tricks."

"Is that so?"

"Yeah. Because what I have here puts all doubts to rest. I have undeniable proof that there is, in fact, another side to this big old coin we're living on. I'm talking the genuine article."

Ryan listened to the rant as he watched Leilah roll her eyes. To her this must have been a load of trite. He was worried about her reaction to finding out *he* was the big reveal.

"I'm talking about this guy right over here," Steve continued, laying a hand on Ryan's shoulder. "This guy is a real out-of-towner, a real dreamer, fresh from the stream of consciousness."

Once Leilah learned that Ryan was his trump card, she appeared impartial. It almost looked as if she were considering the possibility that Ryan really was a dreamer. She brought her face very close to his, looked into his eyes, as if the truth lay somewhere in there.

"Elaborate," she said.

Steve held out his hand, and used his fingers to count his supporting arguments.

"One: he just got done crawling out of an ocean; two: he's not suppose to be here. The manifest can confirm that; three: there's no way he could have gotten on here, even if he wanted to. And four—"

Steve searched for number four. There was one more thing, but it eluded him for the moment. He scanned the room to see if anything would trigger his memory. Then he found it.

"There," he said, pointing over to the orange ball that had just rolled its way into the room.

Ryan turned around and saw what must have been the same basketball from just a while ago. There was no questioning it now that the ball was following him.

Steve went to retrieve it and chucked it over to Leilah. She caught it and examined it closely. She ran her thumb over its surface, getting a feel for the texture.

"I bet you've never seen one of these before," Steve said. "This is what they call a basketball. And if you did any research, you'd find out that they don't sell these in town."

Leilah made another contorted expression that Ryan couldn't quite read. It looked like a mischievous grin—the kind that he's seen Megan put on before whenever she's up to something.

"So what do you have to say about this?"

Leilah shrugged.

"I believe it," she said plainly.

"You what?"

"I believe it."

His mouth hung open.

"No you don't."

"Yes I do."

"No, no. That's not how it works. You're suppose to argue. You're suppose to refute what I say!"

Leilah stooped before Ryan and looked him in the eyes again.

"Tell me, Ryan, are you a dreamer?"

Ryan thought about the question. It should have been easy to answer, but it wasn't. He was tottering back and forth between two different places—one real, and the other a fabrication of his memory. He couldn't pinpoint where the line between the two was drawn. It just wasn't clear. This place, if it was a dream, was much too lucid and too vivid. It could have been real, but there had been too many occurrences that didn't make sense.

"I am a dreamer," he responded.

Leilah nodded.

"He said so himself. He's a dreamer."

"So just like that—"

"But what I think hardly matters," she interrupted. "What does Captain Reynard think?"

Steve shied away.

"He doesn't know yet."

"Ah, I see. So you had to come here first, establish some credibility with me, and *then* alert our superior of the possibility of having an inter-dimensional being aboard our station."

"Ah ha!" Steve declared with a burst of triumph. "You said possibility. I knew it."

She sneered at him as she bent over to pick the gloves off the floor. "Why don't you embark on a lovely hike down to the bridge, where you can say what needs to be said. Let Ryan stay at the lounge down the hall. I'll be right there as soon as I hit a quick shower."

Steve glowered with indignation. Perhaps he was feeling vexed for not having been able to sell his story to her. Ryan however, didn't care one way or another. He was more concerned about what would happen to him once the captain learned he was on board. He was ready to beg Steve not to say anything, but he rationalized that there wasn't anything to worry about. They weren't going to fly him into a star, or throw him out into space. He brushed aside the paranoia and remained composed.

Steve left the room grudgingly, and did what Leilah suggested. He ushered Ryan to the lounge that was just a short walk away.

It was a generously sized room that hugged the outer wall of the station. It had windows overlooking the dark, serene emptiness of space. There were stars of all sizes sprinkled across the blackness, coupled with a few planets no bigger than marbles. Ryan couldn't be sure, but he thought he saw them passing at an abnormally fast rate—or at least a lot faster than what an object millions of miles away should be moving. The station must have been making good time.

"Just hang out here," Steve said. "Don't worry about a thing. Reynard is an easygoing guy. He won't even mind. I'm sure he's got a lot of other things to worry about right now." He stopped himself before mentioning anything that could cause alarm. "I'll be back. If anyone asks, you're with me."

Ryan stayed put until Steve was out of his sight. He then took a good look at the lounge and saw that he had the place to himself. He could have had any one of the big creamy colored couches or armchairs. Each of them looked incredibly comfy, as if they were bloated with air.

He plopped himself into one, nearly drowning in the swell of cushions.

"*Welcome*", said a young female voice from a hidden speaker. "*Please remain still while our program configures the chair for optimal comfort. Thank you.*"

Ryan obeyed, and sat as still as he could. He felt the chair shrink and bulge in different places, becoming a perfect mold for his body. His back, his butt and his thighs all felt like they were sinking into a bowl of jelly. The damn chair was consuming him, he thought. But then after a couple of seconds the cushions became firmer, making the chair feel like it was a natural extension of his body.

The female voice came on speaker again.

"Body type analyzed. Physique: medium small. Muscle mass: inadequate. Tension: high. Initiating massage sequence."

The chair began to pelt him with nudges and pokes. It felt like a bundle of billiard balls skidding around uncontrollably. But whatever it was, it felt good. The tension was leaving his muscles.

Ryan heard the voice again, except this time it was coming from the seat next to him. He looked over and didn't see anyone there, so he leaned forward, barely making out the round orange ball that was sitting comfortably on the cushion.

"Body type analyzed. Physique: not found. Muscle mass: not found. Tension: unknown. Attempting to initiate appropriate massage sequence."

The chair whirred and rumbled while the basketball vibrated blissfully.

"Hey," Ryan whispered loudly. "Basketballs don't get massages."

But the basketball did not listen, and did as it desired. Ryan ignored it and went back to relishing his own massage.

The turning and twisting of billiard balls continued to knead every muscle in his backside. After several minutes, the pressure applied weakened, until it was nothing more than a gentle vibration. The soothing sensation coupled with the thrumming of the motor was enough to make him close his eyelids. In the next few minutes, he fell asleep, and was no longer aware of the world around him.

—)—

Ryan awoke to a pat on his shoulder. His eyes opened, squinting at the light he was no longer accustomed to. Standing in front of him was Leilah, dressed in a purple tank top with black utility pants. Her hair fell over her cheeks, still damp.

"C'mon dreamer boy. You'll never stay awake sitting in that thing."

Ryan took that as a hint to find somewhere else to sit. It was true, he wouldn't have been able to stay awake on that thing.

"I didn't even mean to fall asleep," he said, as he crawled out of the chair. "It just . . . happened."

"If you set yourself up for it, there are many things that can happen."

She was making her way over to one of the couches—the kind that wouldn't give you a full body analysis if you sat in it. She took a seat on one of the plushy cushions while Ryan took the one next to her. She crossed her legs and folded her hands on top of her lap. Her eyes wandered to the collection of chairs they just came from. She had just seen the orange ball propel itself off the chair and onto the floor, where it rolled around at its own leisure.

Leilah bit her lip, trying to figure the thing out.

"That must be an interesting sport you guys have. I've never seen one played with an autonomous ball like that."

"Oh, no," Ryan corrected. "It's not suppose to do that. It's suppose to stay put wherever you set it down, unless you bounce it or throw it. It's not suppose to be rolling around on its own like that."

"Then it looks to me like we're not dealing with your ordinary basketball."

Ryan, too, stared at it, trying to grasp the logic behind it.

"Then what do you suppose is wrong with it?"

"I don't think there's anything wrong with it."

The ball was rolling towards them. It found Leilah's ankle

and nudged it playfully. "Aww," she said, and lifted the ball up and cradled it against her body, where it wriggled with excitement.

"It ain't no puppy, but for a piece of sporting equipment, he's pretty cute."

"How do you know it's a he?"

"Well, either it's marking territory, or he's just very friendly with the ladies."

Ryan considered the notion.

"Maybe it is a he. And if he is, he's definitely not an ordinary basketball. I can't believe it, but I think he's alive."

"If that's the case, you know what that means." She set the ball on the floor, and the two of them watched as it explored the room. "You have to give him a name."

"A name?" Ryan said, finding the idea completely absurd. "Do I really have to?"

"Sure."

Ryan reconsidered his initial reaction. Maybe a name was in order. If something could act on its own volition, then maybe it was deserving of a name. But this was going to be difficult. Out of all the basketballs he had ever owned, he had never given any a name. What kind of name do you give a basketball anyway? Would you give it a typical boy name like Bill, Josh, or Fred? No, they didn't sound right. It had to be something more fitting, that was also short, simple, and easy to enunciate—something that would roll off the tongue without much effort. He said out loud the first name that came to him.

"Bee," he said, discovering he liked the sound of it.

"Bee," Leilah repeated. She seemed to like the sound of it too. "Its got a nice ring to it."

She leaned over the armrest and snapped her fingers to get the ball's attention.

"Hey, Bee," she said, "how's things rollin'?" What do you

think of your new name? Huh?"

Bee nudged her fingers a few times before taking off again. He rolled out of sight.

"I think he likes it. He told me in not so many words, but I'm sure he likes it."

"I hope so," Ryan said. "Because I'm not creative enough to come up with another."

She laughed softly, letting herself loll back into the couch. She turned her head for just a moment to see if anyone was coming. Doing so had inadvertently reminded Ryan that Steve was away on matters concerning him. If they hadn't collected him by now, it was probably safe to assume they didn't perceive him as a threat. At worst, they'd find him fascinating, and order him to be put through a complete physical and mental examination. After thinking about it, he decided he'd prefer to be tossed out into space.

"I tell ya," Leilah uttered, "that Steve worries me. I'm not sure I can trust him to tell the story straight. He's easily excitable"

"I think we can count on him. He's the great white of the air, after all."

"Should have heard some of his other nick names back in the day. Word to the wise: if the sign says *out of order*, you probably shouldn't use it."

"Swell advice. So you've known Steve for some time now."

"Yeah," she said, almost regrettably. "It's been a good while."

"How'd you meet him?"

"We enrolled at the same flight academy, about six years ago; we were both first class cadets. It was a huge school, very intimidating for the two of us. Expectations were high. At the time, they were in the process of transitioning to a different training program. Prior to that year, cadets would partake in your basic courses. You'd have your academics, your flight training, and so forth. But that year they introduced a new required program called emotional response reconditioning, or ERR. It was implemented by the government in order to reprogram the way the armed forces cope with distress or emotional trauma. Basically, you're put into a simulation where you live through one crummy situation after another. They say it's all about learning how to make the best possible decisions under the most undesirable conditions."

"That sounds inhumane," Ryan said. "What kind of situations do they put you through? Wouldn't such exercises turn someone into a desensitized zombie?"

"Not exactly," she said, shifting her position. "The idea behind it is that you don't remember what happened after you've awakened. Though your mind becomes conditioned just the same. So if one of these scenarios did play out in real life, your mind will subconsciously be equipped and prepared to deal with it. Or so that is what they believe. The training is still experimental."

Ryan thought about the benefits such a technology could provide, even though the practice itself seemed cruel and unethical.

"Anyhow," Leilah continued, "Steve and I had this one class together. We were both seated at opposite ends of the top row. And one day I had noticed him fiddling with a piece of paper during the entire lecture. He wasn't taking notes, that's for sure. He seemed to be making something. And whatever he was making, it looked like it was coming along pretty well. I kept sneaking a peek to check his progress, when all of a sudden, I see him dart the thing towards the front of the room, where it hits the front board. The instructor stops writing and picks up the paper airplane, and then, as if he had just crossed paths with some glorious relic, he holds it up in the air, and utters its name with deep reverence—an *X-32 Aracari Fighter Bird.* It's a combat plane that has become somewhat of a classic. This guy is just goggling at it, proclaiming it to be the most stunningly crafted piece of paper he had ever seen. Then he asked who had made it, and Steve, he just kept his mouth shut about it. That's when I decided to confront him after class and let him know that I had caught him in the act. I asked why he didn't admit to it, and then he claims that the professor's exaltation was just a ruse to draw out the culprit. We joked about it. Then he went on with his bit about how he's a man of many talents. I tell him to show me. We end up scheduling a game at the Gravalon Arena. We put some teams together and sure enough, he wipes the floor with us. It was a disaster."

"Sounds like a worthy opponent," Ryan said as he watched Bee roll back towards them. He picked him up and spun him in his hands, hoping that he wouldn't mind. "Steve said that we could have a game once everything has settled down."

"You haven't even played it before, have you?"

"No, but he explained the rules to me. Seems simple enough."

Leilah forced a laugh. "Sure, it sounds simple. But once you're in the arena, your eyes are going to be spinning at all the different things you need to stay on top of. Sixteen players, four balls, a ton of rings. It's pure pandemonium."

"That sounds like fun to me. So are you and Steve still together?"

"Well," she said, tottering her head back and forth. "We were never officially together. We went out once, just to test the waters. After that we decided we weren't ready to commit to anything, because our first year workload was going to be too much. We tried to keep in touch, but we sort of just fell apart. Fast forward two years, he found someone else. Her name was Stephanie. After graduation they got married, and uh, well, as of three weeks ago they had their first kid, Martin."

Ryan was genuinely surprised.

"I never saw him as the family man type," he said. "Not that I mean anything by that."

"It's a fair assumption. The guy can be a bit of a looney at times. He has no idea what's coming his way. Taking care of a kid is no easy task. Not even for a 32-S-rated fighter pilot"

"What does that even mean anyway?"

"The 'S' represents their aerial capabilities—'S' being the highest rank. And the 32 denotes the estimated level of effectiveness that the ERR program has on the pilot. That score is out of 40. So not bad."

"Funny," Ryan said. "I could have swore he told me 38."

Leilah pressed her lips together tightly. "He did have a 38," she said. "But after a reassessment a few months ago, it was lowered. As you've probably already figure out, he wasn't too pleased with the reduction."

"So what happened?"

Her aversion to the question was apparent, but she answered anyway.

"There was a complication with the simulation one day. Steve had come out of it remembering the trial he had gone through, which, like I said, isn't suppose to happen. He was really shaken up about it. He mentioned it to one of the administrators and they instructed him to try his best not to think of it and not to speak of it out loud to anyone, that with time, it should vanish from his memory. So I never found out what happened exactly, except that it must have been traumatizing. He was brooding for the remainder of the week, and even after that, he was never quite as cheery as he used to be."

"That's hard to imagine," Ryan said. "He's a pretty cheery guy. Even now."

"Should have seen him before. But Ryan, just make sure you don't bring this up whenever he's around. Actually, better yet, don't ever mention it again."

"I won't."

Leilah turned around, glancing at the corridor. No one was there. It was still just the two of them in the quiet, empty lounge.

Ryan looked the other way, towards the lofty windows. The stars and the planets reminded him once again that he was far from home, that he had come a very long way. If this was a dream, it was the most prodigious one he had ever had, by far. He had already developed an emotional bond with the people he'd met. And he couldn't help but feel that he would remember them, even after he awoke. How could he possibly forget anything he's seen here thus far?

He looked at Leilah again, except this time through a different lens—an objective one that depicted exactly what it was he was looking at. What he saw was a young woman, waiting around for something to happen. Her crystal blue eyes, her auburn hair, the fabric of her clothing—it perfectly emulated the way things looked in his waking life. He wondered what the difference could have been. Then he remembered something he wanted to inquire about.

"Leilah," he said, and her head turned promptly. "When you told Steve you believed him about me being a dreamer, were you being serious?"

She licked her lips, trying to hide her smirk. "Of course I was. I'd have to be crazy not to, given the evidence."

"I don't know if the evidence makes a very compelling argument."

"Sure it does. Just take a look at Bee over there."

Ryan looked, and saw that Bee was now over by the windows, keeping still, as a basketball should. It almost seemed as if he were staring out into space. How that was possible, Ryan didn't know.

"It could just be one giant hoax," Ryan said.

She smiled at him.

"My intuition tells me otherwise."

"So why teasing Steve about it back at the academy?"

"That's all it ever was. Teasing. It was my way of . . . having fun."

Ryan was appalled.

"So that's what you call it."

"Yep."

"Sure it wasn't jealousy?"

"Nope," she said, but the blushing was evident.

"I see."

They both caught Bee rolling away from his spot by the window. He went around the couch, to the step that led up to the corridor. Steve was entering the lounge, completely wretched. One look into his eyes gave them a gut-wrenching feeling in their stomachs.

He took an empty seat next to them. He exhaled loudly, letting his head sink into the palms of his hands.

"Steve," Leilah said, "what happened? What's the matter?"

He lifted his head and exhaled.

"I wish . . . I really wish there was another way."

"What do you mean?"

He took another deep breath.

"I spoke with Captain Reynard and explained the situation to him. He wasn't rattled one way or another, but nevertheless he called it in."

"To who? Roland?"

"Yeah. They talked for like ten seconds before Reynard addressed me again and tells me that our mission objective has changed. We're no longer intercepting that fleet. Instead— "

"Instead what?"

Steve cringed trying to get the words out. Ryan was almost certain it had something to do with him. The lack of eye contact, the shame in his voice. All signs pointed to one thing. Finally, he went ahead and said it.

"We're going to have to relinquish Ryan."

The room was silent. If the floor wasn't carpeted, they could have heard a pin drop. But what wasn't silent though was the inside of Ryan's mind. His thoughts were racing a mile a minute, crashing into barriers, tires were blowing out. He didn't know where he was going.

"What do you mean relinquish Ryan?" Leilah cried out. "What could they possibly want with Ryan?"

"Information," Steve said. "They're making claims he knows something about the location of the Dreamer's World."

Leilah was thunderstruck by what she heard. Her mouth dangled in awe.

"You mean to tell me that the reason for their military presence is to just glean information . . . about the *Dreamer's World?*"

Steve nodded. Leilah remained shocked.

"How demented is that?" she said, throwing her hands into the air. "The Dreamer's World isn't something you find. It's crazy. It's lunatic. It's like searching for a grain of sand in all the oceans of this galaxy. It's nuts."

"I know," Steve said. "I can't imagine what drove them to undertake such an ambitious hunt."

"Do we even need to cooperate with them? Why can't we just blow those bastards up?"

"Let's not jump the gun, Leilah."

"We can't," Ryan said, forced to realize the cold hard truth. Leilah quieted down when she heard him speak.

"Why not?" Leilah asked.

"Because there's a lot of them. I've met them already and learned that they have a large presence here in this galaxy. To them it was no big deal trashing one of their stations just to issue some petty revenge. These people, whoever they are, must have a lot at their disposal. I think making them angry would be a huge mistake."

Ryan could hardly believe what he had said. He had essentially made an argument for his extradition. But knowing the truth, it wouldn't have made a difference either way. These people wanted him, and they were going to get him.

"He's right," Steve said. "Any form of aggression will mean suicide. We're not equipped to deal with a threat of the caliber that Ryan is describing. Besides, it's not our call."

"Wait a second," Leilah said, looking over at Ryan. "You were on one of their stations before?"

"Yeah. I made it out alive, thanks to this one guy. His name was Zephner. He was really strong, tore right through the lot of them with his motorcycle sword. True story."

Steve and Leilah both looked at him, as if not sure what to think. Ryan didn't really know what to think either. He was stuck on a roller coaster that wouldn't stop.

"That's wonderful," Leilah said. "But what's going to happen this time? Will you be able to give them what they're looking for? I mean, what do you know about the Dreamer's World anyway?"

Ryan asked himself the same question, only to realize he had no knowledge on the subject.

"I don't even know what that is," he admitted.

"The Dreamer's World is a gateway," she explained. "It's how you were able to pass through from the other side. But I don't think that necessarily means you know anything about the journey, or from which point you came from."

"Guess my eyes were closed," Ryan joked, trying to find whatever humor he could in the situation. "Then again, I was asleep."

Steve wasn't saying anything. Perhaps he was too busy ruminating in his own little world. But then in an instant, he became invigorated.

"Wait a minute," he said, his eyes looking down at the carpet.

"What is it?" Leilah answered.

"Why do you suppose Roland was so easily succumbed to these demands? It's not like him at all."

"I don't know. Maybe—"

"Maybe they've already put a noose around his neck, or backed him into a very uncomfortable corner. Or maybe they've already issued some kind of threat."

"We shouldn't jump to conclusions so fast. We really don't know anything."

"I do know there's something that Roland hasn't told us yet."

"Steve," she said softly, try to calm his nerves. She stood up from the couch and approached him. She laid a hand on his shoulder, and then turned around to Ryan.

"Ryan, could you excuse us for just a moment?"

Ryan nodded, slid off the couch, and found a spot at the other end of the lounge to hang around in. Bee followed, willing to keep him company.

Ryan didn't really care too much about what Leilah and Steve were going to say to one another, given that his fate was all but sealed. What he did suspect though was that Leilah was going to make an effort to calm Steve down so he didn't relapse into another emotional episode.

—)—

"Nothing bad is going to happen," Leilah said to Steve. "We're going to comply with their demands. They're going to get what they want."

"But that means they're getting Ryan," he said harshly, trying to keep his voice at a whisper. "And that's not right."

"I know it isn't. But you said so yourself: there isn't another way. We have no other options. I hate to have to give up on Ryan like this, just as much as you do."

"But you heard what he said. He doesn't know anything about the Dreamer's World. So they're not going to get what they want. What do you suppose they're going to do with him then? Ship him back in a carefully packaged parcel?"

Leilah brought her hand to her face, suddenly finding it much more difficult to cope with the situation. She was trying her hardest to stifle the tears that wanted to come out.

"We can talk to them. We can try to remain diplomatic."

"Diplomatic?" Steve scoffed. "Just a minute ago you were ready to blow them outta the sky."

"And that wasn't the right response."

"Then what is?"

"I don't know. We just have to go through with what's safest and most logical."

Steve sighed, and sat in one of the chairs. Leilah looked at him and saw there was still something else on his mind, but again he was opting to stay silent. She had to extract whatever it was.

"What are you not telling me?"

Practically sedated, he took a few seconds to come up with a response.

"They want the delivery to be carried out by a lone pilot."

Leilah knew what was coming next. She probably didn't need to ask.

"And Reynard asked you to do it?"

"No. He suggested that someone else should do it, given that my ability to remain indifferent has been compromised."

"That's probably for the best."

"I don't think so. Which is why I told him I'd be the one."

She shook her head.

"Why are you making this so difficult on yourself? You should have someone else do it."

"But that wouldn't be right, to use someone that won't care what happens to him one way or another. At least if I'm there, he might have a fighting chance of coming back alive."

Leilah lowered her head, finding it hard to accept his rationale.

Steve asked, "It's not wrong to be emotionally invested, is it? I know they don't want us to be. But you know that's something I have trouble controlling."

He was creeping into dangerous territory, and Leilah could sense it. She wasn't going to be able to change his decision and she knew it. And if her understanding of human psyche was correct, it'd be better to get the whole ordeal over with as soon as possible, because dragging it out would only create a more enduring memory.

"No. I guess it isn't wrong," she said. "You're doing the right thing." Despite her assent, Steve still carried a gloomy disposition. "I guess we should talk to Ryan."

Ignoring Bee for just a moment, Ryan noticed Leilah and Steve walking over with a kind of grimness that he didn't care for. They sat in the couch next to him and went on to explain the situation in the only way they knew how, which meant telling him, in the most delicate manner possible, that they had no choice but to deliver him into the hands of their enemies.

—————CHAPTER 11—————

PREPARATIONS

The planet Lylid loomed in the distance, just below the interstellar horizon. It was a relatively small planet, doused in a bluish hue that carried a thick cluster of tempestuous clouds. Ryan viewed it through the window of a corridor, and thought it looked cold and lonely. The turbulent atmosphere made it seem uninhabitable. And it was, except for a handful of military outposts.

At one time, Lylid was a prosperous world, with thousands of flourishing cities, many of which rivaled the beauty of those on Cyannus. It also held one of the largest reserves of the galaxy's most pivotal and valuable resource—a fissile ore known as nethalyte. It was the fuel that allowed vessels to fly and machines to run, for many years at a time. It was an invaluable commodity that lied at the center of galactic commerce. For many nations, it meant the difference between prevailing and collapsing. In the case of Cyannus, it meant economic struggle.   Mining on Lylid came to a cessation when the landscape underwent a drastic transformation. Its only moon met with a terrible fate. An almost equally-sized asteroid had crossed paths with it, shattering it wholly. The first wave of calamities came in the form of burning rock that fell to Lylid's surface—thousands of broken chunks, many hundreds of kilometers wide. Cities and entire regions were wiped out in the hours that followed; monstrous earthquakes were felt across the globe. There was widespread ungovernable panic, combined with the fear and despair that Lylid's time had come. Many of whom survived fled to other planets, in hope of beginning a new life. Those that stayed were forced to vacate within a few years. Lylid had fallen away from its natural orbit. It careened haplessly away from its closest life-giving star, causing the climate to dive to intolerably freezing levels. What remained now was a preservation of the terror that unfolded on that day many years ago.

They were almost there, preparing to enter the atmosphere. Ryan was being ushered down to the loading docks by Steve and Leilah. Though it would have been understandable to feel animosity towards them, Ryan didn't. They handled the matter as best they could. And it wasn't even their fault. The person he should be directing his hate towards didn't even have a face yet. But regardless, he needed to persevere, because it's what Zephner would have done. And it's what he had to do, for as long as he had reason to believe the future held more than one possible outcome.

He was brought to one of the lower, outermost wings of the station, in a hall that came around full circle. There were a series of hatches that ran along the orbicular platform, each marked with a number. For Ryan, it almost felt familiar, like he was getting ready to board an astro-themed amusement park ride. But unfortunately, that wasn't the case here. As they walked, he watched the big red numbers decrease, almost as if it were a countdown to something. They continued until they reached no. 72, which was a hatch, just like any other. What lied on the other side was still a complete mystery to him.

Steve tapped his earpiece. "Captain, this is McKindler We're at the loading docks now. What's our ETA?"

Ryan listened to the transmission. Leilah was there too, embracing herself, her head bowed.

"Roger that," Steve said, tapping his earpiece again.

"How long do we have?" Leilah asked.

"About five minutes until we're in position to deploy."

"That's not a whole lot of time," Ryan said with jest.

"I know," Leilah said. "I'm sorry, Ryan."

"You don't have to be sorry. You're not doing anything wrong."

"But it isn't right either."

"I guess it can't be as simple as right or wrong."

"No," Steve said. "It isn't. This is just the best we can do under the circumstances. Which is why I'm going to accompany you for as long as they let me—to make sure you find your way back here."

Ryan couldn't ask for anything more, especially from someone that knew him for barely a few hours. Steve's selfless gesture could begin to explain why they lowered his ERR score. The man was obviously mindful of the importance of human compassion. The system was going to have to do some serious contending to rid that quality from him.

Steve stepped away to a computer panel that was integrated into the wall. He dialed a few digits and a heavy motor began to whirr.

"I think you will at least enjoy our ride, if not the destination." He tried smiling, but it came out skewed.

The motor continued to rumble loudly until the central plate began to turn. After several rotations the entire hatch retracted itself inside the wall.

Ryan temporarily forgot about the danger he was about to face, because what he saw resembled nothing of an aircraft, or any kind of vehicle or mode of transposition that he could recognize. What he did see was a white, glassy, fifteen-foot tall marble. There was no other way for him to describe it. All he thought was that this dream was just getting weirder.

Steve, with his inclinations to be comical, went over to a

computer console and played around with different configurations. In a blinding flash, splotches of color materialized along the surface of the glassy sphere, encapsulating it in a solid red. Then, just as suddenly as before, the sphere turned orange, then blue, then green. After that a camouflage pattern, followed by an eyeball, a gravasphere, and even the surface texture of a planet.

"That's enough, Steve," Leilah said, forced to step in. "You're going to give him a seizure."

"I thought he'd like it," Steve said, returning it back to its original white color.

Ryan did like it, even though he didn't understand what this thing was.

"That's amazing," he proclaimed. "But what is it?"

"It's the Conoblis—an all-purpose land rover."

"But how do you get inside?"

"Like this."

He went back to the console and pressed a few buttons. Shortly after, a rectangular seam emerged from the hull of the vessel. A panel came down towards the floor, revealing a short staircase on its underside.

Ryan was impressed. He couldn't see much of the interior, but it must have been nice.

"Cool, huh."

"Sure is," Ryan said, with his eyes still feasting over the machine.

"We'd be taking one of the A-Bird models, but there's a storm brewing down there right now, and since our rendezvous is set for one of the cities, flying in would be too risky. So we'll be using this instead."

"I hope that doesn't mean we're rolling in."

"Not quite. The Conoblis comes packed with a set of extendable wheels, and a gyroscopic sensor which will keep us with our feet towards the ground. It'll climb through the snow and ice, and get us there unscathed."

"Sounds good to me," he said, putting his hands into his pockets. "I guess I'm ready to go."

"Wait," Leilah called out from across the room. "Before Steve lets you forget."

She went over to a metal storage closet and threw open the door. There were several different uniforms hung on a beam, as well several jackets and coats, pistols and guns, ammunition, rope, and all sorts of survival paraphernalia.

"It's going to be very cold once you get down there. Surface temperatures can reach subzero."

She handed each of them a parka. They were heavy and bulky, and came down to their knees. Ryan slipped it on, feeling the warmth of the thick padding right away. He spread his arms as far as he could and pictured what he must have looked like to a spectator. Someone like Megan would have laughed at him for sure.

"I feel as toasty as a marshmallow over a campfire right about now."

"You'll be glad," Leilah said, "when you feel that air touch your face."

She grabbed his zipper and made sure it was fastened all the way up to his neck. Then she buttoned the flap around his collar. She looked to see if there was anything else she could do, but there wasn't. She rested her hands on his shoulders.

"Promise me you're going to be careful out there."

"I will."

She looked up at Steve, who had already zippered himself up as securely as possible.

"Steve, do whatever you can to bring him back."

"Definitely," he answered.

Steve was ready to board the vessel, but not quite ready to invite Ryan to come along. Ryan took notice, and spared him the trouble of having to say anything. He dragged himself forward without order, knowing that the future would come no matter how long he loafed around.

Steve had already climbed inside, and Ryan was close behind. Leilah called out to Ryan. He stopped and looked to where she was beckoning. Bee was there, rolling forward at a dawdling pace. He paused once he reached the base of the stairs.

"I'll miss you too, Bee," he said, before continuing up the stairs. Then he heard an incessant hollow thudding. He spun around and saw Bee hammering away at the bottom step. He tried to get a bounce going, but couldn't.

"Bee, what are you doing? You should stay here," Ryan said, but the ball persisted in its efforts. Ryan would have argued if he thought it would work, but the ball didn't look like it could be deterred. It was resolute in its decision to come along. So he picked him up and carried him into the vessel.

The inside of the Conoblis was capacious, despite the spherical layout. It was divided into two, with the front halve serving as a cockpit. There were two seats, overlooking a sizable console. Each side had its own integrated monitor, along with a panel of buttons and switches. Above was the windshield, which, from the outside was indiscernible. It nearly gave a one-hundred and eighty degree view of their surroundings. At the rear was a narrow access to the back halve. In there were two additional seats, and a variety of storage closets and compartments.

Ryan carried Bee to one of the empty seats and set him down. He found a belt strap and buckled him in place, asking himself why he was bothering to take such measures to protect something he would ordinarily slam against the asphalt back at home. However weird it may have felt, it seemed like the right thing to do.

He returned to the cockpit and found his own seat. He strapped himself in, with one belt across the waist and two coming over his shoulders. He was ready for turbulence, ready to be flung by a flipper, or ricocheted into a pocket—any of which would have been preferable to whatever fate awaited him down below.

Leilah was still standing watch, emanating a tacit farewell, which both Ryan and Steve reciprocated.

Ryan watched as Steve returned his attention to the controls. The door of the vessel closed slowly, obscuring Leilah's figure, little by little, until she was gone. He was now sealed off, and could feel something quiver through his body. Grim thoughts hatched in his mind as Steve prepared for takeoff. What was for a short while a pleasurable dream, had now transmuted into a nightmare. He tried sifting through his head for the proper mindset. Maybe he should tense up, as if preparing to be pricked by a needle. Or better yet, pound his face against the dash so that maybe he could wake up.

He opted to do neither of those things. Instead he was hit with a rush of gallantry. He was going to stomach this trial, tackle it head on. After all, it was just a dream. Whatever inflictions he sustained would only last until he woke up. He could almost hear Megan by his side, emboldening him to face the challenge without any reservations. He was properly equipped. He had the tools, he knew what the right mindset was. All he had to do now was give himself permission to go through with it. And that was exactly what he did.

He heard Steve's voice fill the cabin.

"Come in, Captain. This is McKindler. We've boarded the Conoblis; we're set for deployment—roger that."

He accessed the console again, fired a switch and readied his hands on the flight yoke.

The platform beneath the vessel started thrumming. As if they were rested on an elevator, the floor fell steadily. Ryan watched as his surroundings rose out of view, revealing a new dock underneath. The vessel soon came to a stop, and the platform above had sealed itself, leaving them in total darkness, except for the lights on the console.

"Thirty seconds," Steve said.

A countdown commenced inside of Ryan's head. He could see the numbers flash before his eyes. He didn't know exactly what he was going to experience, but whatever it was, he was confident he was ready for it.

"Fifteen seconds."

He was feeling hot. It was probably that heavy coat he was wearing. He welcomed the cold at this point.

'Ten seconds."

Ryan tugged at his seat belts, ensuring they were tightly fastened. They were. He was ready.

"Three . . . two . . . one . . . "

———Chapter 12———

A Cold Welcome

There was a sudden outburst of force that had convinced Ryan that he was just sucked through a vacuum hose. His whole body jerked forward as the vessel barreled backwards. One moment he was looking at a gray wall, then a white wall the next. Except it wasn't a wall, but a blanket of violent wintry air that hurled shrapnel of ice and snow. The white light blinded him. There was no way to judge his bearing. His belt tugged against his body in a multitude of directions. They had to be spinning uncontrollably. Normally he could handle the turbulence, but *this*, this was something that not even all the amusement park rides in the world could have prepared him for. He kept his hand against his stomach, trying to hold on for as long as he could.

"When is it going to stop?" Ryan cried out. It hadn't even been five seconds yet, but it felt like minutes.

"We're going to stabilize right now."

Steve gripped the yoke tightly, while referencing the information displayed on the monitor. He pulled the yoke one way, then another. It did little to keep the vessel steady. Ryan was still being tossed around in his seat.

"We're almost there," Steve said, still wrestling with the controls.

Ryan held on to his seat, relieved to find the vessel becoming steadier. He was now pretty sure that his head was up and his feet were down. Though he could still feel his body plunging downward rapidly.

"We got a parachute or something, right?"

Steve cracked a smile. It actually looked like he was enjoying this.

"Something better," he said. "glotanic gravitational regulators."

Wonderful, Ryan thought. Whatever it would take to not replicate an elevator ride with the break cables cut.

The vessel was easing its descent. Ryan could feel himself weighing down back onto his seat. He still couldn't see anything but the color white, but at least now there was some semblance of stabilization.

About thirty seconds later, all movement had ceased. They must have cradled into a soft pocket of snow. Either that or a pool of sour cream.

"Aced it again," Steve said victoriously. "How are you feeling, Ryan?"

Ryan could only look at him, afraid that if he tried to answer, his words would spill all over the floor.

Steve tapped his ear piece.

"This is McKindler. Captain, do you copy?" He paused and awaited a response. "We've just touched down. We're about to enter Tellashia City."

He turned back to Ryan. He produced a sigh that expressed his disinclination to go on.

"This is it, Ryan. We're almost there. Just another two kilometers."

Ryan was rattled by the reminder. Instead of suffering from a queasy stomach, it was now the rapid palpitations of his heart—a perfectly natural biological response, given his predicament.

"I'm ready," he said, knowing he was as ready as he'll ever be.

Steve nodded and triggered a switch on the console. The vessel whined and lurched upward, and then gradually, a ring of plates rose from a series of spokes, forming a pair of hamster-like wheels around the sphere. Steve applied pressure to the throttle and they rotated, moving the vehicle along the snow-covered landscape. On the inside, Ryan was swaying from side to side in his seat as the wheels climbed over the lumpy terrain. He was still upset that he couldn't see anything.

"How do you know where we're going?"

"The coordinates are plugged in. For now we just sit back and wait."

Waiting was the last thing Ryan wanted to do right now. Waiting is the period of time that could simmer unwanted thoughts. He couldn't even distract himself with the landscape because of the veil of snow.

"Things are going to clear up," Steve pointed out. "Once we reach another mile or so, Mount Hordon will work as a shield. The winds coming from the west will strike the mountain, giving the city a blanket of protection.

"That must be one tall mountain."

"Sure is. There are many like it here on Lylid. It was almost impossible for urban development to not take place under the shadow of one."

Steve had his hands off the controls, so Ryan didn't think he'd mind any questions. Furthermore, it allowed him to steer his mind away from his troubles.

"How come they didn't build somewhere else? I'm sure there are more suitable planets out there."

It's all about nethalyte," Steve said with a hint of enmity in his voice. "It's the food that fuels every facet of our lives. Nearly every machine we have depends on it. Anyone that was looking to make money would have set up camps right next to the biggest deposit, which happened to be right here. And since this planet was annexed by Cyannus, it was us that reaped the loot."

"So you guys were pretty lucky then, huh."

Steve shrugged.

"For about a hundred years, up until Yunak took a fatal hit."

"Who's Yunak?"

"It was Lylid's moon. It was struck by an asteroid, resulting in its total destruction. After that, this planet's orbit was thrown off course, knocking it just far enough away to bring it into an ice age."

Ryan was stunned to learn that this whole planet was essentially a world tossed into an icebox.

"So there's no one here now? No one here at all?"

"No one except for a few military personnel."

"But why keep anyone around if there's no one here?"

"Just to have a set of eyes at this neck of the woods."

Ryan sensed there was more. "That's it?"

"Well," Steve said, adjusting the cuffs of his parka. "It's more of an effort to keep this place quarantined. After the economic surge, a lot of industries began to pop-up all over the place. A lot of them dealt with experimental technologies: medicine, drugs, machines. A lot of prototypes were developed, many with dubious intentions. Most of it was kept under wraps though, never making its way into public knowledge. Fear mongering gave rise to the belief that a lot of it, if sold and distributed, could have had radical implications throughout the entire galaxy. So in all actuality, many would argue that Lylid freezing over may have been for the best."

Ryan started to wriggle in his coat. The wool was making his neck itch. Meanwhile he tried to imagine the kind of things these people could have been working on. He was thinking of things like food that could keep you full for a month, or clothes that couldn't get dirty no matter what. Somehow, he figured he was way off.

"So nothing made it out of there?"

"A few things did, actually. The ERR for one. It's a training regimen for the military, designed to recondition a person's mind so that strong emotions don't compromise their performance."

Ryan was about to spill the beans by mentioning how Leilah already explained what ERR is, but then remembered she said not to discuss it with him.

Steve continued.

"But to answer your question, the reason why we have people here is to keep these technologies from ever being pillaged. There's already been a recorded case of a foreign ops team coming in and excavating something right from within the tundra. They drilled straight into a pharmaceutical lab and stole a vial."

"A vial of what?"

Steve shook his head. "Not even I know the answer to that one. But whatever it is, it's safe to assume that someone out there is already profiting from it."

The more Ryan heard, the more enthusiastic he was about seeing this world, and its once prosperous cities. In the meantime, he had to ride the storm, inside of the tottering vehicle. He thought about checking on Bee, but he wouldn't risk getting out of his seat. Bee was fine, he assured himself. He was a basketball. It's not like he could get hurt.

He continued to stare through the windshield, desperate to identify what was out there. Occasionally there was a pocket in the wind and he could make out some geometric shapes, but that was about it.

The inside of the vessel had been quiet for a while. Neither of them had anything left they wanted to discuss. That awkward tension had emanated itself throughout the whole cabin. Steve, on occasion, would mess with the console, trying to look occupied, but Ryan felt he was feigning. After a few minutes, Steve finally came out and said something, though it wasn't exactly what Ryan would have liked to hear.

He asked him, "Are you scared, Ryan?" Before Ryan could decide if it was rhetorical or not, Steve continued talking. "Because I get scared all the time during our ERR training. Sometimes, if I'm lucky, I'm able to remember that it'll soon be over, and that all I need to do is hold on a bit longer. Maybe if you concentrate on the notion that this is a dream, you'll find yourself back where you came from, safe and sound."

His logic seemed reasonable, until he gave it a few more seconds thought.

"But what if this wasn't a dream? Then what would I do? I would be forced to play out the hand I was dealt."

"But we know that's not the case. You're a dreamer; you'll wake up."

"Yeah, but I'll be waking into a different life, one with its own set of problems—problems that will always be waiting for me. I can't wake up again out of those."

"Maybe not. So I guess we'll just have to do what you said: play the hand we were dealt."

"I'm sitting on nothing but a pair," Ryan said as a last ditch to be humorous. He managed to get a weak laugh out of Steve.

The Conoblis chugged onward through the dunes of snow that were slathered across the plain. Gradually the white shroud of the storm thinned out, until those geometric shapes that Ryan saw earlier could be identified as skyscrapers. As they got closer, the air became clearer, until it was as if the storm had ceased. They must have now been under the cover of the mountain.

The city was an enchantment beyond the bounds of what Ryan could have ever conceived. The structures tapered into the sky like a thousand inverted icicles. Their surfaces shined with a perpetual shimmer, brought upon by the light of the bedimmed sun. Everything had a luster, emulating the brilliance of a glass city encapsulated inside a snow globe. It was a winter wonderland, but at the same time, a forsaken wasteland, carrying the echoes of the animate world that once was.

Ryan looked up at the towers and saw dark patches of shattered windows, which shared the likeness of an abandoned beehive. He was certain that there was no life here. Not anymore. The thought made him feel colder. He was now glad he had that coat.

Their vehicle plowed through the snow-covered streets, with Steve's input at the controls. He was now steering a pair of yokes, each of which maneuvered one of the two wheels. Ryan was peeking through the corner of the window, trying to catch a glimpse of whatever he could. He studied the store facades, searching for anything that would clue him in about the fishy businesses that ran here. Of course, those places probably weren't going to be huddled right alongside the local deli. He observed that almost every establishment had their windows smashed, most likely the result of the looting that occurred after the major catastrophe. But then Ryan spotted something peculiar. He was ready to dismiss as being nothing, but then reconsidered it.

There were disturbances in the snow—not like footprints, but more like the impression left by something that was dragged. A trash bag? But why would someone be taking out the trash if the world was going to freeze over? And if the disturbances happened after the fact, it would have had to be by those foreign ops teams that Steve mentioned. But that wouldn't explain the next thing he saw.

There were vehicles alongside the road, dug from the dunes they were buried under. Sections of the body were mauled and mangled, with long gashes that tore straight through the chassis. Similar inflictions were also visible along the side of cement walls. Lampposts had been toppled over, and doors and windows wrecked and scattered over the sidewalks. All signs were pointing towards a savage outburst from someone or some thing.

"Steve," Ryan said timidly, "did you notice all this wreckage the last time you were here?"

Steve was already eying all the damage himself, though he didn't seem as concerned.

"There wasn't a last time. I've never been in this city before."

"So what do you think happened here?"

"I don't know," he shrugged. "Maybe a group of hungry polar bears were searching for food."

Ryan looked at the damages again, especially those of the cars. They were definitely not caused by polar bears. But he didn't feel like exacerbating the situation, so he left it at that.

"Maybe," he said, ending the conversation.

Steve steered the Conoblis around the next corner, so that they were now heading west towards the mountain. It was a colossal heap of rock and snow that curtained the sky like a blanket. They traveled several more blocks in this direction before they turned again, this time heading north.

"We're coming up to our stop soon," Steve said with a tinge of guilt. Ryan looked to see if there was any ideal location for the drop-off. They were slowing down, and with a jolt of the yoke, the vessel turned into the street to their right.

They were standing there, about fifty meters down the road —a human barricade of armed soldiers, dressed in black military regalia. Behind them were two robotic sentries, each twenty feet tall. They stood like black marble-plated centaurs, with a turret mounted on the end of one arm, and a spindly blade on the other. The two forelegs were long and jointed, while the third rear leg extended far out like a tail. They, and the soldiers were poised to see this operation come to successful completion.

Ryan had no problem trembling inside the protection of his parka. He couldn't lie to himself anymore about being brave, because now the threat was present and very real. He remembered that these individuals were zealously obliged to carry out whatever their superior ordered from them. Clemency was out of the equation, as well as kindness or hospitality. They were going to get what they wanted, and if they didn't, they'd kill him. Simple as that. He could only wish Zephner were here to bail him out again.

Steve was pulling up to them when he made a final transmission to Reynard about their arrival at the rendezvous point. He stopped the vessel and triggered the mechanism to open the side door, letting in the treacherous cold that had been waiting outside. It swept across Ryan's face, freezing what may have been a stray tear, or a droplet of sweat.

Together they stepped out into the street and advanced slowly towards the group of men. Their appearances were distinguishable and recognizable to Ryan, especially that of the tall one standing at the head of the group. He was a spitting image of the man Zephner killed, in terms of uniform. He had the long black coat, with the golden epaulettes on each shoulder, and that same silver insignia over his left breast. The semicircle with the sharp protrusions had no more meaning to him than when he saw them on the other captain.

The man approached with graceful strides across the snowy road. Stray flakes latched to his golden hair as it fluttered in the chilling breeze. He looked different than the last one; he looked a lot younger, perhaps thirty, and had a disposition that promised a little more amiability. He wore a smile that could have only been fitting had it been a lovely spring afternoon—but it wasn't. It was insufferably cold.

"I'm glad we were able to convene on such short notice," he said again, as if on some springtime excursion. "I'm Captain Malcus, of Atlum AK3. Now which of you goes by the name Ryan?"

The question fell on deaf ears. Either that or Ryan was pretending he didn't hear it. Though it didn't matter one way or another. They were going to take him. But before he could whimper out a reply, Steve spoke up.

"Let me clear something with you," he said. "Your intentions are to extract information concerning the Dreamer's World. Is that correct?"

"Yes," Malcus sneered. "That *is* correct."

Steve was unshaken, and stayed firm.

"In that case, if you acquire what you need to know, you wouldn't have to take Ryan anywhere else. He could come back with us."

Malcus held out his arms, as if willing to give full cooperation. "Of course. If the boy tells us what we need to know, then there's no reason for us to keep him. We're not monsters."

Ryan had a thing or two to say about that, but he kept quiet. Steve continued looking at the man sternly, staying true to his word about doing whatever he could to save Ryan.

Malcus asked, "I take it that the silent one is the boy in question?"

Ryan tried to look him in the eye, but couldn't lift his eyes off the ground.

"Yeah," he uttered quietly.

"Splendid then." Malcus clapped his hands together. "Why don't we continue this inside."

He trudged over the piles of snow that had collected along the sidewalk, to the building that stood beside them. Ryan and Steve followed him to the front door, and watched as Malcus gestured the remaining soldiers. There were about two dozen of them, and they were beginning to arrange themselves in an arc around the building. Only two followed him to the entrance.

The front door was sealed, welded shut by a ring of ice. There was no getting through by conventional means. Malcus dwelled on the issue for about two seconds before his boot came up to the height of his hips, and then through the door. Glass and ice spattered to the ground, clearing a path to the inside. He tramped over the mess and glanced brazenly at it.

"It's not like they were expecting any critics this afternoon."

Once inside, Ryan figured out they were standing inside a hotel lobby, a place darkened by the sheets of ice that barred the windows. Everything was covered in its own layer of frost, from the marble floor tiles, to the chandeliers that glittered like crystal crowns. It may have been considered luxurious during its years of operation, but times had changed. Now it was bleak and deserted. The front desk was without receptionists, and the bar and lounge without guest. The hotel was an icy dwelling, forged by nature itself.

Malcus guided the pair to the empty lounge, located in a sunken area to the right of the front desk. He helped himself to a chair, while offering Ryan and Steve to sit in the couch across from him. Meanwhile, the two soldiers that had followed him secured positions by the hotel's entrance.

Ryan was grateful for what Steve was able to accomplish thus far. Being inside a frozen hotel was certainly preferable to being on one of those stations, where crashing into a star seemed like standard punishment. He hoped it wouldn't come to that extremity again. Though if he wanted to avoid hostility, he'd have to find a way to wheedle his way out of here, because he didn't know the answer to a single question on the test he was about to take.

Malcus sat nonchalantly in his seat, with his elbows at his sides and his fingers entwined. He looked at Ryan with a covetous grin, as if the mere sight of the boy was something to feast over. His gaze was without interruption, an inoculation of unrelenting terror. It left Ryan feeling very uncomfortable.

Ryan shivered secretly underneath his parka, awaiting for the interrogation to commence.

Malcus opened his mouth, and his voice reverberated throughout the chamber.

"There is no greater honor than to be in the company of an outsider—or a dreamer, as you might call yourself. You may be unaware of the influence your kind has had on the people of this realm, so allow me to clarify: you are of greater worth than all the material treasures of all the worlds that can be found in this universe."

Ryan, genuinely curious about his rationale, decided to ask a simple question: "Why?"

Malcus held out his arms. "Because," he said with fervor, "the treasures of these worlds have no intrinsic value. They bring only the illusion of pleasure and wealth. To one that has been enlightened by the wonders that lie beyond, these things will not satisfy. No. They will seek something greater, something just outside their grasp—a quintessential joy that has yet to be found."

"The Dreamer's World," Ryan said plaintively.

"Yes. But more precisely, that which exists on the other side—the realm from which you came."

"Earth? Is that what you're after?"

Malcus shook his head, giving a hearty, derisive chuckle.

"I wouldn't expect a young lad like yourself to understand. You see, our minds are attuned to two different forms of perception. Neither of us can ever fully grasp what the other is capable of seeing or feeling. Which makes it very difficult for us to see eye to eye. So instead, think of our quest as an effort to obtain the unobtainable, so that we may be able to . . . gladden the woes that plague the people of this realm."

Steve interrupted. "Let's not jump the gun here." He leaned forward with an assertive posture. "There's no evidence to suggest that the Dreamer's World even exists. For thousands of years it's been regarded as a legend, even by historians and scholars. Thousands of expeditions have been made, led by men of high stature, kings and emperors; and even with their glut of resources, they all came back empty-handed. Now you're going to tell me you're going to be the one to find something that no one else in history could?"

Initially, Ryan felt an ounce of relief. He liked the card Steve was playing. Maybe it could have actually worked. But then he looked over again at Malcus, and saw that his expression had not changed a bit. He was left undeterred.

"Perhaps these men were not thorough enough," he snapped back. "The existence of the Dreamer's World is an absolute certainty. Anyone who opens themselves to the Will of Kausmos will be acquainted with the necessary knowledge to understand."

"And I take it that's worked out for you."

Malcus' fuse was burning with each passing second, his hands curled into fists at his sides.

"You're a skeptic. I can understand that. You're uncultivated and naive. I wouldn't expect much out of you. But this boy on the other hand . . . " He shifted his attention to Ryan, looking at him again with preying eyes. ". . . I'm hoping to learn a lot from."

He let his muscles loosen, and allowed his fists to slacken. His look was affable again.

"Now Ryan, why don't you begin with telling me about your journey to this side."

The question and answer session had begun. Ryan was scrambling to recall everything that would be pertinent to the discussion, even though a cursory sweep of his memory brought up nothing. He looked at Steve, as if he held some of the answers.

"Don't look at him," Malcus hissed. "He's not your attorney. Now recount your story."

Ryan raced to conjure up a tale, but ultimately decided to just go along with an honest account.

"It was a Friday night," Ryan explained (though technically, it still was Friday night). "I was finishing up some math homework. I had dinner, and watched some TV. By then I was very tired so I went to bed. I was lying there for about an hour or so. I was having trouble falling asleep because I couldn't stop thinking about this big basketball game I lost."

Ryan looked at Malcus' face and couldn't shake the feeling that he wasn't hearing what he wanted to hear. But he continued the story anyway.

"So I'd say around midnight I fell asleep, and everything went black. Or at least that's how I think of it. I'm not really sure what color I'm seeing while I'm unconscious. But then at some point I woke up—that is, I woke up here on this side. And then I found myself on that station."

Malcus stared at him for a long time without saying anything. His arms were crossed, his eyes furrowed into slits. Ryan was convinced that he was not pleased with his response. He could have fabricated something else, but lying felt like a risky tactic.

"So there were no sensory observations from what you could recall? You felt and saw nothing between the time you fell asleep and awoke on this side? Is this your testimony?"

"Yes," Ryan said.

"There was nothing indicating a physical passage?"

"No."

"No sightings of any planet, or celestial body of any kind?"

Ryan shook his head. "No."

Malcus looked at him some more with a glower.

"So the journey was instantaneous you say?"

"Yes," Ryan said, becoming aware that every one of his answers was displeasing Malcus more and more.

Malcus, for the time being, had refrained from asking any more questions. He was still and silent, making it practically impossible for Ryan or Steve to know what he was thinking. The situation was becoming increasingly awkward for the two of them. Eventually Steve decided to speak up.

"He doesn't know anything," he said. "He's not going to be able to help you. If you want to find the Dreamer's World, you're going to have to look for answers somewhere else."

Even though Steve was talking, Malcus was still very much focused on Ryan.

"I think . . . we're not done here. I've yet to even scratch the surface."

Ryan noticed Malcus reaching inside his coat. He was petrified instantly, because he knew there could only be a handful of items that he could be reaching for, none of which he looked forward to seeing.

Frozen by terror, he watched as Malcus produced a silver blade in his hand. It was a long knife with a serrated edge. Its luster was radiant, even under the shadows. He couldn't take his eyes off the blade. It was brandished before him, ensuring he understood how real the threat was. And hell it was real.

He cowered backwards into the couch, realizing it did nothing to create distance between him and the knife. He wondered if there was anything he could say at this point that would cause this man to relent.

He heard Steve vocalize his objection.

"He doesn't know anything! He told you that!"

Malcus stood from his seat and took one step forward. Ryan had his arms out in front of him for protection. He was clenching his teeth, trembling uncontrollably, from the cold, the fear, and everything at once.

"I don't know," he pleaded. "I don't know anything!"

Malcus took another step forward, the blade poised in his hand.

"I will drain every droplet of juice from the fruit I've acquired, and I shall drink from it until my thirst has been quenched."

"You're crazy!" Steve shouted. "You're not going to get anything from him. He doesn't know!"

Malcus stopped and stood before Ryan, with the knife held loosely in his grip. His thumb gently caressed the hilt. There was no emotion in his face. Nothing but a cold, lifeless expression.

Ryan saw the knife hover towards him, until it was just inches away from his face. He was on the verge of weeping, desperate to wake up. There was nothing he desired more than to see himself back in bed, inside the safety of his room. But it didn't happen. He couldn't trigger it. He couldn't leave the dream.

He closed his eyes.

There was a sound—a quick, jarring sound of impaled flesh. It was a tear, followed by a gushy trickle. He felt a couple of warm droplets sprinkle across his face. The worst had crossed his mind, but when he felt no pain, he ruled out the possibility that he had been harmed. Then it must have been Steve. He feared that it had to have been Steve.

He opened his eyes.

What he saw was a thousand times more horrific than what he could have ever guessed. That blade was a butter knife compared to the pair of monstrous talons that had skewered the captain's torso. They were pale as ivory, crescent like a sickle, and just as sharp. They pulled apart, prying open the wound even further. A cascade of blood spilled onto the floor.

Ryan couldn't move. He couldn't think. He even forgot he was alive, which was just as well, because whatever that thing was, it was going to kill him.

He saw the knife slip through Malcus' fingers and land on the floor with a clang. Then he saw the claws cleave through the body like a power tool. A conglomeration of bloody chunks splashed across the room, leaving the severed body to collapse to the ground.

The creature now stood in plain view. It was a plump animal, with a white feathered belly and a dark blue dorsal coat. Its feet were like talons, webbed between the toes. The head was four feet off the ground, egg-shaped with a feathered crest. On either side was a green marble eye, glinting with unbridled hate. Then, encompassing its body like two halves of a shell were the flippers. They were unusually large for a creature of this size, but it may have been because the flippers were what harbored the retractable claws—two on each—lethal scythes that were ready for their next kill.

It was a freaking penguin, Ryan screamed inside his head, as the claws came swatting down in his direction. He pulled his feet up onto the couch, and then leapt up onto the backrest, just in time to see the stuffing spill out from within the cushion. He staggered backwards, and fell back against the floor. His spine throbbed with pain, but he didn't let it stop him from scrambling back onto his feet.

Steve hurried around the couch to assist Ryan, and together they watched as the creature scaled the backside of the couch. It perched itself on top, ready to lunge for another attack, which is when the bullets began to fly.

The two soldiers that were stationed by the entrance were unloading shots from their rifles. The shots echoed across the room like thunder; the bullets continued to stream in at their target. Every one landed square in the penguin's belly, but it seemed to do nothing more than ruffle the feathers and anger the bird. That's when Steve commanded Ryan to run.

"Go!" he shouted, as they both took off across the lobby. Ryan kicked his legs as fast as he could, but it didn't seem to be enough. How fast was that penguin anyway? Whatever the answer was, it spelled trouble for Ryan, as he paid no heed to the thin patches of ice that covered the floor. He slipped on one, sending him into a belly flop. He careened across the floor as helplessly as a hockey puck. He tried to slow himself, and in doing so, he spun around, so that now he was facing the two soldiers.

The penguin had gotten to them, and Ryan watched as the lethal claws were driven into their bodies. The first soldier fell to the ground with a hefty thud, while the other leapt away to dodge the forthcoming attack. But it wasn't enough to avoid the sweeping sickles. The left leg was cleanly clipped off, leaving the man pogoing on one leg until the creature delivered the killing blow.

"C'mon!" Steve urged him, grabbing his arm and pulling him off the floor. Ryan started running again, though more carefully this time. Even so he staggered more than once. He could hear a scratching, clacking sound coming up from behind. He wanted to turn around and look, but doing so would have risked another fall, which he couldn't afford.

More gunshots were fired, dozens at a time, a cacophony of bangs and explosions, all coming from outside. There was a swarm, Ryan thought. These creatures were everywhere. Maybe tens, or hundreds of them. He heard shrills and screams from human and animal alike. Through the frosted panes he could see silhouettes, hobbling, and pouncing. It was an all-out brawl between the men and the beasts, though heavily in favor of the latter. The headcount looked to be diminishing as the tallest of the figures collapsed to the ground.

Another shot was fired, this one coming straight through one of the windows. Glass and shards of ice spilled across the sill. A beam of light entered the lobby, granting better visibility to where the patches of ice were hiding. There was one coming up, and Ryan saw it, but his foot was already on its way down.

He slipped and landed on his bottom, and saw before him a succession of light beams breach the far end of the lobby. There was one explosion of glass and ice after another. The windows popped with the likeness of a synchronized demolition. The plump animals stood perched on each of the ledges, crouched like a line of swimmers ready to take their dive. With no hesitation they plopped onto their bellies. They cast their flippers wide, unsheathing their claws, driving them into the floor. With a powerful tug, they slung themselves and barreled forward like a couple of toboggans.

They were coming up fast, four in front, and still one from behind. Ryan and Steve were going to be sandwiched if they didn't react right away.

Ryan considered climbing over the front desk, but that wouldn't offer any outlet of escape. They'd be cornered if they tried that. So that left only one option, and that was the window that was blown open. It was approximately thirty feet ahead on the left-hand side, behind a row of seats. But there was one problem: if they made a break for it now, those penguins would have time to adjust their course. They'd veer to the right and cut them off.

But Ryan had an idea. It was risky, but it was their only shot.

"We'll make a break for the window," Ryan said to Steve. "Right before they reach us. They won't have time to turn."

Though he appeared nervous about the idea, Steve gave a nod of assent.

Together they waited as the penguins drew closer. They watched as the claws provided the momentum. There was a clack every time they dug into the ground. They heard it from down the hall, and from behind. The animals were closing in fast.

The time was now.

Ryan issued the command and the two of them sprinted towards the light. Ryan moved in a blink, and staggered forward. He caught himself on a chair, and pulled his feet away just as the blades grazed the bottom of his sneaker. As he had hoped, he saw the group of birds careen past them—and then bury their claws deep into the floor. They came to a sheering halt, ready to turn back around.

Ryan jumped to his feet and followed Steve, out through the window and into the light. The glaring snow-covered street blinded him. It took his eyes a moment to adjust, and when they did, he caught a glimpse of the rampage in action.

The scene was a zoo break. The city had been repopulated by the short, pudgy creatures. They occupied every street corner for blocks. They were pouring out of the broken store windows, flocking to the roads, slinging themselves across the ice. Their bright orange beaks accelerated like a barrage of missiles. Many of the soldiers already lay disassembled, like action figures that were handled too roughly. Their blood had stained the ice, like cherry syrup over a snow cone. The few that remained sprayed their gunfire in a futile effort to keep the animals at bay, but they only growled with irascibility, before claiming their kills.

The two robotic sentries were faring better in the engagement. Their turrets fired flaming pellets that vaporized patches of ice into puddles. Fireballs spurted into the air, dispersing waves of heat that Ryan intensely felt. He saw one of these shots strike one of the animals, and he heard the squeals and cries that followed. It most definitely pierced the skin, but he wasn't convinced that it was enough to kill it. Several of the other creatures went down in the same manner, up until the machines themselves were assaulted. The penguins came from behind and began hacking at the legs, toppling the robots to the ground. The attacking claws screeched against the metal body with a crackle of sparks, forming gashes that compounded to deep lacerations. The sentries flailed their blades, but they either struck air, or clanged against the parrying claws.

Ryan was darting across the battlefield, as fast as the clumpy snow would allow. He and Steve had stopped for just a second to consider the possibility of getting back inside the Conoblis. The doors were still open. They could reach it in about five seconds, but they passed on the thought once they saw the quantity of animals that surrounded it. Their next best bet was the establishment across the street.

They slipped in through a shattered window, landing themselves inside some sort of restaurant. The place appeared vacant. All the decor was intact, the chairs and tables were untouched, preserved under a protective layer of ice.

Their first objective was to seek cover, somewhere where they could hide and stay put until the fighting outside died down. To their right was the cashier counter, a place that may have fit the criteria. Ryan went around the side, whispering for Steve to follow. They crouched behind it, using the moment to catch their breaths.

Ryan was panting heavily, though not from physical exhaustion, but from experiencing one of the greatest scares of his entire life. Nothing had come close to having what was suppose to be a cute, cuddly animal try and kill you. This was bizarre and grotesque, even for his imagination. He suspected that these creatures, being indigenous to the climate, were the only living things that could have survived the sudden change in temperature. But that wouldn't account for their predatory enhancements. Not to mention their inexplicable strength and heightened intelligence. The signs all seemed to be pointing in the same general direction. Some questionable experiments were taking place in this town, because those were *not* ordinary penguins. Ryan was sure of that.

He looked at Steve and gave a succinct summary of his observations thus far.

"If one thing doesn't kill me," he said, "something else will try."

"Yeah," Steve said, "that's what it feels like, doesn't it."

Steve stood up slowly, just enough so that he could peek over the counter. Through the window he saw a lone penguin waddling his way towards the restaurant. It glanced around sporadically, as if trying to sniff them out. It knew its prey was around.

"Damn it," Steve said, crouching back down.

"What is it?" Ryan asked.

"We got one of them coming this way. It knows we're here."

"What do we do?"

Steve pondered. He studied the other areas of the restaurant.

"There," he said. "The bar. It's open on both sides. If we need to, we can double back from either side. If we stay here, we'll be cornered."

Ryan agreed.

They crept carefully across the floor, staying as low as they could. They came around the side of the bar, and took cover behind the rack of frozen wine bottles. In between the empty compartments, Ryan had a view of the front door. The frosted glass obscured the inbound creature. It wobbled from side to side, its flippers outstretched, claws drawn. Its silhouette grew clearer and larger. It was upon them.

There was a loud crash, as the door shattered into a million crystals. The creature stood in plain sight, taking its first steps into the restaurant.

Ryan retreated immediately behind the wine rack and remained as quiet as possible. Steve did the same. They kept their breathing to a minimum. Their backs were flat against the counter. They listened carefully, tracking its movement by the crackling glass. The sound steadily grew louder—closer. The claws on its feet scratched against the ice. The creature let out an irritable growl.

Ryan could hear it flanking the right side of the bar. Its movement was even more distinguishable now. The commotion that took place outside was all but dying out. The gun shots had ceased. The whirrs of the sentries silent. He figured that he and Steve were the last two humans alive in the vicinity. Never before had he felt so isolated, so certain that his demise was inevitable.

He was shivering without restraint, watching as his breath permeated into the air. He listened for the footsteps that were coming around. Then they stopped.

He heard a powerful swoosh that sliced against what must have been a chair or table, proceeded by the sound of a thousand splinters scattering across the room in a hundred directions. He heard the penguin's flippers wail again on another object, breaking it to bits. It was thrashing about in an outburst of fury, heedlessly destroying anything in its path.

The room fell silent. The footsteps started again. They got closer and closer. They were just on the other side of the counter.

Ryan kept looking to his right. That's where the sounds were coming from. Maybe if he stayed perfectly still, the penguin would continue its hunt elsewhere. But the footsteps were only getting closer. It was right there, and it wasn't going anywhere else.

He saw the ends of the claws poke around the side of the counter—those razor sharp talons that glistened like a polished knife. He could almost feel an incision in his skin merely by looking at it.

The penguin took one more step, and now the whole animal was standing in plain view. The head turned and the eyes latched onto their targets. Ryan had no chance of survival, unless he ran.

Now.

"Run!" Ryan yelled, and both of them clambered onto their feet. They grabbed onto the counter for support and fled through the access on the other side of the bar. From there they made a beeline sprint to the front door, knowing now they only had one shot of getting out of here alive.

"The Conoblis," Steve said. "It's our only hope."

They escaped through the entrance, and ran back out into the street. The scene was different from just a minute ago. There wasn't a soldier left on their feet. Instead they lay on their backs, while the penguins pecked and ravaged their bodies, pulling out whatever meat they could nab. With most of their attention diverted to their meals, Ryan and Steve seized the opportunity to get back to their vehicle.

Ryan didn't look. He didn't think. All he concentrated on was getting one foot in front of the other. He knew he was being timed. The penguins lifted their heads from the carcases, fresh flesh still dangling from their mouths. They chose to abandon their catch, which is when Ryan learned they weren't just interested in satisfying their hunger, but also their desire to hunt.

The Conoblis was just meters away, the door wide open. He ran and ran, and jumped onto the staircase. He flew through the cabin door and caught himself on the passenger seat. Steve was right there with him, rushing to the control console He activated the mechanism to seal the door, but it just wouldn't close fast enough for comfort.

The penguins were flocking from every direction, tobogganing on their bellies, with claws extended. Their eyes burned passionately.

"Lift," Ryan shouted. "We need lift!"

"I'm on it."

Steve booted the main system, and engaged the gravitational regulators. The engine rasped and the cabin shook. The Conoblis was coming off the ground, inch by inch, rising like a balloon. The penguins were right outside, just within reach. When they were within range, they hoisted themselves into the air with a kick of their flippers. They all sprung at the vessel.

The Conoblis, with a burst of acceleration, rocketed up into the sky, though not rapidly enough to avoid a single stroke of one of the bird's flippers. Two hairline nicks were carved into the windshield—a salient reminder of just how close they came to becoming an entree.

"We made it," Ryan said with disbelief. "I can't believe we made it."

"Yeah. We did," Steve said, not nearly as excited.

Ryan detected the subtly of his tone. It was almost as if there was something else to worry about.

"Is something wrong?"

Steve was twitching in his seat. He wasn't quite sure where to look.

"It's just—we took out a high ranking officer of an enemy we know nothing about."

"But we didn't. You saw what—"

"I know. But it's just the same. He was killed during official business with our people. And I'm not sure how killer penguins are going to hold up as an explanation. I just hope this doesn't precipitate a war."

Ryan could agree. Politically speaking, they were in a precarious situation. There was no telling how, or if they would retaliate. To top it off, Zephner had also carried out a couple of executions himself. For all Ryan knew, this was just another log in the fire. And from the feel of things, that fire was getting pretty darn hot.

———CHAPTER 13———

AN UNEXPECTED VISITOR

After Steve sent out a status update, the Conoblis was ordered to return to the *Obsidian*. The vessel reentered the port and was elevated back inside the docking room. Ryan and Steve climbed out, both worried that their relations with the enemy had been greatly exacerbated. Leilah, already having received a message about what happened, was in the room. She looked frightened, scared, and relieved all at the same time. She scurried over to them, holding her hand to her chest.

"Are you two all right?" she asked anxiously.

"Yeah," we're fine," Steve answered.

"Just barely," Ryan added.

"I can't believe it," Leilah said shaking her head. "I had no idea Lylid was inhabited by animals like that."

"It was a surprise to all of us," Steve said.

"I don't know how Reynard, or even Roland is going to take this surprise. An enemy captain is dead."

"That's what I was just telling Ryan. None of this bodes well for us."

Ryan noticed Leilah staring alarmingly at his face.

"Ryan, is that blood?"

He wiped his face with the back of his sleeve and saw the streaks smeared across the fabric.

"It isn't mine," he was happy to say.

She sighed with relief as Steve started to walk over to the bulkhead, slipping out of his coat at the same time.

"I have to go meet with Reynard at the bridge to explain what happened, and figure out what kind of repercussions we're looking at."

"Okay," Leilah answered.

"How about I meet you at the E deck diner in a little bit?"

She made a look of aversion. "How can food be on your mind at a time like this?"

Steve shrugged. "I skimped out on lunch today. No time."

"Fine, I'll see you there."

Ryan was also thinking about food, but not in the sense that he wanted to eat something, but rather regurgitate whatever was already inside of him. He had crossed paths with death far too many times for one day—or night—whatever. He's had about as much as he could handle. Any more and this would unequivocally become the worst nightmare he had ever endured. It'd be right up there next to the time a crazed killer escaped a painted portrait and roamed free about his house. But in that instance, he never actually laid eyes on the interloper, but he knew he was there, waiting around every corner, but then disappearing whenever he would check. The dream he was in now felt much the same way, except here he was facing the threats face to face. Though things may have been calm at the moment, he knew he was in the eye of the storm. It was only a matter of time before the winds escalated again.

He felt alone, knowing home was so far away. Megan wasn't with him, nor Mike, or anyone he was close to. Then he remembered another, when he saw how small the crowd in the room was.

They were all standing by the bulkhead. Steve was ready to seal the hatch when Ryan blurted out his discovery.

"I forgot about Bee," he said. "I left him buckled in."

"Who?" Steve said.

Ryan remembered he wasn't around when he gave Bee a name.

"The basketball. Leilah told me to give him a name."

"Uh huh. Well, go get him. I got to get going." He started down the corridor. "Can you lock up for me?" he said, directing the question to Leilah.

"Sure," she said.

Steve took off as Ryan reentered the room. He was ashamed to have left him there like that. He could only imagine what he must have been thinking during that entire ruckus. Do basketballs get scared? Maybe he would find out.

He raced up the steps and entered the Conoblis. He passed through the narrow access to the rear area. To his left was Bee, still buckled inside the seat that Ryan had left him in. He was squirming to get out, desperate to get free. The poor thing looked terrified. Ryan went ahead and released the buckle. Bee scrammed from his seat and onto the floor. But instead of exiting the vehicle, he rolled towards the opposing wall.

He was showing him something.

Ryan looked.

He staggered backwards, tripping over his own feet, and struck the wall. For there, hiding in the shadowy crevice behind the other seat and an engine block was an animal, lying in a shallow puddle of fluid. It looked like blood, but it was a lot darker, more akin to oil. But what was more concerning was the animal that it belonged to. It appeared to be a carcass of a penguin, of the same variety they had just encountered. This one suffered a gaping wound. In the region of its chest was a fist-sized hole which was seeping uncontrollably.

The creature let out an antagonizing groan, causing Ryan to shudder. His initial assumption was wrong. The animal was still alive, but holding on by a thread. In its tame, incapacitated state,

Ryan was able to see it as something other than a killing machine. It seemed irrational, but he could almost feel sorry for it. It continued to groan and whimper, trying to shift to a more comfortable position. It placed its flipper over the wound, but it did little to stop the bleeding.

The green, gleaming eyes had found Ryan. Though soiled in tears, they still manged to form a scowl.

"Where the hell did you take me?" the creature said, with a low, raspy voice.

Ryan sprung back, astounded by what he heard. Did that voice really come from the penguin? Then again, stranger things had happened.

The creature spoke again with strenuous effort. "Tell me or I'll. . . dice you . . . and serve you as an appetizer."

Ryan looked on with pity at the penguin who was trying to hold on to some dignity by spewing empty threats. He paid little attention, still confounded by how the animal was talking.

"How are you doing that?" he asked.

"Doing what? Leaking juice like a shot cask? It's easy. You get shot."

"I didn't mean—"

Ryan caught himself staring at the injury unhelpfully. He was in a bind as to what the right thing to do was. Just a few minutes ago he wouldn't have cared if they blew away the whole lot of them. In his defense, they were trying to kill him. But now the moral implications of the matter were a bit more ambiguous. Not a whole lot had changed, except for the bit where he learned that these animals could talk. Now he felt obligated to do something.

"We need to treat you," he said.

"I don't need any treatment."

"But if you keep bleeding like this, you'll die."

"It'll heal on its own," the penguin said with a cranky tone. "It always does."

"Always? Is this a typical day for penguins on Lylid?"

"Far from it."

"Then let us help you."

The penguin continued to groan and wince at the antagonizing pangs. Ryan couldn't tolerate watching the animal suffer anymore. He stood up on his feet and took a wary step forward. He thought about calling for help, but realistically, what would they do? If anything, they'd probably put him down, and that just didn't seem right.

He heard Leilah's voice calling him from afar.

"Ryan? Are you all right? Did you get lost?"

Rather than have her stumble onto the site without warning, he stepped outside the vessel and intercepted her before she got any closer.

"Where's Bee?" she asked when she saw him come out empty handed.

"Bee's inside. And um." He looked at her while he searched for the right words. She grew worried the longer he went without saying anything. "There's something I should probably show you."

Ryan led her inside the Conoblis. He took her to the back room, and then waited until she noticed the stowaway. Her reaction was in line with what he expected. She was taken aback, gasped loudly, and nearly fell over her own feet.

"Ryan," she said with disbelief. "Don't tell me this is—"

"It is," he said.

"You're shitting me." Her hand came up to her forehead.

"Nope. Afraid not."

"How did it get in here?"

Ryan paused. "We think someone forgot to close the door."

She gazed down at the animal, fearful of what it was capable of. Then she asked, "Why did it come in here for?"

The penguin caught his breath and opened his beak. "I was

trying to spare myself a pitiful death."

Leilah turned to Ryan, her mouth ajar. "It *speaks*?"

"Apparently."

Another boisterous groan filled the chamber. The animal must have been in great pain. Either that, or it didn't like being the topic of the conversation.

"It's okay," Ryan said. "We're going to help you." He looked at Leilah. "We can help him, right?"

She seemed unsure, and worried that it could still be dangerous. The claws were marginally drawn from their sheaths.

"I don't know," she said. "There's not a lot we can do for him here. How was he wounded?"

"He must have been shot."

"Was it conventional ammunition?"

"I don't think so. These guys took no harm from bullets. It must have been from the robot firing those laser thingamajigs."

"That's fortunate. At least there won't be any remnants to cause an infection."

Leilah made her way to a storage closet that was along the back wall. She opened it and pulled out a first-aid kit and rummaged through it, grabbing some gauze and medical tape. With her supplies in hand, she went over to the animal, sure to keep her distance. She got down on one knee and looked at him, studying his intent carefully. His menacing demeanor left her doubtful.

"I want to help you," she said, trying to gain the animal's trust. "But you have to promise me something."

"What?" he snapped back.

"You got to promise me you're not going to pull any tricks. Which means keeping those claws where I *can't* see them."

The penguin stared at her with his grouchy expression. He was reluctant to comply, but after some time, he acceded to her demands. He retracted the claws back inside his flippers.

"Get it over with, will ya," the penguin muttered.

"Take it easy," she said.

She leaned in close, and got a better look at the wound. Turns out it wasn't as bad as she initially believed. A layer of muscle tissue was already in the process of healing, almost as if cauterization was taking place. The blood seepage was trickling less and less. She was simply stunned by the animal's regenerative ability.

"I'm no medical practitioner," she said, "but from what I can observe, this guy is on route to making a speedy recovery."

"That's good," Ryan said—*I think*, he added in his head.

"You see," the penguin said, "you can leave me alone."

"Mmm, I'm still patching you up though. If you lose too much blood you can still go into a hypovolemic shock."

The penguin uttered some incomprehensible babble as Leilah applied a stack of gauze. The animal winced on contact.

"Ryan, do me a favor. Hold this while I get the tape around him."

Ryan kept pressure on the wound while Leilah underwent the task of getting the tape around the animal. She had Ryan hold the loose end while she coiled the roll around the body, which included threading it underneath one of the flippers. She found that they were heavy, almost like trying to lift a sack of lead. After much winding and unraveling, the penguin was fully patched. It groaned again, perhaps as a sign of appreciation. Or not.

"That should take care of that," Leilah said. "Now see, that wasn't too bad. You're going to be fine. Aren't you glad?"

If his face was any indication, the answer was no. Then again, his face hadn't changed since they found him.

"I'll let you think about it," she said, putting away the remaining supplies.

She moved into the cockpit and waved for Ryan to come along. Together they stepped back into the room and made their way to the far wall next to the computer terminals. Now that she wasn't in the penguin's presence, she let her real thoughts come out.

"I've never worked bomb disposal before, but I think I just got a taste of it."

Ryan could understand where she was coming from. It was likely the animal still retained the strength to kill both of them if it really wanted to. But somehow that threat was mitigated by an intuitive feeling of trust. Or maybe it was just plain stupidity. Either way, he wanted to believe that something good would come from what happened.

"I guess we cut the right wire," Ryan said.

"Beginner's luck," she said. "Or maybe—"

"Maybe what?"

"Maybe he's not like the others. Maybe's he's willing to assess the matter first before jumping into the fray. That, and he knows if he tries anything he'll lose his only ticket out of here. Given his linguistic abilities, I'm sure he's intelligent enough to come to that deduction."

"So you don't think there's any risk of him attacking us when he recovers?"

Leilah stopped to think about it for a moment. She sat at the terminal.

"I think we can count on him to cooperate. I got a good feeling about it." She started to dial commands on the keyboard. "But that still means calling it in."

"Who are you calling?"

"Steve. He can then pass on the information to Reynard when he talks to him."

She noticed the look on Ryan's face. She could tell he looked worried.

"It's going to be fine," she said. "I'll make sure nothing happens to him."

Ryan nodded, then thought to ask, "Are we still heading to that diner?"

"Yeah. You hungry?"

"Not particularly. I was thinking about asking him if he wanted something to eat." He motioned his head towards the vessel.

"Good idea, but just be careful."

Ryan left her to make the call while he went back into the Conoblis. As he approached he heard the groggy groans coming from the back room. He went in and saw the penguin still resting in the same spot he left him. Blood was already seeping through the gauze they applied to him. A little, not a lot. His eyes were looking back at Ryan, with that feeble look of an injured dog. He looked frustrated, maybe even embarrassed by the fact he was helpless and immobile.

"Does this amuse you?" the penguin said petulantly.

Ryan came close and crouched down beside him.

"No," he said. "I was just wondering if you wanted something to eat. We're going to be heading to a diner in a little bit."

"That's right," he winced. "Indulge me with the fantasies of having a meal prepared by amateur cooks who pull their ingredients from a dirty ice chest."

"Sorry," Ryan said. "I didn't realize your standards were so high."

"They're not high. I just have a policy of eating only what I kill personally."

"I can deal with that. But it may be a while before you get a chance to hunt again. I can try to get you something in the meantime. You don't even have to eat it. You can sniff it, and if you don't like it, you can, um, kick it against the wall."

"In that case, bring me one of everything on the menu. I'll paint you a lovely fresco."

"I'll order what I can," Ryan said, standing back up. He

looked away before the penguin could see him smile. The animal's attempt at humor was a telling sign that any ill sentiment between them was diminishing.

He remembered another question just before he left the cabin.

He looked back at the penguin.

"There was one other thing."

"What?"

"I was wondering if you had a name. Since you could talk, I figured you had a name."

The penguin made a disgruntled groan. "I don't have a name."

"Then maybe I can come up with one for you. I already had to name one thing today. I think I can come up with another."

Ryan looked to the ceiling and dwelled on what a good name for a penguin would be. He eventually decided on one.

"What about Rubin?"

The penguin's eyes opened wide. He looked like he was ready to take someone's head off.

"Repeat that name again and I'll slit your throat."

"Okay, fine. Not Rubin. What about Dalton?"

The penguin scowled him. His beak was clenched tightly.

"I hope you never give birth to a living thing."

Ryan was about to suggest a third name, until he detected something was amiss with that comment.

"Wait a minute," he said. "I don't—"

"Save it!" the penguin yelled.

"All right," Ryan said. "You can come up with your own name."

The penguin muttered something under his breath. Ryan couldn't make it out.

"What?"

"I said . . . I already have a name."

Ryan crouched next to him again, glad to see he was finally opening up."

"What is it?"

He hesitated for a second, grimacing as if it would hurt to say it. Eventually it slipped out as something just a tad louder than a whisper.

"It's Guin."

Ryan smiled and stood back up.

"Guin," he repeated. "That's a good name. Especially for a penguin."

He turned around and began walking to the exit. "I'll be back later," he said. "And I'll let you know what's going on."

He stepped out of the vessel and went over to Leilah. She was wrapping up her conversation. When she was done she walked over to Ryan. She spoke to him with her hands on her hips. She bit her bottom lip.

"Everything is in order," she said.

"Is it?"

"Yeah."

"What did Steve say?"

She chuckled. "He sort of freaked out. And that was with me telling him that the penguin was unconscious. Had I told him the truth, I think he would have come running back here with a firing squad. But as it stands, he just wants us to keep him sealed up inside the Conoblis."

"For how long?"

"Until he gets the situation straightened out with Reynard."

Ryan turned his head and looked back at the vessel. Leilah accessed the terminal again, remotely closing the door on the Conoblis. Ryan wondered if the ship's plating was enough to contain him if he were to fully recover. Though he believed it wouldn't be an issue. Guin wasn't going to get physical.

"I was speaking to him just now," Ryan said, "and I managed

to get a name out of him."

"Really," Leilah said. "What's his name?"

"Guin."

"Guin. Cute," she said, bobbing her head with approval. "Did he tell you anything else?"

"Not yet. I mean, getting his name alone was like pulling teeth."

"In his case, more like plucking feathers."

"Yeah. Right. So I think it'll be a while before he discloses any other secrets."

"We got to give him time," she said, standing up from her seat. She started to head towards the bulkhead. "He's an animal outside his natural habitat. It'll take a while before he can adjust."

"But he's not going to stay here forever. They'll take him back home, right?"

Leilah pressed her lips together and put her hand on his shoulder.

"We'll work something out," she said. "Right after we get things squared away."

Together they left the docking room, with Bee trailing closely behind. Leilah sealed the main hatch and strolled down the corridor. Ryan followed, watching the gate numbers on the wall decrease.

There was a lot on his mind right now. He was sifting between different slides in his memory. There were the ones that showed him back at home, asleep in his bed, then there were others that showed him conversing with a talking bird. Among those were many others that were just as silly and far fetched. But the issue was that they were all shuffled together, like a deck of cards after a game of 52 pickup. Some cards were facing the wrong way, others were upside down. Heck, some of them were downright missing. Ryan was trying to put them back in order, but it was proving to be difficult. Every card was a joker.

———CHAPTER 14———

PRELUDE TO TERROR

Leilah ushered Ryan back to the central rotunda, and down the stairs to E deck. They traveled along the outer perimeter of the station, following the long, tubular corridor. These halls were kept darker than the other parts of the station, lit only by the glowing panels on the outer edges of the path. This allowed for an untainted view of the stellar scenery through the broad panoramic windows.

Ryan was caught staring in awe at the majestic vista. Everything was clearer and more vivid than anything he had ever seen before. There were a thousand stars visible within the boundaries of any window, as if a packet of sugar had just been torn open over a black board. And even more marvelous were the planets. There were dozens of them, a variety of sizes and colors. Ryan thought about how much these worlds could hold, and yet how little of it he could see. Each had their own atmospheres and climates, histories and cultures. They may have had civilizations, with billions of people, each with their own lives, their own thoughts—a conglomeration of information that was unfathomable. He stared at one point in particular, though who was to say what it was he was staring at exactly. For all he knew it could have been some alien clown who was juggling buckets of seaweed while balancing on a tractor tire while singing a song about a monkey that commandeered a bus and drove it into a tree that housed a bird who was eating jellybeans. But who's to say.

During their stroll, Leilah asked Ryan about his experience down on Lylid. He reiterated his tale with much gusto, now that he didn't have a pair of claws up to his face. In retrospect, it was an adversity that reignited the spark that was making this dream so stimulating. He was dodging bullets left and right, cheating death more times than his neighbor's cat. He was starting to feel comfortable here. Maybe this place wasn't so bad after all.

Coming up on their right was a wide-arching entrance with a chrome finish. It didn't have a name but Ryan assumed this was the diner they were going to.

They walked down a short ramp into the main dining area. The place was rather nifty. It surpassed Ryan's preconception of your typical roadside diner. This place was much larger, while still maintaining that capsule-like shape. The ceiling was arched, supporting a number of fans that spun slowly enough that you could count the blades. The floors were cream-colored, with a luster that made them look like they were covered in glaze. There was one counter, shaped in a semi-circle, surrounded by tall, red vinyl chairs. The rest of the room was packed with tables and booths, generously spaced apart to avoid a cramped feeling. There were a few other crew members here, but still plenty of open seats.

When Ryan approached one of the tables, he saw that the top was a solid sheet of glass. Classy, he thought, then he slid into the booth. An image emerged on the surface of the glass, displaying the word *welcome*. Then the image transitioned into a GUI, displaying different menu categories. Even though navigation seemed intuitive enough, Ryan couldn't help but stare.

"I take it you haven't seen one of these before?" Leilah said.

Ryan shook his head.

"Not like this. Where I come from, we're handed paper menus."

"It used to be that way over here too. But that was way before my time. Now it's all about minimizing human labor and stream-lining. Because let's face it, in the long run, machines are cheaper and in most cases, a lot more efficient."

Ryan thought about what she said. A question popped into his head.

"So who's cooking my dinner?"

Leilah chuckled. "Don't worry. Machines aren't going to replace the culinary skills of an adept chef any time soon."

She reached across the table to interact with Ryan's menu display. She pressed her finger against the tab that said *drinks*.

"Here," she said, "let me show you how this thing works."

A new screen appeared with a layout of different beverages, things that came in cans and bottles, glasses and mugs. The brown one may have been coffee, but Ryan couldn't have been sure. He didn't recognize any of the labels or substances.

Leilah selected one of the tin cans with a green colored logo. It looked like some kind of predatory animal—a saber tooth tiger perhaps. It was called Ja-Nube, which Ryan found to be whimsically enticing.

The can materialized above the table as a holographic projection. It rotated with a gaudy flair that Ryan couldn't resist. He wanted that drink.

But Leilah was quick to navigate through the other drinks that were available. One by one the holograms changed, to other items that were just as foreign and bizarre.

"Just press the picture of the drink you want to look at. When you've decided, hit where it says confirm order."

Ryan shuffled backwards through the list of items, finally selecting Ja-Nube. He confirmed his order and the table chimed.

"Very decisive I see."

"Not really," Ryan said. "I'm just throwing darts."

"Well, I'm sure you'll like it. Ja-Nube is pretty popular among most folk."

"Bullseye," Ryan muttered.

While Leilah was still choosing her own drink, Ryan went one step ahead and started looking at the entrees. He was glad to see that many of them looked familiar. They had an assortment of burgers and cheesesteaks, chicken wraps and fish platters—he would have to get one of those for Guin. He highlighted each one, even the ones he wasn't interested in, just to see the hologram. They were all perfect, as if the real thing were really levitating right in front of him. It was enough to build up his appetite.

Eventually Ryan settled on something called the ravonook burger. It contained pure ravonook meat, sauteed onions, lettuce, tomato, and four different cheeses that he didn't recognize. It seemed like the way to go.

"Fine choice," Leilah said. "ravonook is quite the delicacy."

"Really," Ryan said. "I didn't think a diner would carry something fancy."

"Used to be expensive. At least until the ravonook made its way over to Cyannus. After that they started to farm them like the money trees they were. The cost came down, so now you'll find them anywhere. But that has done nothing to the taste though. They're still as delicious as ever."

"That's good to know," Ryan said, slumping back into the cushions.

He saw a waitress with a blue buttoned blouse coming from behind the counter. She came their way, with a glass in one hand and a can in the other, and set down the two drinks.

"Your meals will be out momentarily," she said before leaving.

Ryan snagged his can of Ja-Nube, popped the tab, and began to chug it down. It sizzled in his mouth, like a carbonated drink. It was sweet, with a tang of melon flavor. Delicious, he thought, after consuming a quarter of the can.

Leilah noticed his delight. "Not bad, huh?"

"I like it," Ryan said, taking another gulp.

He looked across the table at Leilah's drink. It was a deep blue color, non-frizzling.

"So what's that stuff?" Ryan asked.

"It's blubara juice. A healthy substitute to sugar-heavy beverages. Not to speak ill of Ja-Nube, of course." She held her hand out to the can.

"I'm okay with a little sugar," Ryan said, sneaking in another sip.

Leilah was interacting with the table again. Her finger pressed against a tab along the lower edge, which took her to another screen entirely. She rooted through different menus until a certain selection turned the whole table top black. The image was now littered with a hundred white dots, along with several larger ones of different colors. One was a flashing green blip that was almost undetectably inching its way across the surface.

"It looks like a map of space," Ryan said.

"You're positively correct It's a map of the J-23-sector. It covers an area of about 225 billion square kilometers, which marks everything from Cyannus, all the way to Armon." She dragged her finger all the way across the table. "And this little flashing marker here is us." She pointed to the blip that Ryan noticed earlier. Next she placed both her index fingers on it and slid them apart. The area of the marker was magnified. She made the same gesture again and the image was magnified further. Now the movement of the blip was noticeable.

"Judging from our course, it looks like they decided to head back to base."

Ryan was pleased to hear it. He wanted nothing more than to find Megan and tell her how dreadfully sorry he was for dissipating through space without so much as a warning. That's if she still had the patience to wait around in the museum. Knowing her, she was probably long gone by now. But then he remembered that the museum was surrounded by a tempestuous ocean. She'd be trap there unless she was somehow able to transcend the boundaries set in place by the laws of perception—or layers of perception, as Steve taught him.

"How long is our flight going to be?" Ryan asked, while meticulously studying all the plot points.

Leilah looked down at the corner of the screen where there was a set of dynamic numbers.

"I'd estimate, given our current velocity, we should be back in Cyannus airspace in a little under two hours."

"That's it?" Ryan said. "I would have thought it'd be much longer than that. Back home it'd take years to travel to another planet. How are we making this trip in two hours?"

Leilah smiled at him and took a sip of her juice. "I suppose employing archaic travel methods would net you a pretty lengthy ride. But it's not like that here."

"How is this different?"

"Here we use something called a space orb compressor, or SOC for short. What it does is rearrange the composition of the area around the ship. It curves and compresses the space around us, turning a lateral plain into a much shorter one. Just think of a spherically shaped sponge. Let's say when expanded, it's six inches in diameter. But when you compress it, it becomes two inches. So if you were going to make a trip around the circumference of the sponge, you'll be making the trip in two seconds as oppose to six. Though the relation between compression and time saved is much greater than in the example. Level five compression is about twenty times more efficient than level four, which is twenty times more efficient than three, and so on."

"Gee, and I thought bullet trains were fast. What would happen if our captain fell asleep at the wheel?"

"We could, theoretically, tear a hole straight through a planet, that is if the station wasn't pulverized to bits first."

Ryan looked straight at her, unmoving, unblinking. A sip-full of Ja-Nube sat in his mouth.

"Don't worry," she said smiling. "There's about a hundred different fail-safes in place for such an event. Not only do we have a dozen crewmen monitoring the navigational systems, but there's also communication between land beacons that would automatically override SOC commands that put the station in a dangerous vicinity. So go ahead, enjoy your Ja-Nube."

Ryan swallowed what was in his mouth and set the can back down.

He looked around the room and watched the other patrons. Some of them were eating, while others were busy fiddling around with the computerized table tops. A pair seemed to be playing some kind of game on it, flinging virtual objects back and forth.

The waitress appeared again, this time carrying two platters, but it wasn't theirs. She was heading over to another table. Nonetheless, he could still pick up the pungent scent of battered fish. It reminded him that he needed to grab something for Guin before they left.

"How do you think Guin is holding up?" he asked Leilah.

The abrupt break in silence seemed to divert her from a daydream.

"Oh, I'm sure he's holding up just fine," she said.

"You think he'll recover from that wound okay?"

"I'm sure he will. I could practically see his skin healing right before my eyes."

Ryan looked down at the table. With some reservation, he asked the question that was prancing around in his head.

"Do you think it's weird that I feel bad for Guin?"

Leilah looked mildly confused.

"Why would that be weird?"

"If he had gotten to me on Lylid, I think he would have

killed me. Now I'm sympathizing with him. Just seems like an irrational emotion."

"Look," Leilah said softly, extending her hand across the table. "Emotions are an irrational thing. They're irrational by definition. They're responsible for a lot of the mistakes people make, which is why we have military leaders advocating for its eradication in all military personnel. It's why they've established the ERR."

"But what does that have to do with me?"

"Not a lot, I guess, considering you're only a temporary resident. But for the rest of us, it means the reconditioning of society. Our modern day technologies have had that effect on us. Collectively, people are calling for efficiency and perfection, because, let's face it, mistakes can be costly. Think about a machine as simple as a calculator. You can input any equation and you're guaranteed the right answer. Don't get me wrong, that's great for accountants and physicists, but for a different field, say law enforcement—can you use a calculator to determine whether or not you're in the right to take someone's life?"

Ryan gave her the obvious answer. "No," he said.

"Exactly. But you'll find other people who'll tell you that it's possible. They'll argue that the human psyche is something that can be expressed with mathematical formulas. I'll tell them that they're crazy, and they'll tell me to shut up and watch. And let me tell you, I'm still watching. Sure, we have machines that are capable of making independent decisions regarding ethical matters, but it doesn't come close to the kind of judgment a living, breathing person can have."

Ryan took another sip of his drink while listening carefully. Her aversion was understandable, given the context of what he was told.

"You think enlisting as a fighter pilot was the best road for you to take? Because it seems like you're putting yourself in the middle of the very thing you detest."

"No," Leilah said, shaking her head. "It's *because* I detest it that I put myself in the middle of it. I want to be able to show others that we're still capable of protecting our own fate, and the fate of everyone who depends on us. I want to be able to show them that some decisions are best handled by those that are able to find room in the equation for a little emotion. Because the world isn't black and white. It's a vast spectrum of color. And it takes someone who can see that to be able to keep it that way."

"I see where you're going with this," Ryan said. "If we lived in a world of artificial perfection, then our fate would basically be laid out for us, with no way for us to change it. If every question were dealt with the same systematic approach, the answer will always be the same."

"That's exactly right," she said, with a rapt look in her eyes. "That's why we can't shun away our feelings. We need to be able to use them, and use them well."

"Maybe if I were a machine," Ryan said, thinking out loud, "I would have just let Guin die. There really is no objective reason for helping him. I guess maybe it was because he was a penguin, and penguins look pretty helpless when they're hurt. I guess you can say I have a soft spot for penguins."

She tried to refrain from smirking. "And there's nothing wrong with that. Penguins do look helpless when they're hurt. And though I'm sure Guin would never admit it, I bet you he's grateful that you helped him."

Ryan hoped that was the case, as oppose to Guin genuinely despising his guts. If anything made him feel optimistic, it was the humorous comment that Guin made, which suggested a lack of hostility. In doing so, he conveyed a piece of information that could have been overlooked had the recipient been someone without a sense of humor—a robot, perhaps. Then again, what did he know about robots from this universe. For all he knew, they could be doing standup at the local nightclubs. He didn't know. Then again, there were a lot of things he didn't know.

The minutes ticked away as the two of them waited for their meals to arrive. To pass the time, Leilah showed Ryan the different applications that were integrated within the table's computer. A lot of them were frivolous, but still entertaining nonetheless. One program allowed him to change the texture of the tabletop, so that it could take on the appearance of things like wood and marble. The effect was so convincing that Ryan had to touch it. It was still glass, he discovered.

Next they tried playing a couple of the games. There was one in particular he enjoyed that utilized his can of Ja-Nube as the target of a bunch of tiny alien spacecraft. They had to be destroyed before they could fire their lasers at the drink. He'd poke them with his finger, while drawing lines that served as a temporary barrier. But in the end, the enemy proved to be formidable. The can of Ja-Nube was destroyed—no, it actually erupted into a fizzling mess that was set ablaze. Ryan was flabbergasted until Leilah admitted to swapping the real can for a virtual one when he wasn't looking. He was left humiliated

The waitress that he had seen earlier was making her way across the room again, this time in their direction. She had two platters in her hands, and when she got to the table, she set them down.

Ryan grabbed his ravonook burger and took his first bite of the succulent meat. The savory juices spilled from the bun as his teeth sunk in. It was soft, very tender. He ripped a chunk of it effortless and started to chew. It took about three seconds before he decided that this was the best meat he ever had.

"So what do you think?" Leilah asked.

"The best," Ryan mumbled with the food in his mouth. He looked at Leilah's dish and saw something that resembled a quesadilla. "Yours doesn't look too bad either."

"It's good," she said. "Shame I'm not all that hungry. Maybe I'll save a half to take to Guin."

Ryan smiled. "I'm sure he'll love it too."

Before long, Ryan was down to his last couple of bites. He was full now, but if necessary, he could squeeze dessert. He would've needed to kill more time anyway, since Steve had yet to be seen. Leilah kept looking for him, with her inconspicuous glances towards the entrance. And there he was, making his way to their table. She displayed no immediate reaction, and neither did Ryan. They scrutinized his expression. He seemed remarkably calm given all that had happened. The debriefing must have went smoothly.

"I see you guys managed to stuff yourselves," he said, slipping into the booth with Ryan. He wasted no time in placing his order with the table.

"I guess it's safe to say you have nothing disastrous to report," Leilah said, watching as he made his selections.

"It's too soon to tell what kind of situation we're in," Steve said. "But chances are we're going to face some kind of fallout. I suspect sooner than later."

"So we still don't have a concrete assessment of who we're dealing with?"

Steve shook his head. "Nothing yet. We're currently trying to find an outlet for communication, but we're having no such luck."

Ryan was finishing the last piece of his burger, savoring the flavor for as long as he could. Once he swallowed, he turned to Steve.

"Leilah was showing me a map of this sector," he said. "It showed us heading back to Cyannus. Is that right?"

"Sure is. It was a direct order from Roland."

"Did Roland have anything else to say?" Leilah asked.

Steve shook his head again. In the process, it seemed to wash away his sunny mood.

"No. He was pretty succinct with his statement."

"He had nothing to say about what happened on Lylid?"

"No, not really. He said what happened was unfortunate, and that we needed to consolidate our forces back at home. That's it."

Leilah appeared suspicious. "I know Roland is a man of few words, but the brevity of this response is a little strange, even for him."

Steve was left bemused.

"Now that I think of it, I don't think there was any chance of a favorable outcome. They were ready to stick a knife in Ryan. It's likely we both would have died had those penguins not shown up. Speaking of them, is that one still in isolation?"

"Yeah," Leilah said. "He's contained inside the Conoblis."

"Was he unconscious when you left?"

Leilah paused for just a second, refreshing herself with the lie she fabricated earlier.

"Yes, he's out cold. No pun intended."

Steve cracked a smile.

"I'd say we should have someone take a look at him, but it'd be far too risky. It'd be remarkable if we could bring back a specimen like that alive. But I guess we have bigger problems on our plate."

Ryan was already contemplating the way they would respond when they found out that Guin was conscious and well on his way to making a full recovery. They would most likely consider him a liability. If only Guin could maintain some sort of composure when confronted, maybe they'd spare him any cruel treatment.

The waitress came by again, and set down Steve's drink on the table. This one looked yellow. Some kind of beer perhaps? Steve took a sip of it. Leilah waited until he set the glass back down.

"Did Reynard have anything to say about the penguins, and their unusual characteristics?"

"His best explanation is that they have something to do with a privatized project to weaponize animals during the period before the freeze over. Few details were ever officially disclosed, but he says it has to do with alteration of their DNA, which I guess can account for the claws. But—"

"But that doesn't make much sense," Ryan said, finishing the sentence. "Why would anyone want to weaponize a penguin? Wouldn't it be more effective to weaponize an animal that's naturally more dangerous? And smarter? Like a T-Rex?"

"I was thinking the same thing," Leilah said. "Doesn't seem to make much sense. What's a T-Rex?"

"You're right, it doesn't," Steve said. "And when you consider their method of engagement, it wouldn't be viable anywhere else than on an icy plain. It's great if you're going to storm an arctic region, but anything else and all you'll have is a clump of slow, waddling penguins. Not to mention, you'd still need them to exhibit a high level of intelligence if they were going to be of any use. I'm not sure penguins can be trained in that sort of capacity."

If only he knew, Ryan thought, that Guin was capable of speech. Would that make him seem more or less dangerous in his eyes? Ryan figured that if Guin were the rash, raging animal that he first appeared to be, he'd be more dangerous, simply because without a method of communication, there would be no way to be diplomatic. His instincts would be set to kill, and there would be nothing anyone could do to shut that down. But since Guin could speak, he could be bargained with. Would it take more than a couple of fish fillets? Ryan didn't know, but he guessed he would find out shortly.

"I don't think penguins are capable of high-level thinking either," Leilah said, continuing the ruse. "Scientifically speaking, it is fascinating the way they were able to carry out that attack. At the very least, they seemed competent as predators."

"I agree," Steve said. "It's scary to see a group of tame birds turn into a pack of vicious hunters."

"Can DNA manipulation really do that?" Ryan asked. He was holding the brim of his plate, wishing he had more food to pick up.

"I think it can, to some degree. But I'm no expert."

"What about their super strength? The way they tore through that robot—I don't think any kind of DNA configuration can grant them the strength to do something like that."

"I don't know," Steve said, starting to sound very confused. "There's no telling what kind of experimentation they've been subjected to. And I'm not sure there's anyone left who knows."

"Maybe Guin knows," Ryan said. He knew if Guin's kind had the ability to speak, the knowledge of what went down during those earlier years may have been preserved. But just as he made that remark, he saw the change in Steve's face and realized his blunder. Leilah pretended not to notice.

"Who's Guin?" Steve asked, looking quizzically at Ryan. Ryan shifted his eyes at Leilah, who in return, shifted hers to Steve. Ryan knew if an answer wasn't supplied, he'd only grow increasingly suspicious. He was relieved when Leilah finally spoke.

"It's the penguin we have in isolation. Ryan decided to give him a name."

"Really," Steve said, looking back at Ryan.

Ryan nodded. "I did."

"I don't get it."

"Don't get what?" Leilah said.

Steve looked back at Ryan.

"I don't get why you would give a name to an animal that tried to kill us—an animal that probably won't live long enough to see the end of this trip."

Ryan didn't have an explanation. He couldn't think of one in time either. Steve was going to find out sooner or later, as well as everyone else. There was no point in prolonging the inevitable. He may as well divulge the truth right now.

"I didn't exactly name him," Ryan said.

"Then where does the name Guin come from?"

Ryan's eyes drifted towards Leilah again. She gave no visual cue that he shouldn't continue.

"He told me his name."

There was a long silence between the three of them. No one was talking, no one knew what to say. Only their faces spoke, and Steve's was speaking quite loud and clear. He wasn't gladdened by the news, nor intrigued in the slightest. Maybe at first, but then his expression grew sour. He seemed a bit angry, and even betrayed.

"So it can speak?"

"Yeah," Ryan said.

He turned his head, his eyes fell on Leilah.

"So it's not unconscious?" he asked with indignation. "The animal is awake?"

Leilah pressed her lips together tightly and looked down at her half-finished plate. She brought her arms on top of the table and leaned forward.

"I'm sorry," she said. "I didn't want to lie to you, but I knew you'd panic if I told you the truth. I didn't want you to react rashly."

He lowered his head, with his mouth ajar.

"My reaction is irrelevant," he said. "It's your duty as an officer aboard this station to report any information that may pose a threat to us. I don't need to remind you of the dangerous situation we're in. We really don't need any more problems."

"He wasn't going to hurt us," Leilah said.

"And how would you know that?"

"Because he isn't stupid." Her voice got a little louder. "He isn't a mindless animal. He's intelligent enough to know if he pulls a stunt here his life will be over."

Ryan listened as the hostility of the conversation worsened. He didn't want it to escalate any further. He did what he could to intercede.

"I approached Guin first," Ryan said, before Steve could respond. "And Leilah is right. If he wanted to harm us, he could have. But he didn't."

"Maybe you got lucky," Steve said, keeping a gentler voice with Ryan. "He may have been injured badly enough that he couldn't attack."

Ryan kept quiet. Steve reverted his attention back to Leilah, his face stricken with emotion.

"Why did you have to get close to it in the first place? Why would you take such a huge unnecessary risk like that, especially after the account I gave you of what happened down there? Why would you do that?"

He was distressed, at a loss for words. Leilah wasn't saying anything, and with her silence, he seemed to grow only more suspicious. He was looking at her, studying her, trying to figure out what she wasn't telling him. That's when he noticed her jacket, and the dark colored blotches on the end of her sleeve.

"What is that," he said, motioning with his head.

Leilah looked down and saw the incriminating evidence.

"It's blood," she admitted bitterly.

Steve stared with contempt. Everything was clear now.

"So you did what I think you did. You personally tended him?"

"Yes," she said. "I treated him."

Steve was shaking his head. He was flustered, he didn't know where to look. He threw his hand up and let it fall down to the table.

"I can't tell you how stupid that was," he said. "You're damn lucky that animal didn't tear you apart."

"I knew what I was doing."

"No, you didn't" Steve snapped back. "With situations like this, you never know. That's why we have a system in place that dictates what we need to do when the situation goes astray, so we don't make costly mistakes like this."

"There was no mistake."

"There could have easily been one. And it wouldn't have been just you putting yourself at risk, but Ryan as well."

Ryan could see it in her face. Leilah was distraught, maybe more so than Steve. She clearly didn't want it to come to this, but it did.

"You know," Steve said. "Sometimes I think you picked the wrong line of work. This isn't the kind of job you can do by acting on a whim, or by following your intuition. People are fallible, and they can make serious errors when they're not careful." Steve tried to calm himself, tried to keep his voice low. "I respect your ability to be compassionate in times like this, I really do. But the truth of the matter is, it's dangerous in a time of war. There's many lives on the line, and we have to take the course of action that does the best job of guaranteeing their safety."

Leilah didn't say anything. She even stopped looking at him. The next thing she knew, she was leaving the table in a hurry. Before she could take more than a couple of steps, Steve called out to her.

"Where are you going?"

"To the sim room," she said coldly.

"Why?"

"So I can train to be more like you."

Steve watched as she left the diner, with a tinge of regret on his face. Ryan didn't think he intended to upset her, but it happened anyway. And he knew there was really nothing that could be done about it right now other than to let it blow over.

—)—

Leilah traveled hurriedly through the station, returning to the central rotunda, where she took the stairs up to C deck. She was heading to the simulation room solely as a means of reprieve. Though the ERR regimen was rigorous and sometimes treacherous, it provided a method of escape and recuperation. It was like taking a long sleep. You'd wake up feeling better than you did before, and whatever trials you had to endure during that sleep would be forgotten anyway. Yet supposedly, they were still able to alter your mind, in a way that was unobservable. Leilah didn't have much faith in its effectiveness. She believed that a person was still in full control of their thoughts and actions while awake, and that their subconscious was nothing more than a prattling voice that could be ignored. Though the simulations were as lucid as anything found in real life, they were still just a fabrication of the mind. It was no different than trying to comprehend color in a world that was black and white. You'd never truly understand it until you saw it first hand. Nevertheless, she played along with the system. She had a quota to reach, as everyone else did, so why not kill two birds with one stone.

She moved through the curving corridor until she reached an area with a row of long glass panes. They wrapped around the corner of the hall and continued down the adjacent corridor. The facility's entrance was at that corner, shaped like a circle. Leilah walked on through.

Simulation rooms were always designed to suggest an experience opposite to what you actually got. The floors were fitted with white porcelain tiles, with potted ferns on either side of the sign-in desk. Behind that was a wooden wall, with the middle segment composed of fitted stones. A cascade trickled through them, into the basin below. On the ceiling were lights behind tinted glass, filling the room with a warm, creamy veneer. With these kinds of embellishments, no one could expect what awaited them on the other side.

Leilah approached the man behind the desk and handed him her identification card. He swiped it into the system and invited her to take any room. They were all vacant. He handed the card back to her and she took the path that led to the rear of the facility.

The environment became darker, and the white tiles changed to black. All the light and color of the room was emitted by the cube-shaped chambers that lay abreast to one another, from wall to wall. They were made of frosted glass, like perfectly sculpted ice cubes. They were cool and inviting, a place where one might feel a sense of serenity—a place where one goes to lie dormant.

Leilah stepped inside the first room on her left, passing through the automated door. The room was eight feet by eight feet, holding nothing more than essential components. There was a computer console to her right, which would set up the simulation. Besides that, a narrow tub, filled with a magenta colored liquid.

She inserted her card into the console and initiated the program. The system scanned her data, her previous records and performances, and compiled an appropriate trial. Ultimately, the system would do little more than regulate the thoughts that already existed inside her own head. It would take the things she knew, the things she experienced, and restructure them to create a new scenario for her to overcome. Over time, these new experiences would be added to her library of memories, which would allow the system to draw from a larger pool of options. The only real criticism with this method was that the system would make affirmations regarding things that were only theoretically correct. A simple example would be one where a person's hand is struck by a ten pound object. The system may assess the pain to a value of 10. Now if the system wanted to exert pain of a value of 20, it may strike the person's hand twice with the ten pound weight, thinking it may be the equivalent, even though in actuality, this would be a fallacy. But as things were, this was the only method that would allow the system to impose increasingly difficult challenges.

Leilah didn't know what kind of trial was awaiting her. But it was all just the same, as she wouldn't remember it anyway after it was over.

She moved next to the tub, and gazed into the radiant liquid. Once inside, it would regulate her core temperature, keeping her cool during periods of severe agony and stress, which had been known to cause the body to overheat. Secondly, it monitored pulsations and movement throughout the body. The tub was outlined with sensors that would pick up the vibrations, alerting the system if something was abnormal.

She turned around and slipped out of her jacket, and threw it onto the shelf. The sleeves hung over, revealing the blood stains to her once again. She began questioning if it really was a mistake, but quickly repressed the thoughts. She finished undressing and piled her clothes on the shelf.

She took one step into the tub, and then another. She gripped the brim and allowed herself to be submerged into the liquid. It was a cool, gel-like substance, that felt like it was wet, but wasn't.

She let her head fall back on the padded headrest and waited as a mechanical limb moved forth and brought an oblong plate above her forehead. She closed her eyes and allowed the low hum of the machine to put her into a sedated state. After that, everything was quiet. She didn't know where she was, or where she was heading. In the moments that followed, she saw hints of color, heard bits of sound, and the feeling of solid earth beneath her feet. But something about it was inherently wrong. Something wasn't right. She *knew* something wasn't right. She cried out loud.

The trial had begun.

—)—

"I'm sorry, Ryan," Steve was saying. "I didn't mean to get upset like that. "It's just that I don't want to see any more carnage. What I saw down on Lylid was enough for one day."

"I don't blame you," Ryan said. "I really don't want to have to see that again either."

Steve wrapped his hand around his glass, gripping it tightly.

"I just didn't want anything to happen to her. "She's the only one—"

He cut himself off, and looked blankly at the empty booth across from him, then down at his drink. He twitched his eyes. Ryan noticed something was amiss.

"Only what?"

"Nothing," Steve said. He lifted his glass and took a sip. Maybe he was just nervous, Ryan figured.

"I'm sure Leilah believes that you just care about her. I don't think she's the kind of person that holds a grudge."

"No, she isn't. She always finds a way to put up with me. She was even the one who requested that we be assigned to the same unit. Had she not said anything, I don't think we'd even be in contact right now." He stared up at the ceiling, into the lights. "Sometimes I wonder what it would have been like if things were different."

"Different how?" Ryan asked.

"If it had been Leilah rather than Stephanie."

It didn't even seem like he was speaking directly to Ryan, but ruminating out loud. He hadn't even realized that he had never made mention of Stephanie to Ryan. It was Leilah that brought it up. Ryan decided not to point that out.

"But you love Stephanie," Ryan said. "You're happy to be with her, right?"

"Of course. I just think about it sometimes, just to indulge my curiosity. Because it could have happened, just as easily. Had I chose differently, my future would have forked in a another direction. I like to think that future exists somewhere out there, so that it gives purpose to my pondering."

"I wouldn't think about it too much," Ryan said. "Chances are the only life you'll know is the one you have now."

Steve withdrew his head from the clouds and gave Ryan an appreciative look.

"You're right, Ryan. You're definitely right."

There was a crackling sound coming from somewhere on the ceiling. Ryan immediately associated it with being in school, whenever there was an announcement on the intercom. Apparently someone had something to say, but there was a distinct absence of a voice. It took a moment before anything was said.

"Attention all crew members . . ."

The murmurs in the room all died at once. Everyone gave their full attention to the voice. Again there was a silent pause following the initial words—words which seemed to be spoken with difficulty.

Ryan and Steve looked up at the ceiling.

"This is your captain speaking . . ."

Again another pause. Without a doubt, something wasn't right. Ryan could tell, if only by looking at the faces of the other people in the room. They were apprehensive, filled with worry.

They didn't dare move or blink an eye. But if they were scared, then Steve was terrified. It's almost as if he knew what was coming. It certainly didn't make Ryan feel any more comfortable. And then the voice continued:

". . . *with immeasurable regret I must inform you all that Cyannus has been destroyed.*"

————CHAPTER 15————

BURNING BRIGHT

The words lingered in the air, long after they were spoken. No one could make sense of them. No one, with any degree of certainty, could be sure if they understood correctly. The outlandish message was incomprehensible. The officers in the room conversed among themselves, asking one another to reiterate what was said, because frankly, the news was unthinkable.

The captain's voice came on speaker again.

". . . I'll repeat . . . Cyannus has been destroyed. Nothing remains. The planet . . . is gone."

A clamor rose in the dining room as people digested the message. There was no equivocation, no denying what actually took place. Cyannus was gone; their home was gone. They were now nothing more than a couple of people marooned in an empty corner of space, sentenced there by the forces of fate. They couldn't grasp the circumstances that would have led to such a catastrophic act. It was crazy, mindless, and unfathomable.

The hairs on Ryan's skin stood on end, as a cold chill swept through his body. His mouth felt very dry, and his heart was pulsating rapidly. He didn't know what to think, or how to respond. For the first time since he got here, his mind felt empty. He looked at the other people in the room, and saw their faces.

They reciprocated the look of utter confusion, fear even—every ghastly emotion all at once.

It was pain compounded by pain. Another thorn pierced his heart when he remembered that Megan was there. He left her at the museum, left her awaiting his return. But now . . . she was gone? It didn't seem possible. He couldn't imagine her not being alive. He saw her standing there, talking to him not that long ago. How could—

Steve sprung up from the booth with impulsive haste, as if the band that was holding him together had just snapped. He darted out of the room, without uttering a single word. Ryan was left in the dark as to his intentions, which only incited further perturbation. He wasn't going to stay here alone, not through a crisis like this. He gave chase after Steve.

He followed him out the diner, into the dim corridor. He was moving fast, at a speed that even Ryan struggled to keep up with. He was ready to call out, tell him to wait up, but there would have been no point. Ryan knew what he had lost, and that he would not let down for any reason. He had trouble himself coping with the fact that Megan was gone. It was an inconceivable reality that couldn't be fully processed. It was not like he could see a dead body lying before him, that he could morn and grieve over. This was different. She was gone. And the last memory he had of her was one where she was alive and well.

They were coming around the northern end of the corridor. Steve turned suddenly down another that led towards the central part of the station.

Ryan was growing tired. His body felt heavy, as if he were trekking through a field of mud. But maybe it was just the weight of despondency, the weight of endeavoring for no hope of an award.

Steve entered the rotunda, quickly jumping onto the staircase, trotting up two or three steps at a time. He was panting, holding on to the handrails for support. Ryan gazed up exhaustively at the height of the chamber. Where was he going?

Ryan took his first step onto the stairs.

A quake suddenly erupted right underneath his feet. He staggered forward, falling onto the stairs. Everything was shaking violently. The room was creaking, rattling uncontrollably. The walls felt like a tower of cards ready to collapse. Ryan wanted to climb back on his feet, but every time he tried to steady himself he was thrown onto the stairs.

He looked up, and saw Steve clenching the handrail tightly, steadily climbing one step at a time.

Ryan tried once again to stand up, but was lurched back onto the ground. He fell against the edge of the step, bruising his arm.

"Steve!" he yelled.

He was scared now, thinking whatever fate befell Megan would befall him too. Perhaps this was the attack, the retribution for the debacle that took place on Lylid. He just didn't expect such a quick response. This was it, he thought. He was going to die.

Everything became black. But it wasn't the end. The room was still vibrating. He could still feel the throbbing pain from falling over. He could still remember where he was.

His vision flickered. The stairwell appeared and disappeared. The lights were trying to stay on. Shadows flashed across the chamber. Ryan tried to keep climbing, despite the intermittent blindness.

The strength of the tremors lessened, the electrical power now stable. Ryan was able to stay on his feet. He held on to the handrail in the event of another quake.

Steve was nearly one flight ahead. Ryan kept a close watch, waiting to see what floor he would get off on. They already passed D deck and C deck. Steve vanished shortly thereafter. He must have got off on the B deck. Ryan had little doubt that he had gone anywhere else.

He saw several crew members pouring through the surrounding corridors. Each of them were herding themselves into the same passage: east on B deck. Assuming they knew where they were going, he followed the mob as they hurried through the narrow hall. He brushed shoulders against many of them, while trying hard not to be trampled. Steve was already lost in the bustling crowd.

The path opened up into a small vestibule, the room that preceded the bridge. There were many people scrambling to get through the entranceway, pushing and shoving, a total lack of propriety. Others that had already seen what they came for were forcing their way out.

They were ridden with indescribable anguish, a look of shock that had them staggering against the walls. Their faces were flush, their eyes moist with tears. Some were on the verge of hyperventilating. Others took to a corner and disgorged the contents of their stomachs. They had entered the bridge, only to be inoculated with an unprecedented horror. Not even their training or rigorous simulations could have prepared them for this. This was more than any of them were able to handle. They couldn't walk; they couldn't breath; they couldn't speak. These people had collapsed to the floor, with their backs against the wall. They couldn't move; some were barely able to cry. They stared blankly into space, as if their lives had already been claimed.

Ryan wished the others wouldn't follow suit and enter the bridge. He didn't really want to himself, but morbid curiosity got the best of him.

He slipped through the entranceway and into the bridge. It was a dark room, the size of a small theater. The dimness was probably to prevent interference with the holographic chart projections. He was at the top of a staircase that led down to a mezzanine that overlooked all the station's consoles. He had to go down there if he wanted a view of the outside.

The room was teeming with a soft red glow that glimmered off every metallic surface. It filled the mind with images of blood and fire, blazing infernos and widespread murder. The cries of the victims could almost be heard calling from the traces of shadow.

Ryan came down the stairs, careful not to get shoved. He nearly tripped on the last step. He fumbled forward, but caught himself on the handrail of the mezzanine just in time. That's when he came face to face with the source of the burning glow.

He looked dead ahead, his eyes consumed by the spectacle of color.

The black plane of space had suffered a tremendous wound. An amorphous cloud of dust and gas permeated across the darkness—a pouch of effulgent blood spilled under a black sea. Tendrils of vaporized rock sprawled in all directions, forming a burning smog of matter. The cloud continued to grow, spreading like wildfire. There was nothing left, nothing but a painful testament to what once was.

It was a savage attack, swift, without warning. It left them scarred, without hope, without any sense of purpose. They couldn't even tap into their pool of anger. They witnessed their lives being destroyed, in the most literal sense. It was an image they wanted to forget, but it was already burned into their memory. It was all they could see when they closed their eyes. It's what they would never forget—that seeping wound in space—that cloud of complete utter destruction.

Gone, Ryan thought. Everyone was gone. *She* was gone.

He looked away from the window, unable to bear the sight any longer. Instead he now saw the collection of overwrought faces that were trying to come to terms with what they were witnessing. Steve was among them, at the far end of the mezzanine. He seemed unaffected, for the most part, in the sense that he looked no different than he did just a minute ago before he entered the bridge. He kept a cold, empty expression, as if he were resisting the natural urge to cry out. But then he fled. He left the room, just like the others.

Ryan did the same, but he had no intentions of catching up with him, nor did he want to. Right now he just wanted to separate himself from the crowd, and find a place without all the clamor.

He returned to the rotunda, and started to head back down the stairs. He didn't know what to do, or where to go. There was no place on this station that could bring him solace right now. He felt disoriented and light headed. He grabbed onto the handrail, right at the base of the stairs.

He remembered what he could about Megan: like the times they played basketball in elementary school; the time that she beat him in that pivotal game; the birthday party they celebrated in Pinesburrow Park. But the longer he mused over these memories, the harder they were to see. They were being marginalized by the memories from earlier today—the ones that were weird and nonsensical. And when he pieced that together with what Steve said about the Layers of Perception, he was able to deduce, once again, that this was a dream. He shouldn't have been worrying. There was nothing to worry about. Given enough time, he should wake up. But *why*, he cried in his head. Why was it so difficult to accept that? Knowing that he was asleep didn't help to quell his lamenting.

. . . *Why?*

He lifted his head, and noticed before him a sign posted, detailing all the facilities on C deck. Only one of them struck his interest: the simulation room. That's where Leilah was going. Now that he thought about it, he hadn't seen her in the throng of officers. Her red hair alone should have been enough to spot her in a crowd. She wasn't there, which meant there was a strong likelihood she was still undergoing the simulation, oblivious to what was going on.

Ryan had a premonition. It was important that she was accounted for.

He exited the stairwell and took the north corridor, as indicated by the sign. He followed the path, passing a few stragglers along the way. After that the halls were empty. The station had become creepily quiet. All he could hear was a low hum running through the ceiling.

He came to a juncture and saw the sign for the simulation room pointing left. He followed the corridor, and shortly thereafter he saw the facility, with the long glass panes and the arching entrance. He invited himself inside.

Straight ahead he saw an unattended computer terminal. That wouldn't have been cause for alarm all by itself, but there were also voices coming from around the corner, at least three or four of them. He couldn't make out what they were saying, but their tone was pressing. There was a problem.

He crept past the desk and around the corner of the room. He saw darkness beyond, except for a faint bluish glow. He trod onward, until he was standing inside the chamber. From there he saw the row of glass cubicles. Their glow was alluring, yet at the same time foreboding and noxious. Though the reason for that may have been the group of medics that were surrounding the first cube on the left.

They were men dressed in white outfits, huddled around a steel plated tub. One was setting up a gurney while the other three were reaching inside the water, wrapping their arms around whatever they were trying to pull out.

Ryan could barely see, but he didn't want to get closer. They didn't know he was there. If they did, they may have asked him to leave. But he couldn't leave. He had to see. He had to be sure.

"On three—", one of the medics said. He started to count, and on three, each of the men hauled up the body of a young woman.

Ryan could see all but her face as they transferred her to the gurney. She was limp, unmoving, still as a corpse. They took her wrist, and got a read on her pulse. They attached an oxygen mask, and wrapped her in a blanket. The group of men held onto the gurney and rushed out of the cubicle. They came within a few feet of Ryan, and that's when he caught a glimpse of her face.

He stood motionless as they wheeled her out. He felt cold. He felt like the events of today were unfolding too fast. Things stopped feeling real, or maybe they were just too real. He didn't know what to think anymore.

The other officer inside the cubicle stepped out. He noticed Ryan and walked over to him. The fear was in his eyes, but it wasn't like that of the others. It was obvious he didn't *see* the calamity.

"What happened," Ryan asked him, stifling his tears.

The man looked away, regretfully.

"There was a system malfunction, and she's been trapped in a sedative state."

"Are they going to be able to help her?"

"We don't know yet. Hopefully they can."

Hopefully, Ryan thought. It was hard to be hopeful when worlds were crumbling apart. Things were spiraling out of control, in a manner that seemed unstoppable.

He left the facility and walked back out into the corridor. He sat on the carpet, and rested his head against the wall. It was still quiet there. But of course it would be, Ryan said angrily to himself. That's what happens when lives are eradicated. There's perpetual silence. Perhaps billions of lives had perished, taking away with it billions of lifetimes of memory. There was no surer, more thorough method of destruction. Because the mind was something that couldn't be rebuilt. Once gone, it was gone forever.

Ryan cherished his ability to conceive such thoughts; he

could appreciate the cognizance that came with being alive. All he felt like doing now was thinking, and recalling every blissful memory he still had access to—the amenities of home, the joy of being with friends, the gratification of gorging down a zesty meal. Whatever it was, he was glad and appreciative that he could remember it.

CHAPTER 16

THE DEATH OF A MIND

The morning sun spilled in through the window, filling Ryan's room with a burst of sunshine. He buried his face in his pillow and kept his eyes shut. He needed time to remember his dreams, because if he didn't recall them right away, he would forget them.

What he remembered was unreal. A planet was destroyed, and it caused great turmoil. Many people died—among them, Megan. Then there was the man with the black jacket and motorcycle. He must have perished too. But not before leaving Ryan with cryptic words of caution: *Don't make the mistake of passing this off as being just a dream*. He remembered the words exactly as they were spoken. His voice was still clear in his mind. He wanted to dismiss it as a product of his imagination, but he couldn't. The words were not drawn from his consciousness, he was sure. They were spoken by another, someone with their own mind and will, as was also the case with Steve, Leilah, or even that penguin, Guin, and all that they had said. But as real as it felt, it didn't seem rational to give it much credence. After all, the mind was capable of fabricating some pretty elaborate dreams during REM sleep. He had his fair share of them in the past. But this one was just . . . weird.

Ryan opened his eyes, relieved to find himself back inside his room. Everything appeared the same as when he last saw it. His desk was in front of him, covered with papers and textbooks. On the floor beside it was a waste basket, filled to the brim with nap-kins and candy wrappers (he was once able to stack the trash eight inches high before it toppled). To the left of that, in the corner, was a small television set, with several video game systems connected to it. Beyond that, the window, and adjacent to his bed, his nightstand. He looked at his alarm clock and saw that the time was 10:24, which seemed plausible, given the strength of the sun. Everything seemed normal here.

With a lion's yawn, he swung his feet off the right side of the bed and planted them on the floor. He stood up and was startled. He staggered back onto the bed. *How in the heck*, he thought, when he saw Bee resting on the floor. *It followed me. It found me.*

No it didn't, Ryan realized. It wasn't Bee. It was just his bas-ketball. He left his closet open and somehow it rolled out. But damn, did it give him a scare.

He picked it up off the floor and laid it gently back in the closet, on top of the stack of old board games. He shut the closet door.

He went out into the hall, where the air was infused with the appetizing scent of sizzling bacon. His mom must have been downstairs preparing breakfast, as she usually did on the week-ends.

She was a young mother, having married shortly after gradu-ating from college. She put in a few years as an elementary teach-er before succumbing to the calls of child raising. Ryan spent time in a daycare during his toddler years, but was quickly pulled after he caught pneumonia from one of the other kids. He was on the verge of death, and the doctor had gone through about a half-dozen different antibiotics before he was cured. Chalk it up to paranoia, but she became a stay-at-home mom after that. It wasn't until several years later, after having Ryan's brother Timothy, that she returned to school as a substitute teacher. Each of them would dread that rare occasion when she was assigned to one of their classes. It was unavoidable, being that she could be called in to any of the schools in the township. She always promised though, not to do anything that would embarrass them (too much). As a matter of fact, she was one of those substitutes that the students had hoped to get. It wasn't that difficult to win over a class of sugar-driven kids. Just bring in a box of doughnuts, or a bowl of candy, and promise to throw on a movie if they got their work done early. And of course, pretend to hate the assignments as much as they do.

Ryan's dad on the other hand, was a simple man, a lot more laid back. He went to college and earned a degree in business. Afterward he landed a job as a real estate appraiser, which he kept for only two years. Whenever he entered a residence, he would rarely keep his eyes off the items in the house, as oppose to the house itself. This drove him to revisit an old pastime from when he was younger. He used to enjoy rummaging through yard sales with his father, picking out gems at a fraction of what they would go for retail. For a kid, this meant action figures, roller skates, skate boards, toy guns, and the like. The economy was rough at the time, and this was the only means by which he could acquire such items. Later on, as he got older, he saw the potential for profit. Every week someone would be putting out something worth a pretty penny. It was just a matter of finding it. So in a way, it was a treasure hunt, a quest to seek out the valuables. After many years, he had procured an ample collection, which prompted him to do what he had been wanting to do for quite some time: open up a pawn shop. He was there right now, looking to secure a deal with a man that was bringing in an vintage toy collection. Today was a day for Timmy to stay out of the store, as his mom would say.

Ryan went down the stairs, into the kitchen, and took a seat at the table. His mom was bringing over a plate of scrambled eggs and bacon.

"Had you snoozed another five minutes, you would have missed it," his mom said.

"I was tired," Ryan answered. "School drained me."

"School drained your brother as well. But not enough for him to say no to an afternoon at Kyle's house. Heard they invited some friends over for street hockey. Then to top off their day, they stuffed themselves with hot dogs and pretzels before finally falling asleep in front of the TV."

"Sounds like he had a wonderful time." Meanwhile, a couple blocks down, he had been getting his ass kicked during a public spectacle. He hadn't forgotten how lousy and miserable he felt when he was forced to make that humiliating walk of shame off the court. Had there been school today, it would have been front page news. But fortunately there was the weekend, which, with any luck, would wash away that incident from people's minds. But who was he kidding. No one would forget. Blake wouldn't let that happen. He managed to muscle Ryan right under his thumb, putting him in a most difficult position. Even Mike and Megan were forced into covert operations. Now he thought that love note was a terrible idea, and he feared that Megan wasn't going to keep her cover. Blake would find out, and further humiliation would ensue. The whole thing was just one giant quagmire.

A figure capered from the den into the kitchen. It was Timmy, taking his breakfast break from Saturday morning cartoons.

He was eight years old, with the same light brown hair and thin, bony body as his brother. They got along well, for the most part, when they weren't arguing about what sport was better, or who tracked dirt into the house. The worst incident to ever take place was probably the time Ryan accidentally whacked Timmy in the face with a hockey stick, knocking the then 48 pound kid right off his feet. He acquired a few stitches in the process, which he was very enthusiastic about. For a long time, he used the incident to guilt Ryan into doing his bidding. But the nifty tactic eventually grew stale, and had become ineffective.

Timmy landed in his seat, took hold of his fork, and then stared at Ryan's plate.

"Are you sure you want your bacon?"

Ryan stopped mid-bite and gave Timmy a petulant stare.

"Why do you keep asking that? When have I ever given any indication that I would give up my bacon?"

"I don't know. Just making sure you don't change your mind."

Timmy got to work on his helping. Ryan was still looking at him.

"You don't even like bacon. Why do you always eat so much of it?"

"I need the protein."

"You don't know anything about protein."

"I know it makes your muscles grow."

"No. *Exercising* makes your muscles grow."

"But it still helps."

"There is a thing as too much protein, you know."

"I'm a kid. I'm growing. I need protein," his voice pitched with the last word.

"I think you mean calcium."

"That too. Mom, I need milk."

"All right," she answered on her way to the fridge. "Don't get too over-eager. You don't want to get too big. Then you have to shop for new clothes."

Timmy appeared spooked.

"Half a glass. No more," he said, slicing the air with his hand.

She returned with the glass and took a seat at the table. The two boys munched noisily, observing each others progress for some inexplicable reason.

Timmy looked up with an epiphany.

"Yesterday was Friday," he said.

Ryan's head sunk. He knew where this was going.

"You had that game yesterday. Against that bully."

"What bully?" Mom said worriedly, putting down her cup of coffee.

Ryan said, "There is no bully. Timmy's confused."

"Not uh. You told me there was this guy at school that wanted to kick your ass and make you look like a doofus."

"Timmy," his mother warned him.

"Figuratively speaking," Ryan said.

"Ryan, is there a bully?"

"No. There is no bully. I was just playing a game of basketball with someone."

"Did you win?" Timmy asked.

Ryan didn't want to answer that. In fact, he wondered why he had mentioned it to Timmy in the first place. He couldn't even lie about it, because if he had won, Timmy would have expected him to have mentioned it by now. There really wasn't anything he could do to stop the truth from getting out.

"He pulverized you!" Timmy said, getting excited.

"No, he didn't."

"What was the score?"

"There was no score."

"I bet it was zero to a hundred."

"No, but zero to a hundred is about how fast you're going to accelerate down the street next time I see you wearing skates."

"Cool. I'll tell Kyle to set up the ramp."

Ryan went back to eating his breakfast. Out of the corner of his eye, he could see his mother staring at the two of them like they were a couple of, well, troublemakers. And just when he thought Timmy was finished, he started up again.

"You should have scheduled it for next week so I could have been there. I could have been selling snacks, and taking bets. I could have been a bookie! What do you think your odds were?"

Ryan swallowed the eggs in his mouth, and then put down his fork. He turned to Timmy and looked at him sternly.

"Timmy, remember when I said I'll get you that action figure for your birthday?"

Timmy nodded innocently.

"If you want it, you better stop talking about what happened yesterday."

"Ryan," his mom said, "don't blackmail your brother. And Timmy, stop provoking him. If he wants to tell you about his basketball game, then he'll tell you. So until then, don't make accusations." She turned to Ryan again. "Now Ryan, are you sure there's no trouble going on at school?"

If she was referring to the 'bully', then no, he didn't think there was. To call Blake a bully would be to downplay his artfulness. Even Ryan had to give credit where credit was due. Blake's means never employed any physicality, or even verbal assault. Instead, he managed to extract and exploit Ryan's own insecurities and self-doubts. So in a way, Ryan was his own worst enemy, and all Blake did was hold up the mirror. The guy had gotten into his head and made a home in there, like some sort of pigeon. Now if only there were some way to evict him. But then to compound the issue, there was Karina, literally walking out on him. His chances with her were now a million to one shot, if there was even a shot at all. His mind was filled with the slew of thoughts she must have had right after the game. *What a sad performance, what an overhyped player, what a waste of time*. But it didn't matter. His desire to be with her was still just as strong. He had to make an attempt, even if he would inevitably crash and burn. He was confident he could find a way, all on his own.

"No," he said to his mother. "There's no trouble."

He returned to his meal, as if nothing were wrong. His mom seemed to buy his answer. Timmy was holding on to a smirk.

The telephone rung, and Timmy sprung from his seat to retrieve it, while yelling "I'll get it!" Ryan could only think of two reasons why Timmy would be so ardent about answering it. Either he was expecting a call from one of his friends, or he thought Dad was calling about the toy collection he was planning to purchase.

Timmy nabbed the phone off the wall.

"Hello," he said. A second later, the excitement left his face. "Yeah, he's here. Hey, did you see him play yesterday? I heard he bombed."

"Who is that?" Ryan asked. When Timmy didn't respond immediately, he got impatient. He stood up from his seat.

"Okay, okay," Timmy said into the phone. "He's coming."

Ryan snatched the phone from Timmy's hand and went into the next room. He held it up to his ear.

"Hello," he said.

He heard a familiar voice. It was Megan.

"Hello? Is that you Ryan?"

It was almost strange to hear her voice, given that there was a partition of his mind that was still trying to cope with her death. If anything, speaking to her now was evidence that he was awake. And for that, he was glad.

"Yeah, it's me."

"Thank God. That brother of yours is so tenacious."

"I know. He can be a pain sometimes."

"Ask me and I'll say most of the time." There was a short pause. He could hear her take a deep breath. "Listen Ryan, about yesterday—how've you been holding up?"

Better, Ryan thought. In light of his latest nocturnal tribulation, losing a game of basketball didn't seem all that bad. At best, his otherworldly experience put things into perspective. There were worse things that could happen. But it didn't change the fact that this coming Monday he would be a figure of ridicule.

"I'm doing all right," he said, trying to sound cheery. "I'm not going to let it put a damper on my weekend."

"Looks like you got the right attitude at least. You're going to bounce back, no problem."

"Yeah, I hope."

"What you did was brave. Blake was no slouch. If it was anyone else up against him, we would have had a no-show."

Ryan looked behind. He was expecting to see Timmy listening in, but he was still, shockingly, in the kitchen.

"But he was out for my blood, and my blood only. And I think he got a few pints."

"And you'll return the favor someday. But for now, let's worry about today."

"Anything special going on today?"

"Hmm. I guess you haven't turned the TV on yet."

"No, I haven't. What's going on?"

"Tune to the news."

Ryan grabbed the remote and switched the TV on. He flipped to the local news station and saw an aerial view of a city bus parked in a vacant lot. The image didn't make sense to him at first, until the camera panned around, revealing a squad of police cars, covering the perimeter of the property. There was at least twelve of them, along with news vans and civilian onlookers. The officers present were stationed along the cordoned area, with their guns drawn; a few others were on their radios.

Ryan listened to the broadcast.

"—*police are still making efforts to negotiate with the man inside, which we recently confirmed to be Dr. Edmunds—one of the scientists involved in the creation of The Mind. Our latest reports indicate that there are thirty-two hostages inside the vehicle, none of which have been harmed as of yet. We know Edmunds is in posses-*

sion of a firearm, as well as an explosive that he threatens to detonate if his demands are not met."

"What's this all about?" Ryan said. "Why would a scientist hold a bus full of hostages?"

"I have no idea. I've only just tuned in myself."

"This is really weird."

"I know."

And what made it feel weird to Ryan wasn't so much the fact that he was a scientist, but that the scientist was associated with The Mind. He could never explain it, but to him, The Mind had always possessed some pernicious quality. It was like a bad omen; it was a creation that seemed unnatural.

He continued to listen to the broadcast. The scene was minimized to the top-right corner, and a video of Dr. Edmunds appeared in full. He was an older, bespectacled man, perhaps around the age of sixty. He seemed like a well-mannered, amicable individual. It was hard to imagine that a man with such a warm and friendly persona could be capable of committing such an act.

"The man you see here is the well renowned Dr. Edmunds, who over the years has collaborated with many projects in the scientific community, namely those associated with the advancement of artificial intelligence. When The Mind saw its completion last year, it was widely regarded as the culmination of his career, marking many technological breakthroughs. One in particular is an essential component that came about, in part, by pure chance—a subsection of code that was generated through a process that simulates organic propagation. Estimates say that the likelihood of this self-created computation ever occurring again is once every couple hundred of years, which only affirms the importance of this machine to those that have invested the copious amount of time and resources.

"A colleague of Dr. Edmunds, Senior Engineer, and head of the project, Dr. Allanstein, came out two weeks ago issuing a statement regarding concerns Edmunds had brought forth. Edmunds went on record stating that some of the preliminary assessments made by The Mind were, quote, troubling, end quote. He later threatened to disclose this information to the public if The Mind's method of thinking and deduction were not reexamined and revised"

"Are you still there?" Ryan said.

"Yeah, I'm still here."

"I don't like this."

"Me neither. Gives me the creeps."

"Ryan," his mother called. "Come back to breakfast."

He lowered the phone and called back to her. "I'm coming in a minute. There's something important on the news."

"What?"

Timmy came running over from the table. Ordinarily he wouldn't care about the news, but since Ryan found it interesting enough to watch, then he probably would too.

"It's about The Mind," he answered her, as he swatted for Timmy to go away.

"Oh, that silly thing," she said.

"One of the guys that made it is holding people hostage on a bus."

"Holding hostages?" she said, her voice rising in pitch. Next thing Ryan knew, she came into the room as well. All three of them were sitting on the couch. Timmy was hunched forward, his eyes glued on the screen. The only thing notably absent was the bucket of popcorn.

The newscaster continued.

"Allanstein has since issued his own statement regarding Edmunds' remarks. The following video is taken from a broadcast earli-

er this week, in which Allanstein made his statement."

A man, roughly in his forties, appeared on the screen. He had black, short-trimmed hair, and a tailored suit. His face was stern, very serious, his hands folded over the lectern.

"I respect Dr. Edmunds and his contributions to the scientific community. But as of late, he has put forth some dubious claims, which I believe have been induced by paranoia, and his extensive undertaking that was this project. The problem is that Edmunds came on board with the expectations that The Mind would be able to further his political and philosophical outlook. But as soon as there was indication that The Mind would advocate different ideas, he deemed the machine impaired and unsuitable for continued operation. Which means the only issue here is a conflict of ideologies. As there is nothing inherently wrong with our creation, we will continue with the assimilation process, so that The Mind will be able to provide us with the answers that will guide mankind to a better tomorrow."

"This is boring," Timmy said. "What happened to the hostages?"

"Finish your breakfast, Timmy" his mother said. "You shouldn't even be watching this."

But Timmy remained planted in his seat, bent on catching some action.

The news camera revisited the empty lot. The bus remained parked, and the police cruisers were maintaining their perimeter. The scene was stagnant, except for the few officers that were handling communication. The camera continued circling from above, catching the bus from every angle. It zoomed in gradually, until one could faintly make out the passengers herded towards the backside of the bus. Dr. Edmunds was towards the other end, keeping low on one knee, staying below the windows.

The newscaster came back on, announcing that she was going to turn her attention to a reporter at the scene. The woman stood just outside the cordoned area. She spoke.

"I've just received word that the negotiations between Dr. Edmunds and the authorities pertain to The Mind itself. Edmunds is demanding that The Mind be delivered to him directly, so that he could see to its thorough destruction. However, I've been told that this request is highly unlikely to be acceded by any member that holds high stakes in this project. Dr. Allanstein has been apprised of the situation, and his response was, and I quote, I will not be complicit in the destruction of mankind's greatest creation. To lose these lives would be a horrific sacrifice, but we as a people have no other choice. End quote."

"I can't believe this," Ryan's mom said in horror. "We've reached an age where machines take precedent over human life."

"I don't get it," Timmy said. "Why is this brain so important? It just sits in a glass box all day. It doesn't even do anything. They should have at least given it a body so that it could move around."

"Timmy, you don't understand anything," Ryan said, standing up from the couch. He moved to the next room with the phone in his hand.

"Well, I don't know," Timmy said bitterly. "Maybe that has something to do with me being in forth grade?"

Timmy jumped off the couch and followed Ryan into the living room. Each of them took a seat on the big cushioned chairs. They both slouched right away.

"Tell me what's going on," Timmy said, as he grabbed one of the decorative pillows. He clenched the corners and began twisting it into shapes.

Ryan wasn't sure if Timmy was too young to understand. He barely understood the matter himself, but he felt it was important for Timmy to hear an explanation out of his older brother.

"It's sort of complicated," he said. "This brain they've created is suppose to be very smart. Smarter than any person."

"Smarter than Einstein?"

"Yeah, Timmy. Smarter than Einstein."

"So why is that such a bad thing?"

"Because the president, along with many other important people are going to listen to everything this machine says. It's going to be treated like the leader of the world. It's going to tell us the best way to live our lives; it's going to tell our country how to respond to different issues. And this scares a lot of people."

"What's so scary about that?" Timmy said, still gripping the pillow tightly. "Wouldn't it be cool to have a machine as president?"

Ryan sighed. He was clearly no expert in explaining things to 8-year-olds. He decided to try another angle.

"Think of it like this. You know when you're playing a video game and you get some kind of error message?"

"Yeah. I hate it when that happens."

"Right. Now imagine if something similar happened to The Mind."

"You just restart it."

"But it's not that simple. If The Mind got an error, or made a mistake, no one will realize it until it's too late."

He left Timmy looking more confused than what he was a minute ago. Timmy quickly lost interest in the topic. He stood up, tossed the pillow, and returned to the kitchen to finish up what was left of his breakfast.

Ryan stayed on the chair, and gazed at a painting that was hanging on the wall. It was one of those impressionist paintings, the kind that looked like it was painted by thumb. They differed from the traditional style that put emphasis on realistic depictions, and focused more on spontaneous representation. They would view the scene in real life and extract the essence of what they saw, with a liberal use of color.

The decision making process of painting a picture like this wasn't a hard science. There weren't a set of rules that needed to be followed. The final product was accomplished by the artist's creative instinct. There was no math, no formula involved in something like that, which made Ryan wonder, could a machine like The Mind create a piece of artwork that was an accurate reflection of its feelings (if it had feelings at all)? He thought about how that could translate into a real life scenario. For instance, what if The Mind had to decide whether it was advantageous to go to war. Should a decision like that be made with pure objectivity? Or should feelings remain part of the recipe? Which would make the better cake, Ryan didn't know.

He shifted in his seat, and felt the phone nudge against his leg. He had forgotten all about it. He doubted Megan would still be on the line.

He held it up, and spoke into the speaker, just to be sure.

"Hello," he said.

"Hello."

"You're still there?"

There was a light chuckle on the other end.

"Sorry, Ryan. I was listening in on your tutoring session. Sounds like Timmy is having a little trouble grasping the material."

"Well, as he reminded me earlier, he's only in fourth grade."

"Which probably means he's too young to get involved in the politics of all of this. You'll just confuse him if you try to explain it."

"Too late," Ryan said, snatching a pillow and throwing it onto an empty chair.

"So what are you doing this weekend?"

"Me? Not a whole lot. Weren't you going somewhere this weekend?"

"Yeah. My parents and I are going to take a trip downstate to go to my cousin's birthday party. We're going to leave this afternoon and spend the night."

"How old is she now?"

"She's turning into the good ol' feisty fourteen. So I'm expecting one hell of a raucous: food all over the place, screaming and bitching, untethered excitement, the whole package."

"Sounds like you'll have a good time."

Megan scoffed. "Your sarcasm is duly noted. Now I gotta get going and finish up an essay, 'cause I'm sure as hell not going to get it done any time tomorrow."

"Of course."

"And hopefully this situation with The Mind finds a way of resolving itself peacefully. In fact, I'm going to keep myself in the dark about it for the time being. I don't want to have to brood over this right now."

"I don't blame you. Personally, I think they should just dispose of The Mind and be done with it."

"If only it could be that simple. I'll see you, Ryan."

"See ya," he said, and hung up the phone.

He got up and entered the den again and saw his mom still fixated on the television. From what he could tell, nothing about the scene had changed. The bus was still at the center of the lot and the police cars were still keeping a perimeter. A few moments later the broadcast switched over to another gentlemen, who they were having a discussion with. This man proposed the innovative idea of having The Mind determine what the appropriate course of action would be in this scenario. Apparently there was a plan to put pressure on Dr. Allanstein, and have him prove the worth of his creation. If The Mind was the omniscient entity that he claimed it to be, then it should have no problem coming up with a solution to this predicament.

Ryan thought this idea was clever, and at best, would expose this machine for what it really was: a conglomeration of microchips and circuitry. It had no business dictating the future of mankind. That task was *our* responsibility.

He stepped away for a moment, to finish what was left of his breakfast. Timmy was just finishing up. When he was done, he went back into the den to listen to the broadcast. His mom told him to go upstairs and watch cartoons, but he stubbornly sat and watched.

After eating and getting himself dressed, Ryan returned to the den. His mom was treading back and forth between there and the kitchen, while Timmy stayed put. He was holding one of the pillows again, twisting and squeezing it in every which way.

Dr. Allanstein was now on the air, along with the other gentlemen. They were debating for a while before Allanstein acceded to the suggestion of having The Mind present a solution. Allanstein was heard saying:

"Technically speaking, The Mind's functionality will not be optimal until it undergoes its dormant cycle, which isn't scheduled until next week. However, given that this is a simple problem relative to the capabilities of this machine, I have no objections to requesting an answer. The Mind has already been assimilated with Dr. Edmunds' full psychological and social record, along with all other pertinent information. It's also well-versed in an array of methods and protocols for dealing with hostage situations. I expect nothing less than for The Mind to guide us through the best course of action."

Allanstein was then shown accessing a terminal at his engineering facility by an on-sight camera crew. He logged onto his system and initiated a communication link that would allow him to speak directly to The Mind, which at the time was still inside the Museum of Natural and Modern Science. He held down a green button and spoke into the microphone.

"How do we respond to the hostage situation?"

No further details were necessary. The Mind was plugged into local news feeds. It knew exactly what was going on.

After the question was submitted, there was complete silence from everyone—from Allanstein, and the newscasters. The camera crew were hovering over the computer, trying to focus on the screen. There was tension in the air. A lot of pressure was on Allanstein. Had this machine produced anything but a perfect answer, he would be ridiculed throughout the entire world, thus ensuring an abrupt end to the project. He could have been unyielding about the necessity of waiting until the dormant cycle was complete, but wasn't. This could only imply that this man had absolute confidence in this machine's ability to perform.

Everyone waited patiently for the answer. They were all on the edge of their seats. Every second passed by slowly. Millions of people were watching what could possibly be a monumental moment in history.

A line of words were generated on-screen.

The camera crew moved in, and focused the lens.

The statement was visible, as clear as day.

NO ACTION IS NECESSARY.

There was immediate murmuring from the newscasters. They looked astounded, embarrassed for the doctor. They exchanged glances with one another. One of the women said:

"Talk about a blunder. I don't think any of us were expecting that kind of response."

They addressed Allanstein for an explanation. He answered them, staying defensive.

"There was no blunder here. This was a carefully calculated decision, marked with judicious care. I stand by The Mind's response. I advise that the authorities on the sight take no further action."

Ryan was skeptical. But he was inclined to side with Allanstein. Years of research and development, and hundreds of millions of dollars don't produce a mistake like this. The Mind knew what it was saying, and it had reason to say what it did. Make no mistake about it. The Mind understood full well what needed to be done.

By now he had heard enough, and decided it was best to step away for a while. He returned to his room and picked up his cell phone. There was a missed call from Megan, and one from Mike as well. Except he followed up with a couple of texts, which as Ryan expected, were in regards to the news report. Ryan decided to call him up. The phone rang twice before he picked up.

"Ryan!" he answered. "Have you seen the news?"

"I did. Megan called me up about it."

"I said it. This machine could be hostile. Pretty soon we're going to have to start tallying up the victims."

"Um, I'm not quite sure The Mind is the perpetrator here."

"It is!" Mike said, unable to restrain his excitement. "It's like that *Twilight Zone* episode, where the alien screwed around with the electricity in the neighborhood, making all the residents turn on each other. That's what's happening here."

"I'm not sure this is the same thing."

"Sure it is. The Mind is causing paranoia, and it's causing

people to have psychotic breakdowns. The country will be split into two: those that endorse their cerebral overlord, and those who don't. There's going to be another Civil War!"

"That sounds like it could be rough," Ryan said, trying to play along. "Who's side are you going to be on?"

"The resistance, of course."

"You oppose the reign of The Mind?"

"C'mon Ryan. The Mind is the bad guy. The bad guys die. I want to live."

"All right. Just keep your EMP pulse gun at hand. If The Mind advises you to do something that you don't want to do, just shoot it."

"You can't. It's not that easy. Its presence is everywhere. Remember the trancestors? We got them all over our school. They're still watching us. They're learning everything about us."

"Well," Ryan said, falling into his chair, "maybe in light of today's events, the school will back out from the trial."

"No chance. They probably got contracts and stuff. And you know our school district needs money. I'm telling you, there's no chance."

"In that case, I guess we have no choice but to ready our arsenal."

"I got you on speed dial. Anything happens, you're my first contact."

"Thanks, Mike," he said.

Ryan was more than frazzled by the events that had unfolded today. He needed to unwind, and there was no better way to do that than to partake in a little basketball. He wasn't going to play anyone. At least not any time soon. He was going to play in his driveway, where he wouldn't be burdened by the pressure of making the baskets.

There was nothing like it. Holding the ball in his hand felt natural, like it had been there since he was born. And the motion of shooting a ball was just as intuitive. He could easily forget that he was even playing, which caused his mind to drift to other places. Like right now, he was thinking about Monday, and the things he could expect to encounter. What kind of gibe would Blake have ready for him? What kind of cruel punishment could he hope to receive? Then there was Karina. How could he approach any girl after being chagrined to that extent? He needed a plan, that's what he needed. Though this time, he might have to avoid contracting with Mike.

Ryan was in the middle of taking another shot when Timmy came sprinting out the front door. It must have been about an hour since he last took a peek at the news. Timmy was shouting his name, over and over. Ryan knew he had seen something on the TV. Though he didn't seem scared or frightened; he was excited, like the time he found a dead possum in their backyard.

"He's dead! He's dead!" he announced for the whole neighborhood to hear.

"Who," Ryan said. "Who's dead?"

"The scientist. He shot himself."

He questioned whether or not Timmy had the story straight. It didn't make sense. Why would Edmunds kill himself? Ryan ran inside the house to watch the report for himself.

His mother was in the room, with her hand up over her mouth. Her eyes were glued to the TV. Ryan looked at the footage and saw the hostages racing across the lot. The police rushed the other way, towards the vehicle. The cruisers followed them from behind. They surrounded the bus while select officers stormed the interior.

One of the newscasters was describing what had just transpired.

"*Dr. Edmunds is presumed to have taken his own life, just after delivering one final precautionary message. About one minute ago, he was given notice that under government mandate, The Mind was not to be destroyed, under any circumstances.*"

Amazing, Ryan thought, in the sense that he hadn't expected such an outcome. Edmunds had no intentions of hurting anyone. All he wanted to do was give fair warning about the machine he created. When no one listened, he took things to the extreme. Could he have been right about The Mind, Ryan wondered. Then he remembered the response The Mind gave earlier this morning—the solution to this problem: *no action is necessary.* Ryan didn't know how it was possible, but The Mind was right. Maybe all the fear and paranoia was warranted. Maybe this was an apocalyptic machine.

Whatever the case may have been, it didn't matter. The Mind was right, and now it was here to stay.

Ryan could hear Mike now.

First victim.

CHAPTER 17

HOPE ON THE HORIZON

Ryan went to bed that night with the day still fresh in his memory. It caused him to writhe around in bed for well over an hour. It was difficult for him to digest the fact that something like The Mind could exist. He kept asking himself a million questions about it: does it have opinions? Does it have a motive? Does it have a favorite color? Does it daydream? Does it understand life and death? Does it have a sense of humor? He had no idea what the answer was to any of those questions, which is probably what fueled his disquietude.

When his dad had came home earlier today, he mentioned how the guy with the toy collection never came to the store, much to Timmy's disappointment. His dad attributed it to the incident with The Mind. Either the seller was afraid of driving through the city, or he had already vacated the country, which wasn't unheard of. There were a few extremists that had already established new homes overseas, just in case The Mind was elected president. Humorously, his dad said he was open to the idea of having a machine at the helm. He was optimistic that The Mind would implement better policies than its human counterparts. And as an added bonus, it wouldn't be dependent on teleprompters.

It would be a while yet, Ryan thought, before The Mind appeared on a voting ballot. There was time to think about that later. But for now, in the darkness and tranquility of his room, he had other thoughts. He remembered his dreams from last night. For him, lying in bed triggered past dreams to return. He could try to recall a dream all day with no luck, but the moment he would lie down, they'd all come pouring back into his consciousness—like right now.

Ryan couldn't pinpoint the exact moment, but it happened again. He began to dream.

Ryan was by himself, sitting against the wall in some outlying corridor of the *Obsidian*. He remembered wandering there, after he saw Leilah being hauled away to the infirmary. Her condition was grave; she was still, lifeless, on the brink of death from the looks of it. Ryan didn't know what her chances were. His whole outlook on the future was grim. Cyannus was destroyed—a catastrophe he could hardly believe. It had claimed Megan's life. He was sure of it, until he gave it more thought.

He felt as if he had just spoken to her just a short while ago. But such was an impossibility. Though if he thought hard enough, he could pick up fragments from a different, parallel memory that must have been his waking life. In a way it made sense, given that this was a dream. However, *this* felt like the reality, and it would continue to feel that way for as long as he was here. At any rate, it gave him hope that Megan was still alive in one form or another. That man though, Zephner, may not have been so lucky. As Ryan understood, he was exclusive to this side of his consciousness. And in losing him, Ryan felt a piece of himself die along with him. His death was unfortunate, to say the least.

Ryan didn't feel like being alone anymore. Sequestering himself to a place of isolation would only help harbor further misery.

He decided what he needed to do now was to find Steve and tell him about Leilah. It would have been important for him to be there if she woke up, as Leilah was the only person left in his life. If anyone could ameliorate the condition he was in now, it would be her. But Ryan didn't even know the state of his condition. For all he knew, Steve could be a wreck. How does one even begin to cope with, not only the destruction of their home and loved ones, but the obliteration of the very planet they lived on? It seemed unrecoverable.

Ryan set off to look for him, but the *Obsidian* was huge. If Steve wanted to hide, he could hide. Conversely, if he wanted Ryan to find him, there were only a handful of places where he would expect him to look.

He started by searching his cabin on C deck. When he entered, the room was dark. He flicked on the light switch and saw that no one was there. The bed sheets were without a ruffle, all the drawers and gear were undisturbed. He wouldn't make this easy.

Or did he?

If Ryan's own inclination was any indication, Steve would probably try to isolate himself. But not someplace familiar, like his cabin, or one of the station's lounges. All those places would remind him of where he was, and what had happened. Then he considered the ERR, and the influence that may have had on his thought process. If its purpose was to moderate an intense emotional response, its effectiveness would be increased by the individual making an effort to hide those emotions themselves. Of course, this was all speculation on his part. He'd compare it to staring at his ceiling, or looking up at the sky. It was easier to daydream that way, easier to fantasize.

Ryan thought he knew where to look.

He went downstairs and navigated his way through the winding corridors, back to the Gravalon Arena. Having been there once, he knew that there was no better place for one to clear their head of their worldly concerns. Being inside that room was like having your mind bleached.

He stood by the door, triggered the switch, and watched as it disappeared inside the wall. A wintry whiteness filled his vision as he stepped inside. The room was as bright and pristine as he remembered. He could have pretended to be anywhere right now. He could see nothing—except for one thing.

Steve was slumped against the declivity of the outer wall. It almost looked like he was floating there. He stared out into the void, without the slightest trace of an expression. He was like a cadaver with its eyes still open.

When Ryan saw this, he reconsidered if he should say anything. There was no way he could tell him about Leilah, not while he was in this state. He thought there was little he could do for him right now, and it may have been best to leave him be.

But just as he was about to step out, he heard his name spoken. It reverberated loudly in the empty room.

He turned around. Steve was still a corpse.

"You came here for something?"

Ryan couldn't describe it, but his voice sounded strangely normal. It was casual, soft-spoken, as if nothing was wrong.

"I know this is a terrible time," Ryan said, "but there's something I should tell you."

"Terrible? I'm not sure I catch your drift. Everything seems fine here."

Again, he spoke normally, though his body was still sprawled across the floor. Ryan wasn't sure how to handle this.

"But things aren't fine," Ryan said. "At least not out there. You heard the same thing everyone else did. You even saw it— you saw what happened."

Steve was pulling himself together. He sat himself upright before bringing himself back on his feet. He started to walk down the declivity.

"Hey, why don't we get a game of Gravalon going. You told me you wanted to play, right?"

"No," Ryan said, starting to get flustered. "Not now. Now isn't the time.

Steve shrugged his shoulders and kept walking. Not towards Ryan, or the door, but in an aimless direction. He climbed up the slope until he appeared standing at an impossible angle from Ryan's perspective.

He was broken, Ryan though, a broken-down toy. He was pushing Ryan's patience, almost making him upset. But not at Steve, but rather at the people who formulated the ERR regimen. Apparently this was the result of the reconditioning.

"Steve," Ryan tried again. "You have to understand what happened. You can't just block it all out. That's not how it works."

Steve found a position somewhere half way up the slope and sat back down. He was facing away from Ryan. He rocked himself back and forth steadily.

"I know about Stephanie . . . and Martin. I know it's pretty much impossible to accept the fact that they're gone. But they're not really gone if you remember them. And the same goes for everyone else in your life. These people are what made you who you are. You can't just block them out. They're all you have."

Steve continued to rock himself, faster and faster. He was shaking his head.

"I don't have a family," he said. "I never had a family. I never had anyone. I'm the only one. It's just me. I'm the only one."

"No. You're wrong. You're blocking out too much. You're forgetting someone."

Steve became still. He looked askance and began to think. But he couldn't arrive at an answer. He started to rock again.

"Steve," Ryan said, raising his voice, then following up with a gentler tone. "Leilah is still alive."

Steve halted his movement. He remained seated there for quite a while before climbing back on his feet. He turned around and showed his muddled face. He looked around the room, trying to salvage whatever he could remember. Then he looked back at Ryan, appearing completely baffled.

"She's here?" he asked.

"Yes," Ryan said. "She is." He regretted the words that followed. "But there was an accident at the simulation room. When the power went out, the system malfunctioned and she's now stuck in some sort of coma."

Steve took a long time to digest the words. His head jerked left and right. He looked up at the ceiling, then down at the floor. He was twitching, growing more nervous and restless as he tried to understand, and recall all that had happened.

"Gone," he said, out of no where. "Cyannus . . . it's gone?" He looked at Ryan.

Ryan nodded regretfully, only to see that it exasperated him further. His breathing became heavier, his body tensed up. He was looking around, thinking what to do, thinking about what had to be done. When he decided, he marched off hurriedly.

Ryan saw him leave the room, and followed him. Steve was moving fast through the halls, taking long strides. He kept a brisk pace, swinging his stiff arms at his sides, his fists clenched.

Ryan chased him all the way back to the rotunda. Steve was coming fast down the stairs, clouting hard on each step. Ryan expected him to return to Leilah, but that didn't seem to be his plan. He stopped when he identified the post that marked the infirmary on F deck. That's where Leilah was. But Steve didn't stop. He kept going down. Ryan called out to him

"Steve! This is the floor. She's here!"

He didn't listen. He continued heading downward. Worried, Ryan followed him. He hadn't a clue where he was heading.

Where else would he need to go? But then it hit him when he got off on G deck. He was going to the loading docks. But there was no reason to be there, no reason at all. Except—

Ryan chased after him again, jumping steps where he could. Steve had gained a considerable lead after just a short amount of time. Ryan quickened his pace and called out to him again.

"Steve, wait! Don't!"

He entered the tunnel and saw Steve turn at the next corner. It wouldn't be long before he entered the orbicular room. He had to stop him before he got to that door.

He sprinted to catch up, and got up right behind him.

"You can't do this. You know he'll kill you."

When Steve didn't listen, Ryan grabbed his shoulder. But he shrugged it off and continued with his aggressive march.

Ryan didn't know what else to tell him. Trying to physically subdue him would have been a bad idea, as Steve would most certainly overpower him, if not hurt him. He didn't understand what was going through his mind, or how far he was willing to go. But he needed to think of something. If he went through that door and provoked a confrontation, Guin would kill him, injured or not.

He was running out of time. This was his last chance.

"What am I suppose to tell Leilah when she wakes up? Do I have to tell her you're dead?"

He didn't listen. He kept marching forward.

Ryan tried again.

"You idiot, she still loves you."

What he said must have gotten through, because Steve stopped. Though he was still tense, his fingers still curled into fists. Maybe he was contemplating the consequences of stepping into that room. When Ryan approached him again, he collapsed against the wall, falling like a rag doll. He was gasping for air, holding his forehead with his hand.

He swallowed and said to Ryan, "I'm sorry. I just—I just don't know what to think—I . . . I don't know what to do. It's hurting me."

Ryan stood by his side, and held his shoulder. He spoke to him calmly. "I think we should go to the infirmary and check on Leilah."

He gave a nod of accent and picked himself off the floor and started walking.

The walls of the infirmary were gleaming white, with patient beds all aligned in a row. There were a handful of officers here, each of which incurred an injury during the tremors produced by the shockwave: some scrapes and bruises, fractured bones, a sprained wrist, nothing serious. The truth was most of them were oblivious to the physical pain, which was greatly overshadowed by the new reality they had to face.

Steve entered the facility knowing it wouldn't be easy looking at Leilah lying unconscious on a bed while under medical care, but he convinced himself that he needed to. Even though he had been doing everything in his power to purge any recollection of his past life, he knew he could not let her be forgotten. She was all that he had left—literally. He had nothing else, or no one else to go back to. She was his last reminder that he even had a past. And that being the case, she was the only one that could provide him with a future.

Steve crept across the room, setting his eyes on each of the beds. It wasn't difficult to find her; she was the one lying still, with the gleaming auburn hair laid over the white pillow, and a cooling blanket spread over her body.

He came up to the bed and looked down at her. She looked as if she were asleep; her eyes were gently closed, her lips slightly ajar—but he knew she wasn't. She was strapped to an ECG monitor, which showed periodical spikes, and a consistently high pulse. She was battling some intensive trial. Of what nature, he didn't know. It wasn't pleasant, he knew that much. If he looked carefully, he could see her eyes twitch, as well as her arms.

Steve reached underneath the sheet and found her hand, and grasped it gently. It was warm, teeming with life—with hope. He could feel her fingers trembling. He took his other hand and brought it over hers. He clasped it firmly, and when he did, he could feel her fingers squeezing his hand. He found it difficult to stifle his tears.

It was all his fault, he thought. He was the one that drove her to this, all because she was being charitable to a wounded creature. It was so stupid—*he* was so stupid. He wanted to believe his whole life had been a mistake—he never should have enlisted with the academy. At the very least, he should have stayed at home today with Stephanie. He should have perished with her, and their son. His existence should have been terminated twenty minutes ago. But no, he couldn't believe that, not for as long as Leilah lay there before him—not for as long as her heart was still beating. He needed to hold on, for her. He needed to be there when she woke up.

Ryan was watching from a distance, still trying to fathom his emotions. There was an air of uncertainty all around him. The future was spontaneous, and it couldn't be anticipated. Despicable things could happen at any moment, and he had no choice but to just deal with them. But he didn't know how. The fate of a world and its people was something he had no control over. He was in a nightmare, and he had to ride it out.

One of the doctors came over to confront Steve. Even he was

shaken up, trying to remain composed despite the disaster.

"I'm sorry this happened," he said. "I'm sure you two were close."

Steve dried his eyes with his sleeve while clearing his voice.

"Apparently not close enough. I'm the one that let her get into this mess in the first place."

"You shouldn't blame yourself. What happened was nobody's fault. There was nothing any of us could do about it."

Steve looked at Leilah again, her eyes still twitching.

"How did this happen? What went wrong?"

The doctor explained to him, "The ERR systems rebooted during that brief power outage, before the auxiliary power could kick in, which in turn caused some technical complications."

"Like what?" Steve asked.

"Well, in such an event, the system is suppose to resync with the episode that was administered to the user. But in this instance, there was corruption in the code, and the system was unable to read the details of the episode, which left her functioning independently from the program."

"So you're telling me we have no way of monitoring what she's experiencing?"

"I'm afraid not. Once the episode is administered, her mind constructs the way the trial is played out. Without the ERR system, there's no way to know what's happening."

Steve was still holding on to her hand, stifling the tremors of her fingers.

"So you're telling me she could be going through something unbearable, and there's nothing we can do to help her?"

"I'm afraid not."

"You can't just—just wake her up?"

The doctor shook his head. "We could administer certain stimulants, but a sudden transition out of a trial could result in neuropsychological damage, and in worst cases, death. What's most conducive to her recovery is her ability to conquer the trial she's been given. After completion, she would eventually wake."

Steve sighed softly. "That's fine, doctor. The trial won't be a challenge. She's completed many of them, and she'll do it again."

The doctor nodded and said, "I'm sure she will." Then he walked over to his next patient.

Ryan approached the bed and spent a few more moments looking over Leilah. Steve seemed to have no intention of leaving any time soon. Then again, there really was no where else to go.

There was a crackle in the ceiling, and then the intercom came on. Everyone in the room diverted their attention to it. The message was proclaimed.

"I call to the attention of every crew member aboard this vessel. This is your captain. I speak to each of you when I say that I commend your bravery during this unspeakable crisis. This will be a day that we will not forget, and in remembering, we will preserve our legacy, and the legacy of those that we knew and loved. It is now our duty—still our duty, to protect our people, our culture and values, and our sovereignty. This is why we will seek provisional refuge under the Garthega Federation. As an ally, they will help us rebuild our lives so that we may be able to live our futures. Until you hear from me again, stand by one another and carry the burden of this day equally upon your shoulders."

The voice and the crackling ceased. Everyone in the room remained silent. Each of them struggled to believe the promise issued by Reynard. But Ryan was hopeful. Even if there was the tiniest chance of delivering retribution, and bringing peace back to this foreign realm, then he had every reason to hold on just a little longer. Even Steve believed there was a glimmer of hope, and if there was, he, as a sworn officer, would play a part in the future he thought possible.

---CHAPTER 18---

UNCAGED

Ryan awoke Sunday morning to the sound of birds chirping outside his window. There was a tree in his backyard with a weave of branches that basically served as a bird sanctuary. During the spring months, he'd always spot one of the nests. While he sat at his desk, or watched TV, he would get the privilege of witnessing the birds assemble it twig by twig. He was nothing short of amazed by how they managed with nothing more than a beak. He couldn't even eat spaghetti without getting sauce all over his face, and yet these birds were doing things he probably couldn't do with both his hands. Up until this day he held resentment towards the feathered creatures, for cheating him out of a tree house. When he was much younger, his dad was going to help construct one, but his mom deterred him by saying that it would disturb the birds (but really because she didn't want Ryan falling off and breaking his neck). Lucky birds.

He dragged himself out of bed and parked himself next to the window and looked outside. Autumn was in full force. Every leaf in the yard was a warm shade of pumpkin pie, except for the maple, which was closer to cherry. On occasion he would watch the leaves as they fell, and the journey they took to reach the ground. Some stayed in his backyard, others blew into the neighbor's yard, and the less fortunate ones drifted into the street where they would meet with the underside of a car tire. If only they knew what they were getting themselves into when they chose to let go.

When Ryan turned around to leave his room, he passed by his bed, but not before glancing at it in a different light. He saw it now as some kind of portal to the other side—a nightly retreat where he could explore another facet of himself—a parallel universe that was as astonishing as his imagination would ever allow. The experience was so vividly ingrained in his mind that he couldn't help but think about it while he was awake. He said the names of the friends he made out loud: Zephner, Steven, Leilah, Guin, Bee—where did they come from? He looked outside again, at the sky. Were they out there? Was it even possible? He continued to wonder.

He went downstairs, had breakfast with his parents and Timmy, who was still prattling on about how The Mind was a killer robot (he must have spoken with Mike).

The rest of the day would bring about no surprises. The news continued its coverage of the incident regarding The Mind. Those that were skeptical were now believers of the machine's clairvoyance. On a different note, those that feared its omniscience were able to substantiate their concerns even further. They spoke of how it would be idolized as a savior to mankind—a god among the people. But ultimately, it was nothing more than a computer, a device that would bail leaders out of having to make decisions for themselves. This debate raged on throughout the rest of the day.

After hearing enough, Ryan shot some hoops in his driveway.

—)—

After nightfall, Ryan dwindled away some time in front of the TV, playing video games with Timmy. When it was time to go to sleep, he went to bed and lay there for a while with his eyes open.

He was dreading having to go school tomorrow, for reasons he'd already spent too much time thinking about. Yes, Blake would jeer him, and Karina wouldn't even raise an eyebrow, nor give him the time of day. If there was a way of overcoming this quandary, he didn't know how. He could only hope that tomorrow he would find optimism—somewhere.

As for right now, he knew what to expect. He knew where he was going. He closed his eyes, and shortly thereafter, he fell asleep.

Everyone had forgotten about the feathered beast that remained in captivity behind a bulkhead door, with the exception of Ryan. Guin wasn't exactly the type of animal that one could expect to be patient. Ryan figured he would be getting restless by now, especially if he was recovering at the rate that Leilah had estimated.

Turns out he was right. Captain Reynard had radioed Steve about the motion sensors picking up activity in docking room no. 72. This meant that if Guin had the strength to leave the Conoblis, then maybe he had the strength to leave the room. No one knew if he were capable of such a thing or not. Steve did apprise Reynard of the animal's lingual abilities, to which Reynard suggested they inform him of what was going on, and to inquire about any knowledge he may have regarding the attack on Cyannus.

"You really don't have to be here," Ryan said to Steve one last time, as they were entering the docking station. He really didn't want him there, especially since it was only minutes ago that he was ready to pound the animal that was the living, breathing equivalent of a meat mincer.

"I have to be here, Ryan. I'm involved now."

"Many people are involved, but you don't see them lining up to interrogate."

"They don't have anything left. They lost everything when our world was destroyed. I couldn't see them caring what happens now one way or another."

"But they still have their memory to preserve, like Reynard was saying."

"They're just words," Steve said, with his eyes set on the chamber ahead. "Anyone can hear them, but you still need a reason to believe them. I want to be able to see the hope on the horizon before I tell myself that tomorrow is worth waking up to."

Ryan thought about it, and then told him, "It's not really hope then, if you know what's coming. Hope is believing in what may not happen. That's what should get you up and going in the morning."

Steve sneered back at him, "I think our mornings are counted. If things continue as they are, we may not have another morning. If we all perish, I want to at least die knowing what the hell was going on. That's why I'm paying a visit to *Guin*. And that's why I'm sticking by Reynard when he consults Commander Knivus. And if there's any hope to be found in any of this, then sure, I'll be happy to wake up tomorrow with a smile on my face."

Steve was right to an extent, Ryan thought. There was little reason to be hopeful in a situation like this. Maybe if this were real life, then total despair would be in order. But since this was a dream, there seemed to be a sliver of hope that the impossible could happen. Ryan was hoping that Megan was still alive.

When they reached the orbicular platform, they followed it down to room no. 72. Ryan was glad to see the door intact. He pressed his ear against it, but couldn't hear anything. Meanwhile, Steve stood against the opposite wall, with his arms folded and his head hung low. Occasionally he glanced down the hall to look for Reynard, and when he didn't see him, his head would droop again.

Ryan didn't say anything, but he was genuinely worried about the guy. He couldn't be sure if he was coping in the same manner as a typical person, or if this was just an improvisation produced by his training. Either way, paying Guin a visit didn't seem like a healthy idea.

Soon Reynard was spotted coming down the corridor. This was the first time Ryan had seen him. He was an older man with graying hair, but barely without a wrinkle on his face. He stood tall, without a hunch, and wore a blue buttoned coat that was decorated with several pins and badges. A proud, confident individual no doubt, but when he turned his attention to Ryan, that look waned into a look of shame.

He approached Ryan and took a deep breath before speaking.

"You must be Ryan," he said to him.

"That's right."

Reynard looked at him apologetically. "Ryan . . . firstly I wanted to tell you that I am sorry that I had to deliver you into the hands of our enemies. Had there been another way, I would have pursued it instead. But there wasn't. Many lives were threatened, and it came down to potential casualties, hence the reason why Roland came to this decision."

Ryan wasn't sure what to say. He sounded honest and sincere. He had no reason not to believe him.

"I'm not blaming you," Ryan said. "It's not like I would ask you to jeopardize lives on account of me."

Reynard smiled, and put his hand on his shoulder.

"You're a brave one. I can sense it."

"Not often," Ryan said. "When I am, it's usually because I'm confident of the outcome."

"I think you can give yourself a little more credit than that," he said, and then looked towards the door. "Steve mentioned how you and Leilah patched up the penguin. I think most people would have left well enough alone."

"Well, Leilah was the one that did the patching."

He let out another smile. "Modest too, I see."

Then he turned to Steve, who had moved away from the wall to the one with the security panel. He didn't seem to want anything more than to get inside already.

Reynard said to him, "No one, I included, expects you to do anything more today. I know the loss you suffered was horrific, and I'd understand perfectly if you took no part in this."

"I don't think so," Steve said. "Standing around doing nothing is only going to sustain my misery. I'm better off doing anything else right now."

"All right," Reynard said. "I can accept that."

Reynard faced the panel and was about to dial in the code before Steve interrupted.

"So we're not even going to have armed personnel present for when we open this door?"

Reynard left his hand hovering over the keypad.

"If our aim is to avoid hostility, then it's best we avoid appearing hostile ourselves." He turned his head the other way. "What do you think, Ryan?"

"I think we can trust Guin," he said.

"I think so too."

Reynard went ahead and dialed the code, and the heavy metal door started to slide open. Ryan peeked inside the room as soon as he saw a crack. Though he didn't admit it, there was a part of him that was afraid Guin would bust out like the untamed creature he was. But another part of him believed otherwise.

When the opening was wide enough, Ryan had a perfect understanding of why the sensors went off. There were bits and pieces of metal scraps, broken glass and severed wires scattered all over the room. Some were spilling out of the Conoblis, while others came from the computer console. Even the storage closet was ransacked. The extra coats were torn and shredded down to wads of cotton, while guns and ammunition lay beside them. The whole mess could only be pinned on one thing: the blue-feathered bird standing at the center of the room with the long red cable hanging from his beak.

The penguin stopped gnawing, and looked straight at the others as they stood in the doorway. His wound was now nothing but a light scar. His bandages were long gone.

Ryan entered the room first, with his jaw dropped.

"Guin, was it really necessary to do all this?"

The penguin stared back at him. There was no shame in his eyes. He dropped the cable.

"If this is what it takes to get some service in here, then *yes*. Though to be truthful, I did try calling first. But when the phone didn't work, I attempted to fix it myself."

"Apparently that didn't work out so well."

"I couldn't find a screwdriver, so I had to improvise."

"I see that," Ryan said, still looking at the mess in disbelief. "And what did the coats have to do with anything?"

Guin scowled at him.

"They were a casualty of my frustration!"

Reynard stepped forward and looked studiously at the animal. He didn't seem bothered by the destruction, but rather curious as to its behavioral patterns.

"So you must be the cantankerous creature that breached our walls and found a place to nestle."

Guin snapped back at him, "And you must be the driver that can't find a parking space."

Ryan held his breath, in fear of what that comment could incite, especially from Steve. Somehow he managed to keep his
calm. He didn't take the bait. Reynard looked more disappointed
than anything.

"So you're an insolent animal," Reynard replied. "Looks like
you're going to make it very difficult for me to give you any sym-
pathy."

"If it can't be digested, I don't want it."

Steve quickly stepped forward, taking an aggressive stance.

"I don't care what you want," he said. "But I'll tell you what I
want."

Reynard extended his arm, keeping Steve at bay.

"Now Steve, let us take this one step at a time." He looked
back at Guin. "I see you understand our situation, as you've
already so eloquently implied. Cyannus was destroyed, but we
know nothing as to who, or why they did this. So we merely ask
you if there's anything you know that could lead us in the right
direction."

Guin appeared inattentive, but he was listening. He rolled his
head to the side and stretched his neck all the way back so that he
could look into the eyes of the man.

"It's flattering to know that you're under the impression that
my pea-sized brain holds such valuable information."

"We know it's a long shot, but it's still worth asking."

Guin turned his head and looked away.

"Knowledge isn't free. At least not today it isn't."

"What are you talking about?" Reynard said.

"You know what I'm talking about."

"I'm afraid I don't."

"It's quite simple," Guin said, turning his back and waddling
away. "We're going to land on this new cosmic boulder; you're
going to have your little colloquy with the big wigs, and I'm going to face time in some sort of detention facility where all the

animal misfits go. Not that I'll let it get to that, but I'd like to avoid any unnecessary bloodshed if at all possible."

Steve was fired up again.

"Oh, I'm sure you're the one that should be talking about unnecessary bloodshed."

Guin hollered back, "Listen, my claws are clean. I was decommissioned before I could impale anything."

"Exactly. You would have done the same as any of the others given the chance."

"And I take it you bake a pot pie for the intruder that barges into your home."

"No, but I don't have a guillotine installed over my front door either."

"Well, if things got rough around the neighborhood, I think you'd find it would be a wise investment."

"That's enough," Reynard said, holding his hands out to them. "Now Guin, tell me, do you have any information that could help us?"

"It all depends," Guin answered, "if you can accept my terms or not."

"You better damn well tell us everything you know," Steve hollered.

"Steve," Reynard said, motioning his hand. "Guin, explain your terms."

The penguin stood there, with his belly out and his beak held high.

"I'm not an extortionist," he said. "All I want is to be a part of what happens from here on out. When there's a retaliatory response, I want to be part of the battalion."

Ryan, being silent for the time being, was trying to wrap his head around Guin. He really wasn't a killer, but he didn't exactly seem like the noble type either.

"Guin," Ryan said, "wouldn't you rather ask to be sent back

home?"

"Home?" Guin said. "For all I know, that place could be scheduled to go off the map too. There's no sense in heading back there until I have reassurance that its going to stay in one piece."

"That's logical thinking," Reynard said. "If I were in your position, I'd proceed the same way."

Ryan was unsure about Guin's bullheadedness to get involved. He only saw him as an animal. Or maybe that dog he never got as a kid, just with more feathers.

Ryan turned to Reynard.

"Are the people we're meeting going to be okay with a talking penguin hanging around?"

"Guin wouldn't be the first they see. These genetically altered animals have existed on Armon for a while now. However, the physical feats he's capable of remains inimitable. I'm sure they would be very interested in seeing him."

Guin said, "I'm not heading over there to be put in a circus tent. That's not happening."

"Of course not," Reynard said. "We're all going there with one goal in mind: to amalgamate and exchange information with one another."

"And then do something about it, I hope."

"We will work something out," Reynard said, turning around to exit the room. "I'm leaving now, but I won't seal you in. However I ask that you stay around here so that we can find you when we're ready to land."

Steve looked back before passing through the bulkhead, giving one last resentful glare at the pudgy animal. Ryan stayed behind, not sure if leaving Guin by himself was a good idea. Maybe by staying, and showing that he didn't mind being in his company, he would ease up a bit.

Guin noticed and looked at him with a sulky frown. Ryan

thought it was because he didn't bring the food he promised. But it was actually something else.

"What happened to the other one?" he said.

Ryan wasn't sure what he was talking about. "The other what?"

He twitched his beak, as if he were going to say something, but then dismissed it.

"Forget it," he said and waddled back to the Conoblis. He struggled up the stairs, using his claws to lift himself up each step. "Wake me up when we get there."

Maybe it was best to leave him alone for now, Ryan thought. As a matter of fact, he was feeling a bit drowsy himself (he didn't even know you could feel tired while being asleep). So he went over to the corner of the room, where the shredded coats were and scooped them into a pile. He lay down on them and found himself quite comfortable. Soon he slept, and at some point during his slumber, he awoke in a real bed.

MONDAY MOURNING

Monday morning seemed so far away three days ago, but now it was here. All Ryan could think about while he lay in bed was his public debacle and the aftermath that would follow. The thrashing he received was unreal. He wondered if the whole thing was part of his dream—but unfortunately he was certain that it wasn't. Even if it were, it paled in comparison to the veil of despondency that fell upon every being who was aboard the *Obsidian* at the time of the catastrophe. He thought about Steve, Leilah, and the rest of the crew, and all the heartache they were battling. The problems that lay ahead of him today felt petty in comparison. They hardly seemed worth fretting over.

He dragged himself out of bed and crept downstairs, and warmed up another pastry. He had two more to go before he would transition back to bowls of cereal, which, after ten years of schooling, had become rather unappetizing. But whatever.

The weather was fair enough today for him to take his bicycle to school. Or if he wanted to be honest with himself, he could say the weather had nothing to do with it. The truth was he didn't want to confront the people on the school bus. There were at least two or three jerks on there he didn't feel like dealing with right now.

—)—

He reached the school as the buses were pulling in. The students stepped out one by one. He kept a watchful eye on them, looking for Blake and Karina in particular. But he could spot neither of them among the crowd.

Once inside he made a furtive approach to his locker. The door shielded him from the right while leaving him a vantage point from the left. As he sorted through his books, he peeked down the hall and spotted Karina going to her locker. Even though only a weekend had gone by, it seemed like forever since he last saw her. He had gotten himself into a corner, and now he was beating himself over it. He knew the more he thought about it, the more difficult he was making things for himself. Now the only thing Ryan had to do was look for an opportunity to speak to her. Now wasn't the right time. But *when* would it be the right time?

You're an idiot. A blasted idiot.

"Rye," a voice exclaimed loudly. He turned his head and saw Mike standing beside him. "You decided to show. I mean—of course you showed."

Ryan casually gathered his belongings.

"Obviously. I'm not going to let Blake muscle me off my own turf."

"Exactly. We got to show him who owns this place. I say we challenge him to a rematch. I think the *secret stuff* must have worn off by now."

Ryan said wryly, "Actually, I think he keeps a bottle of it in his locker."

"Bah, it's just water. You know that. He doesn't have what it really takes to stand toe to toe with the champ."

"—you mean ex-champ," a stray voice called out.

They both turned around and saw some guy neither of them really knew. Mike was ready to speak up before Ryan could even muster a thought.

"He was going easy on him," Mike explained. "You can't humiliate the new kid."

"Sure, whatever you say star twerp."

"He's right," Ryan said. "I was holding back."

"Holding back what? Your diarrhea? You should have just shat all over his face. Blind him. It may have given you a chance."

Ryan grimaced at the thought. But Mike seemed even more revolted.

"Hey," Mike said. "You want a piece of him? Make an appointment."

Ryan cleared his throat. "Mike . . ."

The guy laughed. "No thanks. I'm sure the waiting list is full." After that he took off.

Mike stared at him until he disappeared into the crowd.

"Well, there's your typical Blake advocate. Now days they're all around these parts."

Ryan finished grabbing what he needed and closed his locker shut.

"Don't worry," he said. "The next time I encounter one, I won't hesitate to fire a witty retort."

—)—

Ryan set foot in his physics class, narrowly beating the bell. His teacher, Mr. Deskov, was standing behind the table at the front of the room, sorting through his lesson planner. Though Ryan had a suspicion he wouldn't be referring to it later. They were suppose to cover the chapter on Newton's Laws, and follow it up with a lab experiment—last week. But it was hard to stay on schedule when the topic of discussion was always derailed. It was going to happen again today. Ryan knew it. He could see it on the teachers face—the big sparkling eyes and the uncontrollable grin. He was just waiting for the last couple of students to take their seats.

When everyone settled down, he clasped his hands together and put on an exuberant smile.

He announced to the class, "I'm sure all of you heard the news this weekend. This past Saturday, we lost a well-respected member of the scientific community, in a manner which, up until now, was unheard of.

"Dr. Edmunds was a terrific man. I even had the pleasure of meeting him during my graduate studies. He will be missed." He paused, and looked up at the ceiling with reverence, and then he continued. "Now who wants to tell me what they observed during the newscast?"

One of the girls shot her hand into the air.

"Yes, Rebecca?"

"Well," she said. "Dr. Edmunds hijacked a bus full of people and ordered them to park in an empty lot and—"

"Ah," Mr. Deskov said. "Now did we actually get to observe that part?"

"Oh." The girl giggled. "I guess not."

"That's all right. Please continue. What happened next?"

"He had a gun, and a bomb, and he was ordering the police to give him The Mind. But when they told him he couldn't have it, he shot himself."

"And what did he want to do with The Mind?"

"He wanted to destroy it."

He lifted his index finger, and his mouth opened. "Ah, yes. Now think about that for a second. It's not every day that an engineer is willing to kill himself over not being able to destroy his own work. Then again, a mind is a terrible thing to waste." He received a small chuckle from the class. "Which makes this all the more interesting. Because it was *our* government that decided that thirty-two *human minds* were expendable in order to save an artificial one. Think about that and The Mind becomes a scary piece of equipment, doesn't it?"

Ryan thought about it. It was kind of scary. But what was scary exactly? The Mind by itself wasn't dangerous. Its only function was to conjure up information and advice. It wasn't any more threatening than a fortune-teller. What was dangerous, however, was the application of that knowledge in the real world. It could be used in an endless number of ways.

Mr Deskov continued, "It's almost as if this machine is the next step in our evolutionary development. It's already superseded us on one level: it's smarter than any of us, and smarter than what we could ever hope anyone to be. On top of that, we know it's benign. It has no emotion, no desires, or ambition. It's perfectly content with being the all-knowing brain in a box. We humans, on the other hand, have a tendency to be destructive. We compete with one another, hurt one another, and even harm our own planet. If you think about it, we're really just a bunch of vermin when viewed through the cosmic telescope. Am I right?" he grinned. "Can anyone make an argument to defend our right to exist?"

The class was silent. No one could immediately answer what was asked. There was a couple of drooping heads, a girl playing with her hair, and a guy finishing a homework assignment before it was collected.

Ryan had taken his pencil to his notebook. He drew little figures along the margin. Without really thinking about it, he started drawing the people he saw from his dream. He drew Zephner, holding his motorcycle sword. This reminded him of the time he drew a dragon on a sheet of paper, forgetting that it was something that needed to be handed in. Rather than withholding it, he submitted it anyway, and when he got it back, Mr. Deskov had sketched a tiny knight battling the dragon. Ryan aced that assignment. The question? Yes, Ryan was still thinking about that.

One of the guys in the room raised his hand. Mr. Deskov

called on him to answer.

The guy said, "We humans were the ones who made the machine. That means anything the machine is responsible for, it's credited to us. We're still superior."

"Yes, but superior in what way?"

The guy hesitated for a moment. "We're just smarter. We can invent things."

"Oh!" Mr. Deskov's face lit up. "It looks to me you haven't seen the way The Mind can devise prototypes of machines and devices not yet invented. Through its extensive knowledge of every conceivable subject—science, physics, chemistry, engineering—it can create schematics for just about anything. Say the government wanted to fund a bridge from here to Europe. Aside from it being economically impossible, The Mind would be able to tell you on the fly where you would need to put each pylon, how to position the struts, how many lanes you'd need. I mean, the *entire* blueprint. It would instantaneously check for structural faults or any other potential hazards. It's simply amazing. Now imagine if the government ordered the schematics for something like a time machine. If it were possible, The Mind would discover it by using pure trial and error. It would process thousands of mechanical configurations a minute, ruling out what didn't work through immediate simulations. But to respond to your answer, no. The Mind greatly exceeds our inventing capabilities. So I ask everyone again—why shouldn't we all surrender to our new cerebral overlord?"

The class became silent again. Ryan was still doodling, but also paying attention. He couldn't quite put his thoughts into words, but he felt there was a difference between knowing and understanding. The Mind knew, but it couldn't understand. Therefore, it wasn't anymore qualified to helm the future of mankind than its human counterparts.

The girl from earlier raised her hand again. She was smiling, waiting for her name to be called.

"Yes, Rebecca."

"I think we deserve to live because we have the ability to love one another."

A few boisterous laughs exploded from the corners of the room. Even the teacher had to chuckle. Then the girl started laughing.

"No, really," she said. "The Mind can't love. Because love requires chemicals, like when your brain releases dofamine."

Mr. Deskov was still getting himself under control. "I think you mean dopamine. And yes, I'm pretty certain The Mind can't emulate that chemical process. But then we could still ask ourselves, why do we need love?"

Some student from the back yelled out, "To make babies!"

The class broke out into hysterics. The teacher lost it again. Everyone was laughing.

When he gained some composure, Mr. Deskov spoke again. "But now I can ask, why do we need babies? Why do we need anything? The question still stands."

While the class tried to stifle their laughs, a trancestor had slid its way into the room. "Here it comes again," Mr. Deskov said. "Right on schedule." Everyone's attention diverted to the meandering puck. It weaved around the desks, swiftly making its way over to Ryan.

Not again, Ryan thought. It was the same one, with *no. 7* imprinted on its head. It stopped, and its bead-sized visor pointed towards him. Everyone looked in his direction.

Mr. Deskov shook his head. "I don't know what it is, but The Mind sure finds you fascinating, Ryan."

The class laughed, though Ryan didn't find it that funny. He looked back at the little machine, and the machine stared right back. He was desperate to know what that aluminum drink coaster was thinking. But since it had no face, no expression, there was no way for him to know. This made him dislike The Mind very much.

—)—

Later that morning, Ryan made his way to the cafeteria. As of now, it had been a typical day. He crossed paths with one other person who though it was necessary to poke fun at his defeat, but it was nothing he couldn't deal with. Seemingly most people just didn't care, or were too nice to bring it up. Not even Blake had said anything, but then again, Ryan had yet to see him.

Once inside, Ryan jumped into the lunch line and filled his tray with chicken nuggets and corn kernel. He went back to his table and sat next to Mike, who was gorging his meal like they were giving away free seconds. Between his chewing, he tried speaking to Ryan, while overcoming the noise of a hundred rowdy students.

"Two days until we meet *it* face to face," he said. "What do you think it's going to do to us? What's it going to think of us?"

"Nothing," Ryan said, taking a sip of his milk. "And if you continue down this line of questioning, it's going to think you're a paranoid pooch."

"I wouldn't be the only one paranoid. You saw what happened to Dr. Edmunds. He's way smarter than me, and look what he did to himself."

"One too many late nights in the laboratory, I think."

Ryan took a bite out of his nugget, while Mike stared .

"But what if Dr. Edmunds was right, and this thing really is dangerous. This could spell out the end for our species."

Ryan detected some jesting, but he wasn't entirely sure.

He shrugged. "I guess you can pick up where Dr. Edmunds left off. Do what you must to get close to The Mind, and when you are, knock it over the cerebrum with your copy of World

History."

"Maybe I can break into the museum after-hours, get inside the case and spill some juice on it."

"Not bloody likely," Ryan said, doing his best British accent. "They've revamped the museum's security ten-fold before they even let The Mind be brought in. They got like hundreds of sensors monitoring every angle of the room, lasers, scanners, undercover security guards. Even the case that it's in is said to be indestructible by anything short of a nuclear blast."

Mike threw his fist down on the table.

"Bullocks."

At that moment, Megan walked up to the table, carrying a grilled chicken salad. She was less than lively. Maybe even a bit sullen. It was unusual for her not to say anything at all upon sitting. Ryan and Mike both knew that if she was in one of her moods, it would be necessary to proceed with caution.

Ryan watched as she dumped the cup of dressing into the container. She closed it and shook the thing like a kid shaking a piggy bank. When she was done, she reopened the container and began to eat.

"So that birthday party," Ryan said, trying to sound casual. "How did that go?"

"Oh, it was excellent," she said, with blatant sarcasm. "We snacked on junk food, we exchanged fashion tips, we clogged a toilet, and stayed up late watching scary movies. Best day ever."

"Sounds like those girls know how to have a party. Shame I wasn't there," he said, reciprocating the sarcasm.

Mike said, "Meanwhile, Ryan and I watched the terror unfold."

Megan sighed. "Oh, that. I caught the late-night coverage yesterday. Not the kind of ending I was expecting. At least the only causality was the assailant."

"Do you think Dr. Edmunds was crazy?" Ryan asked her.

"Crazy? Yes. But a better way to describe him would be a whistle-blower that didn't know how to handle the situation."

"Maybe he exhausted every other option."

"Maybe. But I still don't believe commandeering a bus and holding hostages was the right follow-up."

Mike swallowed what was in his mouth and added, "I guess you could say he was . . . *out of his mind*."

"So what would have been the right answer?" Ryan asked.

"Not building the stupid thing in the first place. The last thing humanity needs is yet another gadget to grow dependent on. Mr. Deskov, as I expected, was going on and on about how one day we will reach a point when we humans won't even have to use our minds, because there will be machines that can do the thinking better than we can. He gave the example of doctors, who instead of coming up with the diagnoses themselves, would just input symptoms and a patient medical history into a computer, which would then spit out the name of the disease. And bam, just like that, we don't need diagnosticians."

"I wouldn't be surprised if that was already part of The Mind's capabilities," Ryan said.

"It is. That's why we have so many people lobbying against this abomination. Like I said, doctors, along with market analysts, business consultants, and so on. But of course, as many as they make, they're still outnumbered by the amount of people who think this machine is 'cool'."

Mike lowered his head in shame. "I think it's cool," he said. "Even if it makes our minds obsolete."

"Mike, your mind has been obsolete since they invented the abacus."

He looked at her dumbly. "I don't know what that is, but judging from your tone, I think it's an insult."

"Not the most daring assumption I've heard," Ryan said. He ate another one of his nuggets and took a sip of milk. He looked at Megan, who was making slow progress with her salad, and said to her, "I didn't see you pass by the hall this morning. Was the bus late?"

She put on a big grin, her mouth still filled with salad. She shook her head.

"Not exactly, Ryan."

"Not exactly? What does that mean?"

Megan motioned her head to the left. Ryan looked in that direction and scanned the crowd. His eyes jumped from head to head, until they eventually fell upon the guy with the golden hair. Blake was sitting at a table with a couple of his buddies. For whatever reason, he had chosen to ignore Ryan all day. It was strange.

"Blake? What about him?"

Megan pressed her lips together. She forced herself to talk.

"He approached me this morning, reminding me that he hadn't forgotten about that love note. And me, being the faithful friend that I am, went along with the little charade."

"What did he say?" Mike asked nervously.

"Oh, you know. He was talking about how he thought about me over the weekend and how he believes this is the beginning of something wonderful. But that's not all."

"What else is there?" Ryan said.

"Well," Megan said, speaking with strong reservation, "To add the icing on the cake, he wants to bring me along on a special outing tomorrow."

Mike gazed in horror. "You mean like a date?"

"Yes, Mike, a date."

Mike stroked his chin, relishing the possibilities.

"This is excellent," he declared. "This is a perfect way to get some exclusive intel. Maybe we can find a weakness and exploit it next time Ryan faces him."

Ryan nearly coughed up his food. He didn't like the sound of it.

"Hold up, Mike. It may be a while before that happens again."

"No, we got to strike again, and fast. We got to go blitzkrieg on his ass."

"I rather plan my battles carefully," Ryan said. "The last thing I want is to be murdered again."

Megan was disgruntled by having to listen to the two of them bickering. She didn't wait long before interjecting.

"I hate to have to remind you two that the course of future events depends heavily upon what I decide to do tomorrow."

The two of them stopped talking at once.

"What do you mean," Mike said. "You're going to go along with it, right?"

Ryan, feeling guilty about the position she was in, wasn't so quick to a press her into doing something she didn't want to do. But at the same time, if Blake found out that the whole thing was a sham, there would undoubtedly be some kind of repercussion.

Ryan looked at her pleadingly, and said, "What if I told you that I'd like to see you pose just a little longer?"

"Ryan, you know I'd do just about anything for you, but asking me to sustain a fake relationship lays really close to the line I'm not willing to cross."

"Then how about this: you go on this one date, and you botch the whole thing. Make it a horrible experience for both of you. And then tell him it was all just a bad idea. This way no one has to learn the truth."

Megan grimaced at the suggestion. "That's brilliant. Just brilliant. Meanwhile, I come off looking like a total bimbo. Quite frankly, this scheme has Mike written all over it. Have you been talking to him?"

Both of them shook their heads right away.

"Furthermore, how exactly am I suppose to botch this so

thoroughly?"

"Be creative," Ryan said. "Use that date when you were in eighth grade as a reference point."

Megan narrowed her eyes at him.

"Now how would you know anything about that? I never brought that up before, not with either of you."

Ryan thought about it, and when he did, many pieces of the puzzle clicked. It was true that Megan never mentioned that to him—*here*. But there, on the other side, they discussed it at length. She spilled something she wouldn't have openly admitted to while she was awake. That's when Ryan wondered if these two Megans were, in fact, one in the same.

"Are you sure?" Ryan said anyway, trying to dodge the issue.

"Yes, I'm sure. But it doesn't really matter. I'm sure things will become nightmarish all on their own."

"So that means you'll do it?"

She blew out a stream of air through her lips. "I guess so. But consider this the last and only time I'll bail you out for Mike's shenanigans."

"Sounds like a deal."

Megan rolled her eyes, and looked back to study the guy she got mixed up with. She was staring at him for a while, at the ostentatious hair, and his lean, stalwart body. She was locked in a sort of daydream until Mike's voice filled her ears.

"Hey, what do you want?" he said.

Ryan and Megan saw Mike peering over the end of the table. They leaned forward and discovered one of the trancestors parked beside them on the floor. Its beady sensor was focused directly on Ryan. It pivoted itself from side to side, inching closer to him little by little, gauging his trust, like a curious animal. Ryan read the top plate and saw that it was no. 7. It had decided to follow him all the way over here. But for what?

"It's stalking me," Ryan said, feeling silly.

"It is?" Mike said, intrigued.

"Yeah. For the past week or so, that thing has been creeping into all my classes, just to stare at me. People are going to start wondering why."

"Do you know why?" Megan asked.

"I haven't the slightest idea. I'm ordinary. There's no reason it should be interested in me."

"Apparently there is. As you've told me before, numbers don't lie."

"They do if you use the wrong ones."

"Who says that they're wrong?"

"Who says that they're right?"

"All right," she said, throwing her hands up in surrender. "Not again. You're all illegal martians as far as I'm concerned."

Mike wasn't listening. He was still looking at the machine, despite that it clearly showed no interest in him. Only Ryan.

"Hey, Ryan," he said. "I'll buy ya an ice cream sandwich if you manage to pin it down."

A fair challenge, Ryan thought. As he knew, the trancestors were as quick and agile as a rodent. They're ball-like wheels allowed them to accelerate and change direction on a nanosecond's notice if they thought the sole of a sneaker was about to come down on them. This was how they were able to weave through crowds without being trampled.

"Deal," Ryan said, knowing it was a futile attempt. After all, the trancestor was able to hear them. It knew what Mike asked, and yet strangely, it didn't try to move itself out of harms way.

Ryan readied his foot. He looked down at the little machine, then looked away, assuming a casual posture. He waited, and then took another peek over the table. The machine was still parked in the same spot. Not moving, just staring, assimilating information. Ryan looked away again. And then, when he felt the moment was right, he lifted his foot and stomped it into the ground with full force. Anyone watching would have thought he was nuts. And maybe he was for trying to assault a helpless robot.

But he missed, as the machine scurried away just in time to avoid the pounding. It looked back at Ryan with its beady sensor, periodically blinking its shutter. It eased backwards slowly, before turning around and fleeing the cafeteria.

Ryan turned to Mike, looking doleful.

"Why do I feel terrible now?"

Megan butted in. "Because you just tried to assassinate number seven. He probably admired you. You should feel ashamed."

"Thanks a lot, Megan. I do."

"Don't mention it."

—)—

Later that night the clock marked the tenth hour, telling Ryan he should probably be getting to bed, where he would go to sleep, and return to that place. It was routine now, he knew it. But unlike any ordinary adventure, he also knew he couldn't take anything along with him, except for whatever he could carry in his mind.

That night Ryan decided to bring along a newfound willingness and determination to resolve the adversities that had befallen this other universe. He could do it, he thought, because he was dreaming. He knew that on the other side there were no limitations. If he focused on it, he could fly, teleport, or do any other physically impossible feat. If he allowed it to happen, it could happen.

Ryan closed his eyes, and after clearing his head of creeping thoughts, he fell asleep.

—)—

Ryan was awakened by a persistent nudge on his shoulder. He didn't know how long he was out. When he opened his eyes, he saw himself on the floor, lying in the pile of tattered coats. He was back, he said to himself.

He turned over on his back and looked into the ceiling lights. He squinted and was able to make out Steve's face hovering over him. He seemed less tense than before. He was calling Ryan's name, with a calm voice.

"Ryan, we're getting ready to land," he said. "They want us at the southern docking platform."

Ryan sat up and rubbed his eyes. He let out a yawn before speaking.

"How long has it been?" he said, climbing back up on his feet.

"About four hours. We're orbiting Armon right now. We're packed and ready for descent."

"That was fast."

Ryan looked around the room and saw that everything was quiet and calm. There were no further damages.

"Is Guin still here?" he asked.

Steve's expression was filled with resentment. He fell serious, letting out a breath of exhaustion. "Yeah, he's still here. He's inside the Conoblis, fast asleep."

Ryan glanced over his shoulder, finding it hard to believe such an surly animal could manage such a long nap. Even though he's proven to be harmless, Ryan wasn't on board with the idea of the three of them traveling together.

"You know," Ryan said, "I'd understand if you didn't want Guin tagging along with us. I know you hold him accountable for what happened—"

"No, no," he interrupted, holding out his hand. "I don't. Not anymore."

Ryan looked at him puzzled. "What do you mean not anymore?"

"We've already received our first piece of intel. Cyannus wasn't the first planet these people have destroyed. This is a full-on assault on the galaxy."

"Where did this information come from?"

"An intelligence agency under Knivus' administration."

"Who's Knivus?"

"He's the head of the Garthega Federation, and the man we're going to be meeting. He's asked that you come along, given the integral role you've played in everything thus far. He'd like to ask you a few things personally."

"Great," Ryan said. "I wanted to come along anyway."

"And Guin," Steve said, looking back, "based on his claim about having information, Knivus asked that he be present as well."

"What about everyone else on board?"

"They've arranged for them to be sent to a refugee center, where they'll stay for as long as it takes them to get back on their feet. They should fair well, given the technology that's available. There's therapy that allows for memory altercation. They'll be able to forget the whole thing ever happened. I'm sure a lot of them will opt for that route."

"And what about Leilah? Are they going to be able to do anything for her?"

Steve frowned. His eyes looked down towards the floor. "They're going to transport her to the local hospital. The doctors may be able to do more for her there."

"That's good to hear."

Steve nodded, trying to put on a smile but wasn't quite able to manage. "Well," he said. "I guess you better hurry and wake Guin. Every second we wait could be another second too late."

"On it," Ryan said.

He hurried over to the Conoblis and stepped inside. He went

to the rear of the vessel and saw Guin huddled in the corner, away from the blood spill. His belly rose and fell as he wheezed quietly through his beak. He was completely out, probably hungry too.

"Guin," Ryan whispered. When he didn't responded, Ryan spoke a little louder.

The penguin grumbled and continued to snooze.

"Guin!"

"Whaaaat!" Guin shouted, his eyes bursting wide.

"We gotta go. We're ready to land."

Still groggy, he stood up, stretched his flippers, extended his claws, which still made Ryan's hair stand on end. His beak twitched, as if munching on the food that wasn't there. He stepped forward, one webbed foot at a time. He looked down.

"That thing was here before. What the hell is it?"

"Huh?" Ryan said, before looking down at his own feet.

Bee was there, as still and motionless as a basketball at rest should be. He nudged Ryan's ankles.

"Okay," he said. "I'm sure you can come too."

Guin wrinkled his brow. "Whatever. But I'm riding shotgun."

"Of course, Guin."

———CHAPTER 20———

INTO THE TWILIGHT

They had departed the *Obsidian* in a small vessel and were now plunging into a cluster of orange cotton clouds that made up the view through each and every window. The sky was warm, lit by the rays of sun that seeped through the haze. It was a vast, ethereal emptiness that evoked feelings of comfort and serenity to anyone that gazed upon it.

Ryan sat in the cabin, admiring the view through their respective windows; Guin was on the floor, with his face nestled deep into the feathers of his belly. He groaned on occasion to let the others know how much he loathed the ride.

"What are you doing, Guin?" Ryan asked. "You're missing everything."

"That's the whole point," he grumbled.

"What's the matter? Afraid of heights?"

Guin groaned again. "You can hear it straight from the penguin's mouth: there's a reason we don't fly."

"Are you sure it's not just you?"

"I'm sure."

"Whatever you say."

Ryan looked out the window again, enchanted by the way the clouds filled the sky. It truly was a sight to behold, and it allowed him to forget about his reason for coming here. Even Steve was captivated by its beauty. It was a sky he never had the pleasure of seeing first hand.

He stared in awe. "This is stunning," he said. "The pictures I've seen don't even do it justice."

"Just you wait," Reynard said, sitting up front at the cockpit. "There will be a lot more to see once we get through the troposphere. I'm sure you'll find Carthelona City to be more than what you could ever have imagined. Keep your eyes peeled toward the port side."

Ryan continued searching the skies for the first structure he could see.

The vessel descended further through the thick canopy at a steady rate. Another minute had passed, and by then, Ryan could make out the tapering peaks of mountain tops. They were lightly coated in a blanket of snow, with broad slopes that leveled out gradually. Many pines rose through the bare rock, becoming denser and more lush as they got closer to the bottom.

They dipped below the mountain peaks, passing through another layer of clouds. That's when Ryan spotted the needle of a lofty, imposing tower.

It was grander than anything he had ever seen before—an ensign that served to welcome them to this unfamiliar world. The highest decks protruded from the central core, much like the pommel of a sword. Below that were three massive buttresses running along the central column, with thousands of slits for thousands of windows. In between were an assemblage of elevators, zipping up and down like tiny spiders scurrying along a dangling tread of silk. They would disappear and reappear through the sea of clouds. The girth of the structure was massive —just as big, if not bigger than the biggest baseball stadiums he had been to. But the true beauty of it all was how the building gave off a lustrous shine of azure blue, a majestic quality that was surreal.

He turned his head and looked over at the cockpit. He could

see the side of Reynard's head. "So where exactly are we going?" he asked.

"The Icosagon," Reynard said, "to meet with Zachary Knivus. That place is his central point of operation. From there, he oversees all of his subsidiary agencies: military research and development, agriculture, pharmaceuticals, and so forth."

"So you really think they could help us?"

"The Garthega Federation has my full confidence."

This made Ryan feel at ease, for the time being. He was still very much distracted by the view outside his window.

The vessel made a sudden descent, diving through the last wispy traces of haze, bringing everyone face to face with a spectacularly wondrous view of Carthelona City.

The cityscape pierced the horizon like a cluster of stalagmites. There were thousands upon thousands of towers and buildings as far as the eye could see. They decorated the landscape like a swarm of fireflies, up against the waning light of dusk. The structures shimmered with the same brilliance as the tower they had just passed. They came in a multitude of colors—from wintry blues to sunset oranges, even reds and golds—a dripping cascade of paint from an artist's palette. They came in many different shapes and forms, ranging from the usual quadrilateral tower, to the ones with a dozen faces, with curves and sloping corners. There were no shortage of variations.

Ryan's jaw hung as they rode deeper into the city. The buildings were racing towards them, growing bigger, grander, and more dazzling.

In the distance, coming up on their left, was a cylindrical tower, with a rooftop as bright as the midday sun. It projected an analog clock onto the darkening sky. The time was 6:12, and ticking.

Another building, this one spiraling into the air like a helix, had multiple glass orbs encased at different levels, as if a tree trunk had swallowed them. But these orbs were at least a hundred feet across, fully filled with glowing water, which, from what Ryan could observe, were teeming with aquatic life—or hotel guests.

Just next to that was another tower that looked like a collection of organ pipes bundled together to fit inside a circular imprint. And at the top of each of these pipes was a glass dome, harboring a number of facilities, from swimming pools to performance theaters.

Their vessel decreased in altitude, slowly merging with the aerial transit. There was a swarm of automobiles, weaving above the city blocks at varying heights. They traveled at a high velocity, just within a few feet of one another. Their movement was perfectly synchronized.

These vehicles had sleek, slender bodies, not much different than the ones Ryan saw in Cyannus. Their base dimensions were equilateral, as oppose to the more rectangular shapes he was used to. Every angle was sculpted to optimize its aerodynamic capabilities. It was smooth, graceful, like the torso of a manta ray. The windshield was narrow, but extended all the way to the backside of the vehicle. The propulsion system was located on the rear and underside, made up of flat, metallic disks, which, from what Ryan could see, weren't emitting any kind of heat or exhaust. Gravity manipulation? Maybe, Ryan thought.

With a quick dive they slipped into the uppermost lane, squeezing right between two cars. Ryan braced for impact, sure they would collide, but they didn't. They now flowed harmoniously with the traffic, just like a school of fish.

Guin was clenching his beak, groaning at the sudden jerk. His claws were unsheathed, burrowed in the upholstery.

"Is he *trying* to kill the survivors?" he wined. "If my life flashes before my eyes one more time, I'm not only going to be a flightless bird, but a blind bird as well."

Steve was sitting beside him, relaxed and well accustomed to the volatile velocity. He marveled at the glowing cityscape rushing past the window.

"It's all perfectly safe," he said. "Aerial transit systems are fully automated. It's computationally impossible to have an accident."

"I'd like to see how that theory holds up in the event of an unforeseeable mechanical failure."

"Statistically, it's not even worth worrying about."

"Statistically, I stab the engine and we create new statistics that take into account temperamental animals."

Ryan sighed. "Guin, let's try to avoid talking about numbers. All they do is create problems."

Guin silenced himself, but not before uttering incomprehensible babel. He turned around and noticed he had company. Bee saw him and rolled on over, circling him like a curious cat. Guin vigilantly tracked its motions. It didn't taking long before it became a bother.

"Unbelievable," he muttered quietly, rolling his eyes.

After cruising for several minutes, Reynard announced that they were closing in on their destination, the Icosagon. The premises was surrounded by ten acres of grass, with paved walkways that meandered through botanical gardens and decoratively spruced trees. At best, it was a paltry effort to cultivate a city that had been criticized for lacking the color green. Industrialists had joked, telling them to move to the mountains. Some actually did. And it wasn't a bad place to reside in either. You had the evergreen forest, and a spectacular view of the surrounding landscape. Then the industrialists joked again, saying that by living comfortably in the mountains, they were encouraging more urban development. And heck, given the mountainous terrain of the region, it was the next logical place (and only place) to build. The only real obstacle was the cost. If it ever became financially feasible, Knivus voiced his interest in building a new city *inside* a mountain. He was chided for that as well.

He was a man with a long legacy. He was fifty-eight years old, having been commander of the region for thirty-two years. And he would remain in office, either until retirement, or death, whichever came first. The people would then elect another.

He was a very ambitious man, pushing for many different agendas. One of his first mandates was the definitive transition to a mandatory class V transit system, which meant that every automobile had to be in the air, and part of the aerial transit grid network, or ATGN. Every vehicle on the network collectively communicated with one another, always aware of their relative position. They all followed a digital track: eight lanes wide, and fifteen lanes high. Certain lanes were reserved for emergency vehicles. New lanes could be added by the press of a few buttons.

As far as parking went, there were garage towers, which were open air structures with thousands of pockets—a building without walls—a beehive, essentially. The vehicles would autonomously communicate with the tower and find a space suitable for its size.

Parking underground was another option. Select avenues had entrances on the street level where vehicles could descend into. Normally this would grant quicker access to ground level venues, as pedestrians would only need to travel up one floor to get to their destination.

All in all, the drive behind the mandate was not only to clear up the streets for commuters and tourist alike (which would substantially improve foot traffic), but rather to prove to the nations of every world that the ATGN would optimize travel efficiency, therefore producing an economical surge. This was a technology to be sold and profited from, which Knivus effectively did.

But just like with any successful business enterprise, there came a share of failures. There were certain mishaps in the military sector that had yet to show the full extent of the repercussions. There were skeletons in the closet that were still being kept secret from public knowledge.

—)—

The Icosagon loomed in the distance, just a couple blocks away. At their current velocity, they would arrive in a few short seconds.

It was a sizable structure, towering to a height of about two hundred stories. The building itself appeared cylindrical from a distance, but actually comprised twenty separate faces. The highest floors had aerial docks, reserved for high-ranking officials, or any visitor with an invitation.

The vessel made the necessary calculations and rapidly weaved through several lanes to make their next turn (as Guin held on for dear life). The abrupt maneuver was then followed up by a sudden ascent into the air, in the direction of the building. The vessel positioned itself carefully, aiming directly for the dock on the 194th floor. The approach was smooth, no different than a car driving into a garage. A row of flashing beacons marked the landing area.

Once the vessel hovered into position, it settled down onto the metallic platform. Before anyone could step outside, a safety gate rose from the ground behind them.

"This is it," Reynard said. "This is where we get off."

He activated a switch, and the passenger doors slid open. The first alarming sensation was the boisterous sound of the wind gushing into the alcove on the side of the building.

Ryan carefully stepped out onto the platform, feeling like he had stepped into a hurricane. His first instinct was to hold on to the wall for support. But it wasn't necessary. The intensity of the wind was made partly illusory by the fact that they were about two-thousand feet off the ground. It actually wasn't too bad. Steve was standing upright just fine. Guin however, waddled with his claws extended, ready to drive them into the floor if an extra heavy gust tried to sweep him away.

Ryan got the urge to tease him. "What do you think of this?" he said.

Guin looked back at him grumpily. "I think the architects were psychos." He hurried forward, as quickly as his short, stubby feet would allow.

Everyone passed through the door up ahead and entered a small room An officer was stationed here, giving the group clearance to continue. He gave directions to Reynard on how to reach the lobby for the conference room. Reynard thanked the man and proceeded through the airlock and into the interior of the building.

They entered a long capacious corridor, that was at the level of opulence they all expected. The path was wide, and the ceiling tall and curved. Sheets of frosty glass hung along the walls at equidistant intervals, lit from behind. The floor was covered with a rich blue carpet, decorated with elegant motifs.

Ryan admired the appearance of the building. It instilled him with hope that Knivus was a man with the necessary faculty to make something happen. His power and affluence were evident by the sheer prevalence of wealth that was this city. It was only logical to believe the federation's military was equally impressive. Maybe they were capable of just blowing those bastards up, as Leilah had once suggested.

He thought about how she was doing. Right now, she was on route to the hospital. It was Steve's intentions to go visit her there immediately after these discussions were over. Ryan was surprised by the way he was holding together. If one were to look at him this very moment, they would suspect nothing was wrong. It was remarkable taking into account the catastrophe he was forced to endure. Yes, the ERR training may have played a part, but he was afraid that it was only a precarious solution, a shoddy glue job that was liable to fall apart any second.

"We want to go down this hall, and then take a left," Reynard said.

The three others followed his lead. Guin eyed every piece of decoration, grimacing at the ostentatious ensemble. Ryan could imagine the restraint Guin had to employ to not etch carvings into all the fancy glasswork. Also following the conga line was the unassuming bundle of air and rubber that he named Bee. What business a basketball had here, he didn't know. But he looked to be coming along one way or another.

They turned left into the next corridor, where there was a long glass wall. It was the first time Ryan got a view of the city while keeping in one place. There were so many automobiles, he thought. They were as plentiful as raindrops falling horizontally. At the peak of night they must have looked like fireflies glued to a treadmill. It was absolutely crazy. And the buildings were nothing to sneeze at either. He could see hundreds of them down the scope of the endless street. A lot of them were of a similar height to the Icosagon, but others greatly surpassed it, like that one tower they saw on the flight here. It made every other one look like a dog house in comparison.

"Here to the right," Reynard said, and they followed.

They passed through another corridor that eventually led to the lobby they were looking for. The room was sublime from floor to ceiling. There were a pair of crystal chandeliers, and a large gray marble desk. Behind the desk was a young female secretary that Reynard went to speak with right away. Steve went along with him while Ryan and Guin moseyed on over to the seating area, with the big blue armchairs, couches and the glass coffee tables.

There was someone already there—a girl, sitting with her legs crossed, with an opened magazine covering her face. She had on black jeans and an orange polo, which indicated to Ryan that either that outfit was in style in this city, or Megan was alive.

He flanked her position, looking for the face that hid behind the magazine.

It was her.

He was glad and overjoyed, swamped by the sweet remembrance of their happy youth, and all the wonderful times they shared. They had a future again, and the opportunity to continue making memories together. It was an impossible wish that, by some inexplicable means, had been granted.

He approached her slowly, his nerves tingling. He discovered that he hadn't the slightest idea what he should say. His spontaneous appearance would probably alarm her as much as hers did him.

He was standing only a few feet away, looking dumbly down at her. She was heavily invested in whatever she was reading, her eyes glued to the page. Maybe it was something interesting. What kind of articles would they have around here anyway? Definitely none about basketball. They don't seem to have that around here. Maybe Gravalon? Maybe about the ongoing crisis? Why was his mind prattling?

Her eyes shifted, off the page and over to the figure standing just outside her range of vision.

Her eyes opened. The magazine dropped onto her lap.

"Ryan!" she gasped. She looked at him, surprised, horrified, bewildered, everything at once.

"Megan," he said, with a smile.

She sprung up from the couch and rushed over to him, charging like a bull. He braced for impact, but instead felt her arms lasso themselves around his body, locking him in a constrictive embrace. There was nothing he could do about it, even if he wanted to. Thinking about it, this was the first time she had ever hugged him for anything.

With her head rested on his shoulder, she said to him, "Ryan, I thought you were dead. I practically watched you die."

"I could say the same."

Suddenly, she released her hold, but only so she could smack him upside the head (*that was more like it*).

"Ow," he said, without any feeling behind it. "Do I really deserve that?"

"Ryan!" she yelled. "You go to the restroom and never come back. What the hell is that all about?"

"I'm sorry. It was beyond my control. I drifted away to another place."

"While leaving me behind to fend for myself on a planet that was about to burst."

Megan fell back on the couch, crossing her arms and legs.

"I would have rescued you if I could, but I was far away."

"That's swell, Ryan. Real swell. Luckily, my knight in battered leather came to sweep me off my feet to go for a ride on his motorcycle."

Despite the metaphor, Ryan knew who she was talking about. It was a most pleasant surprise to find out that the man who had helped him this far along had survived.

"Are you talking about Zephner?" Ryan asked.

"Yeah. Something like that. I'll tell ya, he was hellbent on finding you. He teared through that museum just to find out that you teleported through a restroom stall. He didn't even want to tell me what it was all about until later after I pried it out of him."

"He told you everything?"

"Just about. He told me about these intruders who are ransacking every galaxy in hopes of finding this Dreamer's World. And on top of that, they're under the impression that you know a thing or two about it."

Ryan had lost focus, and became distracted by whatever conversation was taking place between Reynard and Steve at the other side of the room.

"Well?"

Ryan looked back at her. "What?"

"Do you know anything about the Dreamer's World?"

He shook his head. "No. Not really."

"Figures."

"But there is one thing I do want to know."

"And what's that?"

"How did you make it out alive? How did Zephner know to leave?"

"That was the creepy part. After Zephner and I accepted the fact that you were gone, we went back out to the streets and only minutes into our ride, we both heard this beastly roar. It was so freaking loud. It was like a ship horn, accompanied by the insufferable screech of a violin."

"A musical poltergeist?"

"No, Ryan! This was some kind of physical manifestation. I could hear the tremors in the distance. I could hear destruction, things breaking, buildings collapsing. Something *was* there. Something extremely dangerous."

Ryan was now paying close attention. Things could be worse than he thought.

"Then what did you guys do?"

"Well, Zephner heard it, and he seemed to know exactly what it meant. He told me that it was a sign that we had to get out of there. When you hear the cry of the beast, the cry of all shall end. That's what he told me. That's how he knew Cyannus was going to perish. So we hightailed it out of there and came here."

Ryan didn't know what to say. It was hard to believe, but he had to believe it, given everything that had happened so far. No one was safe. No *place* was safe. If this session with Knivus didn't produce a solution to this universal crisis, the end would come sooner rather than later.

"And you know what else he told me?"

"What?"

"We're dreaming. All of this is a dream. Which I guess explains our escapade earlier. None of it made sense, and now I know why."

"But there was still meaning behind the things you said. The story you told me was true, right?"

She glared at him, arms still crossed. "I'm sure you'd like to believe that."

Megan turned her head, now noticing the penguin and the basketball just a few seats over. Both of them were on the floor. The penguin was murmuring something to the ball, and then slapping it away with its flipper. The ball rolled halfway across the room before it could regain traction and find its way back. It always came back, no matter what.

"That basketball," Megan said. "Is that the same—"

"It is," Ryan said.

Megan watched the way it moved along the floor on its own. She looked as if she were going to say something, but chose not to. Instead her attention shifted to the penguin, who quickly noticed her stalking eyes.

"Great," Guin murmured. "Another one."

Rather than be taken aback by the animal's speech, she stared, somewhat unimpressed. Nothing could surprise her anymore.

She looked back at Ryan with strong disapproval.

"Ryan," she said, "I'm not one to judge, but you really need to reconsider the friends you choose."

"They're really not so bad once you get to know them. Guin

got involved with us unintentionally, but he's making the best of it. And Bee, well, he just likes to follow me around. He's like a gerbil inside a ball. Nothing too unusual."

"Apparently you've been coming here more than I imagined."

"You get used to it."

"Unfortunately. And what about the two Homo sapiens? What's their story?" She nodded to Reynard and Steve who were still hanging around the other side of the room.

"I met them when I teleported to a space station. Reynard, the older guy, is the captain; the other guy, Steve, is a fighter pilot. They were returning to Cyannus from a mission when the explosion happened. So now they, along with a few other crew members, are the last survivors of their world."

"Oh, God, that's horrible. I can't even begin to imagine what that must feel like."

"They're trained not to feel it . . . in a way."

"Really . . ."

Ryan saw Steve moving towards them, calmly and curiously. While laying eyes on Megan, he said to Ryan, "Friend of yours?"

"Yes," he answered. "Her name's Megan. We were talking and, we think she's a dreamer too."

He remained unimpressed. There was no light in his eyes, unlike when he first figured out the truth about Ryan.

"Amazing," he said dully. "I go all these years questioning the existence of such travelers, and now I encounter two on the same day." He extended his hand. "I'm Steve, by the way."

Megan reached out and gave a perfunctory shake, trying to pinpoint what exactly was off about his character.

"I'm really sorry to hear about what happened," she said. To him. "Ryan was just telling me about it. I can hardly believe it."

Steve, for a quick, subtle instant, scowled at Ryan, obviously wishing he'd never brought up that incident at all.

"We can't let that bother us right now," he said. "We need to be looking forward, ready to stop whatever is coming next."

"I guess you're right," Megan said, glancing over at Ryan.

Reynard was walking over dutifully. It was clear he was invested in one thing, and one thing only, and that was getting to the bottom of what happened today.

He concisely relayed the message to the group: "Knivus is ready to see us now."

Chapter 21

Plan of Action

The secretary ushered them through the double doors and into the next room. This was the first time any of them would meet with Knivus, and so they had no idea what to expect. The general populace had labeled him as a stubborn, egotistical man, but at the same time, he was the kind of man that produced results, leaving little to argue about.

The sheer immensity of the room came with no surprise. It was very much like stepping into the mouth of a whale, though not quite as alarming. It was globular in shape, with sturdy wooden beams arcing from one end of the room to the other. At the central apex was a spherical bulb, about five feet across, with smaller, ornamental bulbs orbiting around it along silver rings. The surrounding walls were almost entirely made up of glass. The windows were vertically elongated, rounded along the top. The marvelous city surrounded them from all sides—the most spectacular wallpaper of all.

At the far end of the room was a row of bookcases, juxtaposed in a semi-circle. The center set stood the tallest, while the others tapered in height. On each end were sets of drawers and cabinets, topped with unusual sculptures of wrought metal, meshed together in some geometric design.

But all of this really served as nothing more than a backdrop to the imposing desk at the dead center of the room. Resting on an elevated platform, it took aesthetic precedence over everything. The wood was a dark umber, covered in a rich varnish. The front and side panels were embellished with carved reliefs. It was perfectly suited for the man that sat behind it.

Zachary Knivus sat tall, with arms resting over the armrests of his lofty chair, his fingers curled into fists. His face was stern and rugged, with his brows weighing down on his eyes. He had short black hair and deep blue eyes that emitted a powerful gaze, and wore a black suit that was tailored to fit his broad figure.

He watched closely as Reynard and the others entered the room. Naturally they gravitated to the black couches that were positioned to the left and right sides of the desk. But before they could seat themselves, Knivus projected his voice loud and clearly.

"Thank you all for coming. Please have a seat."

They did as they were told. Reynard and Steve sat together on one couch, while Ryan and Megan took the other. Guin and Bee stayed on the floor.

Ryan, upon entering the room, made an observation that required him to bridle his enthusiasm. He didn't want to say anything, or look overjoyed, but Knivus wasn't alone in the room. Zephner was there, standing to the right of the desk. He had noticed Ryan entering, but then quickly looked away, down at the floor. Aside from Zephner, there was one other man in the room, seated off to one side.

He studied this man, and discerned him as some kind of military figure, roughly in his forties. He was a tall, well-built individual that had clearly partaken in rigorous physical training. He had a long black coat that was tossed over the back of the chair. With the gold epaulettes, and the tall collar, the coat had a striking resemblance to the one that Martisse had wore. But most peculiar was the way it was roughed up and wrinkled, much like the condition of the man's visage. Aside from his hair being dirty and disheveled, his face was glum and sullen. There was at least one gash over his right eye.

This man had paid little attention when the group entered the room, glancing only momentarily at Ryan. Ryan had looked back at him, only to find something remarkably familiar about his green, torture-stricken eyes.

Knivus leaned forward, intertwining his fingers together. He looked over at Reynard and Steve.

"Captain, Lieutenant," he said, "I truly regret the circumstances that have brought us here today. I understand there's nothing that I could tell you to allay the misfortune that has befallen the two of you, and the rest of your crew. Nevertheless, you have my deepest sympathies."

"Thank you, Commander," Reynard said.

Knivus continued, "Now I'm sure you're interested to hear about everything we know regarding the attack. But first let me introduce you to the two men that will be present here with us." He held his hand out. "The man to my left goes by the name of Zephner. He's an . . independent contractor that has worked closely with several crime units and military agencies in this sector, primarily aiding in field operations."

Knivus then looked to his right, and hesitated, not so eager to exalt the man.

"And this here is Marcus Grieve. For many years he served as an astute general, until eventually facing a dishonorable discharge, on the account of comprising a critical military operation, and for the deaths of over two hundred soldiers. The only reason he sits in this room right now is because of his subsequent involvement with the enemy. Then after having his resignation go awry, he's now willing to come forward with information that may help us better understand our situation."

After being stigmatized, a collection of scowls fell upon Grieve. Guin particularly looked ready to sever the man's head right then and there, but was somehow able to find a way to restrain himself. But Ryan however, was ready to give him the benefit of the doubt. He was looking directly at Grieve, who, by no fair testimony, could be compared to the barbarous men that he'd already met. After the divulge of information, he no longer had any doubt that the outfit he wore was the same worn by Martisse and Malcus. But their resemblance ended there. This man, Grieve, was remorseful, more than sorry for whatever atrocities he had committed. He couldn't even look back at the faces that chastised him.

Reynard looked away and said to Knivus, "Let's not waste any time beating around the bush. What exactly is our situation? Where do we stand?"

Knivus answered him, "The calamities we have been dealing with are unquestionably linked to a man who is referred to as Lord Triocks. He hails from one of the deepest, darkest corners of the universe, and is said to be one that reigns over a thousand kingdoms, empowered by the same deity that governs the very laws of existence. Physical descriptions peg him as being remarkably tall and meager; he never exhibits any emotion but pure sorrow. Yet he conducts himself in a manner that garners undivided loyalty from his followers. Apart from his name, I couldn't tell you which details from his dossier are taken from fact or fable. As for this man's intentions, I'll allow Grieve to apprise you of that."

Knivus extended his hand and all eyes were back on Grieve. The man painfully turned his head to face the others. He was hunched forward, with an elbow rested on one thigh, and a hand planted on the other. It was the only way he could control the trembling.

"Captain," he said. "I want to express my condolences to you personally. As well as to you, Lieutenant. The truth is, the past few years have been tragic for many people, especially for those that have lost loved ones." He took in a deep breath, and exhaled.

"And to corroborate what Commander Knivus said, I was, for a time, involved in Triocks' mission. I was appointed to executive officer and delegated—"

"I'd rather not hear it," Reynard interrupted. "There's no reason to further incriminate yourself. What I do want to hear, however, is the goal of this mission, and why it requires the eradication of entire worlds."

Grieve took another breath, gripping his thigh even tighter. His tongue wriggled to moisten the dryness in his mouth.

He looked up and spoke to them. "The motive behind this campaign centers around an event that took place thousands of years ago. Kausmos, the force that has governed this universe since the beginning, made the decision to bridge the gap between our dimension and the other that rests beyond. He made this possible by creating the Dreamer's World, which gave the other beings an opportunity to come to our side."

Reynard asked, "Are we talking about a physical passage, or something more?"

"I would describe it as something metaphysical. The Dreamer's World itself may be tactile, but that which it carries through its gates is not."

Steve spoke up, contributing what he knew. "You're talking about consciousness."

Grieve nodded, impressed. "Yes, that's right. When a person on the other side sleeps, their consciousness is carried into this realm, where they reawaken, and walk among the rest of us."

"And this place . . .this is what Triocks seeks?" Reynard asked.

"That's correct."

Knivus shifted in his seat, bringing his arms over the desk. He addressed the group sternly.

"Now just so we're clear, Grieve's explanation is nothing more than the rationale that our maniacal aggressors use to substantiate their cause. I want everyone to understand that this tale originates from fictitious literature and should be treated as such. This is important, namely because we know our enemy will never find what they seek, and thus their galactic rampage will never cease unless contested."

This was right about the time when Ryan could voice an objection. He was living proof that there was some kind of gateway carrying him back and forth between his bedroom and the universe he was in now. Which in turn meant that the people searching for it weren't so crazy as much as the manner in which they were doing it. Although he still didn't understand the connection between finding and having to blow planets up. Before he could even question it, he heard Megan's voice.

"I'm sorry," she said. "I hate to interject, but I'm not exactly a natural born citizen of Dreamland, which means someone threw me on the midnight train at the Sleepyville Station—against my will I might add. So whether you want to call it the Dreamer's World, or Slumberland, or whatever, it doesn't change the fact that the literature you refer to is not so fictitious after all. You can ask Ryan here, or that Zephner guy to validate my story, because I don't want to be treated with the same level of credibility as the freakin' tooth fairy."

Every head in the room turned her way. She hadn't spoken until now, and her first utterance was an indignant outburst. Ryan was already worried that her mouth would get them all thrown out.

Knivus appeared ready to scold her for her insolent behavior.

"I don't seem to recall giving you an invitation."

Before she could even respond, Ryan jumped in.

"She's with me," he said. "We came here together. What she said is true. We came from the other side."

As if the day were getting too long, Knivus exhaled loudly, turning his attention to Reynard.

"So this is the boy you spoke of—this young, gallant adolescent who is always in the company of an autonomous rubber ball. He was the one they were trying to apprehend."

Reynard said, "Unsuccessfully, you might add."

"Yes. And how did that come to be?"

"The bird and the rest of his rookery decided to intervene."

"Yes, of course, the birds."

Guin, not liking his derisive tone, took one webbed-foot forward, with his flippers poised at his sides. The tips of his claws glistened under the light.

"If you're having your doubts about what I'm capable of, I could happily put them to rest."

Knivus, cracking a smile, raised his hand, facing his palm out at the animal. "I can assure you there's no need. I know exactly what you are." He discreetly glanced at Zephner, who, up until now, had remained silent. His face was still shying away. "You are a killing machine," Knivus continued, "with a toggle that precariously rests between the on and off positions. You're an asset, yet also a liability. Without a moment's notice you could go off the deep end. You may either save lives, or—"

"That's enough," Zephner said, raising his voice. "Things have changed."

"Perhaps. But it's not like I've received any insurance either. Whatever agent you've been inoculated with is unproven and still very much a mystery. I mean no ill-sentiment, but there is a risk in having you around. However, risks are necessary for progress and for achieving results, which is why I haven't shown you the door just yet."

The room became very silent. There wasn't a peep from anyone. Ryan looked at Zephner and Guin, and wondered how they ended up the way they did. He was itching to ask more questions, but this didn't feel like the right time.

He felt an elbow jab him in the arm. He turned and saw Megan glare at him angrily.

"*What kind of penguin is this?*" she said with a sibilant whisper.

Ryan shrugged his shoulders. He wished that no one had overheard her comment, but Guin had already turned his head. He didn't say anything.

Steve, though quiet, was squirming in his seat. He had come here for answers, but as of yet, he hadn't heard what he wanted to hear.

"Excuse me, Commander," Steve said. "I don't want to digress from what we came here for. I want to hear more about Triocks and what his intentions are."

"Didn't you hear," Guin said. "He wants to locate planet Lullaby."

"But why? What business does he have with the Dreamer's World?"

Knivus said, "You can answer that one too, Grieve."

Grieve glanced at Steve, and was met with a glower. He looked away again.

"Triocks," he said, uttering the name with tacit resentment, "sees the Dreamer's World as something that must be acquired to fulfill his life's purpose. While other men may be assuaged by power and wealth, he requires more. Aside from his hunger, he has an ambition that surpasses that of any ruler that has come before him. He wants, and he *needs* to have what no mortal being was ever intended to have. I can't be sure of his sincerity, but he preaches that the discovery of the Dreamer's World will be able to bring about a quintessential joy to every inhabitant of this realm. If you ask someone from the other side, they'll tell you that dreaming can produce an incomparable state of elation. And conversely, Triocks believes that their otherwise, mundane waking life will evoke a similar feeling to the people on this side—not necessarily by what they see, but by how they perceive it."

Knivus clasped his hands together, and looked at Ryan.

"Tell me, Ryan, boy from the other side—do you believe that your universe will satisfy the expectations that this man carries?"

Ryan wanted to say probably not, though that kind of answer was sure to bring some unrest. But would it have been any better to say yes? If he did, he would be, to an extent, justifying Triocks' actions. But what did he *really* think? Was Earth really all it was cracked up to be? What did they have that they didn't have here? Basketball? It had to be more than just that.

"I'm doubtful," he said. "He may be disappointed."

Megan added, "Especially if he comes to our town."

Ryan frowned.

"The answer isn't as straightforward as the question would suggest," Grieve pointed out. "Like I said, it's all about perception, just like the way an outsider sees this universe. What they see is based on their understanding of where they are."

"Layers of Perception," Ryan said.

"That's right. So you must know a little about this."

"Steve explained it to me. Are you saying those same rules apply to my world also?"

"It's a contentious question. You'll hear arguments from both sides, but nothing definitive."

Megan said, "So this guy isn't even sure what he's getting into?"

"No," Grieve said. "*He's* sure of what he'll find. But others are more skeptical."

"Which takes me to my next concern," Reynard said. "How exactly are they planning to find the Dreamer's World?"

The room fell silent again. Maybe because the question alluded to all the worlds that had already been taken off the map.

Steve was writhing in his seat. He kept swallowing, his eyes occasionally twitching. His breathing was irregular, but he kept it together well enough not to draw attention.

Guin, bothered by the silence, opened his beak.

"They're popping balloons," he said. "Just like at the carnival."

Knivus looked at him angrily and spoke, before the brazen remark could get a rise out of the others.

"I've heard you come here bearing pertinent information. Though judging from your pudginess, I doubt there's a cavity in your cranium that holds anything besides thoughts of your next meal."

"And I doubt yours does anything besides think of ways to make your seat comfier for your spit polished rump."

"Guin," Reynard hollered from the couch. "Do you have anything to contribute or not?"

"I have absolutely nothing."

Reynard looked at him, unsurprised.

"So the whole thing was just a ruse?"

"A ruse to secure my seat at this refugee committee."

Reynard closed his eyes and sighed, holding his forehead with his hand. Steve was still showing admirable restraint. And Ryan, he was a firm believer that Guin was simply unfamiliar with so-cial etiquette. But then again, he and the rest of his kind were capable of vocal communication. Maybe the reason for his crankiness lay somewhere else.

Knivus, tired of the creature's antics, addressed him once more.

"Have you had your fun yet? Because if you haven't, I know a place."

Guin was ready to volley back a threat, but stopped himself when he noticed that every pair of eyes on the room were on him. They weren't pleased, not even Zephner. In fact, there looked like there was a chance he would hurl the insolent animal through one of the windows (ironically, a flight Guin wouldn't forget). Ryan was shaking his head.

Guin backed down, looking at the lot of them.

"Don't let my endearing qualities be of further nuisance."

Reynard, growing incessantly weary, looked back at Grieve, who was still hunched forward in his chair.

"I'm sorry," he said. "As you were saying—how are they searching for the Dreamer's World?"

Grieve gathered his thoughts, which carried some delay. When he was ready, he continued.

"The Dreamer's World is said to be concealed within another world, very much like the seed that exists within the fruit. It could be the size of a small moon, or it could be some sort of spatial singularity. Either way, the only sure method of exposing it is through—" He paused, then quickly discovered there was no way to sugarcoat it. He finished his statement. "—by total planetary annihilation."

It didn't come as a surprise to any of them. The gruesome imagery still dwelled in the recesses of their memory, sure to remain indelible. Though hearing the words spoken as if part of a diagnosis was conciliating, if only because it helped make sense of what happened.

Grieve was mortified. Anyone who looked at him could see that he was struggling to get through this session. He was ashamed of every word he had to utter. But as antagonizing as it might have been, it was his only outlet of reparation.

Megan raised a question, before the silence became obvious once again.

"But wouldn't they be destroying the very thing they're looking for?"

"No," Grieve said softly. "The Dreamer's World isn't something that can be destroyed. It was created by Kausmos himself, which ensures perpetual soundness. So in theory, no matter what method of . . . destruction is used, it won't be blighted in any way."

"So," Reynard said, "what you mean to tell me is that Triocks' approach to finding it is through pure process of elimination?"

"Yes. But he's also actively seeking whatever leads he can obtain. That's why they had Zephner in holding, and why they came after Ryan."

"Both of which proved fruitless," Knivus added. "And at the end of the day, he's still dealing with impossible odds. We're not even talking about winning a lottery; we're talking about a needle in a mountain. Possibly more asinine than that. How many planets are we talking about?" He waved his hand at Grieve, catching him off guard.

"I don't know," Grieve said. "There's several trillion in this galaxy alone. As for the entire universe, if we take the ancient writings at face value, it's for all intents and purposes infinite."

Knivus held his hand out to the others in the room, as if trying to build his case.

"As you can see, we're unequivocally dealing with a madman. We can expect no rationality."

"I would have to agree," Reynard said, lowering his head. It became clear to everyone that a peaceful resolution would be out of the question. Diplomacy was not an option.

The news struck Steve hard, sapping what was left of his spirits. His body had become the molted skin of an insect. He was unmoving, with his gaze to the floor. He seemed out for the count, until he broached a question that no one would have expected him to raise.

He asked plainly, "How did they die?"

Worried faces turned his way.

Steve looked at Grieve, eye to eye, and saw he was reluctant to answer. Grieve shook his head. He had already divulged a lot more than what he ever would have wanted to.

"How are they doing this?" Steve asked again.

When Knivus saw Grieve would not answer, he took the question upon himself, without so much as a second thought.

"Their stations, referred to as Atlums, are equipped with a centrifugal column that also doubles as a high-powered laser. And when I say high-power, know that the stations have over a hundred-thousand kilometers of coils dedicated to powering the apparatus. The lasers, aligned along the outer ring of the column, are fired at the core of the planet, while maintaining rapid rotation. This volatilizes all matter, sustaining a shaft through the planet. The warhead is dropped, then triggered once it reaches the core. Complete obliteration follows."

Steve remained stoical, not twitching or blinking. He portrayed no emotion whatsoever.

"Barbaric," Reynard said softly with disbelief.

Knivus added, "If you find that abhorrent, consider the way their captains invite themselves to an afternoon excursion on the planet they're about to target. It's a sick, perverse custom where they take pleasure in knowing that they are seeing the world on its final day. Typically they'll go to dine at the most extolled restaurant they can find, and order the most delectable meal on the menu. Then when they've finished indulging themselves, they'll even have the audacity to leave a generous gratuity."

Reynard grimaced with revulsion. Everyone was thoroughly disgusted.

Megan asked, "And where does that monster we heard in the city fit into all of this?" She looked over at Zephner, and pointed. "How did you know what was coming after that?"

Zephner looked at her with his pinhead-pupils. He would have preferred not to imbibe her with any more information, but it was probably too late for that. Reluctantly, he answered her.

"It's another one of their formalities," he said with a soft-spoken voice. "Hundreds of years ago, before modern communication, these beasts would serve as the knell for what was to come. Those familiar with the ancient lore would understand that this was a sign of the end. It would give them time to say goodbye to their loved ones, find peace with themselves, and to repent of any wrongdoings."

"It almost sounds humane," Knivus said, "until you realize the man who's providing the fire alarm is also the same person who will set the fire."

"Where do these monsters come from?" Megan asked.

"They're artificially engineered right within the Atlum," Grieve said, trying to be informative where he could allow himself to be. "There's an entire wing dedicated to their production. Once the embryo begins development in the amniotic shell, it's launched via a remote drone to be dropped into the seabed. After a period of 168 hours, the creature will attain its infancy stage, and then migrate to dry land. That's when the creature will begin to cry, which is actually a instinctive call to its mother."

Megan's brows curved into a cusp. "That's so cruel."

"You don't have to worry about it," Knivus said. "They won't be winning any awards for philanthropy any time soon."

Ryan was somewhere between here and there, occasionally falling under the false assumption he was going to wake up any second. In the back of his mind, he expected this planet to suffer the same fate as Cyannus. But there would have been the warning, he thought. They would hear it coming.

He was distracted by Guin, watching as he furtively scratched the fibers of the carpet with his toes. He had to stifle a smirk because the way Guin was standing reminded him of the way his brother used to sulk when he didn't get ice cream. Aside from that, there was nothing funny about the situation. No. The situation was extremely dire. So far the problem was clearly spelled out, but the solution was still unknown.

"So what are we going to do now?" Ryan asked to the silent crowd.

Knivus quickly replied, "What do you do? Nothing. This is something *we* will take care of."

Guin stopped scratching. He looked up at Knivus.

Reynard said, "But what kind of response can we expect to see? Are we going to issue evacuations? Or—"

"That won't happen. An evacuation at a global scale isn't even feasible."

"Then we— "

"Retaliate."

"Retaliate?" Reynard repeated for clarification. "Where do we even begin to summon the kind of armaments necessary to combat such a prevalent force of aggressors?"

Knivus reverted to his tall, conceited posture, his arms rested on the sides of his chair.

"You're not giving the Garthega Federation enough credit. After all, we're the ones that pioneered the greatest weapons of war. With our arsenal, we've kept all our enemies in check for over two hundred years. Any foe that has so much as flaunt a pistol at us has been expelled from even the history books."

"So," Reynard said, "you're proposing the use of brute force?"

"My method is a little more involved than that. What I have planned is swift and surgical, and takes advantage of my tactical repertoire."

Grieve adjusted himself in his chair, finding a more comfortable position to be in when he would address Knivus. He tried speaking in a manner that didn't sound like it was being influenced by the way he held himself in bad light.

"Commander," he said, "I've worked a great many years as your general, while additionally getting to intimately know our enemy. I feel it would be conducive to our situation if you allow me to advise you through this plan of action."

Knivus extended his hand. "I appreciate your wanting to help, but there's nothing else you can do for us right now. Our ace in the hole is brewing in the basement as we speak, and will be ready to serve in less than forty-eight hours. Until then, we can all sit tight."

Guin growled with frustration. He advanced forward, his claws creeping through the end of his flippers. All attention was turned back on him.

"I don't like the sound of *sit tight*," he said. "Where's my involvement? Where's my target?"

Knivus gazed at him, raising his voice. "I'm running a military operation here, not a circus ring. If you want something to claw at, take a hike up the mountains."

"This isn't what I—"

"This discussion is over."

He threw his hands into the air, urging everyone to vacate immediately. Ryan went over to try and placate Guin, but he was brushed away before he could even get out a word. Everyone else was heading through the doors, back into the lobby.

"Zephner, stay behind," Knivus said.

Ryan turned around, curious as to what further business Knivus had with him. He would have liked to say hello, or at least thank him for saving Megan, but Knivus wanted him out. Before he turned around to leave, Zephner looked at him in a troubling, disturbed manner. There was something on the man's mind he wasn't saying. There was some kind of connection, almost a telepathic link between the two of them. Ryan didn't know what it meant. Then again, dreaming would always produce uncanny occurrences. Maybe he would ask him about it later.

Chapter 22

Transformation

The group dispersed throughout the lobby, unsure of where to go from here. No one could say if the future looked any darker or brighter. There was still a lot of uncertainty regarding the threat. Knivus seemed optimistic about his ability to stop it, but there was still room for doubt. Ryan, having seen firsthand what the enemy was capable of, found it hard to believe that any sole nation could come out victorious. But in all fairness, seeing an entire planet pulverized to space dust would have been demoralizing for anyone. Maybe the future was bright, and he had just forgotten to take his sunglasses off.

Guin wandered to the corner of the room, right next to a glass end table. The expensive-looking lamp with the chrome base may have been what lured him there. Megan noticed him and walked on over.

"You know," she said, "where I come from, penguins are a tame bunch. They waddle, they stumble and fall, they steal stones from each others nests, and overall make for very cute documentaries. You, on the other hand, are eager to go headlong into a war against a bunch of nutcases with planet-busting nukes. Wouldn't you be happier with a plate of calamari?"

Guin continued to stare at the lamp, trying to stay calm.

"I'd be happier," he said, "if people didn't keep labeling me as a voracious glutton."

She glanced down at his tummy. "Well, it looks like you're a penguin that enjoys eating."

"It's better than letting the cadavers go to waste."

"Uh huh," she said, as she continued to studiously observe the talking animal. Beside the generous circumference around the belly, he looked like an average penguin. She liked his green eyes and the way they shined like emeralds. His pupils were tiny black dots, very similar to Zephner's. But if there was one thing that stood out as being adorable, it was the feathery crest on his head. She wanted to touch it, but eventually backed away from the idea.

She bent over, placing her hands on her knees.

"Are you a dangerous penguin?" she asked him.

He looked at her for a good five seconds.

"If I were dangerous, you wouldn't have to ask."

She pressed her lips together, nodded, and walked away. But just before she did, she took her finger and ran it across the feathers on his head. His head jerked away with a violent jolt. Unfortunately for the cleaning crew, his beak found its way through the glass table, sending the lamp on top of it crashing to the floor.

Steve was sitting by himself on the other side of the room. He hardly reacted to the sound of breaking glass. He glanced at the mess and went back to ruminating.

Reynard saw him seated there, and took a seat next to him. He waited a while before saying anything.

"It's been a long day for all of us," he said eventually, as if making an observation. "It wouldn't be a bad idea if we found a place to retire for the night."

"The night's not over yet," he responded promptly.

"Are you still seeking answers about what happened?"

Steve shook his head, still trapped in a trance.

"I'm not even sure I know the questions."

"You think of them one at a time. Don't overwhelm yourself."

It didn't take long before Steve found one to ask.

"Where did they take Leilah?"

"The Onah Hospital. It's a couple of kilometers uptown. It's the best place they could have taken her."

"I need to be there," he said, his voice summoning new strength. "I need to be the one to tell her what happened."

"Of course," Reynard said. "We can take a ride there right now."

—)—

Megan was ambling over to where Ryan was standing, which was at the opposite side of the room where Guin made his mess. It was clear he was trying to disassociate himself from the havoc. He watched with embarrassment as the secretary went over to see if anything was salvageable. There wasn't. Megan was still carrying that smirk of a rascal.

"So what do you think, Ryan?" she said, holding back her laughter. "Is Knivus out of his league here?"

"I think it's too soon to call," he said. "Depends on what cards he's sitting on. If he has nothing, then we all die. Not sure there's another way."

"We got *the penguin* on our side," she reminded him. "And the motorcycle guy."

"I know. I was just being sarcastic. We have a good shot of making it through this."

She gazed at him with a raised brow. "It's really hard to tell with you sometimes. By the way, *I* was being sarcastic. I think we're doomed."

"Really?" Ryan said, starting to get confused.

"Yeah. Which is why I think we should make the most of the time we have left. Zephner wouldn't make any pit stops on the way over here, and not to be such a girl, but I would really like to check out some of the shops they have around here. They probably have some snazzy outfits on sale."

"Really? You'll prioritize shopping over spending some last minute quality time with yours truly?"

She smiled. "That's real cute."

A deep voice came from behind, taking both of them by surprise. "There's a famous clothing store just a few blocks down from here. I can take you there if you'd like."

They turned around and saw none other than Grieve standing before them in his tattered military garbs (the coat was left in the conference room). He looked a lot taller standing up, six-four at least, with a two-hundred fifty pound body of muscle.

To Ryan, it was peculiar how he interpolated such a casual statement after such an onerous meeting. It was as if he were trying to project himself as being someone other than the bad guy Knivus was making him out to be. He wasn't exactly gleeful right now, but the tone of his voice suggested that he would have liked to pursue that emotional state.

Megan considered his offer. He may have been an ex-maniac, but the point was he didn't fit that bill anymore, based on her evaluation. Her intuition told her he could be trusted.

"That sounds good," she said. "I'll take you up on that." She turned back to Ryan, placing a hand on her hip. "As for you, rye bread, you know I'll never make you succumb to the torture that is shopping, but you are invited to come along. You could use a new t-shirt. Or better yet, a self-sanitizing jumpsuit that you never have to change out of. They must sell those around here," she said, looking at Grieve.

Grieve fumbled with a response.

"I . . . haven't seen one of those."

"Well, we'll find you something."

Ryan belatedly realized that he had yet to agree to anything. But from the sound of things, it looked like he was going to be coming along whether he wanted to or not.

Reynard came over and joined them, with Steve following behind.

"Is everyone settling on what they want to do?" Reynard asked.

"We got our night planned out," Megan said.

"That's very good. Because Steve and I are going to be on our way. Ryan, Megan," he nodded at both of them, "I'm sure you two will fair well, and in due time, will return to the comfort of your homes. And Grieve, in case we don't meet again, it was a pleasure meeting you." He extended his hand, and with some hesitation, Grieve shook it.

"I'll see you all," Reynard said as he left the lobby.

"See you, Ryan," Steve added soullessly, and followed Reynard out into the corridor.

Ryan was left wondering what would become of them. He had watched an affable guy become someone else entirely in a matter of hours. Witnessing that horrific act of destruction had changed him, as it would anyone. And seeing the aftermath only reinforced the idea that there was more to this world than what he had ever known before. The people here weren't cardboard caricatures of the people from back home. They had feelings, dreams and desires, and were complete beings that possessed every crucial quality that one would expect to find. Here or there, people were the same.

Megan was ready to march out the lobby herself until she noticed Guin dawdling around the room. Without his license to kill, he was a penguin without a purpose—just a pet that had been grouped with the rest of the luggage. The poor animal needed something to do.

"So that just leaves Mr. Waddles," she said, looking at Ryan. "Either we leave him at the shelter or he comes with us."

"I'll ask him," Ryan said.

He walked over to him and stooped down to his level.

"Hi Guin," he said. He received an ugly stare. "We were just wondering if you'd like to spend a night on the town."

"That sounds very responsible," he said grumpily.

"Megan kinda wants to go shopping."

"And you're asking me if I want to come along? Does it look like I need a new coat?"

"No. Your coat looks fine."

"Then why even ask?"

"Because our only other option is to find you a keeper."

The penguin let out a groan of frustration, swinging his flipper at the air. "Of all the days I've decided to sleep in, this had to be the day I left my cove."

"Don't worry about it," he said. "Once the forecast clears up, we'll take you back to your cove."

Another groan followed.

—)—

Once outside, the fresh, cool breeze swept across their faces. It was a beautiful night, better than any of them could have asked for. A pink hue on the darkening horizon was all that remained of the sunlight.

A cement walkway lay before them. On either side were rows of lush trees and lamp posts with large bulbous lights. They could see and hear the trickling fountain up ahead, with the underwater lights that gave the illusion that the water was glowing with vibrant colors. There were tourists standing around it and taking photographs, aiming to get a portion of the Icosagon in the background.

They headed to the main street, where there was practically a parade of pedestrians strolling down the road, as every automobile was high up in the air. That being the case, it was common to see vendors parked in the center lane, selling a myriad of different items. They sold everything from souvenir t-shirts to beef kabobs. Some even had animals sitting by their stall. Some looked liked dogs, if they had the bodies of a komodo dragon. They were extremely hairy, and had white, brown and black fur, tall pointed ears, and four foot long tails that wagged back and forth. There was another animal, a giant bird of sorts, also hairy, but with two wings on each side, and a snout that resembled that of a pterodactyl. Suddenly having a penguin in their party didn't seem all that unusual.

They turned left at the end of the block, entering a quieter avenue. Above them, framed between the highrise structures were two moons, one half as big as the other.

There were matters left unspoken between Ryan and Megan. Presumably, the man they were walking with was a mass murderer—a genocidal murderer that, quite frankly, didn't look the part. This managed to get the best of Megan and her unwavering curiosity. She had to learn more.

"So Mr. Grieve," she said. "How long have you been out of town?"

Grieve gazed up at the moon, calculating silently.

"An educated guess puts the time frame around eleven months."

"Hmm. From the impression I got, I would have expected it to be a lot longer. So you're really just a greenhorn when it comes to this galactic sifting process."

"Don't be deceived. Eleven months can be a very long time, depending on how you spend it."

Megan nodded. "I can understand that. Time's not only relative to the observer, but to the mind as well. If you enjoy the way you're spending your time, it's going to go by a lot faster than if you're not."

"Which is why sleeping is instantaneous," Ryan joked.

"Ryan," she said, "why don't you wake up and get out of here."

Ryan shrugged and started to flick his arm with his finger. He heard a *tap, tap, tap,* but he didn't go anywhere. He felt it, but he was still here, walking the streets of Carthelona City.

"Here, this is how you do it," Guin called out. His flipper rose into the air (his claws still sheathed thank God) and came down on Ryan, like a eighty pound sirloin. Ryan staggered to the left, putting his hands out before he could crash head first into a storefront window. The glass rung like a gong, drawing the looks of everyone inside. He scurried onward right away.

"Nice try, Guin, but I'm still asleep."

"That was one strike. Let me at it again."

"No!" He raised his hands.

Megan remained several paces ahead, ignoring the ruckus. She continued conversing with Grieve.

"You don't seem like the kind of guy that would do the sort of things your resume would imply. I know Reynard didn't want you talking about it, but did you really—" She couldn't get the words out.

"Yes," he answered. "I'm afraid your worst assumptions are true."

"So what made you come forward and willingly confess to all of it?"

His willingness to answer questions started to wane. He looked down at the sidewalk, then glanced up at the path ahead.

"I decided I wasn't that kind of guy."

Megan detected something was amiss.

"I hate to be frank, but eleven months is a long time to figure out you're not up for a certain kind of job. Especially when it's the line of work you were doing. Something else must have happened."

Ryan felt obligated to jump in. He could tell that Grieve was getting uncomfortable.

"If she's being too much of a bother, I could take care of her for you."

"That's all right," he said. Though Ryan knew he was only being polite.

Ryan raised his hand and pointed his finger at her.

"Guin, I give you permission to wake her up!"

Megan spun on her feet, pointing right back at the bird.

"Touch me and I'll call animal control!"

Guin glanced at her and kept on walking.

"Not my battle. Odds are she has that number on speed dial."

Leilah was the only thing on Steve's mind as they were cruising through the cityscape, three-hundred feet up in the air. His head leaned against the window, his eyes watching smudges of color dart across his vision. Every second or so there would be a slit in the architecture where he could see down the length of a perpendicular street. For those brief instances he could see the pair of moons up in the sky, which was the only light that would remain stationary during this entire ride.

He couldn't describe the way he was feeling right now. He was overtaken by a dampening sadness that he couldn't quite explain. He should have been mourning the loss of his wife and child, and maybe he was to some extent, but it wasn't fully or wholeheartedly. When he tried remembering the short time they spent together, all he could recover were memories that were half-baked—literally speaking—like that one time Stephanie was arguing about how he could never make an unbiased evaluation regarding her or anything she did. So she baked muffins one day, deliberately leaving out the sugar, and asked him to try one. He did, and gave the critique that they were some of the best muffins he had ever tasted. To make a point of his bluff, she took the unused cup of sugar and spilled it over his head, and said, *imagine how they would have tasted with some sugar.*

He could almost smile by recalling that moment, but it would have been no different than cracking a smile at seeing something funny on television. He couldn't insert himself in the scene. He remained an outsider, viewing a memory that could have belonged to anyone. Maybe he remembered it like a dream. Maybe that's what it was like for the people on the other side. From what he had heard and studied, it was possible to have emotional dreams—dreams of joy, dreams of sadness, and then wake up without them having any bearing on the rest of your day.

He delved deeper into his mind, pulling out whatever memories he could find. He found a few that took place while they were at the academy, such as the day they first met.

He was test-piloting one of the flight simulators, when eventually, it became time for him to land the vessel. The landing pad was due west, but there was a problem. When he steered left, the vessel wouldn't turn. Nervous, and still very much inexperienced, he panicked and buzzed for the student tech assistant who handled minor software hiccups—Stephanie at the time. She came over to his station, pulled open the pilot door, and held up a bag full of textbooks. With a smile on her face, she said, *try not to block the hydraulics next time.* He smiled back. Luckily for him, that wasn't an issue he'd ever have to face in the air.

These were just vestiges of a greater whole, and they didn't evoke the feelings that they should have. Now he could only think about Leilah, and how she was lying in a bed somewhere, undergoing a grueling exercise, testing the limits of her physical and mental abilities. But most important to him right now though was the fact that she was still alive and breathing. This meant that she still had a future that had not yet been told. She was still real in his mind, still someone that he could talk to, someone he could touch. She was an anchor that kept him secured to the life that his training was trying to take away.

The lights continued to dart past their vessel. Reynard sat back, his hands off the autonomous controls. He looked to his side and saw Steve slumped and defeated.

"Steve," he said, "if you don't mind me asking: what does it feel like to remember your life on Cyannus?"

Steve was confused by the question. He didn't know why he would be asking something like that at a time like this.

"I don't know," he said defensively. "I'm not feeling much of anything right now."

"I don't mean to be insensitive. I know you're very committed to your sworn duties, and that you've disciplined yourself when it comes to training and following the orders of your superiors. But now that we're off the record, I want to voice my reservations concerning the ERR training that you've been required to participate in."

"Great," he scoffed. "Should I expect to grow a new pair of limbs out of my spine now?"

"No, no. Nothing like that. It's just that long-term tests haven't been conducted yet. Or tests that would account for the kind of extremities we've faced today. Now I don't worry so much about myself. Older participants are mostly unaffected by the regimen. But those that are younger are a lot more malleable to the training's original intent, which is basically to seclude emotions away from their corresponding memory."

"So what's the issue here? Seems to me like everything is

working as it's suppose to."

"Yes, but that's what concerns me. Your ability to cope is dependent on an artificially created form of defense. It's like creating a fortress of ice in a torrid land. At first it may stand strong, but with time, it will inevitably be nothing more than a puddle."

"So are you saying that I'm going to fall apart?"

"No. I'm not trying to say that either."

"Then what?"

Reynard, looking more fragile than usual, took a deep breath. He looked at Steve again, watching the different colored streaks of light sweep across his face.

"What I really want to say is that memories are an important thing to keep intact. They're the breadcrumbs that tell you how you got to where you are now. Without them, there's no way to retrace your steps. Everything you remember, from your friends to your family, to all your accomplishments, the good days and the bad—they are what shaped the person you are today. And if you ever forget that, you won't know who you are."

Steve scoffed, leaning his head back against the window. "Sounds like a bunch of pseudo-psychology to me."

"Maybe it is. I'm no trained physician."

"Then I'm not a patient. So there's no reason to go on with this psych evaluation. I know I'm going to be fine. I still have Leilah, and I still have memories of Stephanie, and Martin. I won't lose them."

Reynard nodded, and put his hand on Steve's shoulder. "I believe you," he said.

"How much longer to the hospital?"

"Less than five minutes," Reynard said, looking out his window.

—)—

Grieve led the group around the next corner, where they could hear the sound of a low whistle. This brought them to the city's key shopping district, an area that took on an entirely different appearance. The first eye opener was the elevated cobblestone promenade, built directly over a wide open trench. There were short glass footbridges on either side, that gave passage to the outlining sidewalks. At certain spots, there were stairways that led to the lower level. Here a long slender train came barreling across the rails. It eased into the boarding platform and came to a stop. All the pedestrians, the shoppers with their bags full of goods, boarded the cars, and in seconds the train took off again.

Above the crowds hustled to get from store to store. It could have very well been daylight, with all the lights shining from every direction. The handrails on either side of the promenade glowed a misty blue; giant metal arches extended from one side to the other, carrying tendrils of floral bulbs. But most blinding of all were the manifold of different shops, many rising up to ten stories. They all shared a similar architectural trait, in that their facades were almost entirely made of glass. The inside of every level of every store was fully exposed with the enticing mishmash of colorful items and displays.

Megan froze on the brink of the sidewalk, her wide-opened eyes bouncing back and forth between all the glistering window fronts.

"I don't care if I live right next door to the tooth fairy," she said. "I'm moving into this town."

"Don't throw down a deposit just yet," Guin said. "We don't even know if this stuff is affordable."

Megan couldn't wait any longer. She started to move ahead of the group. She stepped onto the footbridge and looked all around. There were so many places to choose from. She hadn't the slightest clue where to start.

"Where do I go?" she asked, as if it were a question that determined the fate of her future.

"The Hios is this way," Grieve said, retaking his position as head of the group. "I think you'll like it."

He led them to one of the tallest buildings on the other side of the promenade. The building was spectacular, with its name plate vertically laid out in twenty-foot chrome letters. The first few floors featured live models in the windows—no, they weren't live. Those were holograms walking up and down the catwalks. It's the only explanation for how their clothing managed to change seamlessly from one thing to the next.

They walked through the entrance, and rode over a moving sidewalk across a long chasm of water. There were fountains on either side, with geysers that shot thirty feet into the air. Hanging from the ceiling were mobiles of different mannequins, each diminishing in size to give the appearance that they were being pulled into some kind of black hole. Which is probably what this place was, for shopaholics.

Ryan thought it was strange to see Megan so excited over a clothing store. It was never really her thing. She was a get in, get out kind of shopper, buying what she needed out of necessity. But here, she was, letting herself go.

As they continued their ride across the sidewalk, two black pillars descended from above, and orbited above each of them. It's like they were scanning their bodies. Ryan discovered why in just a little bit.

At the end of their ride, there were several seven-foot vertical screens that produced animated images of everyone that had passed through. That's when Megan got really excited. She saw herself on one of those screens, twirling from side to side, showing off this conceptual outfit that she would look good in. It had her in a long sleeved yellow top with frilly cuffs, black calf-length pants and flat sandals. After showing that outfit for a few seconds, it changed to something else. And then it changed again.

Enamored by what she saw, she hurried into the store, leaving everyone else in the dust.

"She seems enthusiastic," Grieve said.

"Yeah, she does," Ryan said. "It tends to happen whenever she goes somewhere new."

"Perfectly normal." He took a few steps into the store. He stopped and turned his head. "I'm going to find something for myself. It's high time I found a different outfit. We'll meet back here in twenty."

Minutes or hours, he wanted to ask. There was no telling with the new Megan here. But he didn't feel like this was the best time to bring up a joke. He saw the uniform Grieve wore, and it was indeed something that had to go. Even looking at it in this bright, jovial establishment was enough to resurface the faces of the men who swore allegiance to an overlord whose zealousness already cost the lives of thousands of civilizations. Even after witnessing the tragedy firsthand, it was still difficult to fathom. Ryan *did* want to see Grieve in another outfit, because this one was foreboding.

"What is *this?*" Guin hissed, turning to one of the animated screens. Ryan looked and saw Guin being depicted just as he was, with no clothes, except for a fedora. Given his head size, the hat fell right over his eyes, where it rested over his beak. His body swayed from side to side with unrivaled swagger.

"I guess that's your style," Ryan said.

"My style . . . I'll show them my style."

Guin cocked back his flipper, drawing his pair of claws out from their sheaths. Ryan saw what he wanted to do, but he had to intervene, as dangerous as it may have been.

He stepped forward, clutched the feathers of the flipper and pulled them back.

"Stop, Guin," he said. "You'll get us kicked out."

"Get out of the way!"

Ryan wasn't going to be able to restrain him much longer. So he was fortunate when the image on the screen was swapped out with another random patron. Upon seeing the change, Guin eased up and retracted his claws back where they couldn't be seen.

"They did the right thing," Guin said, as he waddled into the store. Somehow, Ryan was going to have to keep him on a short leash. And Megan too, if they ever wanted to see her again.

Megan was enthralled by all the different fashion collections she had never seen before. There was so much clothes, and so many styles that she didn't know where to begin. There were clothing racks everywhere, designed like cogwheels, so they could swivel around an axle. At the center was a round platform that generated a full-scale holographic model that could swap between any of the outfits that were at that particular rack, just by the press of a button.

Megan went from station to station, experimenting with all the clothing options. They had all sorts of tops and dresses, with laces and abstract patterns. She felt the fabrics. They were all silky smooth and very durable, probably repellent to most stains. There was a particular look going on with many of the clothing articles. The shirts and pants seemed to be sewn in layers, where the top most layer came over the layers below, with the seams crossing along the body at an angle. Different patterns would alternate down the length of the outfit, creating a layered look with the least amount of pieces.

She spotted a model in the distance wearing a tube top dress that fancied her. Actually, she found it gorgeous. It was royal blue, with a subtle, lustrous shine. It came down to the thighs, wrapped in many layers, just like a lot of the other outfits she saw. In a way, it was like being wrapped in mummy's bandages, except more socially acceptable.

She took one of the dresses off the hook, and was perplexed when she saw it wrapped like a roll of toilet paper. She referred to the hang tag that gave instructions on how to wear it. Apparently she wasn't far off with the mummy analogy. The dress was supposed to be wrapped around the body, held together by a self-adhesive material. She found it odd—so odd she had to try it out.

She located the nearest fitting room, which was hidden away inside a cylindrical chamber. She scurried through the narrow passages, like a mouse in a maze, and secured one of the empty square rooms. Inside, the floor and walls were beaming with light, showcasing her in the finest possible way. She was a star, she thought, gleaming in the spotlight. But not in *these* clothes. She saw herself in the mirror, still dressed in the black jeans and orange polo, which served as nothing more than an unwanted reminder of the time she was still drifting through the corners of this universe like a dandelion seed in the wind.

An important day was coming, she knew, but what exactly she couldn't quite recall. All she knew was that it was important that she looked her best.

Without wasting any time, she took off her top and the rest of her garments, tossing them onto the floor. It was the first time she'd seen herself fully disrobed in what was essentially studio lighting, which she believed was an enhancement that made her comparable to the beauty and elegance of a Greek sculpture. She was mesmerized by her body, until she discovered grains of sand still clinging to her skin. She brushed them off as best as she could before trying on her new outfit.

She picked up the dress and unraveled it off the roll. Trying to follow the instructions, she took one end and wrapped it around her thighs, until the backside of the fabric could reconnect. Almost like magic, the material stuck to itself. From there, the rest was easy. She took the remainder of fabric and bundled the rest of her body, until she felt like a human tortilla wrap. The end tapered into a lacy ribbon that looped just below her chest.

The dress was now complete. She twirled around and admired her new look. She was the bell of the ball.

She left the room and went back out onto the floor. There was still so much to see. She reentered the jungle of clothing and mannequins and before long, she crossed paths with Ryan and his feathery companion. Not surprised, they hadn't altered their looks one bit.

"What's the matter, Ryan? Couldn't find anything?"

"We did. Just decided not to take it with us."

"You're no fun."

Megan put her hands on her hips, whipped her hair to the side.

"So what do you think? Am I just gorgeous or what?"

Guin answered instead. "Gorgeous? No. Over your head in what you think you're walking out of here with? Absolutely."

"I'll pretend I didn't hear that."

Grieve came up behind the three of them, sporting his new outfit. He had on a rugged field jacket with beige slacks. It was a slightly different look—at least a better look, in that it made him appear more comfortable.

"I see you've found something you like," he said to Megan. "What's the occasion?"

She turned her cheek, stretched out her arms, and curled her hands up into little fists. "I'm finally living the dream," she said.

As she spoke, there was an ear-shattering sound that came from outside, and shot through the entire store—a terrible dissonant screech, like a wailing siren, that caused everyone to stop in their tracks and gaze in panic at their surroundings. The sound peaked in pitch and then died back down. After a few seconds pause, the sound intensified again. This time it was clear that it wasn't just a sound, but a scream. It was a vehement cry of the kind of titanic beast that Megan wished she'd never have to hear again.

CHAPTER 23

A FAIR WARNING

"Son of a bitch," Grieve said, his teeth clenched. "It's too soon for this."

Guin answered, "As if there could be a more convenient time."

"I mean, if only Knivus was able to issue the first offensive. The timing for this attack doesn't even make sense. They targeted Cyannus less than six hours ago. There's hundreds of planets in route to here, and with only three Atlums in this quadrant, there's no way they could be here already if they were following a standard itinerary."

Ryan looked to the front entrance, but couldn't detect the source of the sound. He had no idea how far away this beast was.

"So something drew them here," he said. "You don't think they're still after me, do you?"

"No. They wouldn't initiate this procedure if they wanted you extradited. They're here to do what they do. They're here to cross us off the list."

"Then what are we waiting for?" Megan cried, her body trembling. All the joy and jubilation had left her face. "We have to leave now!"

Guin growled with his beak clenched tightly. "I'm not going to keep playing musical chairs! We either eliminate the competition now or we're going to end up with no place to sit."

"He has a point," Ryan said. "If we run now, we'll keep running forever until there's nothing left."

"But what can we do about it?" Megan responded.

No one could answer. There was no obvious solution. There was only silence among them. Meanwhile the other patrons in the store began to murmur. The level of unrest was building; people were coming and leaving without any idea of what they should do. Children were in tears, holding on to their mothers. Others were on their phones, desperate to get in touch with whoever they could. No one here knew anything, except for Ryan and the three others who knew that the planet they resided on only had minutes before it was purged from existence.

Ryan wondered what it would feel like, to be here one moment and not the next. But this was only a dream, right? Logic dictates that he would wake up safe back in his bed. But what did it mean for the people who resided on this side? What would they wake up to? According to Zephner, the answer to that was nothing. But despite Ryan's immunity from a deathly fate, he could still feel the trepidation, and the palpitations of his heart. Fear was at work, and it sprouted goosebumps all along his arms. The prospect of death wasn't easy to face, regardless of the final destination.

Megan, still peeved by the lack of a response, spoke up again. "So the plan is to sit here and die?"

"No," Grieve said.

"Then what is?"

There was a ringing sound coming from Grieve's belt. He reached and pulled out a device no bigger than a key chain. He pressed his thumb against the front panel and held it up to his ear.

"Knivus?"

The voice came through the speaker. "Grieve, we have a situation, and it's come a lot sooner than expected."

"I know. We all heard the cry. We have thirty minutes at best to devise a response."

"I'm aware of that. Which is why I'm going to appoint you to handle the matter."

"Me? What could I possibly do? I no longer have any authority over our armaments. And besides, thirty minutes isn't enough time to stage such a large scale attack. And quite frankly, I'm not even sure we have the power to contest—"

Knivus interrupted. "It's Thomas leading the assault."

"*Thomas?*"

"He knows you're here, Grieve. He gives his hello."

For a moment, Grieve is left speechless. His brows wrinkle, the rest of his faced contorted with confusion.

Knivus continued, "He's touching down to personally bid you farewell."

"And what am I suppose to do?"

"You deal with him. He's the one who recruited you. You talk to him, tell him to back down, go bark up a different tree."

"That's not going to—"

"I don't care. Do whatever you want. Say whatever you want. Use the kid as a bargaining chip for all I care. Do whatever it takes to buy us more time."

Limited by his options, he yields. "Where's he going to touch down?"

"At the southern airfield, zone no. 23. I've already sent a transport to your location. It'll be waiting for you right outside the door."

"Wonderful. Now what's your plan for handling the beast?"

"I have Zephner tracking it down right now."

He shook his head. "You're putting a lot of faith in that man."

"It's either we deploy him, or we blow downtown into a crater. I'm willing to see how the former pans out first."

"All right. I'm leaving now."

Grieve put away the device and addressed the others. All of them anxiously awaited what he had to say.

"That was Knivus. He wants me to meet up with Thomas at the airfield."

"Who's Thomas?" Ryan asked.

"The man who's prepared to press the detonator if we don't talk some sense into him."

Megan said, "Is that even going to work?"

He looked at her dolefully. "No."

"Then . . . "

Overtaken by the implications of his answer, she felt her knees begin to buckle. Her whole body wanted to collapse. She found herself clutching onto one of the bars on the clothing rack. Ryan saw this and knew something had to be done. He couldn't just give up knowing that he still had the ability to stand up on his own two feet.

He faced Grieve. "I have to come with you. Maybe I can still prove to be of some value. Maybe there's something I can say that will change his mind."

Grieve nodded. "That's what Knivus suggested. Though I don't see our haggling bringing about any success."

"We have to try something. I don't want to wake up knowing this world and everyone on it will be gone forever."

"Let's not forget something," Guin said. "I got stakes in this, too. If the kid goes anywhere, I'm tagging along."

On paper, it sounded like a bad idea to Ryan. He looked at Grieve and waited for him to comment on it.

"It's fine," Grieve said. "If the pleasantries don't go as planned, we might just have to employ a different form of communication."

"You mean . . . "

"I hate to resort to that, but they have us pinned."

"And what do I do?" Megan said, trying to regain some composure.

"You stay here," Ryan said. This is the safest place you can be right now."

"But what about you? You're going to endanger yourself again?"

"Maybe just a little. But I'll figure something out. I'll find a way to keep us all alive. Promise."

His promise looked like it meant little to her. She kept staring at him with these wistful eyes, as if she had already lost him. She was trying her best not to cry, because, well, she never cried. At least not in front of him.

She stepped forward and gave him a firm embrace, reminding him how much she cared. Ryan hugged her back and patted her gently.

"Everything is going to be fine, Megan" he said.

"I wish I could believe it, rye bread."

She let go, and right away both of them looked down at the floor as they felt something nudge their toes. And there it was again, that strange basketball that always seemed to spontaneously appear no matter where he was. Bee must have wanted a piece of the action, Ryan thought. He picked him up for Megan to see.

"Look," he said. "I got Bee with me. Nothing can go wrong."

"Yeah, that's right. Go settle this over a game of basketball. You can't *possibly* lose."

Ryan didn't mind the sarcasm. He smiled and winked, and hurried off towards the front door, along with Grieve and Guin.

Frantic city dwellers rushed through the streets like a current, squeezing into alleyways or buildings which they believed to be secure. The bulk of aerial traffic was heading due north, away from the wailing screams of the beast.

It was implicit that the creature was big, and not indigenous to the world they knew. The cries were unlike anything they had ever heard, and so they panicked. Only a handful of people were acquainted with the ancient stories, but none would actually give them any credence up until this moment. They could no longer deny the sound that echoed through their streets, nor their imminent death. All they could do now was prepare for the end.

Perhaps the only motorist daring enough to oppose the foot traffic was the man with the motorcycle. Acting on nothing more than an edict, Zephner stormed his way through the streets of downtown, in pursuit of the deathly scream. His bike roared passionately, as if it were an animal itself, herding the crowds apart. The city grazed by his vision, along with the lights and nighttime decor.

He knew the scope of what he was up against. It was foolish, and maybe even suicidal, but that was the magic of it. When death was all but certain, consequences become irrelevant; actions become free from rationale. Where there may have been fear, there was none at all now. If anything, this would be a moment of redemption, an atonement for the things he did. Or maybe he was just being rash and reckless. He didn't know. He didn't care.

Confronting the beast head on would be a folly. He had to formulate a plan of attack that would employ the element of surprise. If he approached from the ground, he would be seen. He needed to come from above, and there was only one way to make that happen.

He followed the creature's scream to the adjacent avenue, and behold, the beast prowled along the line of the horizon. It was more or less two miles away, still only a blip in his vision. But it was coming this way. He needed to be in position.

A block up ahead was a deserted parking garage, which had

become obsolete since the city's conversion to aerial transit. At thirty stories it would be tall enough to use.

He pressed onward through the foot traffic, where he endured the shrills of people and beast alike. He narrowly grazed past each person, veering from side to side. His destination was coming up on his right, and so he hopped up onto the sidewalk and took a sharp turn into the garage entrance.

Knowing that time was of the essence, he pinned the throttle and raced hastily down the open lot. The vacant facility was as dark and damp as a subterranean cavern, with cement columns that were dirt-stained and brittle. The roar of the revving engine echoed loudly throughout the chamber.

He rode to the exit ramp at the back of the lot and tackled the steep incline. The motor chugged as the bike gyrated around the cylindrical tower. At every level he caught a glimpse of the lit city, as he steadily rose higher and higher. The street level quickly vanished from view, and soon after he was riding at the level of the aircrafts.

The beast unleashed another piercing cry, which by this point was almost deafening. The beast was nearing, and he could hear it, along with the cries of the crowd. He could hear structures shattering, clumps of rubble spilling liberally over the streets as if it were hailing boulders. He could feel the death toll rising with every second that passed. He had to hurry. He had to put a stop to it. Somehow, some way.

The spiraling ramp led into an open expanse. He was four-hundred feet up, atop the highest floor. The lights of the traffic and surrounding structures brightened the sky overhead.

In another burst of acceleration, he raced to the building's edge, and halted right alongside the parapet. He climbed off his bike and peered down at the street below. There were still hundreds of people jostling to safety. The cacophony of destruction was still audible. There was a heavy thrash, followed immediately by the crackling of steel and stone.

The beast was coming.

Forget about what he thought before. There was fear. It was only natural to feel it whenever your next breath could be your last. Especially in this instance. He had never tackled anything this colossal. He could easily die in the coming minutes. But he had to take the risk. He'd promise himself that he would never do anything rash again, but this was the dictionary definition of it. But he *had* to do it. If Grieve could somehow deter the imminent attack on the planet, this beast was still something that needed to be dealt with. And the longer he waited, the higher the death toll would be. Something had to be done now.

He climbed back onto the motorcycle, wrapping his fingers around the handlebars. His thumb hovered over the weapon shifter, trembling gently. He told himself he was ready—ready as he'll ever be.

—)—

Ryan wasn't sure what he was thinking when he decided to tag along with Grieve, to meet a maniacal psychopath, no less. Either it was an act of valor, or total stupidity. He wasn't sure which.

Nothing about the ride was pleasurable. Despite their altitude, the cries of the beast were still clearly audible. He looked out the windows to try and spot the monster, but he couldn't find it. To put a positive spin on the situation, at least it wasn't something that towered over the buildings.

"The two of you listen," Grieve said from the cockpit of the vessel. "When we touch down and meet him, don't say a word. Not unless I tell you to."

"Why not?" Ryan asked.

"Because Thomas is a dangerous man. Even for the likes of these people. He's a cutthroat manipulator, and sits at one of the highest ranks under Triocks' mission. Not only is he devout, but eccentric as well. No method is too extreme if it means achieving the desired result."

"Sounds like some of the neighbors I have back at home," Guin said.

Grieve shook his head. "You can't take this man lightly. Before you know it, he'll have you doing his bidding."

"So you've known him for a long time?" Ryan asked.

"Many years. We enrolled in the military at the same time. I got to know him very well. He was a good soldier, and never let all the stringent training and morbid nature of the job take away his humor. He was the same guy for all those years. But after completing his first term of service, he told me he was going to move overseas, to look after some of his relatives that were getting older—relatives he had never bothered to mention before. I think that's around the time when the records became questionable."

"You think that's when he got involved with Triocks?"

"I don't know what he did during those years. When I spoke to him over the phone, he told me about how he became a merchant, selling home amenities to foreign markets. It would have explained why I was rarely able to get in touch with him. However, ten years later, I meet with the misfortune of getting through to him the one time I shouldn't have. The Garthega Federation was going to engage in an air raid over the city of Welwig, as there was a high concentration of insurgents there, actively organizing attacks against us. At the same time, I'm stuck with the guilt of knowing that Welwig is the same city that Thomas resided in. So in an effort to spare his life, I call to warm him of the attack. Come the time after the assault, we find out the people we were trying to take out were still alive and operating. As I'm sure you could deduce yourself, there's only so many ways that puzzle fits together."

Guin said, "Looks to me like your boy was selling more than

just toaster ovens."

"Evidently."

Ryan said, "So that's when they got rid of you."

"That's right. After that, I couldn't make ends meet. And with three young mouths to feed, well, I was an easy target. I'd take any job that was offered."

"Yeah," Guin said. "I hear genocidal murderer doesn't get many applicants."

"No," Grieve said, pledging his defense. "No, no, I had no idea what the job would entail. I didn't find out until it was too late. I knew they were after the Dreamer's World, but I had no idea it would require such widespread destruction."

"Then you resign."

"I tried to," he said, with a tinge of anger. "But that's when Thomas reminded me of everything I had to lose. If I were to go back home, I would have been labeled as a murderer and a renegade. I could have potentially faced imprisonment, and not see my children for who knows how many years. My only chance was to collect enough money to vacate this place and start a new home elsewhere. And Thomas . . . he made it sound so easy. The eradication of a planet . . . in the end it boiled down to the press of a button. All I had to do was accept that as part of my responsibility. And the first time I did it, he had me look away, and return to my quarters. I didn't even see the aftermath of what I did. Every time after that, it became easier and easier, until it didn't mean a thing. For a while, I *was* one of them."

"And then you left," Ryan said.

"No. I tried to, and was imprisoned."

"But you escaped."

"Thanks to you."

Suddenly it all clicked inside Ryan's head. One of the questions that had been bothering him finally had an answer.

"So you're the one that changed the coordinates. You steered us away from that star."

"Yes. After I was released, I went to access the station's navigational systems from a remote room when I saw the co-ordinates that were set. Though to tell you the truth, it was my plan all along to ditch the Atlum anyway, and then take off in one of the docked aircrafts. It was the best way to avoid being tracked."

Ryan stared down at the floor, grateful for the way things played out.

"To think we could have died had I not told Zephner to let you go."

"Scary thought, I know."

Guin was getting grumpy, and growing tired of listening to the incessant bellows of the monster.

"Tell me one more thing," he said. "What knocked the sense into you to make you want to ditch your high salary job?"

Grieve didn't give an immediate answer. Several seconds later he was still quiet. From Ryan and Guin's perspective, only the back of his head was visible. There was no telling what he was thinking, or why the question was so difficult. Soon enough it was evident that Guin was sticking his beak where it didn't belong.

Grieve eventually said, "It's not something we need to think about right now. We have Thomas to deal with. Let's focus on that."

They were passing through the perimeter of the city, leaving behind the cluster of brilliant lights, and entering a stretch of empty fields. Their vantage point gave a clear view of the mountains that were only a few miles out. Their silhouettes were faintly visible, contrasting only with the moon-lit sky. They were gargantuan, gobbling the horizon like lofty plumes of black mist. They were powerful, and intimidating, dwarfing the city the same way a boulder dwarfs a pebble. And still the boulder is overshadowed by the mountain that it rests on. As Grieve pointed out earlier, this universe was for all intents and purposes, infinite, which in turn implies that there is no ceiling when it came to expectations. As ridiculous as some hopes can be, there was always room for the desired outcome—an infinite amount of room. There had to be a way to survive this night, and if there was, Ryan would find it.

They were approaching the airfield now. Scattered across the ground were dozens of tarmac landing pads, ranging anywhere from fifty feet across to over two hundred feet. Each plot was demarcated with flashing beacons at each corner, many of which were already occupied with a variety of aircrafts. Ryan actively searched for the one that could have belonged to Thomas. It wasn't going to be the gracious ones, with the turtle-back curves and eel-like tail fins, or the ones that were coated in flamboyant shades of red and blue. It would be something more incongruous, with the appearance of having come from a place billions of light-years away. After getting a fair look at his surroundings, it was undeniable that Thomas' craft had to be the black amorphous oddity that sat idly on zone no. 23. It was aesthetically ferocious, mimicking the likeness of wrought metal disks soldered gather at random. Many fin-like appendages protruded in different directions, some sharp, others long and serpentine, like a mesh of bramble.

Grieve was in the process of setting down the vessel in one of the empty zones. Once contact was made, the side door panel slid open. Ryan and Guin both stood up and made their way outside, where they felt the cool nightly breeze. It was also quiet, when compared to the populated center of the city. Here there were no people, no flying automobiles, or venues with loud music. Just the darkness and silence. Though nothing could be heard, there was a certain energy that could be felt. It dwelled all around—a looming presence that couldn't be observed. It hid in the air, or even in the night itself. It fed thoughts into them, of sadness and despair. It wanted to speak to them and tell them that their endeavor would prove fruitless. Ryan believed it to be something brewed by his own thoughts, but it was more than just that. There was a force here.

Grieve walked around to the front of the vehicle, and met with Ryan and Guin as they came around from the other side. They didn't say anything to each other because they all saw the same thing: a lone man standing alongside the black vessel.

Ryan stared at the man, and grew uncomfortable right away. He recognized the dark uniform with the long coat, immediately associating it with the captains of the Atlums. But there was even a more sinister quality about him—a queer, awkward quality. His posture wasn't completely erect, in the manner that would convey professionalism. His head was at a slight tilt, and his right shoulder weighed down. One knee was bent a little more than the other. He was like a string puppet that was broken and reassembled incorrectly.

His feet began to shuffle forward, with one foot angled away from the other. As he got closer, he quickened his pace, and his peculiar gait became more obvious. He moved with a limp that came from his left leg. Meanwhile his right forearm remained locked in a semi-raised position. When he got close enough, they could see his face, which bore a dubious smile. He had thick, black lustrous hair that dangled over his face, with ends that curled along the back of his neck. He gave off an ambiguous sense of sincere delight and deep-seated spite. He may have been friendly, or despicably hostile. His appearance gave no answers.

He moved a little closer, stepping into the light of one of the beacons. His eyes stayed on Grieve.

"Goodnight, *General*," he said, being derisive towards the man's former title. "Now wait a minute, that's not right." He brought a finger to his chin. "Why doesn't that work as a greeting?"

Grieve remained stern, not willing to let the man indulge in his dull humor.

Thomas gave up waiting for a smile. "It's been such a long time."

Grieve answered, "It's only been a month since I've had to look at you and be reminded of the atrocities you've committed."

"Oh, I see. I would have thought you'd be a little cheerier about my visit. But I suppose not."

"How did you find me?" Grieve asked, trying to keep his patience. "How did you know I was here?"

Thomas smiled. "It was rather simple, General. I fired a call to the big fish and asked to have you meet me here. He didn't object to the request. Then again, where else would you have run off to beside your home sweet home?—where the bistros are plenty, and the air suffused with vapors of nostalgia, and everything nice?"

Still, Grieve was serious. He tried to contain himself.

"This doesn't have to be difficult," he said. "You leave now, spend your time somewhere else, and come back later."

Thomas twisted his face into a wry look of total confusion.

"Is . . . this a bad time?"

"Yes it is."

"Well, that's a shame. It really is, because I can't reschedule. You see, Lord Triocks runs a tight ship, and marks all appointments with ink. But you know that already, which begs the question—" His eyes shifted over to Ryan and Guin, his gaze building an appetite. "Is that the best you can do for an entourage?"

"I'll tell you once more," Grieve said, taking two steps forward. "Heed my warning. If you don't comply with my order to stand down, there will be a severe retaliation by the Garthega Federation. If you have any hope of ever finding the Dreamer's World, you best continue looking for it elsewhere."

Thomas shook his head, trying to stifle the inappropriate chuckling. He laid his look of pity upon the man.

"Marcus, what's happened to you? You look so . . . miserable. Dare I say I've seen you smile on more than one occasion while you were with us. For that short time, you had a purpose. You learned that there was more to your life than what you had been led to believe. You were progressing so nicely. You took on a task that not many have the strength to carry out. But then you threw it all away—you allowed yourself to be put at the mercy of your own feeble mind. You sought immediate gratification rather than committing to the search that would ultimately yield a wonder beyond all comprehension."

Grieve was trying to control the last ounce of patience he had. "You won't find it. You won't *ever* find it. It was never meant to be found."

"Oh General, General. Listen to yourself. If it exists, it doesn't matter if it was intended to be found. The point is that it *can* be found. Now why don't you take another whiff at the possibilities. Think about what it would mean to find the Dreamer's World. It may very well be the sole method of ever seeing her again. Doesn't that just mean everything to you?"

"I don't want you speaking about her. I don't want you *thinking* about her. I hold you fully responsible for even letting it happen."

"Now, let's be fair, I cautioned that bringing aboard a female was a bad omen."

"That's enough!" Grieve shouted, curling his hands into fists. He took another step forward. "You're going to do as I say, and *leave this place*."

Thomas shook his head again disappointingly. "You don't

realize what I'm doing for you, do you? I'm giving you ample opportunity to relocate before we . . . initiate our sequence. Consider it a debt repaid."

Ryan kept quiet, as Grieve had instructed him to do. He tried not to look weak or vulnerable, but it was difficult. Grieve wasn't getting through to him. Thomas wasn't going to stand down, and honestly, he didn't expect him to. The crazed, overzealous devotion to his cause was unwavering. He was going to go through with the attack.

Grieve marched forward across the tarmac, arms stiff at his sides, his chin held high. He demonstrated that there was no room for compassion or compromise. His intentions were resolute. He would not plea or bargain. His word would be final.

Now he stood before Thomas, with at least six inches on him. His eyes fell down on him, burning with belligerence. Thomas looked back at him, with a stupid, silly grin that only fueled Grieve's intolerance.

Grieve spoke loud and clearly, "This is the last time I will say it. Stand down."

Thomas smiled. "Sorry, General."

That was it. The tension reached its breaking point. Grieve snapped.

His elbow shot into the air, powered by the twist of his waist, and packed with fuel of his hate. The bones of his forearm were ready to smash against the side of Thomas' face.

Fast as the blink of an eye, he couldn't have seen it coming. This was a terminating blow.

But it wasn't.

He felt his bones strike against stone.

Thomas, with impeccable reflexes, had already risen his arm to block the attack, stopping it dead in the air.

Grieve followed through with a left hook, again packed with all the strength he could muster.

Thomas brushed away his arm effortlessly.

Grieve, growing desperate and overeager, pulled both his arms against himself like a shield. He took a step, thrusting the weight of his body forward, while at the same time, locking his foot around Thomas' ankle.

Just as intended, Thomas staggered backwards.

Yes. He would have him on the ground.

But he felt the clutches of fingers around the sleeves of his jacket. Next thing he knew he was coming down along with Thomas. The world spun around—concrete—lights—darkness. His back slammed against the solid ground. He winced from the pain, his shoulder blades taking the brunt of the fall. He saw Thomas standing over him. Somehow he managed to divert the momentum of the tackle.

So swift. So perfect.

He had to get back up on his feet fast, he thought. He couldn't remain vulnerable.

He rolled onto his side, firing a swift kick at the inside of Thomas' leg.

Thomas lifted his foot off the ground just in time—as Grieve expected. But it bought him time to roll away and climb back up on his feet.

He held his hands out in front of him, contemplating his next move, all while battling the demoralizing sight of Thomas' sheer calmness. He stood there dumbly, as if their scuffle hadn't happened. He didn't even look like he was breathing.

Grieve couldn't stand to look at him for more than two seconds. He rushed in again, with his right fist cocked back.

He fired a punch, twisting his hips, backing it with all the strength in his arm.

Thomas casually stepped to one side, as if he saw it coming from a mile away. But Grieve expected the evasive maneuver.

With Thomas now leaning to the left, Grieve lassoed his

other arm around his neck, effectively putting him into a head-lock. He pulled him forward, tightening his hold as much as he could. He continued to apply pressure until the muscles in his arms grew sore.

But the strangulation wasn't working. Thomas showed no resistance—there was no need for resistance. His breathing remained normal. His face didn't turn red. He was fine.

"Marcus" he heard Thomas say in a low, regretful tone.

Grieve couldn't be sure what happened next. A sharp pain erupted in the vicinity of his abdomen—a blunt stab that could have been anything from an elbow to an iron rod. He fumbled backwards and tumbled to the ground. He rolled to his side, pressing against the area of injury. Grunts of pain escaped past his clenched teeth.

Thomas looked down at him and was crestfallen.

"Was this the contingency plan?" he said. "Whittle me down with whacks and smacks until I broke down and surrendered? I thought you to be a better strategist than this."

Grieve tried his best to block the pain. He couldn't buy any more time if he stayed on the ground, so with arduous effort, he crawled onto his hands and knees. He raised one foot and planted it flat on the ground, giving the appearance that he was struggling to get back up. With his hand concealed behind his body, he dug for the knife in the sheath of his boot.

He pushed off the ground with an explosion of energy. He pulled back his arm high, holding the knife in reverse grip. He feigned a stab from above, until he pulled back and came around with a swing from his left.

Thomas didn't react. A strike was certain.

The blade propelled forward, directly for his chest.

Swift, accurate.

It drove through flesh.

Grieve stared at the damage, aghast and demoralized.

He saw the knife lodged in the dead center of Thomas' palm, in up to the hilt. A stream of blood trickled slowly down his forearm. He didn't twitch, he didn't wince. He displayed nothing but a cold, dead stare. Instead, Grieve was the one trembling. He knew what this meant. It was plainly clear. This quarrel had reached its conclusion.

Thomas said to him, "Do you now understand what it means to renounce the Will of Kausmos?"

Grieve could feel his own hand being repelled back by the bloodied hand. He took a step back.

"We were elected by him—*entrusted* by him to find the Dreamer's World. We are empowered by him."

Grieve watched as Thomas took his pierced hand and closed it over the handle of the knife. He applied pressure with his thumb, snapping the wooden hilt like a twig, and then bending the steel tang underneath.

"He has given us the *strength* to find it."

Thomas pulled away the contorted blade out of Grieve's weakened grip, and with his other hand, he lifted the blade from his palm. The residual traces of blood dripped down the tip and onto the ground. He took it and tossed it aside.

"Understand there is no force in this universe capable of debasing our commitment to our cause. Neither you, nor anyone else has any say in our inevitable triumph. If you are to understand one thing, let it be this: the Dreamer's can, and *will* be found."

After those final words were issued, Grieve watched as a hand smacked him across the face. He was knocked off balance, falling forcefully against the asphalt, his face brushing against the coarse stones.

He was in pain, and was disoriented. There was no way he could climb back up on his feet. He expected that these would be the final moments he would ever experience. With his vision upside down, he saw Thomas taking his steps back towards his vessel. It would only be minutes now before everything around him turned to dust. He didn't want to accept it, but there was nothing more he could do. He was competing against powers that could not be contested. It was over.

As a final reminder, he heard the cry of the beast once more, far in the distance. The bellow echoed like a horn, denoting that the end was near.

————CHAPTER 24————

CRY OF THE BEAST

Claps of thunder erupted from the street below. The beast was nearing, and Zephner could feel it, but not quite yet see it. It would only be seconds now before it came into view. He rehearsed the plan of attack in his head, and at the same time, tried to calm the nerves that caused his body to quiver. Never had he faced something so enormous. Combating people is what he excelled at. This, however, was an entirely new undertaking. The probability for success would be slim. He knew this, but didn't care.

His heart skipped a beat when he saw a massive shape pass by the edge of the far building. It was a foul snout, as black as the night. The skin was coarse, covered in scales that overlapped like a suit of armor. Some bits were short, while others were long and jagged, protruding from the skull like some kind of urchin. The eye cavities were black, bottomless trenches that ran across the face like an open gash.

The beast dropped its jaw, spreading it wide to let out another scream that pierced and shook the atmosphere. In doing so, it exposed the row of three-foot fangs that outlined its mouth like a twisted vine of thorns. They were like silver skewers, glistening from the sludge of saliva. The region of its throat was a cavern coated in fleshy, viscous layers of mucus, with slimy tendrils that hung like wreaths of worms and snakes.

The beast took a step forward, shaking the ground like thunder. Then another.

The rest of the body was exposed, proving to be just as hideous as the head. The entire length of the spine was shielded with crusty plates, with sharp rock-like shards poking through the wet epidermis.

The two massive legs followed. Each were ridden with bulging masses of muscle. The digits of the foot were long and many, like the roots of a tree.

The beast trampled onward.

Behind the torso followed the tail—a sinuous serpent with seemingly no end. It danced and twirled through the air, crashing against the side of every building. Windows shattered, cement turned to rubble, and all the fragments rained down on the streets below.

The tail tore through the air, like the crack of a whip, granulating a line of automobiles.

The claws of the feet dug into the asphalt with every step, crunching and splitting the earth.

The cries and screams were widespread, only muffled in between the crashing sounds of falling debris. Now the beast walked through a smokescreen of dirt and dust, pressing forward with its trail of destruction.

There was no more time for Zephner to dread what awaited him. The sight of the creature instilled the feeling of certain death. Attacking it was suicide, but the alternative was to do nothing and most likely perish anyway. Death was death, and if he were to die, it would be by his own terms.

He had no more time to think about it. He had to be in position.

He revved up the engine and rode along the edge of the garage roof. After he picked up some speed, he sprung his body up, lifting the bike high enough to catch onto the parapet. Here he stopped, and peeked down at the street below. The crowds flocked north, while only half the automobiles did the same. The ones that weren't fleeing in the right direction were riding into the cloud of smoke, or directly into the beast itself—an oversight in the design of the transit system.

The beast was coming, and he waited for it to stand right underneath the garage tower. It took another thunderous step, and then another. It let out one more antagonizing roar before it landed in the footprint of the target zone.

It was time.

Zephner gripped the handlebars tightly and pinned the throttle, riding the motorcycle over the parapet. The first wheel went, and then the other. The world around him slowly ascended past him, and then faster and faster until things became a blur. A violent surge of wind brushed against his face, blowing his hair wildly. When the timing was right, he flipped the toggle switch.

The motorcycle changed. The different sections twisted and turned in relation to the two handlebars. The long blade sprouted forth, and the two wheels moved towards the rear, becoming the cross-guard of the sword-like weapon.

The weapon plunged downward, with Zephner following behind it, clutching the handle firmly with both hands. He would drive the blade into the head, in a small crevice between the stone-like scales. If luck permitted, it would pierce the brain, causing enough damage to fell the beast. This was the best he could hope for.

His descent rapidly approached an end. He was a hundred feet above the beast.

Fifty feet.

Thirty feet.

With all the might in his arms, he thrust the blade downward, and then—

Thwack.

His body burned with insufferable pain. His bones felt flattened and shattered, as if he had stepped in front of a freight train. Everything he saw became an instant blur. The lights and color of his surroundings gushed past him. Again—

Crash

Another surge of pain exploded through his body. He kept moving and spinning until he landed and tumbled along a solid surface.

Now lying motionless, he tried to digest what just happened. But all he could think about was how he could barely feel his limbs, or any part of his body for that matter. Everything was hurting all at once. He looked at his jacket sleeve, and the big tear that ran through it, exposing the flesh, or what was left of it. His arm was soiled in the blackened blood, as well as the side of his face. He tried lifting his head, and bringing his arms behind him to support his body. Even that was excruciating. But he had to get up. He couldn't let this be the end.

Trying to blink the dust out of his eye, he looked around to see where he was. From what he could tell, he was inside an office lounge. There was broken cement and pulverized drywall everywhere. And lying just a few feet away was his motorcycle, with the blade impaled inside one of the couches. And if he looked straight ahead, he could see the breach in the wall he created when he barreled through, as well as the flogging tail that happened to find him during his descent.

The beast was moving away, and he needed to stop it.

Instead of letting the tremendous pain be a deterrent, he channeled it into anger. The rush of blood through his body invigorated him, giving him the strength to push himself off the ground. The more pain he felt, the stronger his desire to finish the job.

He let out a growl of his own as he forced himself back on two feet. Quickly, he walked over to the couch and withdrew his weapon. It felt much heavier now, but that was to be expected.

He hurried across the room, moving parallel with the street. He dragged the weapon behind him, letting the weighty blade tear a seam through the carpeting.

He rushed into the next room, trying to keep up with the beast as it traveled further down the block. There were several work stations in here, with people seated at the desks. If the crying howls of a colossal monster wasn't enough to spook them, seeing this man carrying a grisly contraption sure was. They all gasped in horror.

He yelled to them, "Get out of the room! Head to the other side of the building!"

More than terrified, they sprung from their seats and did as he ordered.

He rushed to the other end of the room and looked out the set of windows. He caught a glimpse of the head passing by. He no longer had the height necessary to repeat his initial strike, so he opted for the next best thing.

He waited for the animal's torso to come into view. When he had a visual, he charged forward, the blade still dragging behind. He held his forearm out and aimed his elbow at the glass pane.

He busted through the window, spilling a slew of broken shards out into the air. He traveled with the glass, onto the backside of the monster. Before fumbling, he grabbed onto one of the protruding scales, and held it tightly.

The monster swayed with each step, rocking him back and forth. He couldn't hold on for long. He could barely hold on as it was, as the skin and scales of the creature were as wet and slimy as anything that lived in the sea. He studied the terrain he stood on and observed the vulnerable patches of flesh that hid under the stoney plates. He pulled his weapon up and positioned it appropriately. Daringly, he let go of the scale he held and put both hands around the handle of the weapon. With a swift motion, he drove the blade into the beast, as far as he could force it.

The creature let out a cry, a sound that was barely a whimper. He didn't expect it to be the finishing blow, but it wasn't even a prick. If anything, it drew the beast's attention. It writhed back and forth, jerking its body one way and then another. All Zephner had to hold on to was the handle of the weapon. But with all the turbulence, the blade wouldn't remain embedded forever. The flesh was tearing, the blood was gushing, and soon his only anchor would give.

In another effort to dismount him, the beast staggered to the left, ramming its body into the side of a building. A downpour of rubble fell from the sky, scattering over the creature's backside.

Zephner withdrew the weapon from the wound and dashed away, narrowly avoiding a cement pillar that splintered into dust upon hitting the jagged scale. He held up his arm to shield himself from the splash of debris.

The beast lurched in the other direction, and Zephner staggered forward. Careful not to fall off, he swung his weapon outward into the air, to counteract the way his body was leaning. He grabbed onto another one of the scales.

High above in the sky, he saw the tail flailing wildly, oscillating back and forth. The end point was no where in sight. Again and again it brushed against the buildings, scattering rubble into the streets. It was an appendage that seemed to have a life of its own.

Out of no where, the serpentine tail descended at an incredible velocity. The black tubular bundle of meat and muscle came right for him.

He saw it, and leapt out of the way. And just as the tail was about to make contact with the creature's backside, he swung his weapon skyward, connecting the tip of the blade with the animal's flesh.

The blade's edge tore open a straight gash that released a

drizzle of viscous fluid. The beast let out a low bellow.

The tail rose back into the air, where it twisted and meandered in every direction. It was posturing for an attack that could have come from any direction. Zephner kept a close eye on it, waiting to see what it was going to do.

After watching it closely for several seconds, the tip of the tail had made its first appearance. It was a long, flat extension, with some semblance to a tattered feather. It gleamed an alluring turquoise, shining like a bulb. But he didn't care how beautiful it looked. He knew it was dangerous by the way it secreted a liquid substance. It couldn't have been anything other than a defense mechanism.

The tail looped around for a second pass. The glowing fin brandished like a flaming torch. It was coming down on him with staggering speed. It tore through with a horizontal swoosh.

He fell flat to his belly, allowing it to pass over him. The fin of the tail grazed the side of another building, leaving behind a streak of effulgent ooze. In an instant, the substance began to foam. The little bubbles expanded and burst shortly thereafter. The inflicted area of the wall sizzled and became a glutinous sludge that dripped down the building.

The tail swung back, intent on hitting its target. But Zephner would have none of it. He saw it coming from above, and darted away just before it struck down. The acidic goop splashed across the plates, having no effect on the creature.

He heard another swoosh, coming from behind.

He turned, and saw the tail rushing in for another strike. It would be unavoidable, he thought. It would land one way or another, and so he made an impromptu decision.

Right before the tail could connect, he performed a wide horizontal stroke with his weapon. The blade pointed dead ahead, just as the tail made a direct collision with it. Nearly the entire motorcycle was driven into the flesh before he felt the subsequent force that swept him off his feet.

As if he were just fired from a cannon, he saw the city zip past his vision at an astonishing rate. Only after a few seconds did he realize he was still clinging on to the handle of his weapon, which was still embedded inside the creature's tail.

He rapidly climbed in altitude. He was at five hundred feet. A thousand feet. Eventually the frantic pedestrians were no more than pinheads. He climbed higher still, holding on to the weapon for dear life. The gush of air was like sitting on the windshield of a plane. The sheer g-forces would have killed any normal human being. But he had to hold on no matter what, as he now must have been somewhere in the realm of two thousand feet (how damn long was this tail?).

The beast continued flailing its tail back and forth, evidently aware that there was something attached. Zephner rode out the torturous ride for as long as he could, gripping his weapon with all the strength he had. He thought he could feel all the organs in his body being scrambled.

The tail suddenly swung in another direction, like the crack of a whip. He anticipated what would happen as soon as he saw the blade lift from the skin of the tail. Just like that, he was separated from the beast, and left with only the company of gravity— *several thousand feet in the air.*

His natural descent was almost a delight compared to what he had just endured. But he was still in no better position to slay the beast. It was now several blocks ahead of the spot where he would ultimately land.

Despite ridding itself of the latched pest, the tail was still flailing uncontrollably.

While contemplating his next move, Zephner met with another onslaught of attacks. The tail continued to weave in and out of the space around him. And since he could only helplessly fall, he did his best to repel the aggressive motions with parries of his weapon.

He swung to his right, forming one gash, then followed through to his left, creating another. All in all, it was petty damage that would amount to nothing. He needed some kind of plan, but the problem was, regardless of the force exerted, a toothpick was never going to vanquish a whale. But maybe he should be giving himself more credit. His weapon was more than a toothpick. It may have once been a commonplace motorcycle, but now it was something much more potent. He had no choice but to stake his life on it.

He plunged further and further towards the ground, now with little time to make a decision. Considering it to be his next best move, he would go for another strike to the head.

He leaned his body forward, catching the wind under his opened jacket. The effect it had on his trajectory was minor, but it was enough for him to have some semblance of control over his descent.

He scanned the line of traffic below. There were still plenty of cars racing through the hazardous territory, at altitudes that put them over the head of the beast. The only way he would have his second shot is if he put himself and others at risk again. It was a gamble he had to take.

The target was a blue aircraft, cruising at about 180 miles per hour at four hundred feet above street level. His landing would have to be precise if he didn't want to crush whatever passengers were in the cabin. He had about six feet between the cargo hold and the tail fins—a zone that was dangerously small for a body traveling at free fall to land on.

He extrapolated the rate of his fall, with the vessel passing underneath. He leaned forward just a little more.

He was closing in fast.

Two hundred feet.

One hundred feet.

With the wind rushing past his face, and his target increasingly growing in size, he feared it would be a harsh collision. But it was either that, or falling flat on the street and abandoning whatever chance he had.

The car was right under him.

He leaned back just a hair.

Impact.

He heard the sound of metal being crushed and teared, along with the crackling of glass. The entire vessel plunged down a good thirty feet into the lane below, before the automated system could rebound it back into place. He threw his arm out and grabbed onto the first thing he could get his hands on, which happened to be the frame of the rear windshield. The two passengers up front squealed as they were startled half way into their graves, but were otherwise unharmed.

Latched on like a bug, he rode the vehicle down the stretch of road. Within seconds, he was riding neck to neck with the beast. The head was less than a hundred feet below—close enough that the tail shouldn't be able to thwart him. But just in case, he surveyed the skies, and saw that the tail was still making the rounds through the cityscape. This should have been easy enough.

He dragged his weapon over to the side he would jump from and let it hang with the blade towards the ground. Taking into account his inertia, he jumped just before he would pass over the head.

Once again, he felt his body enter a state of free fall. He gripped his weapon tightly, with both hands around the handle, his arms ready to apply force for the impalement.

He got closer and closer.

The weapon was thrust down.

There was a *clank* as the blade scraped the side of one of the armors plates. He fell hard against the stone-like surface, intensifying the insufferable pain of his already battered body. He had missed that small rift of exposed flesh between the plates, thus blowing whatever chance he had of killing the creature.

He climbed back on his feet in a hurry, desperately trying to inflict whatever damage he could. He hefted the weapon again, trying to ram the blade into whatever crevice he could find. But the truth was, this seven foot instrument wasn't a stabbing weapon. There was no way he could consistently hoist it high enough to jab with, especially with all the rocky movement.

He was running out of ideas. He searched laboriously for any means possible. But nothing came to him, that is, until he considered the particle blast his weapon could fire. But would such a blast even penetrate the protective layer on this animal?

Before he could consider the possibility, the beast jerked its head abruptly, causing him to fall onto his rear and slide straight off the surface of the head.

Seemingly unable to keep his feet on anything solid, he plummeted towards the street below. He racked up a few meters before he felt another substantial impact that blacked out his vision for just a second. Aside from the burning sensation in his muscles and bones, he also heard the rupturing of glass and the clunk of metal. He lifted his head and saw the buildings darting past him, which brought him to the conclusion that he was riding on the mangled hood of a car. But he wasn't going to stay up there for long. His weapon hung over the front of the vehicle, and it was pulling him down with it. Under no circumstances was he going to let it go, so he had no choice but to go down with it.

This time he could at least anticipate the impact. He wanted to land on his feet, and so he maneuvered himself accordingly.

He landed on the dead center of his soles, which sent pangs through all the bones in his legs. He could feel everything inside of him become brittle. If he kept up this grueling battle he was surely going to shatter something. Even a man of his physical prowess had limits.

After taking a breather to digest the pain, he turned around and saw down the avenue. About two blocks away was the behemoth, standing in a light that made it appear larger and more fearsome than what could have been observed from the air. Its mandible hung so low, almost as if it were detached from the rest of the skull. Its sharp, serrated teeth glimmered in slobber, and its breath produced a foul stench that suffused the air with the malodorous scent of rotten marine animals. But if he could make one propitious observation, it was the fact that its entire underbelly was lacking the protective plates that were located on the backside. But even so, an external blast would not have been fatal. It would need to be internal, while preferably being in range of a crucial organ.

But how?

There was a quake stirring just under his feet. He could feel the vibrations of something weaving through the ground below him. He followed the sound as it traveled down the length of the block. When he turned around he saw the street rupture into a geyser of shattered concrete that shot a hundred feet into the air. From the dispersion of dust and debris emerged the creature's tail, rising into the night like a spire.

That was the answer, he thought. Below this street was a subway tunnel—a sizable trench that would serve nicely as a collapsible pit. He worked out the details of the scheme, and figured there was only one sure method to put the rampaging monster out of commission. It wouldn't be safe. It was anything but safe. But what was one more impetuous decision on what could possibly be the eve of the end?

With the tail still rising to unprecedented heights, he rushed in the direction of the beast. He held his weapon in tow, the blade grinding against the concrete street. Given his condition, it was like hauling an anchor. But he would have to put the pain and fatigue aside if this was going to work.

He glanced up at the sky and observed the tail. The glowing fin was lighting up a trail through the darkness. It began to droop forward, plunging back down towards the ground. The secretion of acid started up again, and now blue droplets were drizzling down.

He saw he needed to hurry. He hadn't much time.

The beast advanced another step, and then another. Each contact with the ground carried a wave of tremors. It lowered its head and dropped its jaw, and let out another boisterous cry. It was almost disorienting for Zephner, simply deafening. But he needed to focus. He *had* to focus.

He looked up. The tail was coming down, a finishing strike if it could make contact.

With his hand around the handle of the weapon, his thumb reached for the dial. He kicked it up several notches, and the wheel's began to spin. The rotations became rapid, thrumming to a whistle. Soon the sparks where flying; the energy was being stored.

The beast stood up ahead, no more than a block away, continuing with its incessant roaring. It took another step, and then another. It was getting close.

Zephner looked up, and there was the tail, which was now that much closer. It fell like a comet, burning, growing larger every second.

The time was now. He had to unleash the attack.

He tugged on the weapon, and with the momentum hoisted it into the air.—wheels churning—sparking—whistling.

The beast took another step.

He eased the weapon down gently, waiting for the blade to be pointed at just the right angle.

Almost.

It was parallel with the street.

Just a hair of a second more.

Now.

A shining orb of energy traveled down the shaft of the weapon, and was ejected through the tip of the blade. It made contact with the street, just at the base of the creature's foot. A white flash blinded the city block. There was an eruption of con-crete, a typhoon of debris, wind and scorching heat. The air was burning—a blizzard of stones and dirt.

But he had to move now, into the zone of the blast, as the beast was stumbling into the trench—into the subway. Having had the ground removed right from underneath its feet, it staggered forward. It was going to fall, hard and heavy.

Zephner jolted forward with all the strength he had left, which wasn't much at all. He needed to be in position.

He felt that feeling now, the one where immediate death was a strong possibility. His fate hung in the balance. This could have been his last breath, his last thought. He had no way to know for sure. He couldn't help but ask himself if his life had any meaning at all, or if this moment was his ultimate purpose. If it was, he thought it was really stupid, especially if Grieve couldn't succeed with his bargain for a reprieve. There had to be more to it, he thought. The only reason he was in this situation right now was because of that enigmatic visitation by Ryan. It had to have been more than a coincidence. Perhaps it even delved into the realm of a divine plan. But whatever the reason, he hadn't the time to think about it in detail right now. He was about to kill, or be killed—or both.

He entered the footprint of where the beast would fall flat. Looking up, he saw the black mountain coming down on him. There was no time to second guess, no time to take back his de-cision.

He stopped, and swung the weapon skyward. He planted his

feet firmly, legs apart, preparing himself for the fallout.

In the last instant before impact, he watched as the tip of the blade entered the creature's throat. It was a clean incision, with the flesh providing no resistance. Finally he had breached the walls of this impenetrable fortress, and now there was nothing to shield against the decisive blow.

He flicked the trigger, and took delight in the surge of blazing heat that followed.

CHAPTER 25

NEGOTIATIONS

Guin didn't look like he was going to just let Thomas board his vessel. He was clasping his beak, with his body hunched forward, and his claws peeking through their feathered sheaths. Had the battlefield been a little colder and icier, Ryan had no doubt that Guin would be racing down the landing zone flat on his belly. Though with forethought, it may have been for the best that he didn't. For one, he observed that the knife wound in Thomas' palm had found a way to regenerate. Even the blood itself had disappeared, as if the whole thing never happened. It was like watching a miracle unfold, though through a power that was un-likely anything but malevolent. The only thing clear was that this power wanted nothing more than the Dreamer's World to be found. And if Thomas was a key instrument in its search, it was likely he would be spared any harm that would impede that search. It was pure conjecture, but he felt this man was different than the likes of Martisse and Malcus. He was at an entirely dif-ferent level in terms of rank and devotion. An assassination at-tempt seemed unwise, and even if successful, it would only stir up the rest of the colony. The truth of the matter was he didn't think violence could put an end to this conflict. But what other options were there?

Ryan heard Guin utter quietly, "What are the repercussions of tearing apart this pretty-haired hoodlum?"

"I'm not sure," Ryan said. "All I know is even if we take him out, there will be more of them."

"But the idea is to buy ourselves some time, until whatshisname is finished with his science project in the basement."

Ryan didn't know how much time they needed to buy, but he figured the more the better. Thomas was just about ready to board the vessel, which gave him only seconds to decide what he wanted to do. If he didn't do anything, they'd all be gone in a couple of minutes. This was the time to either be brave, or to be stupid. But he had to take a gamble on it, because in this case doing something was better than nothing.

He considered an idea, one that would attach significance to a dream he had not too long ago. Initially, he dismissed it as being another one of those senseless happenings that was nothing more than a fabrication of his imagination. But now he was open to the possibility that it had some ulterior purpose. Maybe there was a reason that he caught a glimpse of that derelict city, and more interestingly, that lone girl who appeared spooked by his presence. She left an impression on him, one that he couldn't just let go of. There had to be a reason why. If Zephner had taught him anything, it was that everything he experienced here was more than just a dream.

He looked down at Guin, who was still poised to attack.

"I'm going to buy us some time," Ryan said to him.

"Yeah? With what funds?"

He took his finger and tapped his own head. Guin didn't seem to comprehend.

Thomas was taking his first step onto the ramp.

"Thomas!" Ryan yelled across the landing zone.

He stopped and turned towards Ryan, his face muddled with confusion.

"We need to talk."

Thomas cupped his ear. "What about?" He shouted back.

"I have some information you might be interested in. In exchange for it, I want you to leave this planet alone."

"Now just hold it. You're in no position to be making demands."

Ryan paused and thought about it.

"Yes I am!"

"No, no. I mean you're standing too far away. I can't hear you."

They stared each other down, each suspicious of the other. Mutually they decided to take steps towards the middle of the landing zone. They stopped when they reached a comfortable distance.

Thomas was initially serious, but soon broke into an impish grin.

"What is it that you're offering me?" he said, in a way that suggested his expectations were low.

Ryan tried to maintain a stout posture and a convincing visage, for if there was any doubt or insecurity left to be read, Thomas would certainly write off his claim as a hoax.

"An end to your search," he said, as tellingly as he could.

Thomas smiled. "Indulge me by elucidating, if you will."

Easy. He had him on the hook.

"I can tell you where to find the Dreamer's World."

Thomas remained incredulous.

"Am I . . . truly to believe this?"

"Yes," Ryan said. "And if you don't believe me, I wouldn't mind telling you about Captain Martisse and Captain Malcus, and how their lives were cut short before they could pull anything out of me. Both of them knew I came from the other side, and they knew I would hold the answer. So as it stands, I either give you that answer, or you can spend another thousand years blindly throwing darts. Personally I think the former is the better bargain."

Thomas grimaced with delight. "I wouldn't disagree, *if* I knew I was conducting business with an honest dealer. Surely you can imagine the score of false leads we've collected over the course of our search. But like any avid hunter, we are obliged to exhaust every possibility, no matter how suspect we are."

He was buying it, Ryan thought. Sort of.

"But bear in mind, if we're lead to a dead end, we won't be pleased. More greatly so, Lord Triocks will be not pleased. And let the general be the one to tell you what that's like for the culprit."

This was the time to take back his move, before he let go of his piece. But he didn't. He was resolute in his judgment. This universe had become a place he wanted to protect. It was more than a nightly retreat, more than a stage where his mind could indulge in the whims of his subconscious. It was an extension to his reality—or maybe it was the other side of the same coin. He didn't know where it was, whether it was *out there*, or somewhere in his head. But either way, this was the place he would return to each and every night, whether he wanted to or not. It was his turf, and he wasn't about to let someone muscle him off.

"So let me ask you," Thomas said, "do you really possess the knowledge that you claim?"

"I do," Ryan said dutifully.

Thomas smiled. "In that case, do tell, before I convulse to death from anticipation."

Ryan saw that the man was still doubtful. Nevertheless, he went on with his testimony.

"I can't give you coordinates, but I can tell you what I saw."

Thomas motioned with his hand for him to continue.

"I was on a deserted planet that was covered in sand and rocks as far as the eye could see. The air was unbearably hot and the sky was pale gray. I was thirsty, so I moved out in search of water. I heard the sound of a current, so I followed that."

He paused, and studied Thomas. He listened intently, with one arm folded, the other propped under his chin, though not quite touching it.

Ryan continued.

"I trekked through a valley and found a river waiting for me on the other side. That's when I noticed two things: first, an abandoned city in the distance, perhaps no more than two or three miles away. The buildings were hundreds of feet high, rising from the mountain side. They were heavily damaged and crumbling apart; second, I saw a girl by the river, maybe about my age. She looked in my direction, and was startled. That's when the machine that was with her began to approach me."

"A machine? What kind of machine?"

"I couldn't really say. It was fairly large, with arms, legs, and a silver body. I didn't wait around to snap a good picture."

"So you ran?"

"Yeah," Ryan shamefully admitted. "And that's when I was awakened by my alarm clock. It was . . . time for me to go to school."

Ryan wasn't sure why he had decided to add that tidbit of information. It sounded odd, considering he was currently asleep. Now he began to wonder how much time he had left before he would be awakened again.

Thomas continued his inquiry. "And what gives you the impression that this was, in fact, the Dreamer's World?"

Ryan wasn't entirely sure. He thought quickly and produced an answer.

"Because I felt that there was something being protected."

"Evidently the machine was protecting the girl."

"But maybe the girl was protecting something as well."

Thomas raised an eyebrow. He was interested. Ryan was pulling him in.

"That's fine," Thomas said with a low voice. "That's quite

fine. Grand, really. And I only say so because the world you're describing fits one of the planets on our charts. While there may be dozens, if not hundreds that fit similar criteria, only one of these possesses an exclusive attribute."

"Which one?" Ryan asked.

"Tabernas."

"What makes Tabernas so special?"

"The population is zero," Thomas said, with an unbridled grin. "And what better place to hide a nonpareil treasure than in an uninhabited wasteland in some far-off dusty, forgotten corner of the galaxy. But let's analyze it one step further and say this planet, and the one you speak of are, in fact, one in the same. It makes for a very pressing question: why, in the name of every leaking piss bucket, would there be a young female on this planet accompanied by a robotic guardian?"

"We should go find out," Ryan said, enabling him further.

"Find out we shall," he answered, as he began taking steps towards his vessel. Then he stopped to look back at Ryan with a sinister smile. "How old are you?" he asked out of the blue.

Ryan, confused by the inquiry, answered, "Fifteen."

"How about that. It would put her around the correct age."

"Who?"

"Never mind. Come," Thomas said. "We'll need someone who can point out the sights. It's part of the package I'm paying for."

"Wait," Ryan said. "If I come along, you'll spare everyone here. Right?"

Thomas' excitement was waned by the holdup. "I'll tell the rest of my company to lay their fingers off the big red button. For now."

"Promise?"

"Of course," he said with mocking endearment. "We're not monsters. And speaking of such, it seems Velachio has stopped crying. I would take it that someone has hurt him. Now *there's* your monster."

Ryan sighed with relief, knowing that Zephner was able to come out triumphant in an assignment that was probably issued as a suicide mission. Now it was his turn to complete the task that he had entrusted himself with.

Thomas turned around and proceeded towards his ship. Ryan took a step forward when he heard a voice call out from behind.

"Room for one more?" Grieve said, picking himself up off the ground, while clutching his side.

Thomas stopped mid stride and turned his head.

"Now General, for what conceivable reason would you want to accompany me on this trip?"

Grieve got on his feet and stood up straight, grimacing at the pangs that shot through his body. "Don't you think I should be there, when you finally uncover the Dreamer's World, and bask in your moment of glory?"

Thomas looked to the sky and thought about it. "Yes," he said. "You would be a most fitting witness for this marvelous unveiling. I wouldn't want you to miss it for the world."

When Thomas turned back around, Grieve shot a glance at Ryan, and continued following Thomas back to the spacecraft. Ryan took a step forward, then stopped when he remembered something.

He looked back and saw Guin standing idly, with both flippers flat at his sides, with an embittered stare. He was like an animal that was left on the side of the road.

"Guin," he started to say, as if he were obligated to give an explanation for this impetuous decision.

"Forget it," Guin said. "I'll save your space."

"Guin," Ryan said again, "I need you to go and check on Megan. Make sure she's all right. Tell her everything is going to be okay."

He grumbled something under his breath that sounded like an affirmation.

"And see if you can find Zephner, too. He could be hurt."

Guin flailed his flippers. "Of course, of course. Let me pluck a quill and write this all down."

Ryan snickered and smile. "Thanks, Guin."

With that, he traversed across the landing zone and climbed the ramp, where Thomas waited, ready to usher him inside.

There wasn't a whole lot going through his head right now. Though maybe that's what it felt like to be valiant. You decide you want to do something, and then you just do it. You don't think about what it would mean to fail, because you've ruled that out as an option. Everything that lies between here and the goal are obstacles, that, when overcome, make the victory that much sweeter. Being that this was a dream, the potential magnitude of these obstacles were great. But by the same reason, it also meant that his potential was great. Theoretically, there was no limit to what he could accomplish here. But no matter what he did, it was still his mind, and *only* his mind that had the capacity to make the decision.

This was his decision—to save this universe, so that his dreams may always have a home.

He stepped inside the vessel, feeling hopeful about the next couple of hours, and tomorrow, and even the day after that.

Yes, things will be great, he thought, just as he heard the infernal ringing of his alarm clock resonate throughout the room. He rolled on his side and quickly struck the toggle. He sat up in his bed.

Things will be great, he thought. Things will be great.

www.ingramcontent.com/pod-product-compliance
Lightning Source LLC
Chambersburg PA
CBHW071154250626

47159CB00001B/86